THE VIPER'S KISS

AMY BEATTY

STICKPIN
PRESS

THE VIPER'S KISS

Edited by Julie Frederick

Published by
STICKPIN PRESS
Amy Beatty Studios, LLC
www.amybeatty.com

ISBN: 978-0-578-59729-4 (Paperback)
AISN: B07ZJ28CKY (Kindle Edition)

First Edition

For those who know
they're in over their heads,
but who go on loving anyway.

THE
VIPER'S
KISS

PART 1

Chapter
1

HANNA BLINKED. TWICE.

Jon was still there. She must really be awake this time.

His cheek rested on his arm, which was draped along the edge of the bed in which she lay, his forearm fin concealed under a long black sleeve. His other web-fingered hand was folded gently around one of her own, warm and reassuring. The rest of his long, lean, fighter's body sprawled in a massive armchair pulled up beside the bed.

Even in sleep, his face looked worn and tight. Tendrils of dark hair had escaped from his multitude of tiny braids, falling loose over his cheek. Carefully, Hanna disentangled her fingers from his sleeping grasp and nudged his hair behind his ear, then traced the firm line of his jaw until she reached his full, frowning lips.

He had come for her. In the darkness, and pain, and confusion, Jon had come for her, a defiant shadow dancing with death—The Viper in the Night.

And now he was here. Wherever here was.

The room beyond him was not at all familiar. Wainscoted walls stretched up to a high, coffered ceiling. A marble fireplace occupied one wall, and a large bay window with a cushioned window seat dominated another, framing a picturesque view of a sunlit garden. It was all taste- fully and expensively decorated in tones of taupe and cream and a pale green that accentuated the elegant carved wood furniture. Certainly not her own house. Or Jon's.

A sharp intake of breath from behind startled her, and Hanna turned her head to see Narista sitting in another armchair on the opposite side of the bed—which, Hanna realized, was at least king sized, with a canopy and pale green velvet curtains pulled back and tied to tall posts at each corner. *Definitely* not her own bed.

Narista closed the book she held and pointedly laid it on an ornate side table. "Miss Bradley," she whispered with a reproving frown, "please do not wake my brother. This is the first sleep he's had in three days."

"Three days?" Hanna whispered, thinking back, trying to account for that much time.

She and Jon had talked. She'd told him everything. And he had believed her. Her throat tightened. Jon *believed* her. In fact, he'd had answers to questions that had plagued her for years.

He had walked her home. Kissed her goodnight.

And after that . . .?

The nightmares. Dalathek's face in her bathroom mirror. Dalathek's hands on her body. The same nightmares that had haunted her dreams since she was seventeen.

Except . . . this time, it had been real again. *Dalathek's hand in her hair. Dalathek's knife at her throat.*

Pain.

But this time, Jon had been there. He'd stopped the rest from happening. Still . . . three days? She couldn't make it fit.

"You asked him to stay," Narista hissed, recapturing Hanna's attention. "I told him you were delirious, but he didn't care."

Stay with me . . .

The lab. Or maybe it was a hospital. Had that part been real?

"And you sat with me too." Hanna whispered.

Narista gave her head an exasperated shake. "The rest of us took turns. But Jon wouldn't leave."

"Still," Hanna whispered, "you didn't have to do that. Thank you."

"*Someone* had to. We couldn't very well leave the two of you alone together for that long."

"Why?" Hanna frowned. "What did you think Jon would do?"

Narista's eyes flew wide with outrage. "My brother's honor is without question!"

"I'm not questioning Jon's honor," Hanna whispered, "I'm just wondering what you thought would happen. After all, I was unconscious. Or did you think I was going to seduce him in my sleep?"

Narista's eyes narrowed. "Jon would *never* lie with a woman who was not his wife. He follows the Sower. And he knows his duty to his House."

Hanna blinked. "Do you mean to tell me Jon has never—"

"Humans," Narista made the word sound like a profanity, "will lie with anyone. I've seen your entertainment media. For you, it's a mere matter of physical gratification, sometimes mixed with ephemeral emotion. You think no one else is affected by your actions."

"Humans aren't all like that," Hanna said.

Narista made a dismissive gesture and continued as if Hanna hadn't spoken. "Talessanins know that when two people come together it isn't merely a light matter between two individuals; it's the union of Houses, of bloodlines, reaching infinitely into the past, and into the future. It affects parents and grandparents, children and grandchildren, the flow of wealth and power, the transmission of customs and traditions to the next generation, and the generations beyond. The seeds of life are sacred, to be planted with deliberation and nurtured with care, not strewn heedlessly and abandoned. *Of course* Jon has never. But I very much doubt you can say the same for yourself, *human*. And I will not have you involving my brother in vicious gossip."

"Enough!" Jon surged to his feet on the other side of the bed, startling both of the women. His furious gaze was locked on his sister. "You will apologize, Narista. Now."

Narista rose to her feet, face defiant, jabbing an accusing finger in Hanna's direction. "She's a *human*, Jon. I've said nothing untrue." She was no longer whispering.

"Yes, she is a human," Jon retorted. "A human I have never seen behave dishonorably in any way. A human who is recovering from a nearly fatal wound given to her by a Talessanin man who drugged her, kidnapped her, and threatened to rape her. Would you like to explain again how much more virtuous Talessanins are than humans?"

"Surely you're not suggesting the entire Talessanin kinship should be condemned because of the actions of one deviant individual!" Narista snapped.

"Surely *you* are not suggesting," Jon said with icy calm, "that one individual human should be condemned based on the actions of others in her kinship."

"So what you're saying," Hanna interrupted calmly, "is that a chaperon was considered necessary because you wanted to protect both of us from the hastily formed opinions of ignorant people, not because you thought anything untoward might actually happen if we were unsupervised. I can see how that makes sense."

Both of them stared at her.

"Well, I did ask, Jon. Narista was just answering my question. And maybe a few other questions I hadn't thought of asking yet. We didn't realize you were awake."

"I was not." Jon scowled. "But I am now."

"Me too." Hanna grinned.

An answering smile spread across Jon's face, and he began to laugh. "You *are* awake!" he exclaimed. "And we are bickering like children." He shook his head ruefully and sat on the edge of the bed. "How are you feeling, Hanna? We were most anxious."

Hanna considered. "Not as bad as I'd expect after . . . what happened. A little shaky. Also hungry. And I have no idea where I am."

Narista made a soft, disgusted sound.

Jon cleared his throat. "You are safe, Hanna. You are in the human wing of the guest quarters at the Talessanin Empire's North American Continental Embassy on Earth."

"The embassy?"

That would be somewhere in the Rockies on the border between the United States and Canada, although the news reports always said the exact location was a closely guarded secret.

Jon nodded. "You seemed to find the medical complex distressing, so you were kept sedated until your injuries had healed sufficiently to move you here."

"Distressing?" Narista muttered indignantly. "She tried to kill the medics."

Jon glared at his sister. "You would probably do the same if you woke up surrounded by strange humans. She will be much more comfortable as a guest of the embassy until Dalathek is caught."

A cold prickle ran up Hanna's spine. "They haven't caught him?"

Jon's jaw clenched, almost like a flinch, but his voice was steady enough when he said quietly, "Not yet. But it is only a matter of time."

The prickle twisted in her throat. *Dalathek's mouth on her mouth. Dalathek's knife in her gut. Dalathek's harsh whisper: "This is not finished!"*

Hoarsely, she asked, "How *much* time?"

"Perhaps a day. Perhaps several weeks," Jon said. "It is impossible to say."

"*Weeks*?" Panic clutched at Hanna's insides. "No. I have to go home. Rachel and Tiffany are probably frantic. And Harold Purcell is expecting more of my paintings at the gallery." She knew she wasn't being entirely rational, but she needed to have this be over. She needed to get back to her regular routine so she didn't go crazy. Routine was what kept the nightmares at bay.

She pushed herself into a sitting position, trying not to wince at the pain that flashed through her belly when she moved.

Jon placed a restraining hand on her shoulder, just long enough for her to feel the comforting warmth of his skin through the thin white gown she was apparently wearing, then pulled it back as if afraid his touch might break her. Carefully, he cradled her hand between both of his instead.

"Tomin has informed your friends. Rachel said to tell you everything is taken care of." He let out a tired sigh. "This is my fault, Hanna. I should never have allowed him to escape. Please, you must let us keep you safe until he is caught."

"*Allowed* him?" Narista snorted. "Jon, you were unarmed, unarmored, outnumbered nine to one, and had your hands tied together. It was a foolish risk. You're lucky you didn't get chopped into stew meat." Her glare made it plain she considered the whole thing Hanna's fault.

Jon's lips pressed together. "Narista," he said through gritted teeth, "perhaps you could go tell the medic on duty that Hanna is awake."

"So you can kiss her when I'm not looking?"

"I have been given permission." Jon raised an eyebrow at his sister. "I could kiss her when you *are* looking if you would prefer."

"Really." Narista scoffed. "Permission. Knife and everything, I suppose." She directed a contemptuous glare at Hanna. "She's *human*, Jon. Does she even know what giving permission means?" Without waiting for an answer, she added pointedly, "I'm coming right back," and left, slamming the door behind her.

Hanna scowled at Jon. "What does she mean, do I know what giving permission means? What *does* it mean? And what was that about a knife?"

All the haggard exhaustion returned to Jon's face. "It means I have been impertinent again. I am sorry, Hanna.".

He sighed regretfully as he released her hand and moved from the bed back to his chair. "The knife is a Talessanin courtship custom. A woman presents her suitor with a knife bearing a symbol of herself or her House on the pommel. If either she or the suitor wishes to end the relationship, the knife is returned. While a man possesses a woman's courting knife, it is contemptible for him to pay court to another woman. And it is vulgar for a woman to behave too intimately toward a man wearing another woman's knife." He shrugged one shoulder. "But you are not Talessanin. The knife does not matter."

"I see." Hanna frowned. "And permission?"

"Ah. As to that . . ." Jon scrubbed a hand over his tousled braids and drew a deep breath. "I was only . . . guessing. I know of no human equivalent to the granting of permission. Human customs seem remarkably confusing and contradictory to me, and perhaps I have misunderstood your intentions. But you had kissed me once already that night, and I do not think you are . . . casual . . . with your kisses."

He shifted in his seat, leaning forward with his elbows propped on his knees and his eyes focused on his clasped hands. "That night, you said perhaps our friendship could include a romantic claim of the sort that would allow me to kiss you whenever I liked." He shot her a quick glance before focusing his gaze back on his hands. "Among Talessanins, a woman may sample a man's kisses whenever she pleases, provided he is unattached and willing. But a man must never kiss a woman without asking unless she has granted him permission. A suitor who has been formally granted permission may be somewhat more forward in his expressions of affection than one who is merely a private supplicant.

"Humans seem to arrange things more . . . informally . . . so when I walked you home, I took a risk and kissed you without asking first. When you did not protest, I decided to interpret that as permission. Of a sort."

"I see," Hanna mused. "And if it *was* permission, what would that mean?"

He turned his face toward her slightly, watching her from under his long lashes. "It would mean you officially accept me as a suitor. That you recognize our relationship as one that could, after a suitable period of getting to know one another better, potentially lead to . . . to betrothal and marriage."

Betrothal? Marriage? Hanna's heart flipped over and her cheeks warmed. *Was he really that serious about this?*

Jon must have noticed her reaction, because he sighed and looked down at his hands again. "Or not. The privilege may be withdrawn as easily as it is granted. But it would not obligate you in any way. A Talessanin man may court only one woman at a time, but a woman may accept as many suitors as she wishes."

"Is . . . is that what you want, Jon?" Hanna's voice came out a little breathless. "Permission?"

One of his shoulders rose and fell. Shy. Vulnerable. His hazel gaze flickered up to meet hers. "I think I have wanted permission to court you ever since you named your conditions for watching a movie with you." A boyish grin tugged at his lips, then turned into a pensive frown as he looked down. "But I have no wish to pressure you into a relationship you do not desire."

Hanna's heart pounded in her throat. What *did* she want from their relationship?

To see where it went.

She hadn't thought any farther ahead than that. There hadn't been time.

But . . . that was really all he was asking for. Wasn't it?

Her hesitation must've dragged on too long, because Jon rose from his chair and paced over to look out the window, back stiff, shoulders tense.

"Forgive me," he said softly. "You have just woken up injured in an unfamiliar place. I should have waited to speak of this. I *meant* to wait. I have had three days to consider what you said that night before Dalathek came and . . . and after. But for you it must feel like only hours have passed. Moments, perhaps." He turned back to face her, brows drawn, mouth resolute. "Some things should not be said in haste."

"Some things should not be said *at all*." Narista's voice was sour and clipped.

How long had she been standing in the open doorway? Hanna hadn't heard the door open.

Jon's sister stepped the rest of the way into the room, and two other women silently followed. The short one with graying hair wore a red tunic and trousers, and the other, a slender blond, hardly more than a girl, wore a green dress that looked like a uniform.

Jon glanced over at the three women, scrubbed a hand back through his braids, and turned back to Hanna.

"She is right," he said softly, brow furrowing. "I should not have spoken of this. Perhaps you do not even remember all that passed between us then. And I . . . I am not even human. Why would you want . . . . Perhaps I misunderstood." He shook his head. "I have been a fool. Forgive me. I . . . I should go."

Grimly, he headed for the door.

"Wait!" Hanna flung back the covers, intending to go after him, but the twisting motion of her body as she heaved her legs over the side of the bed sent a sharp pain through her abdomen. Her startled gasp was punctuated with a dull thump as something pink rolled out from the tangle of blankets and landed on the carpet.

Jon spun into a crouch, a slender blade glinting in his grip, eyes locked on the thing on the floor.

Hanna's pink teddy bear stared balefully back at him.

It was the gray-haired woman's soft chuckle that broke the tension and made Jon relax. He shook his head sheepishly and made the knife disappear before he moved to pick up the bear and press it into Hanna's hands.

Her brows rose. "You brought Mr. Bickles?"

He shook his head sheepishly . "I wanted you to feel safe. But perhaps I have been impertinent in this as well."

He sighed and turned back toward the door.

"Jon, *wait*."

He stopped and half turned, face carefully impassive as he studied her with those dark eyes of his.

She probably looked like a child, standing there in her white cotton nightgown, clutching her teddy bear by one lumpy pink leg.

It didn't matter. She cleared her throat. "You didn't misunderstand. My lack of protest when you kissed me goodnight meant exactly what you thought it did, and I'm pretty sure I remember everything we said to each other that night. I haven't changed my mind. You just caught me off guard, that's all."

A slow, wondering smile spread across Jon's face, and he turned more fully to face her. "Truly?"

"Truly."

"I have permission to court you?"

"Yes, Jon." Hanna laughed. "You're not being impertinent, you're just being a little exasperating. You said you were going to kiss me, and you haven't yet."

His smile morphed into that crooked grin that always made Hanna's pulse beat faster. "You would allow me to kiss you? Now?"

"Only if you want to."

He stepped closer and laid one web-fingered hand against her cheek, then hesitated, making sure she really meant it, before leaning down to give her a tender, lingering kiss that sent tingles all the way down to Hanna's toes.

Narista emitted a gagging grunt.

Jon paid his sister no mind at all, finishing the job quite thoroughly before he straightened with a contented sigh, gathering Hanna even closer, tucking her protectively against his body. "I am glad you are awake, Little Mouse," he murmured. "I have been wanting to kiss you again for days."

"Sower save us!" Narista left the same way she'd come in, slamming the door on her way out. Apparently, the other two women would suffice as chaperons.

Hanna laughed into Jon's chest and murmured. "Well, you did warn her."

Jon stroked the fingers of one hand down the middle of Hanna's back to her waist. "Perhaps she should have taken a little longer fetching your medic."

Then he sighed regretfully. "However, your medic has arrived, and she will want to check your wound."

Releasing his embrace, he shifted back half a step so he could see her face. Softly, he asked. "Do you still wish me to stay?"

"Um . . ." Hot blood rushed to Hanna's face. Had he stayed before when they checked her wound? *How much of her had he seen?*

Her alarm must've shown on her face. Jon smiled reassuringly and brushed the backs of his fingers against her cheek. "I would turn my back or wait in the sitting room. In the medical facility there was a screen. I have no wish to violate your privacy, Hanna. It is only . . . when you woke before, you were so afraid. You asked me to stay with you. And I want you to feel safe."

Hanna studied his face. He was clearly exhausted. And she wasn't sure she even remembered what safe felt like well enough to recognize it if she felt it again. The medic and her green-uniformed companion seemed harmless enough. For aliens. And Jon clearly trusted them.

Drawing a steadying breath, she said, "I'm all right. You should go get some sleep. And maybe a shower." She shifted so she could look up at him. "And when was the last time you ate?" She poked him playfully in the ribs. "Have they been feeding you?"

Jon chuckled. He moved one hand up to cradle her face and ran his thumb up her cheekbone, then bent to kiss her again—a small one this time, but no less tender. Then he touched his forehead to hers and murmured, "I have missed you, Little Mouse."

Chapter 2

WHEN JON STEPPED FROM HANNA'S bedroom into the guest suite's sitting room, Tomin was pacing back and forth in front of the glass-paned double doors that led out to the private walled patio and the courtyard beyond. At the sound of the door closing, he stopped and looked up.

"Report." It came out more abrupt than Jon intended.

Tomin shook his head. "They lost him somewhere in Singapore. But they've got his jump ship and the orbital port is locked down. He won't make it off planet in that shuttle. They'll find him."

So Dalathek was still out there. Part of Jon longed to join the hunt, to be the one to bring his former mentor to justice for what he'd done to Hanna, both this time and . . . before. But he couldn't leave her. What if Dalathek doubled back?

As if reading Jon's thoughts, Tomin said quietly, "They'll find him. And this is a high security suite for visiting heads of state. She'll be safe here until they do."

He gestured toward the door Jon had come out of. "How is she?"

"She is with her medical adviser. They want privacy."

A snorting laugh came from the other side of the room—Chance was sprawled on one of the sofas in front of the marble fireplace with his boots up on the armrest. "Three days sitting by her bedside, holding her hand, fluffing her pillows, snarling at her medics if they didn't jump fast enough, and the first thing she does when she wakes up is throw you out? Isn't that just like a woman."

Jon shuffled over and dropped into one of the armchairs next to Chance's sofa. "It was not quite the *first* thing she did." He tried to hold back the smile that was tugging at his lips.

Chance twisted his head around to look at Jon. "No?" He sat up and leaned forward, resting his elbows on his knees. "Tell." His amber eyes laughed in his dark face.

Jon shrugged one shoulder and took a deep breath. "Well, she . . ." He stopped to wrestle the smile into submission and failed utterly. It broke across his face as an idiotic grin. He decided he didn't care and let it stay there. "She let me kiss her."

"Of course she did." Chance leaned back into the sofa. "Fair payment for services rendered. You did save her life, after all."

That sobered Jon fast, and the smile died. "Barely. It was close for a while." He shook his head and looked down at his hands. He had never felt so helpless in his life as he had sitting beside her, watching her bleed out on the street. And then on the medic shuttle when her heart had stopped . . .

His fault. He'd made her a target.

Tomin lowered himself onto the other end of the sofa. "They wouldn't have moved her to the guest quarters if she was still in any danger from her injuries. I'm sure she'll be herself again in no time."

Jon startled himself by laughing. "Oh, she is very much herself." The idiotic grin was back, too, though softer now. "She said she had to go home and paint more pictures."

Tomin grinned back at him and relaxed. "There you go," he said. "That sounds *exactly* like Hanna."

"What else did she say?" Chance was watching Jon's face again. Sometimes Chance was a little too perceptive.

"She said I need a shower."

"She isn't wrong. What else? There's something you're not telling us."

Jon was almost afraid to say it out loud. It was still too new. Too incredibly precious. And he wasn't certain how his friends would react.

But if he *didn't* tell them, the joy of it might burn a hole through his chest.

He cleared his throat. "She gave me permission to court her."

Chance nodded in satisfaction. "Sensible girl."

Tomin sighed, frowning thoughtfully. "Courting a human. You're really going to do it then? I mean, I'm quite looking forward to the fireworks myself, but your sister looked ready to tear someone apart with her teeth when she blew through here a minute ago."

"His brother won't mind," Chance put in helpfully.

"Probably not." Tomin nodded. "He might even encourage it if he thinks it'll forward his agenda. And Jon's mother will most likely come around eventually. His step-father will be harder to—"

"He has no say in this," Jon snapped. "I retired from the Winds, I am no longer his to command."

Tomin raised his eyebrows. "Look, Jon, I don't know what passed between you and the Emperor that created this latest rift, but you know as well as I do that courting a human will only make it worse." He shook his head. "Your choices affect other people. More so than most, because of who you are. You need to choose carefully."

Jon scowled. Quietly, he said, "I have spent my life choosing what was good for the Empire. For my House. For my family."

Tomin sighed. "I know that," he said gently. "You even abdicated your claim to the Throne because you think your brother would be a better emperor. All I'm saying is—"

"Is it too much to ask that in this one thing I might choose what is good for myself?" Jon's frustration showed in his voice. He scrubbed a hand back over his loosening braids and slumped back in his armchair, scowling at the carpet.

"What about Hanna?" Tomin persisted. "Is she ready for this? Does she know what she's getting into?"

Jon was saved from having to answer by the sound of door chimes and a perfunctory knock at the suite's main entry. Tomin went to open it, and Chance rose respectfully to his feet as Kamm swept in from the corridor with Narista on his arm.

Jon rose too and strode over to accept his brother's customary greeting, clasping Kamm's upraised hand and dance-stepping close until their shoulders touched, followed by a brotherly embrace.

Narista just folded her arms across her chest and glared at him. He ignored her.

"I thought you were stuck in meetings all afternoon," Jon said, stepping back so he could see his brother's face.

Kamm grinned. "Narista was good enough to pass me a note to let me know Hanna was awake, so I called a recess." He glanced toward the bedroom door. "How is she? Is she accepting visitors?"

"She is with her medic. I think it might be a while. But she seems well enough, considering the circumstances." Jon couldn't stop the silly grin from making another appearance as he thought of the look on her face when she scolded him for not kissing her. He rather liked being scolded by Hanna.

Kamm grinned back at him. "I'm glad to hear it."

Narista cleared her throat meaningfully.

Kamm's grin turned a little sour, and he shot a look at her before clapping a hand down on Jon's shoulder. "Narista tells me Hanna granted you permission to court her."

Narista's glare turned smug. She must've brought Kamm here to try to talk Jon out of it.

That wasn't going to work.

Jon's chin came up and his grin faded as he looked his brother squarely in the eyes, daring him to object. "She did."

Kamm's serious eyes studied Jon's face for a long moment, weighing whatever he saw there. Then he nodded, and his smile came back, a little tired this time, almost sad. But he gave Jon's shoulder a companionable pat as he let go and said, "Then I'm happy for you. May she bring you all the joy you hope for."

"You're *what*?" Narista unfolded her arms and put her hands on her hips, sharing her outrage between her brothers.

"You can't be serious," she said to Kamm. Clearly, she'd expected him to take her side.

Kamm pinched the bridge of his nose and said tiredly, "She makes him happy, Narista. Can't you just let him be happy?"

"She's a *human!*"

"Some of my favorite people are humans," Kamm said calmly. "Have I introduced you to—"

"Salenia hasn't even left the planet yet." Narista turned her anger on Jon. "If you're going to play this obscene little game, you could at least wait until Salenia isn't looking."

"Salenia is *your* guest, Narista, not Jon's." Kamm's voice had taken on an edge of impatience. "It's not his job to keep her happy. And I have more important things to do than—"

"You know as well as I do why Salenia's really here." Narista snapped. "She wanted to see Jon." She jabbed a finger at Jon to emphasize her point. "And if Jon had *any* sense at all, he'd want to see Salenia."

"He had enough sense to stay alive all those years as Commander of the Nine," Kamm said sourly. "I think he can manage this."

"Not so far." Narista folded her arms across her chest again and addressed herself to Kamm, pointedly turning her back on Jon. "Salenia is *Ahnat* to House Trakanaleth, second only to our own House in power and wealth. The friendship between our families fosters stability within the Empire, and a union with her would secure our family's claim to the Throne for generations. A rift with Trakanaleth could throw the whole Empire out of balance. And yet *he* wants to play games with that little . . . that . . ." She waved an agitated hand at the bedroom door.

"Woman he loves?" Kamm said wryly. He drew a deep breath and grasped both of Narista's shoulders so she would have to look him in the face. "A union between Jon and Salenia would also put Trakanaleth one step closer to the Throne. And Salenia's father doesn't want to destabilize the Empire any more than we do. The tide of power ebbs and flows, often in ways we can't see and couldn't change if we wanted to. Jon deserves a little happiness. Leave him alone, and let this sort itself out."

Chapter 3

HANNA BARELY HAD A CHANCE to catch her breath after the bedroom door closed behind Jon before the woman in red stepped briskly forward. "Miss Bradley," she said, "my name is Arastan. I will be acting as your medical adviser while you recover from your injury." She offered her hand to Hanna palm up. The submissive greeting.

Hanna hesitated. It didn't feel right to claim social superiority over this woman. But of course, Arastan knew more about the proprieties of such things than Hanna did. She decided to follow the medic's lead, tentatively extending her own hand palm down for the wrist clasp.

The woman nodded approval and gestured for the blond girl to join them. "Susan has been assigned to be your maid during your stay at the embassy."

The girl's wide blue eyes shifted from Hanna to the door where Jon had disappeared and back before she stepped forward and dropped a curtsy. "I'm pleased you are awake, my lady."

Hanna blinked. A *maid*? What would she do with a maid? Especially one who curtsied and called her 'my lady.' But, when in Rome.

"Um. Thank you, Susan."

Arastan gestured for Hanna to take the chair Jon had occupied. "Do you remember what happened?"

Hanna shrugged. "Dalathek stabbed me in the belly with a dagger. It's a bit muddled, but I think I remember as much about it as I care to."

The medic used a hand-held scanning device to examine Hanna's wound, which had already healed to a thin, reddish purple line that snaked across her abdomen from the edge of her rib cage on the upper left to just below her waist on the right. The skin over the wound was healing well, Arastan explained, and the scar should fade quickly. The deeper injuries, however, would be slower to mend, especially where Dalathek's knife had taken a good-sized chip out of one rib. And it might be even slower for Hanna, since she was human.

All humans, according to Arastan, were deficient in myoglobin (whatever that was), which affected oxygenation protocols. They also had excessively high levels of something-or-other that slowed the action of bone stim nodes (whatever those were) considerably. Hanna didn't understand all the technical terms, but she got the general gist—humans were uncannily similar to Talessanins, and many advanced medical techniques could be used on them, but there were some differences in body composition and chemistry that required adjustments in treatment, which Talessanin scientists were still in the process of refining.

When she finished her exam, Arastan nodded once. "You seem to be recovering more or less as expected. We'll try a small meal, but I'm afraid your diet will be somewhat restricted until your digestive tract has recovered more. After that . . ." She frowned. "A soak in the hot pools would help the regeneration fluid work more quickly, but there's still too much sedative in your system for that. Tomorrow, perhaps. We shall see. We normally use a different sedative for humans, but you . . ."

She pursed her lips and studied Hanna's face. "You remember the attack. Do you remember the medical facility as well?"

"Sort of." Hanna thought back. "It's a bit hazy. You were there?"

Arastan nodded. "Kamminalithen *Ehrat* insisted. I am one of the foremost experts on human physiology." She raised one eyebrow. "You nearly took a slice out of me with that surgical blade."

Hanna's cheeks warmed. "I'm sorry about that. I was—"

"The fault was ours, not yours." Arastan waved Hanna's apology away with a dismissive hand. "We miscalculated. That sedative is safe and effective for most humans, but there is a small subset who are resistant, for whom it wears off too quickly. We neglected to test you for that in advance because we were in a hurry, and it isn't very common." She offered Hanna a wry, apologetic smile. Then her face went more serious. "One might think, after all these years of studying humans, I would know better."

The way the woman was looking at her sent a sudden chill down Hanna's spine. "How many years have you been . . . studying humans?" It had been eight years since the Talessanin embassy ships landed. But Hanna knew the aliens had been around for at least five years before that.

Arastan gave her one more long, penetrating look. Then she closed her eyes. "You remember *that*, too, don't you." It wasn't really a question. She shook her head and drew a deep breath. "Your DNA scan matched a record in our data banks. One of the first test specimens brought in by the Winds during the early days. Non-reproductive female. Late adolescence. Repair of minor abnormality in the formation of the left kidney."

Hanna's heart lurched. She couldn't breathe. Her head began to swim, and she swayed dizzily sideways, pressing the heel of one hand against her forehead. Gentle hands caught her shoulders and helped her onto the bed. Arastan used some of the pillows to raise Hanna's feet and tucked Mr. Bickles against Hanna's chest. After a moment, the dizziness began to subside.

"Try to breathe slowly and deeply," the medic murmured. "We had to give you a rather large infusion of synthetic blood. It can sometimes cause lightheadedness or vertigo if a patient overexerts herself or becomes startled." She gently stroked Hanna's shoulder with her webbed fingers. "The effect may be more pronounced for you, because you are human. Myoglobin deficiency."

As if that explained anything.

Hanna wrapped both arms around her teddy bear and squeezed. Her voice came out small and frightened. "Is that what they did when they cut me open? Kidney repair? I never knew."

Arastan patted Hanna's shoulder one more time and went back to the armchair. "You weren't supposed to ever know any of it had happened. We used the same sedative back then, along with a paralytic to keep our subjects from shifting in their sleep during the comprehensive bioscan. But it wouldn't have worked properly on you then, either. I suppose you woke up in the middle of it all and found you couldn't move."

She sighed. "I'm so very sorry. If we'd realized back then, we could've patched your memory. Now, though, too many other memories will be attached to that one, and it wouldn't work. She shook her head. Your collector was meant to have observed you for several days after your release and reported any problems."

Oh, Dalathek had observed her, all right. Up close and personal. Hanna drew a steadying breath and opened her eyes. "I'd rather know. It's part of my reality whether I remember it or not, and I'd rather know."

Arastan nodded slowly, still studying Hanna's face. "Your scans revealed something else, too. You have a great deal of old micro-scarring, Miss Bradley. All over your body, but particularly in the skin over your chest. The injuries were healed using Talessanin medical technology, but the alignments were slightly off, so it was probably not done by a medical professional."

She waited for Hanna to say something, but Hanna's pulse was making her whole head throb, and her voice was caught at the back of her throat.

"Would you like to tell me what happened, Miss Bradley?" Arastan's voice was soft. Sympathetic.

Hanna's heart pounded harder. Even *thinking* about the things Dalathek had done to her in that shed all those years ago brought back the scents of old wood and gasoline, the taste of blood in her mouth, the ghost of the white-hot terror of being unable to move as her tormentor's hands brushed a stray lock of hair from her cheek . . . closed around her throat . . . moved down her body.

"No," she managed to whisper.

Arastan waited a moment, letting Hanna collect herself before asking, "Does . . . your suitor . . . know?"

"Yes."

The medic thought that over. "You are in a difficult position, Miss Bradley. And this new assault can't be helping matters." Her lips drew into a troubled frown. "Still, you seem to be adjusting remarkably well." Again, she studied Hanna's face. Searching. Analyzing.

Hanna picked at a frayed place on Mr. Bickles's ear. "I should probably be more . . . upset. Shouldn't I?" She shrugged. "But it mostly feels like just another one of my nightmares."

"You have nightmares?" Arastan's frown deepened. "Regularly?"

Dust motes in sunlight . . . her back against the wood slat wall . . .

Hanna coughed out a grim chuckle. "And flashbacks, and panic attacks, and sometimes hallucinations. Don't worry, though, it wasn't the non-consensual kidney surgery that did it. At least not most of it. It was . . . the other thing. But I manage."

That must sound convincing, coming from a grown woman clutching a teddy bear.

After a long, silent moment, Arastan said, "Very well, then. I'll have Susan bring you something to eat. Get as much rest as you are able. Some mild pain is to be expected at this stage of recovery, especially with sudden movement, but if it becomes severe, report it to Susan so she can summon a medic."

She rose and offered Hanna a parting bow. "I will check on you again tomorrow."

After Arastan left, Susan began bustling about the room. She straightened the chairs and pushed back the curtains on the bay window to let the sunlight in. Then she set up a small folding tea table and carefully laid out a china dinner service on a crisp white tablecloth. She was older than Hanna had thought at first, probably only a few years younger than she was herself. The woman's slender build and nervous hesitation had made her seem younger.

And Hanna realized something else, too, as she watched Susan arranging the flatware. Although the woman moved with the smooth, precise grace Hanna associated with Talessanins, she had no finger webbing. Human, then. It shouldn't have surprised her, she supposed, with a name like Susan, but it did.

While Hanna dutifully ate her supper of sweet, flavorful porridge, Susan prepared a scented bath in the adjacent bathroom (which had a tub big enough to fit four people as well as a walk-in shower that was larger than Hanna's entire bathroom at home) and found a fresh white nightgown in a massive carved mahogany wardrobe that stood against one wall. She helped Hanna bathe and dress—any amount of twisting sent a jolt of pain through her insides—and then tucked her back into bed with Mr. Bickles. Hanna wanted to see Jon again, but she was exhausted, and he was probably sleeping. Soon, she was too.

She woke again two hours later, screaming and choking, with the feel of Dalathek's hands fresh on her skin from the nightmare. At her request, Susan brought her a cup of herbal tea and took her out to the small service kitchen off the sitting room to show her the control panel for the guest suite's security system.

The second time the nightmares woke Hanna, Susan helped her check each window and door in the suite to make sure it was really locked.

The third time, which must have been some time after midnight, Susan found Hanna in the bathroom, sobbing from the horror of the dreams and the pain of vomiting up her porridge. The maid's hands were gentle as she cleaned Hanna up again and put her back to bed with Mr. Bickles clutched tight against her chest.

It was a long night for both of them.

When the first gray light of morning began to filter in through the bay window, Hanna finally fell into a deep, dreamless sleep from which she didn't wake until well after noon.

When she did finally drift back into consciousness, Susan, who looked fresh and cheerful despite the disruptions of the night, brought more herbal tea and another bowl of porridge—savory this time, with shreds of flaky fish mixed in. As Hanna ate, the maid told her Arastan had come by that morning to check on her patient and left orders for her not to be disturbed. The Viper, she reported in a trembling voice, had come twice, refusing refreshment, but waiting in the sitting room for nearly an hour each time before he was called away to other duties. Tomin and Chance had made one polite inquiry each, and Jon's brother, Kamm, had sent a nice arrangement of tiny pink flowers, but had not come himself—unsurprising, since the heir to an intergalactic throne undoubtedly had stacks of far more important things to do than wait around for his brother's girlfriend to wake up.

When Hanna finished eating, Susan summoned Arastan. The medic ran her scanner over Hanna's abdomen again and had her sit, stand, and walk about the room. The scan, which indicated that the last of the sedative had cleared out of Hanna's system, was the only part of the procedure that didn't hurt to some degree, but the pain seemed less than it had the day before, and the scar had faded to a sickly-looking pink. Arastan declared herself satisfied with Hanna's progress and gave strict instructions for her patient to go soak for as long as she could manage in the hot pools in the compound's courtyard.

Chapter
4

AFTER CLEANING UP A LITTLE, Hanna emerged from the bathroom to find that the bed had been made up with fresh linens, and Mr. Bickles was propped cozily against the pillows. Susan stood in front of the enormous wardrobe, studying its contents. Most of its interior was taken up with an assortment of Talessanin dresses that looked new, expensive, and about Hanna's size. On one side, though, several hangers held baggy t-shirts, a couple of pairs of old sweatpants with paint stains on them, and one or two other items of familiar clothing. Hanna ran a hand over them, wishing she could slip into the softest of them and curl up on her couch at home with a good book.

"Those were in a case sent from your home, my lady," Susan said with an apologetic half smile. "There are some underclothes and other personal items as well, but no bathing suits were included." She pulled open a small drawer on one side. "I would have laid one out for you from the selection provided by the embassy, but I wasn't certain about my lady's tastes."

Hanna chuckled. "Rachel and Tiffany probably thought I just needed comfortable alternatives to hospital gowns. Healing from something like this would take a lot longer at a human hospital." She sighed and added, "I'm not certain about my tastes either, to be honest. I haven't even owned a swimsuit in years."

Deep water was not a safe place for a panic attack—and she *would* have a panic attack anywhere she couldn't breathe freely. And … well, she didn't like men looking at her body. But this was only a soak in a shallow pool. By herself. She could do this. Doctor's orders.

Susan laid all the bathing suits out on the bed for Hanna's inspection. One of them was a traditional Talessanin design called a *lanan*, which consisted only of two long strips of cloth. Susan explained that one strip draped around the neck, crisscrossed over the chest, and then tied around the waist, while the other strip passed between the legs and was secured by tucking it under the waist wrap in front and back, and letting the ends hang down like a skirt. Hanna couldn't imagine appearing in public in such a get-up. If one knot slipped, the whole affair would fall right off. The other suits weren't much better. There was a skimpy bikini that seemed to be more string than fabric, and a one-piece that didn't look too bad until Hanna held it up and realized it had far too many strategically placed cut-outs for comfort.

The one Hanna finally settled on was a plain black one-piece with a halter style top and a built-in skirt clearly designed to mimic the drape of the breechcloth portion of a *lanan*. The suit's back was open from neck to waist, probably designed to accommodate a Talessanin woman's dorsal fin, but apart from a slightly too deep neckline—which Susan quickly adjusted with a few well-placed stitches from a needle and thread she evidently kept in her pocket—the front covered all the important bits, including the scar across Hanna's abdomen.

Moving slowly, Hanna was able to put the swimsuit on by herself, but she couldn't quite manage the kind of twisting needed to get her arm into the second sleeve of the long, clingy silk robe Susan produced to go with it, and was glad of her maid's help.

Susan had just begun combing the tangles out of Hanna's hair, when a chime sounded from the sitting room to announce visitors at the guest suite's front door. The maid bustled out to answer it, and returned moments later, flustered and wide-eyed. "They're here, my lady!" she gasped. "Both of them! In the sitting room!"

Hanna blinked at her blankly. "Both of . . .?"

The maid blushed furiously and dropped a deep curtsy, then folded her shaking hands at her waist and bowed her head. Penitent. "Forgive me, my lady. I—" she cleared her throat, trying to collect herself. "My lady, the Imperial *Ehrat* and his brother the Kanestelan *Ehr* beg the p-privilege of waiting upon you in your sitting room at your convenience," she gulped. "And they said their retainers would admit the Kanestelan *Ahn* and the Trakanaleth *Ahnat* when they arrive so I may assist you without interruption."

"Jon is here?" Hanna's pulse quickened, and she couldn't repress a smile as she glanced toward the door.

"Yes, my lady." Susan snatched up the silver comb and began pulling, twisting, tucking, and pinning as if her life depended on it. "And his brother. I'll be as quick as I can, my lady."

Hanna squirmed under the onslaught. "Um . . . Susan," she said, "it makes me nervous to be called 'my lady.' I don't suppose you could just call me Hanna?"

Susan's hands froze. She cleared her throat. "I'm not sure I could, my lady, with half the imperial family in the sitting room." She swallowed hard. "And one of them the Viper himself."

Hanna laughed. "They're just people, Susan." The maid didn't look convinced.

When Susan had declared her suitably presentable, Hanna drew a steadying breath and opened the door to the sitting room, heart pattering at the prospect of seeing Jon.

Before she could even look around for him, a squealing bundle of lavender ruffles flung itself across the room and wrapped its skinny arms around Hanna's midsection. Hanna stifled a gasp and tried not to wince as she looked down into the beaming face of Tala, Jon's little niece.

"Miss Bradley!" the child piped, "I am glad you are better now. I was so distraught!"

"Distraught?" Hanna chuckled and hugged Tala back.

"Tala has been studying her English vocabulary." Kamm, younger and slighter of build than Jon, rose from one of the elegant sofas by the fireplace and strode over to lay a calming hand on his daughter's shoulder. "Having a new English-speaking friend seems to have improved her motivation. Welcome to the embassy, Hanna."

Hanna felt suddenly awkward. She wasn't even sure how she should address Jon's brother under these circumstances. Tomin hadn't coached her this time. She decided to err on the side of caution and held out her hand in the submissive greeting, palm turned upward. "Thank you for letting me stay here, Honored *Ehrat*."

Kamm tilted his head and raised his eyebrows. Instead of accepting her greeting with the appropriate palm-down wrist clasp, he took her hand in his own, palm to palm, raising their joined hands and dance-stepping closer until his bicep brushed her shoulder—the greeting between good friends. "We decided you'd call me Kamm. Remember?" He bent to place a brotherly kiss on her cheek. "It's good to see you so much recovered."

Hanna's face warmed, and she tried to think what to say, but Kamm stepped away, making a response unnecessary. Almost immediately, his place was taken by Tomin and then Chance, who also greeted her as a good friend, though without the kiss. Unlike Kamm, who was formally dressed in an embroidered longcoat, Tomin and Chance wore long, loose robes that hung open down the front, exposing breechcloths like the one Jon had worn in his hot tub at home.

Tomin saw her noticing and shot her a confidential grin, leaning close to murmur, "Arastan mentioned you were heading for the soaking pools, and we thought you might like some company."

So much for a quiet soak alone.

As he stepped away, the door chime sounded again, and Susan went to answer it. Narista and Salenia glided in, both wearing billowy silk wraps in the same style as Hanna's.

"I hope we haven't kept anyone waiting," Narista said cheerfully.

"Not at all." Kamm stepped forward with a smile to greet his sister. "Hanna only just arrived."

A dramatic sigh came from over by the French doors. "Yes, and she has greeted everyone but me. You wound me, Hanna." Jon stood with one shoulder propped against the door frame. His long black robe had snakes embroidered in gold thread writhing up the borders, and the way he stood made it fall open down the front, showing his bare, muscled chest and a black and gold loincloth. His mock pout turned into a disarming grin, and Hanna couldn't help laughing, even as her heart quickened.

"Why, there you are, Jon!" she teased back. "I thought maybe you'd gotten tired of waiting and had gone off to hunt giant venomous sloth creatures or something."

He crossed the room to greet her, and when he dance-stepped close, it wasn't just their forearms that touched; his thigh pressed against her hip, and his free hand came to rest on her back, coaxing her even closer. Surprised, she looked up at him, and he leaned down to kiss her firmly on the mouth. "Today, I am hunting little mice," he said with a slightly wicked grin.

A shocked gasp came from behind Hanna, and Jon looked up, scowling.

Hanna turned to see Narista looking slightly sick at the sight of her brother kissing a human again. The gasp, however, had come from Salenia, whose face had gone pale, lips tight, eyes narrowed. Hanna suddenly realized that the greeting she'd just received from Jon was the kind Salenia had so confidently, and unsuccessfully, attempted to elicit from him at his dinner party—the lovers' greeting.

The copper-haired beauty pasted on a long, cold smile, her eyes assessing Hanna as if really seeing her for the first time. "I'm so pleased you're feeling better, Miss Bradley," she purred. "We all hope you will recuperate quickly, so you can return home very soon. I'm sure you had other plans."

Return home soon? Other plans? Did Salenia think she was being subtle?

Hanna smiled sweetly back. "Thank you, Salenia, I'm sure you had plans of your own that I have interrupted."

Salenia's cheeks flushed, and her eyes flashed to Jon and back.

Across the room, Chance coughed and turned away.

Kamm cleared his throat. "Tala and I wish we could join you at the soaking pools," he said, sounding genuinely regretful. "But we have a previous commitment this evening. We just stopped by to wish you well now that you're awake." He held out a hand to his daughter. "Come Tala, we mustn't be late. You can visit Miss Bradley again another day."

Instead of taking her father's hand, Tala scampered over to hug Hanna again, more gently this time, then she was out the door, quick as a flash, leaving Kamm to catch up. He shook his head and smiled wryly as he followed her.

"May I escort you, Hanna?" Something in Jon's quiet voice as he offered his arm made Hanna look sharply up at him. His eyes held an intensity that stopped her breath—she could fall into those pond-shadow eyes and never find the bottom. Then he blinked, and it was gone.

When she tucked her fingers into the crook of his elbow, the wide sleeve of his robe shifted, giving her a glimpse of his half-unfolded forearm fin beneath.

Something there wasn't right.

"Wait," she said, tugging him to a stop as he turned toward the doors. She pulled the edge of the sleeve back, exposing the fin. A pale line ran across it from arm to edge.

"What's this?" she asked. "This wasn't here before."

"A minor injury. It is nothing to worry about." Jon folded his fin and tugged his sleeve back in place.

A prickling suspicion crept up Hanna's spine. "Let me see."

"It is nothing, Hanna," he crooned reassuringly. "We should—"

"Let me *see*," she insisted, stepping in front of him and placing both hands on her hips.

He sighed and pulled his sleeve back, extending his fin for her inspection. She ran a finger lightly along the line of the wound and turned his arm over so she could trace it back up the other side. There was a noticeable swelling at each of the fin spines, and one of them bent slightly.

"This cut went all the way through your fin," she said. "What happened?"

"I forgot for a moment that I was not wearing armor and blocked a dagger with my arm," he said gently. "It is not important. The scar will fade very soon, and Arastan says I will be back to swimming with it in another week. Maybe two."

He folded the fin and reached with his other hand to tug the sleeve back over it. As he did, the open front of his robe shifted, and Hanna caught sight of another new scar running back along his ribs under his arm.

She pushed back the edge of his robe so she could see it better. "And that?"

"A clean slice, easily repaired with a cell aligner and a little regeneration fluid," he said. "You will not even be able to see it in a day or two. It would be gone now if I had not waited so long to get it treated. It is nothing."

"Nothing?" Hanna's brows drew together. An odd emotion that seemed composed of both fear and indignation welled up in her chest. "That *nothing* is at least eight inches long. How did this happen?"

"Hanna—"

"This was for me, wasn't it?" It came out like an accusation. "When you were fighting Dalathek's men. Why didn't you tell me they hurt you?"

"I did not wish you to worry."

"I'm not a child, Jon. There's more, isn't there? What else are you not telling me? What did they do to you?"

"It does not matter."

"It matters to me. Show me."

Jon hesitated, studying her face, reading the determination in her eyes. He shrugged. "A scratch here." He pulled his other sleeve up and pointed to a barely visible white line on his upper arm, "from a throwing knife that mostly missed."

"And?" Hanna demanded.

"A small puncture here, where a throwing knife did not miss." He pushed back the edge of his robe and twisted to expose the back of his shoulder. "But it was not even poisoned. It is nothing, truly Hanna."

"And?"

"Hanna—"

"What else?" she insisted.

He sighed and showed her a smooth patch of pink skin on his other shoulder. "A mostly healed burn. It will probably not leave a permanent scar."

Hanna gasped. "That's as big as my hand, Jon! How did—"

"A pulse pistol," he said, his voice becoming defensive. "But it does not hurt anymore, only itches."

"They *shot* you?" Hanna stared at him. "And you didn't think I'd want to know that?"

He scowled. "It barely grazed me. It is nothing to fret over."

She folded her arms across her chest.

"What else? I want to know."

"Hanna—"

"I'm not kidding, Jon."

He glared back at her for a minute, stubborn defiance in his eyes. Then he reached over and pulled out a carved wood chair that sat next to an ornate tea table by the sitting room wall. Keeping his eyes locked with Hanna's, he thumped his foot down on the chair's seat and pulled back the side of his robe. The fabric of his breechcloth was wide and had been draped in a way that covered everything from his waist almost to his knees, leaving only a narrow gap at each side. In this position, however, the fabric fell away to front and back, and left his leg exposed to the hip.

Streaks of the deep purple, green, and yellow of healing bruises spread from his hip down his thigh and up under the wide belt of his breechcloth, forming ugly concentric curves around a roundish patch of paler skin and a sickly red lump in the middle of the mess.

"Jon . . ." Hanna's whisper trailed off in cold disbelief. "How?" Her hand trembled as she touched one fingertip, feather soft, to the injury.

His expression softened. "A bullet," he said simply. "Under normal circumstances my armor would have absorbed and dispersed the entire impact, and I would not have even noticed it. But much of the impact management is handled by a particle field that clings to the surface of the armor and skin during combat, and it was not active at the time because I had taken off my jacket and *enkalan*. The inactive lower body armor I was still wearing stopped the bullet from penetrating, but a sizable portion of the kinetic energy passed through the armor and caused some bruising. That is all it is, Hanna, just bruises. The regeneration fluid doesn't do much for bruises once they've set. You just have to wait for your body to clean them up. It is a little sore, but nothing is broken or permanently damaged." He shrugged. "I have lived through much worse."

Hanna studied his face until she was sure he was telling her the truth. Then she swallowed hard and squared her shoulders. "What else?"

"That is all of it," he said gently, "My honor, Hanna, there is nothing else."

Again, Hanna studied his face. Then, she nodded. "Thank you for showing me."

Jon gazed down at her a moment as if waiting, then tipped his head to the side. "You are not going to tell me I was foolish to rush in without weapons or armor?" he asked, sounding skeptical.

"You did it to rescue me. I'd be pretty ungrateful if I scolded you for it now. But it hurts me to see what they did to you. And it makes me sick to think what might've happened if that bullet had hit just a little bit higher." She laid her hand against his side, just above his waistband.

At her touch, Jon's muscles flinched taut beneath his skin, and he drew a quick, sharp breath. His brows drew together as he took her hand in his and lowered his foot to the floor, tugging his robe back into place. Softly, he asked, "You are not going to tell me that I must not engage in battle?"

Hanna sighed. "I imagine that would be as useless as you telling me I shouldn't worry. You're the Viper. You fight. I get that. I'm your girl-friend. I worry. It's the nature of things."

That word, *girlfriend*, felt strange in her mouth, awkward and sweet, and made her lips twist into a shy smile as she added, "But I will admit to being very glad you're retired now."

Jon shrugged sheepishly, looking down at her hand, which he still held cradled between both of his own. "There are good reasons I left the Winds. I am getting old and slow in addition to being foolish. Narista is right. I am very fortunate they did not cut me up into stew meat." He glanced over to where his sister waited, arms folded, face grim.

Hanna glanced around at the others; in her concern over Jon's injuries, she had almost forgotten they were there. Tomin and Chance looked amused. Salenia decidedly did not. Susan stood frozen in the bedroom doorway with a bag slung over one shoulder and an armful of towels, looking as if she might faint. All of them were staring at Hanna. Her face went hot, and something twisted inside her belly.

Jon must have felt her tense, because he gave her hand a reassuring squeeze before dropping a kiss into her palm and tucking her fingers into the crook of his elbow. He made a broad, sweeping gesture with his other arm and said, "Shall we go?"

The others trailed after them as he guided her through the French doors and across a small patio to an elaborate wrought iron gate. From there, they emerged into an enormous public courtyard, where brick-paved pathways wound between decorative rock formations, artistically arranged clusters of trees and shrubbery, and small fishponds, creating enchanting vignettes beneath the backdrop of the mountain peaks that encircled the entire enclave. The slanting golden light and soft shadows told Hanna sunset was rapidly approaching, and the evening air was cool against her skin.

She was still gaping at the scenery when the path curved between a huge boulder and a tiny forest of trees with bark that looked like fish scales and ended at a broad stretch of flagstone scattered with clusters of wicker chairs and loungers, beyond which lay the pool.

To call it a pool seemed a ridiculous understatement. At the far end of the massive water feature, a high, stone outcropping jutted out of the ground, backing a wide, clear, man-made lake. Vines dripped down the wall from planters tucked into crevices, and stairs and diving ledges had been carved from the stone. Men and women, and even a few children, called out to each other as they dashed up the stone steps and flung themselves from the wall in dives that incorporated complicated acrobatics.

The near end of the pool consisted of a seemingly random series of small fjords, lagoons, and intimate grottoes separated by stone planters and rock formations that gave an illusion, at least, of privacy to the occupants as they soaked in the steaming water. It was like a grown-up version of Jon's hot tub back home, and Hanna smiled as she imagined Rachel and Tiffany trying to throw a hot tub party here.

Jon wove his way across the flagstones to a small grouping of unoccupied rattan lounge chairs. "Will this do?" He pointed out into the jumble of heated pools. "There is a small lagoon there that seems not to be in use."

Hanna saw the one he meant and nodded. The others trailed up behind them, and Susan began laying out her assortment of soft towels and other useful items. Hanna's stomach twisted. She had longed to see Jon, but this was something she would rather have done on her own. The idea of standing in front of all these people wearing nothing but a bathing suit made her feel ill and a little shaky.

The Talessanins clearly didn't share her self-consciousness. Tomin and Chance shucked off their robes and headed for the small lagoon, apparently to stake a claim. Narista slid out of her silky wrap and dropped it on one of the loungers. Under it, she wore a deep indigo *lanan* that nicely complemented her thick, dark hair, and Hanna was surprised to see that the two strips of fabric actually provided quite a bit more coverage than she'd have expected. Maybe she should have Susan show her how to wear one after all.

Salenia sighed. "The water has been calling me all day," She stood and turned her back to Hanna and Jon as she slipped her shimmering wrap coquettishly off her shoulders, gazing back at Jon as she let it slither off her backside and drop to the ground. Then she raised her arms above her head, and stretched, gracefully and elaborately like a cat, extending all her fins as she did so. Her fin membranes bore a subtle pattern of delicate swirling lines, like lace, that matched the coppery color of her hair. Her body was perfectly sculpted and beautifully tanned. Her *lanan* was a rich burgundy with embroidered edging and a soft fringe and must have been made with narrower strips of fabric than Narista's, because it certainly didn't cover as much. A dangling piece of jewelry had been attached to the lower edge of Salenia's dorsal fin, dripping a spill of fine gold chains from her waist down the back of her breech-cloth, where it ended in a large gem that caught the evening light and flashed the color of fire. It reminded Hanna of a fishing lure—especially when she glanced over and saw Jon watching Salenia's little display.

A shiver of doubt crawled down Hanna's spine. What could he possibly want with a dumpy little human like her when a beauty like Salenia was making herself so obviously available? Was he already regretting asking for Hanna's permission instead of Salenia's? The two of them had seemed so right together when they danced at Jon's dinner party. Midnight and fire.

He turned his head and met Hanna's gaze. "Are you ready?" He sounded oddly uncertain. Tentative.

Was she ready? Ready for what? Ready to take her robe off in front of him so he could compare her body to Salenia's? Ready to show him she had the kind of curves that came from eating too many sticky buns, and the sort of uneven tan a girl acquired by sitting for hours in the sun wearing jeans and a t-shirt while swatting bugs and pushing paint around on a canvas? What was this, the swimsuit competition?

But she was overreacting, and she knew it. He meant only to ask if she was ready to go soak in the pool. She took a deep breath and forced her lips to smile. "As ready as I'll ever be, I guess."

Susan appeared at her elbow. In a soft, shaky voice, she asked, "My lady, shall I help you with your wrap?"

Hanna tried to make her smile reassuring. "Thank you Susan." Moving that way still hurt. *So did the thought of Jon's eyes on her body. What if—*

Susan froze, went pale, and dropped a shaky, blushing curtsy as Jon moved behind Hanna instead, and his hands settled on her shoulders, warm against her skin through the thin fabric of the robe.

"Let me help you. Please, Hanna." His voice was soft and deep and held the same intensity she'd seen in his eyes in the sitting room.

She nodded once, slowly, and tried to keep her hands from shaking as she tugged loose the tie at her waist. His big hands slid gently down her arms, taking the silky fabric with them. The feel of his gaze on her body was almost tactile as she stood there, tense, tears pricking at the backs of her eyes. She jumped when his fingers brushed her skin at the base of her neck and trailed down her spine, exploring the absence of a dorsal fin, and a ripple of dizziness made her head swim. She heard him draw a slow, deep breath.

And then he started to laugh.

Chapter 5

ALL OF HANNA'S BLOOD SEEMED to rush to her face at once, bringing another ripple of dizziness. She whirled, staggering a little to catch her balance. "Are you *laughing*?" she demanded. Tears of humiliation welled up in her eyes, and she pressed her fingers to her forehead. "You're *laughing* at me?"

"What?" Jon's expression lurched from amusement to confusion. "Hanna—"

"I'm a human, Jon. This is what I look like. It might seem weird to you, but you don't have to *laugh!*" Hanna's voice broke as the tears spilled down her cheeks.

She spun away so he wouldn't see, gritting her teeth against the pain from her wound, and stalked two wobbly steps toward the small lagoon. Then she stopped, swaying.

Tomin and Chance waited there. Their stares made her feel naked. And deformed.

Well, she was *not* going to go soak in a hot tub with Jon's friends, the only human in the bunch, and have to endure that smug expression on Salenia's face the whole time. It was too much.

It was *all* too much. The attack. The nightmares. The stupid artificial blood that was making her head swim. Salenia. All of it. She was done. She wanted to go home.

But Dalathek was still out there; going home was not an option. And Arastan had said she needed to soak in the hot water to heal. She gritted her teeth. From this angle she could see another small, unoccupied pool a planter or two beyond the one she'd originally been aiming for.

She stumbled to the empty pool, conscious of all the eyes on her back as she went, and lowered herself carefully onto the stone bench that curved around the inside edge below the water line. Sliding around sideways, she wrapped her arms around the ache in her middle, letting the hot tears wash away some of the anger and embarrassment while the hot water eased the pain in her gut and the dizziness settled.

He had *laughed*.

A scuffing noise made her look up. Jon stood on the opposite side of the narrow pool, watching her. His face was solemn, his stance rigid, hands behind his back, feet slightly apart, like a soldier—or like a small boy called on the carpet. The dying sunlight glittered off the gold embroidery on his robe and slid across the smooth muscles of his chest. He looked even more like a sea god than he had when she'd gone to see him about Narista's note and found him soaking in his hot tub at home. *Of course* he'd laughed. How could such a magnificent creature not laugh at a stupid, awkward little thing like her?

"May I speak with you?" he asked quietly, when her eyes met his.

Hanna shrugged and shifted around to face forward on the bench, gesturing vaguely at the space next to her.

Jon came around to her side of the pool and stopped behind her for a moment. His robe flumped onto the flagstones, and then he lowered himself to the edge of the pool, dangling his feet in the water next to her.

She couldn't look at him, so she focused her gaze out across the soaking pools, across the gardens that mostly hid the alien architecture of the embassy compound, to the mountains beyond. Wispy clouds drifted above the peaks, catching the golden light in a pre-sunset glow. Naples yellow. She wished she could paint it, that she could drift into that other way of seeing where all that mattered were light and shadow, color, texture, and line. Painting always made everything else—the pain, the fear, the *confusion* of living—fade into something distant and bearable. But even that escape was denied to her here, and she was stuck in the reality of the moment.

"I am so very sorry, Hanna." Jon's voice was gentle. "I did not think how that would seem to you. But I was not laughing at you. Truly."

He caressed the damp hair off the back of her neck, and she scrunched down in the water, pressing harder against the edge of the pool, hiding her finless human back from him. His fingertips trailed up the side of her neck and down her jawbone, coming to rest beneath her chin, where they coaxed her into turning her head to look up at him.

"I was *not* laughing at you," he repeated, leaning closer to look her in the eyes. She only looked back at him, not trusting herself to speak.

"It was just . . . I could not help but think of the strawberries."

Hanna frowned. "Strawberries?"

"I am afraid so." His mouth curved into half a wistful smile, and he shrugged. "I remembered what you said the first time you saw my dorsal fin, and it came into my head that if you crept into my room at night while I slept, as you threatened to do, and painted all my *enan* to look like wild strawberries, I would have no way to retaliate. That is what made me laugh, not you. I was not laughing at you."

His fingers tickled against her neck as he smoothed back a stray lock of hair. "Hanna . . ." he began, his voice dropping into a coaxing croon—but stopped. "I should go. I truly am so very sorry." He shifted as if to rise.

Hanna caught his hand. "You weren't laughing because you think my back looks funny without a fin?"

Jon hesitated, then slid into the water and moved to stand in front of her, taking both of her hands in his and gazing earnestly into her eyes. "I think your back is perfect just as it is."

"You do?"

"Your back is fascinating." He drew her to her feet and slipped his hand around behind her as if they were dancing, resting it in the small of her back, stroking her skin with his fingers. He leaned down to whisper, "And I would like very much to see it again, if you would allow it."

She laughed, a choking, half-weepy giggle, and studied his face. Slowly, she turned away from him. His fingertips traced her spine again, from the base of her neck to the top of her swimsuit at her waist, and she shivered. "That tickles."

"Does it?" He sounded delighted. He did it again, and she squirmed. "Hmm," he mused. His fingers moved her damp hair away again, and he leaned down to place a kiss on the back of her neck. She squealed and wriggled around to face him, ignoring a quick flash of pain.

"Neck too," he said smugly. "I am making a list, you see, Little Mouse. For later."

Hanna laughed again, and this time it was a real laugh, loud enough to echo softly among the rocks.

Jon sighed and laid his hand against her cheek. "That is the sound I most wanted to hear. Do you think you can forgive me for laughing about the strawberries?"

"Only if you forgive me for misunderstanding you so badly," Hanna said. "And if you tell me one more time you don't think my back is hideous."

He grinned and turned her around again so he could trace her spine with his fingers, then leaned down to wrap his arms around her waist and pull her toward him, cuddling her into his chest.

Hanna was abruptly, electrically aware of his body, of the muscles moving under the bare skin of his chest, pressing against the bare skin of her back, as he embraced her. Of the sudden catch in his breathing and the shudder that passed through his whole body before he pushed her suddenly, almost violently, away from him.

Hanna flailed, pain knifing through her gut, caught her balance, and turned, confused. Jon stood with his back to her, head bowed, one knee on the stone ledge, hands braced against the edge of the pool as if about to lever himself out of the water. His fingers were splayed, and his arm fins fully extended, the mottled patterning on the underside more pronounced than she remembered in the dimming evening light. His dorsal fin stood erect down the middle of his back from neck to waist. His breath came hard and rapid as if he'd just been running.

"Jon?"

He didn't respond.

"What's wrong, Jon?"

"Nothing is wrong," he gasped. "I think your back is enchanting." He gulped in a great, shuddering breath. "And I think I had better not do that again when you are not my wife."

Hanna stepped closer to him. "I don't understand. What's happening?" She reached a tentative hand out to touch his arm.

As soon as her fingers brushed his skin, he flinched away from her. "I will explain, Little Mouse, I just need a moment." She stepped closer to him again, and he shifted away. "And I need you to sit over there and wait." He waved a hand toward the other end of the small pool. "Please."

The pool narrowed so much at the far end that Hanna could sit on the bench on one side and prop her feet on the bench opposite. The stone seats had been carved with a gentle, curving contour that was actually comfortable as she leaned back, resting her head against the edge of the pool. Behind the mountains, the lowering sun shifted the slanting golden light into the rosy end of the spectrum, tinting the clouds a delicate shade of coral. Titanium white, she thought, with cadmium orange and just a blush of alizarin crimson. They still offered her no escape from the burden of present reality.

After a few minutes, the water sloshed as Jon lowered himself to the bench beside her feet and propped his feet up on the bench next to her.

"Better?" she asked.

His smile was small and shy. "Better. Thank you."

Hanna edged upright in her seat and frowned, peering at him in the dimming light. Several dark streaks curved from the corners of both of Jon's eyes up to the hairline at his temples and down over his cheekbones toward his jaw. The skin between the streaks bore the mottled pattern from his fins. "What happened to your face?" she asked, leaning forward for a closer look.

"Please," Jon said, holding up a warning hand, fingers splayed, "just stay there. I will explain." The webbing between his fingers had gone darker too.

Hanna settled back against the stone bench, her frown deepening.

Jon wrapped his arms self-consciously around his middle and tipped his face so his hair fell forward, covering some of the marks. "It is my *tehilethkalan*." He hesitated, looking up at her from under his dark lashes. "In English, it would be called a mating mask. It is one of several physical changes that occur when a Talessanin male experiences a sufficiently high degree of sexual arousal. You understand so far?"

Hanna said quietly, "I understand."

Jon cleared his throat, and his eyes dropped away from hers, focusing instead on the surface of the water between them. "It generally accompanies a very strong urge to . . . to lie with the woman who . . . who inspired the arousal. But . . ."

He was silent for so long that Hanna ventured a soft, sad, "But you don't feel that way about me? It's okay, you can just say it."

Jon lurched into a more upright position, his hair falling back again, revealing the dark markings around his eyes, and his words came out in a rush. "Gentle Gardeners, Hanna, look at me. That is not what I was attempting to say. Just now I want you more than almost anything else I can think of, and it would take very, very little for you to make me forget for a while that there was even anything else to want. But I need you not to do that, because afterward I would never forgive myself, and I would find it very difficult to forgive you."

He stopped again and rubbed at his face with one hand. "I am sorry. I am uncertain how to approach this. I thought there would be more time. I did not anticipate . . ." He shook his head and slouched back down in the water, tipping his head so his hair fell forward.

He drew a deep breath and began again. "We come from different worlds, different cultures. And there are . . . other complications. I do not know what to expect from you with regard to physical intimacy. I do not know what you are ready for. And I do not know what you expect from me. I do not wish to frighten you with my . . . my reactions to you." He gestured vaguely at his face before he looked up again, searching Hanna's eyes, gauging her response to his words. "I am not Dalathek. My honor, Hanna, I would never force you, no matter how . . . eager . . . I may become."

Hanna frowned. "I don't think I ever saw his face do that," she said softly. "It doesn't make me think of him."

Jon's eyebrows rose. "He never . . . ? But I thought he—" He stopped. Shook his head. He had promised not to ask about her time in the shed with Dalathek. Some wounds, he'd said, were too tender to uncover overmuch. But it was there between them anyway.

"Nerve damage, perhaps, from the injury." His hand sketched a line down the side of his face where Dalathek's scar would've been, and Hanna was struck again by the realization that Jon really had known the man who had stolen her innocence and inhabited her nightmares all these years. Dalathek had been Jon's mentor. He'd led the Nine Winds until Jon caught him torturing another human girl and challenged him for command.

She shivered and drew her legs back to her own side of the pool, bracing her feet against the solid stone at the bottom while she wrapped her arms protectively around her belly and shifted her gaze outward again to the distant mountains. The clouds had shifted from blushing coral to the color of a candle flame. She wanted desperately to paint them.

Jon said gently, "I am not like Dalathek, Hanna."

That was true. Dalathek hurt people. Jon protected them. The tightness in her chest was not Jon's fault.

"I know you're not," she whispered. She drew a steadying breath and unfolded herself, stretching her legs across the gap again, resting her feet on the bench beside him. His hand moved toward them, but he didn't touch her. He always seemed to know when she needed space.

"Thank you, Hanna," he said. "Your trust is precious to me." He held her gaze for several heartbeats. Nodded once. Said gently, "I also wish you to understand that I am not like the men represented in the chick flick we watched. I am not as . . . casually affectionate. There are some kinds of physical intimacy that I am not ready for—that I will not be ready for except with my wife, when I have one." He paused again before saying softly, "Can you understand this too?"

Hanna chuckled wryly. "Narista did mention that Talessanins take sex very seriously."

Jon frowned. "Narista is . . . concerned about my interest in you. But yes, the cultural expectation among Talessanins is that the full expression of sexuality is reserved for marriage. And by and large that is also our reality." He shrugged. "There are, of course, individuals who think this is foolish and repressive, and who choose another path. But Hanna, I cannot do that. I *will* not do that."

"Because you follow the Sower?"

"Yes," he said. "Because I follow the Sower, and life is sacred to me. I will not be frivolous either with its taking or with its giving. That is one reason. There are others." He regarded her seriously. "Because I have a duty to my House. Because I do not wish to risk fathering a child I might not be allowed to raise. Because I have always wished I might tell my wife, someday, if I ever have one, that I have been faithful to her even when I did not know who she was. Because . . . well . . . there are other reasons." He stopped and drew a deep breath, shaking his head. "Can you accept this? It is not because I do not want you now. Please do not think I am pushing you away because I do not want you."

Hanna nodded. "I understand."

Jon relaxed a little. "You are not angry?"

"Why would I be angry?"

"Some women are, when I tell them these things." He shrugged. "As I said, some people think waiting is foolish and choose a different path. A more . . . *human* path. Some such women feel that when a man shows her his *tehilethkalan*, she is entitled to lie with him."

Hanna blinked. "Not all humans are like that. And I thought it was an involuntary response."

"It is," Jon said. "But a man can feel when it is getting close and can take measures to stop it from happening." He shot her a shy glance from beneath his lashes. The dark markings around his eyes made their deep hazel even more striking. "This time, it began when you came out of your bedroom in that wrap, and I caught a glimpse of your legs as you walked."

His gaze flickered to her legs, lingered there a moment, then jumped to her face. Abruptly, as if afraid he'd crossed a line, he stood and turned away from her, head bowed. His dorsal fin was folded now, the knobby *enan* at the ends of the spines trailing in a line down his back like a row of dark beads.

Wild strawberries, she thought, and smiled.

"Forgive me," he said.

"For what?"

His shoulders rose and fell. "For not knowing where your boundaries are. Your legs are as fascinating as your back. It is difficult not to look."

She laughed. "I don't mind if you look." And strangely, she realized, she didn't. In fact, she rather liked it when Jon looked at her. It was an odd sensation after all these years of trying not to be looked at.

He sighed and turned around again, sitting on the edge of the pool with his feet on the bench, and leaning his elbows on his knees as he spoke. "I have been trying to learn about human courting customs, but there seem to be no rules. Especially in your culture. It is all very confusing and contradictory."

"For us, too. And I know nothing about Talessanin customs. We might have to make this up as we go along. Talking about it is good."

He nodded slowly, studying her face. "For me, too."

"So, your . . ." Hanna gestured vaguely at her face.

"*Tehilethkalan.*"

"Yes. That. It started because you liked my legs?"

"Yes." He gave them another appreciative once-over. "But it would have gone away again had you not taken such an interest in my injuries." His eyes met hers, and he grinned. "I liked the feel of your hands on my body even more."

The blood that rushed to Hanna's face made her a little light-headed.

"I could have let your maid help with your wrap," Jon continued, "but it is proper for a Talessanin man to assist a woman he is courting. And if I am to be entirely honest, I must admit that I was very curious to see what was underneath. Up close." He shot her a shy smile. "And I thought we would go sit in the pool with the others, and talk of other things, and it would distract me enough. But then, like a great fool, I laughed, and you thought . . ."

He sighed. "I knew I was taking a risk when I came to you, but I could not let you think I was laughing at you. I thought I could stand on the other side of the pool and tell you, but you were crying, and it seemed so cold not to comfort you. It was a truly rash thing to put my arms around you after that, but I was feeling very rash at that point, and I wanted so badly to hold you. Still, I could have stepped away at any time. I *should* have stepped away at some point. But I did not." He looked down at his clasped hands. "And some women would think that after all those opportunities to step away, I ought to . . . follow through . . . once I exhibited my *tehilethkalan*. Especially since . . ." He spread his hands, palm up—a gesture of helplessness. "Well . . . I am the Viper. People invent stories."

Hanna frowned. "But that's ridiculous," she said. "It's *your* body, Jon. You have a right to say no any time you want, no matter what. If you want to wait, we'll wait."

"You are not angry?"

"What is there to be angry about?" She shrugged. "I have my own reasons for moving slowly. You know that. And now that you've explained this . . . *tehilethkalan* . . . to me," her tongue tripped over the unfamiliar word, "I'll know what it is if it happens again, and I'll know you'd prefer for me to back off for a while."

Jon rose and stood gazing silently down at her for a long moment. Then he stepped slowly over and cautiously lowered himself to the bench beside her.

"Are you sure that's a good idea?" Hanna edged away from him.

"No," Jon said with a shaky grin. His gaze shifted from her eyes to her mouth and back again. "But I feel safe with you, Little Mouse. I can tell that it is fading now, but you may look at what is left of it if you wish."

"I would like that very much," Hanna murmured. "If you're sure."

Jon nodded. "I am sure." His slow grin slid across his mouth again. "We are courting, you and I. It is not improper for you to see. But I did not want to frighten you. And I wished to be certain we understood each other's limits. Because if you kissed me just now I might . . ." His words trailed off as his gaze focused on her lips again, and then dropped shyly to the water, making his hair fall over his face.

Hanna froze, breathless, heart pounding, until he looked back up at her and smiled. He was right, the marks were fading, and the light was growing ever dimmer, but she could still make out the dark streaks across his skin. The ones she'd first noticed were the largest and darkest—six of them curving up and down from the outer corner of each eye. But there were fine lines in between them that wove around each other in complicated, symmetrical designs that overlaid the mottled patterning.

He closed his eyes, and she saw that there were streaks and lines on his eyelids as well. She leaned closer, trying to trace one of the beautiful, intricate lines with her eyes, as it wound across his cheekbone, but his hair had fallen over it. She reached out a tentative hand to nudge it out of the way, and Jon tensed as her fingertips brushed his skin, but he didn't move away. Hanna tucked his hair behind his ear and traced the line lightly with her finger until Jon drew a ragged breath and opened his eyes.

"That's amazing, Jon," Hanna whispered. "Thank you for letting me see."

He nodded once, and the way he looked at her made Hanna think again that she could fall into his eyes and never find the bottom. After a long moment she looked away, and Jon shifted on the bench beside her, propping his feet up on the bench across from them and leaning his head back. "And now," he said softly, "perhaps you will show me what you keep looking at up in the sky."

"Mmm . . ." said Hanna, leaning her head back next to his. "It used to be a duck, but the wind has blown it around a bit, and now I think it looks more like a bat. Do you see it?" She pointed up at one of the wispy clouds. "Or possibly a hippopotamus."

Jon laughed. "I am not an expert on the fauna of Earth, but I do not think a bat looks like a hippopotamus."

"No," Hanna said, "but that cloud does now. If you look at it from the right angle."

"And what does that cloud look like?" Jon asked, pointing to another one.

Hanna regarded the sky thoughtfully. The clouds had gone a smoky gray color, their edges glowing crimson with the last rays of the setting sun. In between them, the stars were beginning to show in the night sky. "Burnt mashed potatoes," Hanna announced solemnly. "With red gravy."

Jon laughed again. "You are good for me, Hanna," he said softly, and his hand closed around hers in the water between them, giving it a caress that sent shivers chasing up and down her spine. And the silence that settled between them now was soft, and warm, and smelled of night flowers.

As the last traces of sunset faded from the sky, other lights began to shine among the pools. Underwater lamps made the water glimmer softly in different shades of blue and green, orange, red, and violet. Cunningly concealed spotlights illuminated the walkways and the flagstone terrace. In the darker corners of the planters, the gentle glow of bioluminescent flowers, ferns, shrubs, and mushrooms created haunting fairyscapes. Jon's webbed fingers twined with hers, and she leaned her head against his solid shoulder.

Maybe this was what safe felt like.

A blue-green lamp Hanna hadn't noticed before flared to life in the pool wall just behind her elbow. She squealed softly and jumped, then scooted up onto the edge of the pool so she could lean her head down and wait for the wooziness to pass.

"Are you all right?" Jon asked.

"Dizzy." Hanna said into her knees. "It startled me."

"Ah." He reached over to stroke her shoulder comfortingly with his fingertips. "Synthetic blood. It does that to me every time."

Hanna tipped her head to look at him. "Every time? How many times have you needed blood transfusions?"

He shrugged one shoulder. "Several."

Her eyes narrowed. "Like you have 'several' scars?" She skimmed her fingers over the new one on his forearm fin.

"Something like that."

The colored light shimmering from below gave the angles of Jon's face an elegant, almost ethereal beauty. The dark markings had entirely faded from his skin, and a musing smile played across his lips.

"What are you thinking?" he whispered.

"I'm wondering why Narista hasn't showed up yet to make sure I'm not doing anything that might bring out those gorgeous markings on her brother's face."

Jon chuckled and pointed. "I think that is because Chance is spying on us for her from that rock."

Hanna followed his gesture and saw a dark figure perched on top of one of the decorative rock formations where he could see their little pool, but far enough away not to be able to hear what they were saying.

"How thoughtful of him." Hanna laughed.

"He is a good friend," Jon said firmly. "But with the sun gone, he must be getting cold. Perhaps it is time for us to rejoin the others." He waited for her to nod before asking, "How does my face look?"

Hanna used her fingers to tip his chin up so she could see better. "Like you never looked at me twice in your life."

Jon gave her a wicked grin and eyed her up and down. "I very much doubt I would have to look twice, Little Mouse."

Hanna hoped the dark and the colored lighting hid her blush. "I only meant the marks are gone now."

"I know what you meant." Jon winked and ducked to kiss her on his way out of the pool.

Chapter 6

H ANNA SLEPT MOST OF THAT night undisturbed by nightmares and woke late again the next day, a circumstance that
pleased Arastan immensely. According to the medic, sleep was
nearly as good for healing as hot soaks, and Hanna should try to sleep
a lot over the next few days as she continued to recuperate. Though
it might be more than a few days—it was hard to say since, as always,
Hanna was human and possessed all the annoying medical deficiencies
thereof.

The soreness in Hanna's abdomen had lessened noticeably, though
any amount of bending or twisting still sent pain stabbing through her
abdomen, and she needed help dressing in the Talessanin-style gown
Susan had laid out for her. The dress itself was unexpectedly comfortable—soft, cream-colored fabric cut to cling just a little, but not too
tightly. Delicate beaded embroidery curved along the neckline and
graced the soft points of the handkerchief-hemmed skirt that swirled
around her ankles. The sleeves hugged her arms down to the elbows,
where long flounces fell away to blend in with the skirt, leaving her forearms bare in a way that, Hanna realized, would highlight a Talessanin
woman's arm fins. She tried not to feel self-conscious about being human and not having any. Funny, that had never bothered her before.

Her breakfast—or perhaps more accurately, her late lunch—consisted of more porridge, and by the time she was finished, the others had gathered in her sitting room once again.

Jon met her at the bedroom door with a lovers' greeting that left her breathless and blushing. She half expected another glimpse of his *tehilethkalan* as he leaned back from the kiss, but his face was marked only by a satisfied smile.

"We thought you might like to see Kamm's menagerie this afternoon," he said. "It includes a number of rare specimens from across the Empire, and there are places to rest if you become too fatigued."

After that greeting, Hanna would much have preferred some private time with Jon, but she couldn't help smiling back at his enthusiasm. "Sounds like fun."

Kamm led the way out through the French doors, with Tala tugging at one hand and Narista's hand tucked into his other elbow. Jon laid one hand firmly over Hanna's to anchor it in the crook of his arm and followed his brother. Salenia quickly fell into step with the two of them, laying claim to Jon's other elbow, and Tomin and Chance brought up the rear with Susan. As their little procession entered the courtyard, black-armored bodyguards slipped inconspicuously among the trees and rocks, shadowing them. At Jon's house, Kamm and Tala had always had at least one bodyguard hanging about, though sometimes it was only Chance or Jon. Was the increased number because they were at the embassy now? Or because Dalathek was on the loose?

Hanna walked slowly to keep the flickering pain at bay, and Jon matched her pace as they followed the winding brick paths, taking different turnings from the ones they had followed to the pool. When the first fenced enclosure came into view, Tala came skipping back along the path.

"*Bahta* Jon," she sang merrily, "will you come and help me find a *talengu*? Please, *Bahta* Jon? I can never see them until you point."

Jon looked from Tala's imploring face to Hanna, and back again. Hanna laughed at his torn expression. "You should go on ahead, Jon. You can show it to me too, when I get there."

Jon grinned and bent to kiss her cheek. "Thank you, Hanna," he whispered.

Tala squealed in delight as Jon swept her up onto his shoulder and strode rapidly down the path. Salenia shot a satisfied smirk back at Hanna as she glided along at Jon's side. The three of them looked like a family—a perfect little Talessanin family. A knot formed in Hanna's stomach as they rounded a bend in the path and disappeared behind the enclosure. How could she compete with that?

Her thoughts must have shown on her face, because beside her, Tomin chuckled and said, "Don't worry, Hanna. Jon knows what he wants, and it isn't her."

She offered him a wry smile. "Maybe someone should tell that to Salenia."

An answering smile flashed across Tomin's freckled face as he offered Hanna his arm, and the two of them started walking again, leaving Chance to walk with Susan.

After a moment, Tomin asked, "What do *you* want, Hanna? Where do you think this thing you've begun with Jon is headed?" His conversational tone carried undercurrents Hanna couldn't decipher.

"I don't know," she admitted. "I just . . . I just know I need to find out." She sighed. "Maybe it would help clarify things for . . . everybody . . . if I had a courting knife to give him. Jon said it isn't important, but maybe it's important for other people, even if it's not important to him."

Tomin stopped walking. "You would give a courting knife to a Talessanin man?" His smile was gone, but it was hard to tell from his blank expression what that meant.

Hanna laughed nervously. "Well, I wouldn't give one to a human man, he wouldn't have any idea what it was for." She sighed and started walking again. So did he.

After a few minutes, she asked softly, "Do you think Jon would even accept something like that from me? A courting knife?"

Tomin thought that over as they walked. "I don't know. I've never seen him wear one before, but being in the Winds can be hard on relationships. I've seen him become close to a few women, but evidently things never progressed as far as courting knives."

Hanna frowned. "Never?"

Tomin patted her hand reassuringly. "I've also never seen him watch a woman the way he watches you." He smiled, but something about his eyes looked vaguely troubled. "And he did ask for your permission. Maybe he'd wear one, if you offered it to him."

Hanna shook her head. "I don't suppose it really matters. I haven't got a courting knife to give him, and I have no idea how to go about getting one. We'll just have to make do with the permission or whatever and see where it goes."

"Permission. Or whatever. Right. Hanna, are you certain—"

"Look!" Hanna gasped. They'd arrived at the first exhibit in the menagerie. The enclosure was just large enough to contain a single straggly tree with a gnarled trunk, knobby, contorted branches, and broad, leathery leaves. Long-tailed, bright-winged creatures the size of Hanna's hand fluttered among the branches and sprawled across the sturdy leaves, soaking up the sun. When Hanna stepped up to the mesh enclosure and looked more closely, she saw that the creatures were vaguely reptilian—tiny bat-dragon creatures with gemlike eyes, and slightly translucent wings, like stained glass butterflies.

The next enclosure housed a herd of deer-like creatures about the size of house cats, with large, doleful eyes and miniature forking antlers. An artificial brook trickled merrily through their carefully tended meadow and into the pen next door, where it became a pond full of flashing silver fish. On the shore and hanging partway into the pond was a sort of burrow or nest built with mud and sticks. Hanna could see something peering back at her from a hole in the nest, but the shadows concealed the creature too much for her to make out what it looked like.

After rounding another bend or two in the path, they found the rest of their group clustered in front of another enclosure. Three of its walls were made of stone, and the fourth seemed to be made of metal bars, but as Hanna joined the others standing in front of the cage, she saw flickers of blue light spark between some of the bars and realized there was some kind of particle field there as well.

The ground inside the enclosure consisted entirely of sticky, black mud. Spiky bog plants poked up out of the muck here and there, and in some places a greenish scum floated on oily-looking puddles. Water seeped out of cracks in the stone walls, making an eerie drip-dripping sound that, combined with the musty smell of the place, made Hanna feel as if she'd wandered into the back end of a very old sewer. Insect things of various sizes and shapes buzzed, fluttered, and crawled around inside the enclosure, and at first Hanna thought they were the primary inhabitants. However, as she nudged her way closer to where Jon knelt on the path next to Tala, she realized there must be something else in there with the bugs.

Everyone's attention was focused on a clump of half-rotten plants to which Jon pointed. "Under that big leaf in the front," Jon said. "The twig on the right with the fat, furry, orange grub crawling around on the end."

Tala clapped her hands in delight and leaned forward eagerly.

"Oh, that's repulsive!" Salenia exclaimed. "What is that thing?"

Jon chuckled. "That is the *talengu's* lure. And I think it has attracted some interest. Look to the left about two hands' breadths."

A fist-sized cross between a crab and a fungus was picking its way across the surface of the mud with careful, sporadic movements, stalking its fuzzy orange prey. As it drew nearer, a tense silence settled over the watchers. Closer. The thing had drawn within a hand's breadth of its quarry. Closer. A finger's span only. Slowly, carefully forward.

It pounced, seizing the orange grub with all three pincers. The mud beneath it erupted, as a tangle of spiky tentacles lunged from below, wrapping around the crab creature and pinning it in place.

Hanna jumped, startled, and dizziness washed in on the resulting wave of adrenaline.

Tala burst into a fit of triumphant giggles and threw her arms around Jon. "You were right, *Bahta* Jon! It *is* a *talengu*!"

In the enclosure, the mud surged again as the creature dragged the rest of its body out from under the muck to enjoy its meal. It looked a great deal like a huge, lumpy toad with milky white eyes and tentacles surrounding its beak of a mouth.

Hanna shuddered. Her dizziness made the ground seem to rotate jerkily, and pain twisted in her gut as she staggered half a step sideways to catch her balance.

Chapter 7

J ON BENT TO RETURN TALA'S embrace, heart thrumming in time
with the little girl's innocent enthusiasm. Grinning, he glanced up to
share the moment with Hanna—only to see her stagger sideways and
clutch at her belly with one hand.

Instantly, he was by her side, steadying her. "Are you all right?"

"I think I need to sit down," she whispered shakily.

"Of course you do. What a fool I am."

Synthetic blood. And he had allowed the talengu *to startle her.*

He supported her with an arm around her shoulders as he led her
around the corner of the *talengu* exhibit to a place where the path widened into a broad oval surrounded by brick walls and stone benches. She
slumped onto the nearest seat, and he knelt on the bricks in front of her.
"Lean your head down," he advised, and when she did, he guided her
forehead to his shoulder and stroked the back of her neck with his fingertips. Her skin was soft and warm, and her neatly plaited hair smelled
faintly of flowers.

She let out a long sigh.

The sound was echoed by a gasping hiss from behind Jon, followed
by a clicking chuckle, and then—as Hanna lurched upright—by shriek-
ing, maniacal laughter.

Jon caught her shoulders as she swayed, bracing her. "Do not be frightened, Hanna. It is only the *kalakanek*." He couldn't blame her, though; the creature's cry could be rather disconcerting.

She closed her eyes and rubbed at her forehead with her fingers. "What's a *kalakanek*?"

"It is a predatory animal from a jungle on the moon of a distant planet. They are quite rare in captivity, and Kamm is excessively proud to own one." Jon turned and pointed to the heavily planted enclosure behind him.

It took Hanna a moment to find the creature, crouched as it was in the shadows created by the drooping trees and dense undergrowth; the catch in her breath told him when she spotted it.

To her, it must look like a great black dog—except its heavy, muscled forelegs were longer than the hind legs, giving it a stance more like that of the gorilla he'd seen in an Earth zoo than a dog. Its skin was bare but for a mangy-looking mane along its shoulders that from this distance appeared to be made of either spiky fur or feathers but up close, Jon knew, was something in between. Its snout was mashed in, and its lips pulled back around four protruding tusks in a permanent leering grin. Its bloodshot eyes were fixed intently on Jon and Hanna, seeming to hold a mocking, malicious cleverness. As they watched, the thing yawned insolently, its lips drawing even farther back to display a disturbing number of needle-sharp teeth arranged in a double row like those of Earth's sharks.

"I think it wants to eat me," Hanna said.

"Do not take it personally." Jon took her hand in his. "It wants to eat everyone it meets. But its cage has several layers of extra security, so there is no danger of that happening." Two fences with a moat in between surrounded the enclosure, and those were only the most obvious security measures.

Hanna shuddered and swayed. "I hope this isn't a deal-breaker for you," she murmured, leaning her forehead back onto his shoulder, "but if you and I ever do get married, you are not allowed to have a pet *kalakanek*. That is the creepiest sound I ever heard in my life. And nobody needs that many teeth."

Her breath tickled against the side of Jon's neck, making his pulse quicken and sending a pleasant shiver down his dorsal fin. A warm flush of unexpected delight trailed after it, as the part of his soul that chafed at being ordered about by the Emperor rolled over on its back and began to purr, just as it had when Hanna had told him to wash his hands and get out the popcorn bowl the first night they'd met. What was it about her that made him want to dance to her command?

Jon chuckled, but his voice came out soft and serious when he spoke. "That is something you might actually consider, then? I was not certain you truly would."

She shifted her head so her ear pressed into the fabric of his shirt, and her forehead nestled against the side of his neck. "A pet *kalakanek*? Absolutely not. I just said."

Jon turned his head slightly. "No, Little Mouse," he murmured, "I meant marrying me. You would truly consider it?"

Hanna sat up again, cheeks pink with embarrassment. "I . . . I thought you said that was the point of courtship for Talessanins. Not that I'm ready to do *more* than consider it, I just . . . I mean . . ." She looked down. "Unless you'd rather I didn't."

Jon laid a careful hand against the side of her face and let his thumb trace her cheekbone. Part of him still marveled that she allowed him even that much. "I would very much rather you *did*, Little Mouse. But you are not Talessanin, and human customs are confusing to me. I am not always certain what you—"

Footsteps on the path.

He dropped his voice to an intense whisper and leaned closer. "I am very glad to know you recognize my courtship as sincere, Hanna."

A sharp gasp announced Salenia's arrival, and Jon looked over to see her standing at the corner of the brick wall by the *talengu* enclosure, lips tight, eyes bright with a fury she had no right to.

Narista rounded the corner next, stopping short at the sight of their little tableau. "Jon! Have you lost your mind? A son of House Kanestelan kneels before no one. Least of all a *human*!"

Hanna tensed.

Jon gave his sister a quelling glare—not that it would do any good. "It is my heart, not my mind that I have lost, Narista. And I hope every son of House Kanestelan is man enough to bow before that."

The angry flare of Narista's nostrils was subtle, but gratifying.

Hanna giggled, and some of the tension went out of her body. "You say things like that just to annoy your sister, don't you?" she murmured under her breath.

He shrugged. "Sometimes. Which is not to say I do not mean them." He winked at her and stood as Tomin came around the corner followed by Chance, who escorted Hanna's timid maid.

Hanna smiled at Narista. "I got dizzy. He was just keeping me company while it passed."

Jon sat next to Hanna and draped an arm across the back of the bench behind her. "I believe we will rest a few minutes longer." His tone held more challenge than he'd intended. "However, we have no wish to detain the rest of you."

Salenia's eyes narrowed, but she had managed to stuff her outrage out of sight behind a smile. She gracefully lowered herself to one of the other benches and said, "I'm a bit fatigued myself. I'm sure you won't mind if I sit with you."

Narista joined her. "Kamm and Tala are likely to be admiring that *talengu* for a while yet; we might as well all wait together." She smiled sweetly at Hanna. "Though I'm sure Miss Bradley's maid could show her back to her rooms, if she is feeling unwell. She could continue her tour tomorrow."

The little maid took half a hesitant step forward, but stopped, flinching slightly, when Chance quietly caught her elbow.

"Oh, that wouldn't do at all." Salenia's mouth pouted prettily, but her eyes calculated, and she didn't lower her voice as she leaned confidentially close to Narista. "Jon won't be here tomorrow to show his little neighbor all the best exhibits."

Hanna tensed on the bench beside Jon and turned to look a question at him.

Salenia always knew which triggers to pull. Jon clenched his teeth and drew a slow breath to keep himself from saying anything regrettable to Salenia. Arranging a conciliatory smile on his lips for Hanna, he said gently, "The High Council has summoned me to the Capital. I was going to tell you."

Hanna studied his face for a moment, then looked over at Salenia and back to him, a troubled crease forming between her brows. "I see."

Her tone told him what she saw—he was *going* to tell her, but he hadn't. And Salenia already knew.

He could tell Hanna that Salenia only knew because she and Narista had happened to be with him in his rooms when the message arrived, but that wasn't likely to help matters—he hadn't invited Hanna to his rooms yet either, but Salenia had been there. That fact would only feed whatever suspicions Salenia had just awakened in Hanna. A cold knot formed somewhere in the back of his chest.

Tomin cleared his throat. "You're not even on the Council anymore, Jon. What do they want from you this time?"

Jon shifted uncomfortably. This just kept getting worse. But he hadn't had time to tell Tomin either, so Tomin wouldn't know that question led to a minefield. Slowly, he said, "They have asked for a recommendation on the human question, now that I have lived among them for a time. A resolution is about to be brought to a vote by the Assembly, and the Council has been asked to endorse the proposal."

"The human question?" Hanna frowned, puzzled.

Salenia spoke first, lips pulling into a self-satisfied smirk. "The question," she said, "of whether humans should be legally designated as persons under imperial law. Many people feel humans are not sufficiently advanced as a species to qualify. Some of you still live in nests made of mud and sticks. Some of you kill your own unborn young. Whole groups of you slaughter each other over skin pigmentation and access to natural resources. It's bestial."

Hanna shifted uneasily and looked questioningly back to Jon.

"That's very much a minority opinion," Tomin interjected. "Almost all of the delegates are prepared to accept that humans qualify as persons even if they do still have some issues to work out—children and barbarians are still persons. It's only a few Talessanins who don't see it that way." He shot a frown at Salenia. "I guess sometimes it's easier to embrace people who are so different that they seem exotic than it is to accept those who are just different enough to make one question one's own identity and superiority."

Salenia's eyes narrowed again, and she shot one of her meaningful glances at Jon, then Tomin, and back again. She had never approved of the way Jon allowed his lowborn friends to speak like they were his social equals. But some things that happened on a battlefield transcended social rank, and even as only an Imperial *Ehr*, Jon was still Salenia's superior, so she'd bow to his preferences—at least on a surface level. He waved for Tomin to go on.

Tomin raised a smug eyebrow at Salenia and sat down on Hanna's other side as he explained. "To most of the Empire, humans have always been just a finless variety of Talessanin. The real question at this point is whether humans are, in fact, a Talessanin subspecies, or if they're a separate species altogether. Earth would have delegates in the Assembly either way, but there is debate about allowing them a seat on the Council as well, since some people feel that would unfairly grant Talessanins an extra vote in a Council that is already dominated by Talessanins. And of course, there's the question of sub-governmental structure if humans are declared to be a variant of Talessanin, since humans have no recognized Houses." He shrugged. "It's a fascinating debate."

"It is a *dangerous* debate," Jon cut in, leaning forward on the bench to look at Tomin. "Whether the law recognizes it or not, the fact is that humans *are* persons. The differences between us and humans are so negligible that to claim *they* are not persons is to claim *we* are not persons. Whether they are the same species or a different one is largely irrelevant—they are persons either way. But right now, the only thing preventing the mass export and exploitation of the entire human population is the fact that the Kanestalen *Ehrat* has claimed the entire planet as his private reserve, and so far, no one has had the impudence to openly challenge him. Even with Kamm here, the poachers get more aggressive every year, and more and more humans are turning up in the black market. Without citizenship, this entire population of persons has virtually no way of defending themselves on an intergalactic scale, and virtually no legal rights or protections. As long as the Assembly and the Council keep dragging out this ludicrous debate, the captive humans cannot be reclaimed, and the dealers and owners cannot be prosecuted for slave trafficking."

"Slave trafficking!" Salenia surged to her feet. "That's nonsense. Legally, humans are *not* persons. The mere fact that *you* think they should be doesn't make it so, and some of the most powerful people in the Empire disagree with you, including your own stepfather. And his opinion carries a great deal more weight than yours. Yes, humans are clearly *sentient*, but they're not sufficiently *sapient* to qualify as persons. By definition, a creature that is not a person cannot be a slave. It is a pet. Or perhaps livestock." She shot Hanna a contemptuous look.

"*Livestock*?" Hanna's face went white.

Salenia ignored her. "It is not illegal to own a human, Jon. And if you pay that much for a pet, you're not going to mistreat it. My father keeps one, and it wants for nothing. It's ridiculous how he spoils the thing. Yes, there's a superficial resemblance, but that's just a fluke of evolution. It's not a *person*, Jon."

Jon rose to face Salenia, glowering down at her with his arms folded across his chest. "What your father does is *wrong*, Salenia."

"You are such a hypocrite." Salenia's eyes slid meaningfully toward Hanna. "If you're going to do this, at least be honest about it. A creature captured from the wild and tamed is as much a pet as one purchased from an exotic animals dealer—though, of course, a reputable dealer will at least check the thing for diseases."

The hot blood drained from Jon's face. His fists clenched. "Stop this Salenia," he hissed. "Now."

Salenia's face flushed even redder than her hair, and her eyes flashed fire. She opened her mouth to retort, but Narista shot an uncomfortable look at Hanna and cut her off.

"Have you read the new resolution, Jon? What are they proposing this time?"

Jon glared at Salenia, his jaw muscles clenching and unclenching as he tried to decide whether to respond to Salenia or his sister.

Tomin leapt into the breach.

"We had a brief in the public relations office. The new resolution would establish humans as a subspecies of Talessanin and would create a sub-governmental committee to facilitate integration with the rest of the Talessanin kinship. They would likely be allowed to maintain their current practice of territorial nations under supervision of one or more of the Talessanin Houses, so most humans would hardly notice any change. They wouldn't have their own seat on the Council, which is unfortunate, but at least the debate would be resolved, and the population of Earth would be eligible for imperial military protection."

"What about the humans who are already . . . detained?" Chance asked quietly, with a nervous glance at Hanna.

Tomin cleared his throat. "This resolution calls for the establishment of set rates based on various factors such as age, sex, and household function, at which such a human may reimburse his or her owner in order to terminate the . . . relationship. If they choose."

"They have to *buy* their own freedom?" Hanna sounded incredulous. "If they *choose*?"

Jon couldn't read the expression on her face when she looked back up at him. Horror? Outrage? Betrayal?

He went cold all over.

Before he could think what to say, Salenia snapped, "The Assembly should not be given the power to rob citizens of legally purchased property without reimbursement. Where would it stop?"

Tomin said, "The last resolution contained a clause that would exclude existing pet humans and their offspring from personhood in perpetuity. Purchase of freedom is a vast improvement." He sighed and leaned back against the bench. "This is a more complicated matter than it may seem, Hanna. Some of the detained humans will feel that they are better off as they are now. As pets, they're legally entitled to receive adequate food, housing, and medical care from their owners. As free citizens, they'll have to fend for themselves. Of particular concern to the Assembly are the hybrid children of human women who have been kept by married Talessanin men for . . . entertainment and companionship."

Hanna made a small choking sound. "You mean they think humans are animals, and they sleep with them anyway?"

Tomin frowned. "Not animals, exactly. Just underdeveloped. Like . . . Neanderthals. Proto-Talessanins, so to speak."

Hanna just gaped at him, so Tomin went on. "As Salenia has pointed out, these women are generally well cared for, and often an emotional attachment has formed between them and their owners. But if the women and their children are declared to be persons under the law, existing anti-slavery laws will come into effect, and their owners will no longer be permitted to keep them. The women may not have marketable skills with which to support themselves and their children. Should they be forced into homelessness and maybe starvation just so the delegates to the Assembly can feel good about themselves for freeing all the humans? This resolution attempts to address this situation by allowing the humans to choose for themselves. It's not a perfect solution, but the longer the debate goes unresolved, the more humans will be bought and sold on the black market as pets."

Hanna stared at him for a long moment. Then she rubbed at her forehead with her fingertips. "Why haven't I heard about all this before? Why isn't something that affects humans so deeply being reported and discussed in the human media all over the world?"

Tomin shrugged. "Most humans are aware that full citizenship is still pending. It wasn't felt they needed to know all the details of why. Particularly if that knowledge might cause unrest that would interfere with the orderly transition to imperial rule. Small advancements in medical treatments, energy technology, and agricultural techniques can purchase a great deal of silence. And there are always memory patches."

Chance quietly took the seat Jon had vacated on the other side of Hanna. "Or more permanent solutions, like the assassination of the Bolivian president three years ago," he said. "If we're going to tell her all this, she might as well know that too." He turned to Hanna. "Keep in mind that there's more than one way for a transition of power to happen."

Tomin glared at him and then said solemnly to Hanna, "Earth is on the intergalactic charts now, and if it isn't absorbed by the Empire, it will be absorbed by one of the other powers. And believe me, they would not be kind to anything resembling a Talessanin. Militarily, Earth is outmatched on a scale humans can't even imagine. But the current imperial regime prefers diplomatic integration over military conquest, so the Empress sent embassy ships instead of warships. Everyone would prefer a smooth transition, and the diplomatic corps felt this was the best way to achieve it."

Silence descended as Hanna's horrified gaze shifted from Tomin to Chance and then settled on Jon. Hurt. Questioning.

He tried desperately to think of something to say.

"What would you choose, Hanna Bradley, if the resolution passed?" Salenia's voice was smooth silk colored with an undertone of triumph.

Hanna blinked. "What do you mean?"

Salenia raised an elegant eyebrow. "Have you become so attached to your owner that you'd choose to remain his pet, or would you wish to purchase your . . . freedom?"

"Salenia!" Jon snapped.

She only raised a defiant eyebrow at him and went on speaking to Hanna. "I'm sure Jon would provide your price if you *asked* him nicely." Her tone implied something more than just asking.

"Salenia," Jon growled, "you will stop this *now*."

Salenia ignored him, speaking slowly and precisely to Hanna as if to a small child. "You are living on a Talessanin estate in an enclosure that's been adapted to resemble a human's accustomed habitat. You wear what they give you, and eat what they feed you, and come when you're called, and do as you're told. Are you a person? Or are you a pet? Kamm's guest, or a gift to his brother from his ridiculous little private reserve?"

"Enough!" Jon took a step toward Salenia.

Sweet Sower. Was she right? Was he doing what Salenia accused him of—making a pet of Hanna? The idea was obscene.

Salenia shot him an obstinate glare and continued. "You should bear in mind, Hanna, that Jon will eventually wish to marry. What will you do if his wife will not allow him to keep a pet for companionship? Hmm? What do you think?"

Hanna looked back and forth between Jon and Salenia. "I think," she said slowly, "that humans are not the only ones who can be barbaric."

The thrumming fierceness that lay beneath the studied calm of Hanna's voice made Jon's pulse hammer with dread.

"And," Hanna went on in that same even tone, "I think I've walked a little too far today. I'd like to go lie down." She rose to her feet. Jon took half a step toward her, but her eyes pinned him in place. "I can find my own way back to my rooms."

Jon's heart clenched and stopped beating. "Hanna—" he choked.

"Wait." Narista's voice cut into the tension. "I think perhaps it is Salenia and I who have gone a little too far this afternoon. You stay, Hanna. Please. We'll go." She directed a glare at her friend.

Salenia gave Jon a long, intense look before following Narista back around the corner of the *talengu* exhibit.

Hanna stood frozen in place, her face entirely pale except for two angry pink spots high in her cheeks.

Jon's mind churned. *How could he fix this?* He *had* to fix this. He couldn't lose her now. Not like this. He opened his mouth, but nothing came out.

Chance's chuckle broke the stillness. "Hanna, you do realize, don't you, that Salenia is here on exactly the same terms you are. She is living on someone else's estate in rooms designed for Talessanins, eating the food she's given just the same as you. And you saw her do as she was told when Narista said it was time to leave. There's no difference between her status and yours."

"Except most of us like you better." Tomin winked at her.

Hanna choked out a bitter laugh and sank back onto the bench. "It's not the same. Salenia is a person. An imperial citizen protected under the law." Her voice was small and hollow. "And apparently, I'm property. Like that *kalakanek*. Not that anyone bothered to tell me." She rubbed at her forehead with her fingertips again. "No wonder Narista was offended when I showed up at that dinner party."

"Hanna, no." Jon dropped to his knees in front of her again, heart pounding. "It is only a minor legal technicality. No one told you because it does not matter."

"It certainly matters to Lord Trakanaleth's . . . pet." Something else occurred to her, and her chin came up. "And what about Susan?" she demanded, waving a hand toward her maid, who still stood near the wall, hands folded, lips pressed tight, eyes focused on the flagstones. "Is Susan Kamm's pet?"

"Susan is my *employee*, Hanna." Kamm stood at the corner by the *talengu* enclosure. Tala wasn't with him; she must have gone back with Narista as well. "Just as Tomin is my employee. He gestured with one hand, and Tomin moved out of the way so Kamm could sit beside Hanna on the bench. "Susan is appropriately compensated for her work and is free to stay or leave as she chooses. If you want to know more than that, you'll have to ask Susan."

His gaze met Jon's, seeking his permission, and Jon gave him a slight nod. The tightness in his chest eased a fraction. Kamm was the diplomat; he always knew what to say to fix problems. Jon only knew how to kill them.

Kamm took one of Hanna's hands in his and spoke earnestly. "Jon came to me for help after the Winds completed their work collecting research specimens for the exploratory expedition. He had much to say about humans. And he was very convincing." His gaze flicked to Jon and back to Hanna. "The reason I claimed Earth as my private reserve was to protect humans from those who would exploit them until their status as wholly sapient beings was appropriately acknowledged by the Assembly and they officially received citizenship and full protection as persons under the law. And if the Assembly doesn't come to its collective senses, the Throne has power to overrule their decisions. If that doesn't happen during my mother's reign, it will happen during mine. I promise you, Hanna, it's only a matter of time."

Hanna appeared to be mulling this over, but she said nothing, so Jon could only guess at the direction of her thoughts.

After a moment, Kamm prompted gently, "Do you understand?"

Slowly, Hanna removed her hand from Kamm's and looked up at him. Her jaw was set, and her eyes smoldered defiance—a small, wounded human woman facing down the Imperial *Ehrat* of the Empire Among the Stars, a man second in power only to the Throne itself. Jon's heart twisted in his chest. It was almost the same defiance he had seen in her eyes that first day when she rang his doorbell. So much courage for a little mouse.

"I understand," she said with quiet intensity, "that right now I am the property of the Imperial *Ehrat* as part of his private reserve. I understand that humans lack the technological ability to object to that arrangement. I understand that legally, I am—"

"Free to live as you choose," Kamm interrupted, his voice matching hers in tone and force. "And under my protection, as are all humans within my jurisdiction." He looked her solemnly in the eyes. "And my brother will kill anyone who tries to make you otherwise."

The two of them sat like that, eyes locked, taking one another's measure, until Jon said softly, "Hanna?" and she turned to look at him, there on his knees on the pavement. "I have made a mess of this." He let his voice carry the full measure of his desperate misery. "I am so very sorry."

A small line appeared between her brows, and her jaw muscles tightened, but she didn't say anything.

Moving slowly, carefully, he took both of her hands, cradling them gently in his own. When she didn't pull away, he bent to place a kiss in each of her palms, folding her webless fingers closed around them.

She didn't move. She didn't speak. He couldn't read the expression in her eyes. Was she angry with him? Was it over between them? Was Salenia right, and he had become part of the problem?

Softly, he asked, "Have I treated you like a pet, Hanna? Have I behaved as if I own you?"

Still, she said nothing, just sat there, perfectly, terribly still, her chocolate eyes looking back at him. Please let her see beyond all this to his heart. Please let her still care for him. Even just a little. Enough to start again.

When the silence grew too heavy, Chance muttered, "If you ask me, it's the other way around."

"The Lady Who Leashed the Legend," Tomin added dramatically.

"Please, I am serious," Jon insisted. "I need to know, Hanna. Do I make you feel like property?"

Slowly, Hanna tugged one of her hands free of his. Then the other. A heavy, black pit yawned open in the center of his chest.

He'd lost her.

But she only used her delicate webless fingers to push his loose hair back from his face. "Jon," she said gently, "no one has ever made me feel more like a person than you have."

She leaned down and kissed him. And Jon's soul . . . *sang!*

When she straightened again, relief poured out of Jon in a long sigh, and he rested his forehead for a moment against her knee. Then he recaptured her hands and rose, drawing her up to stand with him, keeping her fingers twined with his. "Thank you," he said, looking her earnestly in the eyes. "And if I ever treat you with anything less than the respect you deserve, you must tell me. Do you understand? And I will fix it."

Hanna was quiet again for a long moment, searching his face. Then she squared her shoulders and tilted her chin playfully. "You don't own me, Jonantathinel of House Kanestelan *Ehr*," she said. "You can't tell me what to do"

Jon threw his head back and laughed. Then he wrapped his arms around Hanna and held her tight. "That is exactly right, Little Mouse. Never forget that."

Chapter
8

"I'M SORRY, MY LADY," SUSAN murmured, ducking her head, "h-he asked me not to wake you."

Hanna brushed a fingertip over the white petals of one of the dark-eyed daisies in the vase on the sitting room tea table and read the note again.

> *Please think of me. I will be thinking of you.*
> *—Jon*

He was already gone. His shuttle to the orbital port had left in the early hours of dawn, and the long-distance transport that would take him to the City of Eternal Radiance, the capital of the Empire back on the Talessanin home world, had left the port shortly after.

"It's all right, Susan." Hanna forced a smile for the flustered maid. "I was just hoping to say goodbye."

She'd wanted to say a little more than that. Needed to, really. She should have said it while he knelt in front of her on the hard bricks of the menagerie path. She'd said he made her feel like a person, but there was so much more to it than that. From the first time he'd smiled at her when he answered his front door, Jon had made her feel like she *mattered.* Like she had real value. Like her opinions were important and her life was worth sharing. She hadn't felt that way since . . . well . . . since before the shed. She should have told him.

But everyone had been looking at her. And at the time, the revelation of "the human question" was still too new. Too raw. It had left a lingering tension between the two of them that manifested as a careful politeness while they toured the rest of the menagerie. Still, she'd thrilled inside when he took her hand to help her up a short flight of steps. And after he'd walked her back to her rooms, when Arastan came to shoo him off so Hanna could rest, the look he'd given her before he kissed her cheek had melted whatever was left of the cold dread that had clutched at her when Salenia called her livestock. Jon obviously didn't see her that way. And neither did his brother. The two of them were working to fix things, and it was only a matter of time. Maybe not very much time, if Jon's meetings went well.

And then what?

She didn't know; all of it was still too new. But she knew she wanted to be with Jon.

She'd fallen asleep with that thought in her mind, with the warm, spicy memory of his strong arms around her and the echo of his whisper: *I am very glad to know you recognize my courtship as sincere.* And for the first time in a long time, she'd slept without waking until morning.

The chime of the guest suite's doorbell interrupted her thoughts, making her heart leap with completely irrational hope, and then plunge in senseless disappointment when her visitor turned out to be only Tomin.

When they were seated comfortably on the sofas in front of the fireplace, Tomin held out a large envelope. "Kamm asked me to deliver this, since I was coming to see you anyway."

The envelope was made of thick paper, stamped with a fancy border of gold leaves, and sealed with a fat blob of dark green pearlescent wax. It contained an elaborately embossed card bearing an engraved invitation to a Grand Imperial Ball to be given at the North American Embassy in two weeks' time, in honor of the Empress Among the Stars and her Imperial Consort, the Emperor.

Susan made a small noise in her throat when she saw it, and Hanna looked at her, brows raised.

The maid's cheeks flushed. "I beg your pardon, my lady. It's just . . . that's a personal invitation signed by the *Ehrat* himself. I've only ever seen the regular kind his secretary sends to all the visiting nobility and important diplomatic representatives. It's a great honor, my lady."

Tomin grinned. "It is, indeed. And you'll want to have Susan display that on your sitting room mantle so all the great ladies can see it and envy you when they come to visit. It's tradition."

Hanna laughed. "Nobody is going to come visit me."

"Salenia might." Tomin shrugged. "She'll have gotten one too, of course, so she'll be less impressed with it than some others would. Although, now that I think of it, hers was still sitting on Kamm's desk when I left. That's a shame, of course, because it would mortify her to know you received yours first. And you know how maids can talk." He winked meaningfully at Susan, who choked down a laugh.

"I will bring tea for your guest, my lady," she said. Then, watching Tomin's face carefully to make sure she'd correctly understood his request, the maid added, "It may take a few minutes if I need to run down to the main kitchen for . . . for something."

Tomin gave Susan a knowing wink and nodded. "Take your time," he said.

The maid curtsied and went out through the door to the service kitchen.

"I hope I never get on your bad side, Tomin." Hanna shook her head. She turned the invitation over in her hands. "How can I go to a ball? The only dance I know is that *aylencanat* you taught me for Jon's dinner party."

Tomin shrugged. "If you can learn one dance, you can learn more. I'll teach you. How do you feel about meeting the Empress and Emperor?"

"Meeting—" Hanna went cold all over. "You mean they're coming *here*?"

Tomin chuckled. "The ball *is* being held in their honor, Hanna."

She stared at him for a moment, then put her face in her hands, bending over to let a wave of dizziness pass while the horror of being presented to the rulers of an intergalactic empire waged war in the pit of her stomach with the slightly more ordinary terror of meeting her new boyfriend's mother.

Tomin waited patiently, not saying anything while she counted her breaths in her head, making them slow and even, as her latest therapist had taught her for dealing with her panic attacks.

When she straightened, rubbing at her forehead, he was watching her with a sympathetic smile. "That bad?"

Her shaky laugh held a thread of hysteria. "What am I doing, Tomin? This is crazy. I'm just some artist from a small town in the middle of nowhere. I'm not even a very good artist—there's no deep, esoteric meaning in my work, I just paint landscapes that go well with someone's couch. Until Jon's dinner party I hadn't owned a formal gown since my junior prom. I get my clothes from the discount racks at the thrift store. I walk around barefoot, and put my feet on the coffee table, and half the time I have paint in my hair. How can I be sitting in the guest quarters of the Talessanin embassy waiting for my maid to bring tea and talking about going to a Grand Imperial Ball at the personal invitation of the ruling family of the entire intergalactic empire? I can't do this. It's crazy. I should be home stretching canvases." She shook her head and closed her eyes. "But of course, I can't go home. I don't even know how to *get* home from here."

"You're not a prisoner, Hanna," Tomin said softly. "Susan can show you where the shuttleport is. Or you can ask me, and I'll take you home myself any time you want. But Dalathek is still out there."

"Right." Hanna sighed. "Dalathek. Have they found him yet?"

"Several times. Most recently off the southern coast of Madagascar. But he's slippery. He's using some kind of modified jamming technology, and the trackers suspect he either has collaborators on planet that we haven't yet identified, or he's in contact with some of the poachers who occasionally make it through the orbital port's security onto the planet, and they're guiding him to cached resources. But the hunters are closing in on him, and they've nearly worked out how to hack his tech, so it shouldn't be long now."

Hanna sighed. "None of this feels quite real. I mean, things like this just don't happen to people. I don't know if I can do this, Tomin."

Tomin studied her seriously, as if trying to judge whether her mental seams would hold, or if she was going to fray apart under pressure. She couldn't tell what conclusion he came to.

"It's going to be all right, Hanna," he said. "We'll teach you what you need to know. Just take one thing at a time. And think about Jon."

Jon.

I will be thinking of you.

If she could really be with Jon, if she could feel the way she felt when he held her in his arms and called her Little Mouse, even just *some* of the time . . .

She sighed and went to the fireplace to set the invitation on her mantelpiece. "Teach me, then. I have nothing else to do today. Just take it a little slow. I'm feeling a lot better, but it still hurts if I twist too far." At least it would keep her mind off the growing ache in her chest that had nothing to do with her injury and everything to do with the unexpected magnitude of the hole Jon's absence had left in her insides.

Tomin didn't answer until she turned to face him, letting him see the determination in her eyes. He must have liked what he saw, because a slow smile spread across his mouth, and he nodded once to himself, as if he'd been right about something.

"Okay. If you're sure about this." He paused, as if giving her one last chance to back out. When she said nothing, he nodded and launched into full lecture mode. "The first thing you should know is that there are likely to be an increasing number of Talessanin nobles, as well as aristocrats of various other citizen races, wandering about the embassy in the upcoming days as the guests begin arriving for the ball.

"Since you're human, they'll probably mostly ignore you, at least until Jon gets back and they realize how you fit in around here. But just in case, you should know that you're entitled, as things stand, to greet anyone short of the Emperor or Empress as at least an equal. However, it might still be a good idea to offer a submissive greeting in most cases, as it will make you seem gracious and will not risk offending certain parties who are still unable to view humans as equals. But that's up to you, not them. No one can *force* you to submit. If you want to be greeted as an equal, just stand there with your hand out straight until they take it or leave. They'll probably take it, since backing down from a human would be an even greater disgrace than greeting one as an equal.

"Also, each race and culture has its own structure of aristocratic titles, and you'll probably hear some of them being used. But you don't need to worry about remembering them because it's common practice in the Empire to address any high ranking diplomat as 'your dignity' and any aristocrat as 'my lord' or 'my lady.' Except the Emperor and Empress, of course. The Empress should be addressed as Your Grace, and the Emperor as Your Magnificence, and you should add a deep curtsy to your submissive greeting. Unless they instruct you otherwise when Jon introduces you to them after they arrive next week. Have you got all that?"

The look on Hanna's face made him laugh. "Don't worry, we'll practice."

Then he straightened, apparently remembering something. From some pocket or other, he produced a small, round box that seemed to be made of ivory, and tipped the lid back to display a lump of what looked like pink plastic about the size of a peanut.

"And you'll have this," he announced triumphantly. "Sorry, I almost forgot."

Hanna blinked at the lump. Then at Tomin. Then at the lump again.

He laughed softly and shook his head. "It's a translation module, Hanna. You put it in your ear. Kamm sent it along with the invitation."

She must have looked as apprehensive as she felt, because his voice was more sympathetic when he added, "Don't worry, it's very safe, and you can take it out yourself any time." He held the box out invitingly. "Shall we give it a try?"

When she nodded cautiously, he showed her how to tuck it into her right ear canal.

"See?" he said. "Just like that." Then he added something in Talessanin. As he spoke, the Talessanin words were overlaid, after the slightest of delays, with a deeper male voice that said in English, "It can take some getting used to, but after a while, you'll hardly notice it."

Chapter 9

THE FOLLOWING DAY PROVIDED MORE distractions. During her morning visit, Arastan declared Hanna ready for solid food, and Susan took her to the embassy's main dining hall for lunch.

The dining hall provided a perfect opportunity to test-drive the translation module. As Hanna sampled fruits and cheeses imported from other worlds and nibbled on a rich, nutty bread the embassy's baker had learned to make in Europe, she eavesdropped on several nearby conversations being conducted by embassy staff members in Talessanin, French, and a handful of other languages she didn't recognize. The translator seemed to be able to detect which conversation she was focusing on, and it rendered the words into perfect English, complete with appropriate slang and idioms. Still, the exercise would've been a lot more fun if the module hadn't been limited to one male voice and one female voice for its English translations, and if the conversation topics had been more interesting than broken plumbing, medical benefits, and someone's three-year-old's startlingly colorful vocabulary.

It would've been even better to have someone to converse with herself, but Susan stood stiffly behind Hanna's chair, every inch the proper, efficient lady's maid, and there was no one else in the room that Hanna even recognized. She longed to talk everything over with Tiffany or Rachel, but when she'd asked Tomin about calling home, he'd said it was a bad idea, since human communications technology was easy to hack and trace, and calling her friends might lead Dalathek back to her them. As much as she wanted them to help her daydream about Jon, the last thing she wanted was to drop the nightmare on their doorsteps.

She had almost finished eating when Tala, looking bored and a little cross, arrived in the dining room accompanied by a woman who turned out to be her nursemaid, along with one of the ever-present bodyguards. As soon as she spotted Hanna, the little girl's face lit up, and she skipped across the room to climb, giggling into Hanna's lap.

With the nursemaid's slightly disapproving (though obviously re-lieved) permission, Hanna spent the rest of the afternoon touring the embassy under the guidance of Tala and Susan. They showed her an enormous library, where Hanna could sit and read any time she liked, as well as a small theater, a collection of ancient artifacts from various plan-ets, a quiet chapel with a soft spiciness in the air that made Hanna think of Jon, and a game room where Tala tried to teach Hanna how to skip smooth stones across an antigravity field and make them land in a white stone bowl on the other side. A climate-controlled room housed a fas-cinating display of extraterrestrial insect life, and a long gallery housed some spectacular works of art from the far reaches of the Empire. Be-yond the art gallery, echoes chased each other around the corners of a grand ballroom where dust covers draped over small tables, chairs, and folding screens provided a fantastic setting for a game of hide-and-seek. After that, the three of them returned to Hanna's room. Susan produced milk and cookies from the service kitchen, and Tala fell asleep on one of the long sofas, her head pillowed on Hanna's lap. All things considered, it had been a good day. And even with all that scampering around after Tala, her belly had hardly hurt at all, except for a twinge now and then when she stretched her arms too high above her head or twisted her torso a little too far.

Hanna stroked the little girl's hair, fascinated by her long eyelashes, dainty ears, and the flush of soft pink in her cheeks. One of Tala's arms rested across Hanna's knees, and Hanna traced a finger down the child's forearm, caressing each of the slender spines of her delicate, half-un-folded fin. After a moment, she looked up to see Susan watching her intently from the other side of the room, seemingly frozen in the act of carrying away the dishes. Hanna felt a self-conscious smile tug at her lips, and explained, "I was just thinking about what it might be like if I had children with fins." She looked down again, retracing the delicate bones with her finger.

Susan set down the plate she'd been holding and came to perch on the edge of an armchair across from Hanna. "Some human women find they don't like it very much, my lady." Her words were simple enough, and her expression was calm, but there was an intensity in her voice that hinted at layers of meaning beneath the placid surface.

Hanna met Susan's gaze. For a long breath, the two women just looked at each other. Then Hanna said softly, "You can tell me, Susan."

Susan studied Hanna's face for one more long, tense moment. Slowly, she unbuttoned one of her cuffs and pushed her long sleeve up to her elbow—and extended the forearm fin it had concealed.

Hanna stared.

Speechless.

Susan cleared her throat. "If I keep them covered, I can pass as full human, since my fingers and toes have no webbing." She folded the fin and began to tug her sleeve back over it. "I'm not sure who is more bothered by them, humans or Talessanins."

Hanna found her voice. "I'm not bothered, Susan, just . . . surprised. May I see?" Careful not to wake the sleeping child, Hanna slid forward a little on her sofa.

Susan hesitated warily, then pushed her sleeve back up and held her arm out. Hanna took the maid's hand in hers and gently stroked the slender fin spines one by one, base to tip, as she had done with Tala's. The delicate webbing was the same rose pink as the blush rising in Susan's pale cheeks and covered with a fine filigree of white lines.

"Your fins are beautiful," Hanna murmured. "Please don't feel you have to hide them on my account." Her finger paused at a barely noticeable bulge near the end of one spine, then again at a place where another bent slightly out of proper alignment.

"My mother used to break my fin spines between her fingers when I was bad." Susan explained softly, "The other arm is missing a spine entirely because she cut it off with a pair of scissors when I was about Tala's age. There wasn't enough left for the doctors to regrow it when I came here and they tried to repair the damage. I think she would've cut more of them, but the cook heard me screaming."

Hanna's horror must have shown in her face, because Susan pulled her arm away. "Please don't judge her too harshly, my lady. She was very young to be a mother and had a difficult life, but I think she loved me in her way. She was one of the first humans taken by the smugglers in the early days, before Earth was 'officially' discovered. I don't think she ever knew who my father was. It couldn't have been our owner, since he wasn't Talessanin, but he sometimes loaned my mother to his friends." She shrugged. "I don't remember her very well. I was sold when I was old enough to be useful."

Sold.

Hanna cleared her throat. "Is that when you . . . came here?"

"No, that was years later. I had three owners before the Viper found me and—" She stopped, flustered, stared at Hanna for one long, frozen moment, eyes round with some remembered emotion, and cleared her throat. "He saw what I was and told the woman on the refugee shuttle to have me sent here." She looked down as she continued, smoothing her long sleeve back over her forearm, hiding the fin. "It's better here. The Honored *Ehrat* says I only belong to myself, and I'm not made to do things I don't want to do. He says I may leave whenever I like, but . . . where would I go?"

She looked back up at Hanna again. Shy. Maybe a little afraid. "Perhaps it would be different for you. Your— He—" She cleared her throat again. "I'm *sure* it would be different for you. And for your children." She stood abruptly and curtsied. "Please forgive me for intruding in your private affairs, my lady."

As Susan bustled back to clearing the dishes, Hanna stroked Tala's hair and touched her tiny, fragile fin spines again. What would it be like to *be* a child with fins? With, perhaps, the wrong kind of fins? There weren't many hybrids on Earth—Talessanins and humans mostly kept their distance from each other outside official delegations. According to the tabloids and celebrity gossip magazines lining grocery store checkout aisles all over Earth, the first hybrids in existence were about to start kindergarten. But how many more were there like Susan? Did anybody know? If Hanna and Jon had children, what would life be like for them? Was it fair for her to choose that for her children?

A chime sounded, and Tala stirred awake. Susan arranged her face into a bland smile and moved to open the entry door. Tomin was there, along with a young Talessanin woman whom he introduced as Tala's music tutor. Tala gave Hanna a sleepy hug and kissed her cheek before thanking her nicely and leaving for her music lesson.

Tomin smiled after her for a moment, and then turned to Hanna, holding out a package. "This came for you on the afternoon packet."

The outer wrapping, which reminded Hanna of thin, flexible coconut husks held in place with twine, fell open to reveal a wooden box with carved leaves encircling the sides and a tree carved into the hinged lid. Inside the box rested a large book bound in thick, soft leather. The cover had a flap that folded around the pages and tied shut with a leather thong. Hanna lifted the book carefully from the box, savoring the buttery texture of the leather.

A tidy collection of narrow, colored sticks with pointed ends had been arranged inside the flap, attached with loops that kept them from falling out. Next to the sticks were a long, thin knife, something that looked like an old-fashioned pen with a metal nib, and three paintbrushes in varying sizes. A pocket near the bottom of the flap contained a small glass vial and an oblong metal plate with indentations around the edge and a larger well in the middle. A water bottle and palette? Underneath the flap, tucked in on top of the thick, fine-grained white pages, was a folded note.

> *My dearest Hanna,*
> *After all these empty hours the transport has stopped halfway for fuel, and I can think only of how far I am from you now. I thought perhaps a stroll in the port bazaar would distract me. I was wrong.*
> *The shopkeeper says this is a good gift for an artist stranded without her tools. Dry, the colors can be used like pencils. Dipped in water, the marks are more like ink. The pigments dissolve in water to make paint. I hope you find them suitable.*

I will think of you sketching in the court-
yard, with Earth's sun kissing the back of
your neck since I cannot.
Please think of me.
Jon

As Hanna refolded the note, she caught a faint scent of leather and spice, and couldn't help thinking that Jon's hands had made the creases. A wave of longing washed through her, and her breath caught in her throat. From the corner of her eye, she saw Tomin watching her and stopped herself from raising the paper to her nose.

This was absurd. How could she possibly miss him this much? She hadn't even known him very long.

Still . . . how far away *was* he? Hours by flutter drive, and he'd only been halfway. Flutter shuttles could travel to the other side of the world almost instantaneously. The distance was unimaginable.

She swallowed hard, then cleared her throat. "When are you people going to invent a long-distance cell phone?" she asked Tomin, with a shaky attempt at a smile. "Do I really have to wait until he gets back to tell him thank you? That's wrong, Tomin. It's just wrong."

Tomin shook his head sadly. "A lot of us wish the same thing, Hanna, but you can't send a communications signal through a flutter fold, and that's all there is to it. Something about mass, I think, but I wasn't really paying attention in class that day."

"So we're stuck with intergalactic snail mail," Hanna said morosely. "Who would've thought? It's practically medieval."

"So is dancing." Tomin rose, grinning, and held out a hand to help her up. "Come, let's get you ready for that ball."

Hanna laughed weakly and put her hand in his. Somehow Jon had become enough a part of her to make the distance between them hurt. That might be the only thing she was sure of. But it was something. The rest she'd just have to figure out when she got there.

Chapter
10

THE REST OF THE DAY dragged slowly by, as did her lonely soak in the hot pools in the evening. Especially after Narista and Salenia joined her, with their sly, sidelong looks and giggling whispers; that was a worse kind of loneliness than being alone. Even on the rare occasions when Narista seemed to tire of the game, Salenia pushed it brutally on.

At night, the nightmares came, with their adrenaline-fueled dizzy spells and retching fits that tore at her healing insides. Once, Hanna even thought she saw Dalathek standing at her bedroom window in the darkness, looking in—but of course that was ridiculous, since Tomin said the trackers had him cornered somewhere in Taiwan, and he wouldn't have been able to break into the embassy anyway. She supposed she shouldn't be surprised that the hallucinations were back again, though. Stress always made them worse.

Daytime was better. She spent the morning—after Arastan came and tsked at her for healing slowly because she was human—carefully pressing and drying one of Jon's daisies in the service kitchen microwave. She sandwiched it between two pieces of stiff paper and tucked it into the envelope with Jon's note. When she got home, she'd make it a proper glass frame, but for now, this should keep it from getting broken.

She spent all of the long afternoon and most of the following day adding drawings to the sketchbook's pages; it helped her pass the time and clear her head. When she drew, everything else receded and time seemed to fold in on itself, becoming nothing more than line and shape, light and shadow, and her worries faded into a soft peacefulness. Did Jon know what a gift he'd given her when he sent her this book?

She sketched the plants in the courtyard flowerbeds and the animals in the menagerie. She spent at least three hours drawing beetles in the room with the insects, and the furry little man who curated the collection helped her write down the name and origin of each of the creatures she drew. She went to the art gallery intending to copy bits she liked from the works on display there but ended up mostly drawing the other people who wandered through the exhibit.

Tomin was right, the embassy was beginning to fill with exotic guests. Although most were Talessanin, Hanna began, here and there, to catch her first glimpses of members of the Empire's other citizen races and to catch fascinating snippets of their alien languages, all of which were rendered into perfect English by the translator she wore in her ear. She had seen pictures of aliens before, of course, but it was different seeing them in real life. Most were at least roughly humanoid—Hanna had seen a scientist on TV once explaining something about how convergent evolution produced apex animals with an upright posture, the ability to grasp and manipulate objects with their appendages, elevated optic organs, and a number of other human-like adaptations.

Although, now that she thought about it, the term "humanoid" did seem a bit narcissistic. Who was to say they were shaped like humans, instead of humans being shaped like them? Maybe they were all "Talessanoid" in form. Which of the sapient species had evolved first?

Tomin had been right about something else, too. They all ignored her. And really, she thought she preferred it that way.

She did make one friend among the newcomers, however, one lonely afternoon in the library.

The third day after the sketchbook arrived dawned to a heavy overcast, and by lunchtime the gusting wind in the courtyard tasted like impending rain, so Hanna decided to spend the afternoon indoors. The library was cool and quiet, and Hanna was delighted to discover Tala having a lesson there with one of her tutors. With her dark little head bent over her books at one of the tables, Tala actually held still long enough for Hanna to make several sketches of her young friend. There was something sweet in the pensive frown that drew Tala's lips down when she was deep in thought, and a delightful twinkle in her eyes when she triumphantly offered a correct answer to a question her tutor had asked. But eventually the lesson ended, and Tala's tutor took the little girl away.

Most of the other occupants of the room drifted away soon after, as rain began to patter against the library's windows. Hanna tired of sketching and decided to find a book to read curled up in one of the big overstuffed chairs. It took her a few minutes to locate the section with books written in English, and then to find one that seemed like it might have a plot interesting enough to keep her mind from dwelling too much on Jon, but which still used simple enough language that her brain could process it in her distracted state.

When she returned to the table where she'd left her things, Hanna was surprised to discover an elegant middle-aged Talessanin woman standing beside the table, slowly turning the pages of Hanna's sketch-book. Hanna froze, staring, uncertain what to do. She was still hesitating when, a moment later, the woman looked up and saw her standing there. Hanna's cheeks warmed.

The woman said something in Talessanin, which Hanna's earpiece translated as, "Is this your sketchbook?"

"Yes, my lady," Hanna said, relieved to find she remembered what Tomin had said about how to address the nobles if one of them should happen to speak to her.

The woman gave Hanna a long, penetrating look, then returned her gaze to the book. She turned over another page. "Your work is quite good," she said, musing. "Especially these last pages when you were drawing the little *Al Ahnat*." She turned another page. Then she looked up at Hanna again, examining her minutely from head to toe. "You are human," she stated flatly. "I am not familiar with human customs. Is this work your profession, or merely your amusement?"

Hanna hesitated. "I'm an artist by profession, but these sketches are for my own amusement. I'm pleased you like them."

The woman turned another page. "I would be curious to see your professional work. Have you any pieces in the embassy gallery?"

"No, my lady, I don't have that honor." Hanna hesitated, then added, "However, one of my paintings was recently purchased by Jonantathinel of House Kanestelan *Ehr* for his private residence."

The woman raised her eyebrows. "Indeed," she said. Again, she scrutinized Hanna closely. "Do you ever work on commission? I have been considering having a portrait made of my granddaughter."

"I do sometimes accept commission work," Hanna said carefully. "Unfortunately, current circumstances prevent me from being able to begin a new project immediately. However, if you'd be kind enough to write down your name and contact information, I'd be happy to let you know when I'm available."

The woman blinked slowly. Her eyebrows rose. "You don't know who I am?"

Hanna felt more blood rush to her face, and she looked down. "Please forgive my ignorance, my lady. I've only very recently become acquainted with any Talessanins at all. I still have a great deal to learn about a great many things."

A smile spread across the woman's face. "How delightful! I cannot tell you how long it has been since I had the opportunity to make a first impression on a new acquaintance." She turned the sketchbook's pages until she came to the first empty page after the sketches of Tala, and thoughtfully selected one of the colored sticks. Then she looked back up at Hanna. "Do you read Talessanin? I'm afraid I've not yet learned to write in the language you use here."

"I regret I don't read Talessanin, my lady, but I have a friend who is very good at translating."

"Excellent." The woman wrote several lines on the page in neat, flowing Talessanin script, then tucked the stick back into its loop and closed the book. She looked back at Hanna. "I wonder if you would indulge me . . ." She frowned. "We have not been introduced, and I have no idea what to call you." She held her hand out, palm down. "You shall call me Kieran. At least for now." She smiled indulgently.

Hanna hesitated. Tomin had said she could greet anyone short of the Empress and Emperor as an equal. Should she insist on that? Would this woman be offended? Tomin had also said the submissive greeting would make her seem gracious, and it wasn't smart to go around offending potential paying customers. She reached her hand out, palm up, to grasp the woman's wrist, subordinate to superior. "My name is Hanna Bradley," she said. "I'd be honored if you'd call me Hanna, but Miss Bradley will do if you prefer."

The woman gave Hanna's wrist a little squeeze before releasing her grip. "You know some things about Talessanins, I see." She looked pleased.

"I'm trying to learn, my lady." Hanna inclined her head.

"Kieran," the woman corrected. She waved her hand toward a pair of armchairs in one corner. "Do you play, Hanna? I wonder if you would indulge me with a game."

It took Hanna a heartbeat to realize the woman was actually gesturing at a game board that rested on a low table between the two chairs. It was the same game she'd watched Tomin and Chance playing the night she took Narista's note over to have Jon read it to her—the one that looked a lot like Chinese checkers. *Jennan.*

"I had the game explained to me once," Hanna said uncertainly, "but I've never actually played."

Kieran looked delighted. "Good," she said, "perhaps I will win for a change. I'm told I am too impatient to play really well."

The two of them spent the next hour or two with their heads bent over the game board. At first, they talked only about the game as Hanna learned, first the basic rules, and then a little strategy. But after a while the conversation drifted to other things. Kieran spoke about her younger brothers, who had always been so smug when they won against their big sister. Then she told Hanna how they had put bugs in her bed one time, and she had retaliated by tying their hair to the headboards of their beds while they were sleeping.

Hanna laughed and told Kieran about the time she and Tiffany had put a toad in their fourth-grade teacher's underwear while it was drying on the clothesline.

Kieran told Hanna about her secret infatuation with her poetry instructor during her adolescence and laughed nostalgically about how heartbroken she'd been when the man ran off with the baker's assistant.

Hanna told Kieran about the time when the boy she liked kissed Tiffany behind the cafeteria dumpster, and she hadn't forgiven her friend for five months, even though it wasn't really her fault.

Kieran told Hanna how her oldest son had fallen in love with her dear friend's daughter, and the hopes they'd had for a union of their Houses. Her son had worn the girl's courting knife for two or three years during his basic military service, but when he decided to stay in the military beyond basics and accepted a command position, she asked him to return it. First love, they decided, was a hard thing no matter which world one grew up on.

Kieran had just begun to tell Hanna how she'd met her first husband, when another elegantly dressed Talessanin woman glided around the corner and stopped at a respectful distance, evidently waiting, her face carefully blank. Kieran sighed. "Ah, Hanna, here is my maid to tell me I must go prepare for dinner. It has been most enjoyable to have someone speak to me as if I were just a person again. I sincerely hope you will continue to do so when next we meet." She stood and strode to the door without looking back. The maid glided in her wake, and after a moment two bodyguards Hanna hadn't even noticed followed her out of the room.

As soon as they were gone, Chance stepped out from behind a bookcase. He wore his black bodyguard uniform and had a big grin on his face. "Well, that's something you don't see every day," he said with a chuckle.

"Chance! What are you doing here? How long have you been there?"

"I've been following you all day. Tomin and Susan and I decided you should have your own bodyguard."

Hanna scowled at him. "I thought you said I was safe here."

"You are. So are all those other great lords and ladies. Bodyguards have more uses than just the obvious, Hanna. We make very decorative status symbols too." He flexed his muscles dramatically.

Hanna rolled her eyes. Then she leaned forward in her seat. "And you know who that lady is?"

"Hanna, everyone knows who that lady is."

Hanna waited for him to tell her. "Well?"

Chance laughed and shook his head. "Well what? If she didn't tell you, I'm certainly not going to. Are you ready to go dress for dinner like everyone else?"

Chapter 11

TOMIN ANNOUNCED DURING THEIR DANCE lesson the next morning that Jon's transport was scheduled to arrive at the orbital port late that night, and he should be back at the embassy by morning. Hanna botched all the dance steps after that and was entirely unable to focus on the etiquette lesson he tried to give her instead, so he gave up and left.

She barely picked at her lunch because her stomach was in knots, and her hands shook every time she tried to draw.

Jon was coming home!

Being away from him had made her realize how big a space he occupied in her life now. How much she wanted that to continue.

What if being away from her had made him realize what a mess she really was and decide she wasn't worth all the drama? Maybe listening to all the Council's arguments about why humans shouldn't be considered people had convinced him they were right. Or, what if this had all been a game to him in the first place? Maybe he was just slumming with a human to see what it was like, and he fully intended to settle down with Salenia once he finished playing around with Hanna. A thousand maybes danced through her head to wreak havoc with her heart.

But he had said his courtship was sincere. And most of her believed him.

Dinner that night turned out to be a last-minute formal affair in the main dining hall, complete with a fancy invitation from Kamm. Susan got all in a fluster over Hanna's hair, arranging and rearranging it three different ways before she was satisfied enough to start on the makeup which, to Hanna's profound relief, was quick, elegant, and understated. The anxious maid had just finished lacing her mistress into a red silk evening gown that had magically appeared from whatever wardrobe department had been supplying Hanna's clothes during her stay at the embassy, when the door chimes sounded.

Tomin's eyes scanned Hanna from head to toe as he entered the sitting room. "I guess you'll do," he teased. His approving grin told her Susan had done her job well. "I just came to see if you need any quick refreshers on table manners before they throw you to the sharks."

Hanna grimaced. "Am I the main course tonight, then? Petrified human under glass?" She gestured toward the sofa and they both sat down.

He laughed. "Not this time. They know they're on Earth, humans at the dinner table are only to be expected."

"Not *this* time?" Hanna rolled her eyes. "You really know how to comfort a girl." She drew a deep breath and shrugged. "Don't worry, I remember. Sit up straight. Don't splash in the finger basins. Never leave a beetle fork on your plate belly up."

He gave her a satisfied nod. "You'll do just fine. I can't wait to hear all about it."

Hanna frowned. "Won't you be there?"

"Hardly. Lowly media relations officers aren't nearly important enough to dine with such grand company. But Chance will go as your bodyguard."

"A lot of good that'll do me when nobody wants me as a dining companion. Who am I going to sit by?"

"Probably some Hikanu lordling who couldn't find someone to sit with either. Don't worry, you'll get used to the smell." He chuckled at the look on Hanna's face. And then went serious.

"Actually, there's something else I wanted to discuss with you." From an inside breast pocket of his diplomat's robe, he produced a narrow box made of fine-grained black wood, smooth and polished. He cleared his throat self-consciously. "Before you open it, I just want to apologize if I've overstepped myself in this. You said you thought you needed one, but when I had an opportunity to speak to a maker out on one of the orbitals, I was unable to contact you because you were sleeping. I decided to just have one made and surprise you. The maker said she'll take it back if you don't like it."

The knife that rested against the padded, deep green silk of the box's lining was about six inches long from its leather-sheathed tip to its exquisitely crafted pommel. The detail in the embellishments made it seem more like a piece of fine jewelry than a tool or a weapon.

The silvery grip was crafted to look like a bit of tree branch, bark still attached, with two smaller twigs angling out from where it joined the blade, forming the knife's crossguard. From one of the twigs, a lobe-edged leaf curved around the grip, making a sort of decorative knuckle guard. On the base of the branch, as the knife's pommel, sat a silvery field mouse, its head tilted questioningly, its long tail winding down around the grip. The fur of the mouse was etched so beautifully it almost looked as if it would be soft to the touch, and its bright, inquisitive eyes were made of a deep green gemstone that matched the lining of the box.

The black leather of the knife's scabbard had been worked to depict more lobe-edged leaves, overlapping as if they had fallen to the ground. Peering out from under some of them were several intricately detailed beetles, and pressed into the leather between the leaves was a row of tiny animal tracks, as if the mouse had walked up the scabbard to reach its perch.

The blade, when she slid it from its sheath, was not at all what Hanna expected. It was a slender, polished piece of the same deep green gemstone that had been used for the mouse's eyes, thin and sharp at the edges, but more rounded down the center of its length. As Hanna held it up to the light, she caught her breath; a four pointed star made of light seemed to float within the stone blade, shifting position as she tilted the knife, changing the angle of the light.

"It's beautiful!" Hanna breathed. She slid the blade back into its sheath and set it carefully back in the wooden case. "Is this . . ." She hesitated. "Is this a courting knife, Tomin?"

"It is," Tomin said gravely.

Hanna touched a careful finger to the top of the mouse's head. "It's really amazing," she said softly. "I've never seen anything like it. But

Tomin, I can't possibly pay for something like this. Just the blade alone is probably worth more than I ever earned in my life. Put together."

"The maker isn't expecting payment," he said. "At least not in money. She offers it to you as a gift, with her compliments."

Hanna gave him a skeptical look and waited for him to explain.

He sighed. "Assuming he accepts it, that knife will be worn by Jonantathinel of House Kanestelan *Ehr*, himself—the man who gave up the Throne of the Empire Among the Stars, who became Commander of the Nine Winds, the Viper in the Night, Subduer of Worlds. I don't think you really understand what that means. He is the most famous, most eligible bachelor in the Empire —possibly in existence. And he doesn't just go around courting women all the time. If he accepts a knife from you, that is the knife the Viper will wear. A maker of courting knives can't possibly get better publicity than that. Once word gets out, every daughter of every Talessanin House in the Empire will be begging for a knife by the same maker. If you asked her, the maker would probably pay you to accept this knife. It could easily be the making of her fortune."

Hanna stared at him. She opened her mouth to speak, hesitated, then closed it again and looked down at the knife in her lap.

Tomin cleared his throat. "There are a few things you should know about that knife before you decide whether to accept it. First, there are two kinds of courting knife. One is highly ornate, but rather generic, with just the woman's family crest on the pommel and a lot of filigree and gemstones. They might be passed down within a family and used by more than one daughter, or even by more than one generation. These are by far the most common.

"The second kind is more personal and less common. Instead of a family crest, the pommel bears a symbol specific to the woman herself. They're generally used when a woman wishes to accept a suitor without making her identity as the object of his affection a matter of public discussion. But sometimes they're given in order to let a suitor know his courtship is of particular value to the woman."

Hanna ran a careful finger down the length of the knife in its case. "And this is the second kind."

"It is. I didn't know if you even had a family crest, but I know Jon calls you Little Mouse, so I thought that might work for a personal symbol." Tomin shifted uncomfortably. "I didn't ask for all those *taless* leaves, though. I promise. I only told the maker that a lady who was being courted by the *Ehr* wished to commission a knife with a mouse on the pommel and asked her to choose appropriate accompanying embellishments."

"What's wrong with *taless* leaves?"

Tomin stared at her for a moment, then shook his head. "I forget sometimes that you wouldn't know these things. In most traditional origin stories among the Talessanin cultures, the first people grew from the first seeds of the first *taless* tree. That's why we're called Talessanins—we're the people of the *taless* tree. Those who still follow the traditional ways, like Jon follows the way of the Sower, often burn *taless* seeds as part of their religious rituals. The leaves are generally viewed as symbols of life and fertility, and they're a common motif on courting knives in general. And maybe that's all the maker meant by using them. But they're also a symbol of the ruling House—of House Kanestelan. They're all over that invitation to the ball, remember?" He jerked his chin toward the mantle, where the invitation was still on display.

Hanna shrugged. "I didn't know that's what they were."

Tomin gave her a long look. "I don't suppose you would. But surely you can see now that this knife combines your mouse symbol with a symbol of Jon's House that has a double meaning of fertility. It's practically a public declaration that you want to be the mother of his children. Especially when you throw in all those beetles. Which is fine in a personalized courting knife if the relationship is really that serious, but it's not a thing to taunt a man with if it's only a casual bit of fun for you. And then, of course, there's the blade." He shook his head.

Hanna's brow furrowed. "I think the blade is amazing!" She took the knife out of its case and slipped the blade free of its sheath so she could examine it again.

"Oh, it *is* amazing," Tomin agreed. "Star stones are often used to embellish courting knives, because they represent good fortune, but I've never seen one used as a blade before. Actually, I've never seen one big enough to make into a blade before. But Hanna, that color of green is another symbol of the Imperial House." He fingered his dark green diplomat's robe. "It's a bit brash for you to use it on your knife at all, since you are not, yourself, of Kanestalan. That's mitigated somewhat by the fact that this is a highly personalized knife intended specifically for Jon, but you couldn't really give that knife to a different suitor without having the blade replaced—except maybe Kamm. And that very fact could be taken as an insinuation that you intend to never have another suitor besides Jon. It hints that you're ready for betrothal."

Hanna looked at Tomin, then back at the knife. The four-pointed star gleamed out at her from the heart of the blade. "That does sound pretty intense. Especially with the *taless* leaves."

"The maker said she could replace the blade with platinum to match the hilt and give you a less . . . suggestive . . . sheath. That would take the intensity down a few notches."

Hanna looked up at him again. His face was carefully expressionless.

"She also said she thought any woman brave enough to give a courting knife to the Viper at all would be audacious enough to give him *that* knife. And she made me promise to show it to you before I ordered changes."

Hanna slipped the knife back into its sheath, admiring the amount of detail worked into the tiny beetles peering out from under the meticulously crafted leaves. She didn't know what to say.

A pause. Then, "It's your knife, Hanna," Tomin said softly. "You need to tell me what you want."

What *did* she want?

She placed the knife back on its bed of shimmering silk and ran a finger over the mouse, down the *taless* leaf knuckle guard. She thought of the tingling thrill of kissing Jon. Of how safe she felt with his gentle arms around her. Of the wondering tone in his voice when he had asked if marriage with him was something she might actually consider. Of how breathlessly close he'd been when he allowed her to trace the dark lines of his desire on his face. Of how achingly far away he must be now.

If she were completely honest with herself, she already knew what she wanted. She wanted the kind of relationship with Jon that this knife represented. In this moment, she wanted it so much she could taste the smoky, spicy scent of the longing. But did she have the nerve to *ask* for what she wanted?

And if she did, would that be fair to Jon?

What about the nightmares? The flashbacks? Could she be that intimate with a man without the dark terror surging up to overwhelm and suffocate her? She had tried a few times over the years with other men.

The results had been disastrous. Just thinking about it made her want to weep again with the humiliation of it. But this was different. Jon was different. Maybe . . . Maybe . . .

Tomin leaned forward in his seat, suddenly intense. "You don't have to do this, Hanna."

She looked up.

"In fact, you should think long and hard before you do. If you're not really serious about Jon, it would be best for both of you if you just walked away completely. Now. Before this goes any deeper."

"Tomin—"

"You don't see all the moving parts on this, but they are there all the same. And they're spinning faster all the time. I thought it would just be . . ." He stopped. Pressed his lips together. Drew a deep breath and continued, "You learn fast, Hanna, and you handle yourself well. Jon needs someone like you. But you're in over your head, and sooner or later you're going to realize just how much. When you do, you'll have to learn to swim or head back to shore. One or the other, or you'll drown in this. I don't want to see that happen. And I don't want to see Jon get hurt. That man has been through enough pain for several lifetimes already. As his friend, I'm asking you. Don't toy with him. Don't give Jon that knife unless you truly mean to see this thing through. This isn't frivolous for him."

Hanna stared at him. Sink, or swim. Fish, or cut bait. And all she could think was *deep water isn't a safe place for a panic attack.*

Tomin held her gaze, his eyes serious and intense.

Then he sighed and leaned back in his seat. "All of which is none of my business. I'm sorry."

Hanna drew a deep breath. "Can I have a few days to think about it?"

Tomin tilted his head to one side and regarded her. "Of course you can. Take all the time you need." He was quiet for a moment, looking at her. Then he stood abruptly. "I believe that takes care of all my business here," he said with his usual cheerful smile, as if nothing out of the ordinary had passed between them. "And now I should probably go. I wouldn't want to make you late for dinner with the Imperial *Ehrat.*"

Chapter

12

HANNA NEEDN'T HAVE WORRIED ABOUT finding someone to sit with; Kamm came to solicit her companionship as soon as the door steward announced her arrival. When he greeted her as his good friend, a murmur of surprise chased its tail around the hall, but everyone was exceedingly polite as he introduced her to his higher ranking guests—the Heads of three Great Houses, several Delegates to the Grand Assembly, and a handful of ambassadors from worlds Hanna had never heard of.

She had hoped to see her new friend from the library, or perhaps Mrs. Milgram or her son David, who had both been in attendance at Jon's dinner party back home. Besides Kamm, however, the only familiar faces in the crowd were Narista, who was acting as hostess for the evening, Salenia, and Salenia's parents, Lord and Lady Trakanaleth, whom she had met briefly—and awkwardly—at the Future Vision art exhibition. They were clearly even less amused by her presence at this event than they had been at that one.

During the meal, Hanna was seated to Kamm's left, as the host's dining companion. He did try several times to engage her in conversation, but Narista, seated on his other side, kept interrupting and seemed intent on monopolizing his attention, leaving Hanna to fend for herself. From her vantage at the high table, Hanna had an excellent view of the other guests—and an increasingly uncomfortable awareness of just how often their eyes rested on her. Judging. Speculating. By about the third course, however, when the human interloper had failed repeatedly to do anything particularly shocking, their attention drifted to their food and to their neighbors, and the low murmur of hesitant conversation grew into a healthy rumble.

And Hanna wasn't entirely neglected; she spent most of the meal chatting with the honored guest who occupied the seat to her left, a short, odd-looking alien named Cerulean Stone, who managed to seem dignified even while using the long, thin tentacles surrounding his beaked mouth to manipulate his eating utensils.

Hanna was, at first, rather startled by his visual mode of communication, which involved rapidly evolving changes in the pattern and coloration of markings in his damp, translucent skin, and reminded her of videos she'd seen of cuttlefish. However, he had a device that rendered his communication into Talessanin speech, which Hanna's translation module then translated into English punctuated with soft verbal hints as to the emotion intended to accompany the words, such as "uncertainty," "intense interest," "sarcasm," and "pleasure." And when Hanna spoke, colors and patterns flickered over the surface of a smooth, oblong object the alien cupped in one fingerless appendage that Hanna thought of as his arm, though it wasn't in quite the right place for that and was definitely not the right shape.

Cerulean Stone, it turned out, had been to nearly every planet in the Empire during his long political career, which spanned more than a century in Earth years. He possessed a dry wit that gave spice to his stories of other people and places, and Hanna soon found herself quite absorbed in conversation with him. And since he was by far the most exotic person in the room, making friends with Cerulean Stone somehow made all the other guests seem much less strange and intimidating. Had that been Kamm's intention in arranging the seating this way in the first place?

As the final course of the dinner was served, Cerulean Stone leaned back in his chair, a soft blue wavy pattern flickering over his skin before it returned to its more habitual oscillating brown blotches. Hanna's translation module announced, "Affectionate sincerity. I have enjoyed your company this evening, Miss Bradley; you laugh at all the right parts of a story. Too many Talessanins neglect laughter."

Had he just called her a Talessanin?

Hanna's cheeks warmed. Did human facial expressions and other body language cues translate through Cerulean Stone's device at all, or was he operating purely on the verbal content of the conversation? What would happen if she inserted the kind of verbal hints his translator was feeding to her? "Sincerity," she said. "I haven't met many people who aren't from Earth, but so far I must say you're one of my favorites."

Cerulean Stone's skin flickered white and then darkened to a muted grayish color. "Startled," Hanna's module said. "Uncertain." There was a pause, a quick flash of green, and the brown blotches reappeared. "Miss Bradley, did you intend to insert an emotion cue into your speech?"

"Yes," Hanna said tentatively. "Did it work? I hope I didn't offend you."

"Delighted!" Hanna's translator reported, as Cerulean Stone flushed a deep blue-green. "It worked wonderfully. But I have not met many Talessanins who thought to try, so I was uncertain if it was intentional. I always feel as if I am missing half of the intended meaning when I speak with Talessanins. Please do continue."

"Relieved," Hanna said.

He'd called her a Talessanin again. Or at least, he'd lumped her in with them. Why? Was he testing her in some way? Or was it just that he couldn't tell humans and Talessanins apart? Fins did seem like a pretty superficial difference compared to tentacles, color-changing skin, and . . . that arm thing. Was he only being nice to her because he thought she was Talessanin?

He seemed to be waiting for her to say something else. She cleared her throat and tried, "Um. Commiseration. I often feel that way myself when I speak with Talessanins. We humans are still learning how to understand offworlders."

A rippling quiver passed through Cerulean Stone's tentacles, as his skin pulsed through pale turquoise to a ripple of pastel green. "Affectionate approval," the translator murmured. "You do very well, Miss Bradley. I have not met many humans from Earth, but so far I must say you're one of my favorites."

Hanna's cheeks warmed again with a blush. "Flattered," was all she could think to say.

After a small pause, Cerulean Stone said, "Friendly curiosity. Is it true that the Viper himself offered you surrender, and you just walked away?"

"Oh." Hanna blinked. How had he heard about that? "Startled," she said. "I suppose he did, technically. But I didn't know that was what he was doing at the time. And he didn't mean anything by it."

"That is not what he told me." A fluttering ripple moved through Cerulean Stone's face tentacles. "Deep amusement. Candor. I like you Miss Bradley. You must come see me if ever you visit the Capital."

He knew Jon? How well? Well enough for Jon to tell Cerulean Stone about that ridiculous stunt he'd pulled at the art show, apparently. They must have crossed paths while Jon was in the Capital.

The Capital. Hanna's eyes flicked involuntarily toward Lord Trakanaleth before she forced her gaze back to her nearly empty plate and from there to Cerulean Stone's eyes. "I would like that very much. I've enjoyed hearing about your travels, and I would love to hear more."

"I would love to tell you. No one wants to hear my stories anymore. Annoyed. Everyone I meet with only wishes to lecture me about the virtues or deficiencies of their pet Assembly resolutions. Affection. You would be most welcome."

"Pleased," she said. Again, Hanna's gaze drifted toward Salenia's father. A man who kept a human woman as a pet. "But I don't think it's very likely I will ever see the Capital. I'm not sure a human would be safe there."

Cerulean Stone's eyes narrowed, his slitted horizontal pupils contracting as he glanced in the same direction. His skin darkened almost imperceptibly, then flickered through a series of blotchy brown patterns. "Miss Bradley," the translator intoned solemnly, "please know that you do have friends in the Capital if you need them."

A response was rendered not only unnecessary, but nearly impossible by a flourish of music from the back of the room as the after-dinner entertainment began. Hanna hung back from the dancing, afraid of making a clumsy mistake, but the three times she was coaxed onto the floor she managed to survive the dances without catastrophe and with less pain than she'd feared. Tomin was a good teacher. And apparently all those soaks in the hot pools were doing their job too.

It was a relief when the dancing ended, and Kamm offered to escort Hanna back to her rooms. Everyone stared as she left the dining hall on his arm. The corridor felt strangely empty as they walked, despite the escort of bodyguards, including a stoic Chance, that spread out before and behind. Maybe that was because the man she usually walked with like this, with her hand tucked into the corner of his elbow, was Jon. He could fill a space all by himself just by breathing.

Kamm chuckled softly and smiled down at her. It was almost Jon's smile, but not quite. Kamm's smile was more open, less guarded. "You were wonderful, Hanna. I was concerned when the Chancellor asked to be seated next to you; he can be rather unsettling. But the two of you seemed to find plenty of things to talk about."

Hanna stopped dead in the middle of the corridor. "The Chancellor?"

"Cerulean Stone," Kamm clarified. "He's the Chancellor of the Grand Assembly. Didn't you know?"

Hanna shook her head and began walking again. "No. You people always seem to cleverly leave out the most important information."

Kamm chuckled. "That's because to us it's the most obvious information. Forgive me, Hanna. I'll try to do better."

They stopped in front of the door to Hanna's guest suite, and Hanna began to move her hand away from Kamm's elbow—but stopped when his fingers closed gently over hers.

"Thank you for your elegant diplomacy tonight, Hanna," he said, his face and voice suddenly serious. "You confirmed all the good things I've been telling the Assembly about humans, and none of the bad things they've heard from others. I couldn't have asked for a better ambassador for humanity. And as always, I enjoyed your company." He paused for a moment, his expression turning pensive, and he looked as if he wanted to say something else. But he only shook his head and brushed a light kiss against her cheek before he whispered, "I wish you well, Hanna Bradley," and left.

Chapter

13

JON SHIFTED ON THE LUMPY, wobbling, fold-down jump seat behind the pilot's chair, as the supply pod released its docking coupler and drifted away from the orbital station. The pilot glanced back over his shoulder again, his face tense and pale. Jon couldn't really blame him; as if having an unexpected passenger forced on him at the last minute wasn't bad enough, Jon could only imagine the man's distress when the passenger turned out to be the Viper. Well, he'd have a story to tell his children.

In the blackness outside the pilot's viewport, Earth floated, a blue and white crescent. Hanna was up there. Somewhere. He would see her soon.

He'd thought himself fortunate when his transport was bumped ahead in the queue at the fueling station because the one ahead of it had mechanical problems, allowing him to arrive at the Earth orbitals ahead of schedule. But then the station master informed their diplomatic party that the passenger shuttle for the North American Embassy had departed only moments before their unexpected arrival, and they would have to wait for its next trip. The other diplomats merely shrugged their shoulders and went off to the small station bazaar to find a meal, or a massage, or a gift for whoever was waiting at home.

But Jon hadn't slept well for days, and all the flutter shifts of the long journey had made the ache of his old wound throb mercilessly under the healing bruises on his hip. He just wanted to get back to the embassy and see Hanna. If she was still there. If she still wanted to see him.

Flutter travel tended to distort time a bit, but he figured five days had passed here since he left. A lot could happen in five days. Maybe Kamm's security forces had captured Dalathek, and Hanna had gone home. Maybe Salenia had said something to Hanna that would irreparably damage his chances with her. Maybe she'd just come to her senses and realized that allowing the Viper to court her was rash to the point of imprudence. Maybe, now that she'd had time to fully process "the human question," she wanted nothing more to do with him. There had been an awkwardness between them when they parted after the tour of the menagerie, and she had still been asleep when he left. He wished he could be more certain how things stood with her now.

Perhaps more showed on Jon's face than he intended, because the station master had swallowed hard and began tapping at his display, checking for other options.

Now, the cargo pilot's hands moved over the pod's controls as he reoriented the pod into alignment with the gravitational direction of its destination. Earth drifted out of the viewport, leaving only blackness dotted with distant stars. Then the grinding thump of the pod's flutter drive throbbed through the hull, making Jon's seat vibrate uncomfortably, and pain knifed down his leg from his hip again as the fold formed and released. Cargo jostled slightly and settled in the restraining webs as Earth's gravity took hold, and then the pilot was negotiating the short descent onto the wide pod field at the far side of the embassy's shuttle port. Rain beat against the viewport, and gusts of wind kept trying to shove the pod out of its assigned trajectory. At last, however, the pod settled onto the ground, the pilot powered everything down, and the rear hatch hissed open.

Cargo handlers in rain gear stared as Jon strode through the bay, bag slung over his shoulder, trying not to limp. It was raining hard enough to make the main passenger terminal difficult to make out, crouching as it was on the far side of the field, but he could see the lights from its windows shining out into the stormy night, and he set off in that direction. Mud sucked at his boots as he walked, and soon his black velvet longcoat was so wet it dragged at his shoulders. His bag kept swinging against his sore hip, and he paused to shift it to his other shoulder. Maybe he should have waited for the passenger shuttle after all. But it wasn't scheduled to depart for another four span.

Where would Hanna be? She wouldn't be waiting for him, he wasn't due for hours yet. She certainly wouldn't be sketching in the courtyard in this rain. Maybe she'd be in the art gallery. Or in the game room with Tomin and Chance. Or Narista and Salenia. He shivered. Maybe Hanna was in her rooms curled up in front of a chick flick in those shapeless gray trousers she liked to wear, hugging Mr. Bickles and a bowl of popcorn. Maybe she'd let him join her. That thought made him smile.

His boot slid in the mud, and pain shot down his leg from his hip again as he caught his balance. He gave up trying not to limp and focused on keeping his footing in the slick mud. Finally, he reached the flat-topped pavement where the passenger shuttles set down. He scraped off as much of the mud as he could manage and shoved his dripping hair out of his eyes so he could see how much farther he had to go before he reached the passenger terminal. It wasn't far. Light shone out warm and welcoming from the big windows next to the wide, round door that had been an airlock before the embassy ship settled to the surface here.

And there she was.

Hanna stood framed in one of the windows, one small hand pressed against the glass, looking out at him. For a moment, his heart stopped, and he just stood there, frozen in place while some wild emotion he could not quite name washed over him. And then he started walking again, his strides growing longer and faster with each step on the solid footing until he broke into a jog for the last few lengths.

Hanna turned from the window as he pushed in through the door, and he froze, feeling abruptly foolish. She was beautiful—regal even—in a rich red gown with gold embroidery shimmering at the borders and a belt that spilled long gold chains sparkling with beads down among the folds of the skirt. Her hair was swept back and up in one of the latest Talessanin styles, and a deep red gem on a gold chain sparked against the skin of her throat just where the curve of her neck met her collarbones.

Jon's boots squelched as he shifted on the doormat, and the water dripping from his coat made a distinct plink-plopping noise in the sudden silence as the door hissed closed, shutting out the sounds of the storm. He wanted to go to Hanna, to hold her, to kiss her, to tell her how much he'd longed for her. But in this state he felt as if he soiled her just by looking at her.

"Jon!" Hanna's voice was soft, perhaps a little breathless. "It *is* you. I thought I was imagining." She hurried to close the few steps between them, and he stepped back, not wanting the hem of her skirts to brush against the muck that caked his boots. She stopped, a look of frightened confusion flashing across her face. She looked down, blushing most becomingly. "I'm sorry." She took a step back. "I thought . . . I'm sorry. I won't bother you."

She spun away, and Jon realized she'd misunderstood his hesitation. "Wait!" he called. She stopped with her back to him, shoulders tight. "Hanna, please do not go." His mind was having difficulty shifting back to using English again, and he could not find the right words. "It is just . . . the mud." He floundered. "Your dress."

She half turned toward him, looking back over her shoulder, her eyes scanning him from head to toe. A smile bloomed across her face, and she turned fully toward him. "Mud?" She folded her arms saucily across her middle. "Is that all?"

Jon let his bag slide off his shoulder and drop to the floor, then took a tentative step toward her, careful not to get too close. "I missed you, Hanna."

Hanna eyed him up and down again, scowling. Then she pointed a commanding finger at him. "Don't move."

Jon blinked at her, confused, but nodded.

Hanna stepped closer to him, and he looked down to see the gold-embroidered skirt hem drag across his boot and come away filthy. She ran her fingers over the embroidered lapels of his dripping longcoat, then pushed the coat open and, tucking her hands between the coat and his mostly dry shirt underneath, wrapped her arms around him, and pressed her cheek into his chest. "I missed you too," she murmured. "Mud doesn't matter."

Hesitantly, Jon put his arms around her, holding her close, watching the water from his heavy cuffs roll down her dress, leaving dark tracks on the rich red. Then he closed his eyes and buried his face in her hair, taking in the scent of her, the feel of her body pressed against his, the sound of her steady breathing. She was still here. She was still his. She turned her face up and kissed him, long and lingering, and a little bit hungry, and he knew he was truly home.

After a long, sweet moment, Hanna pulled a little away from him. "Welcome back, Jon," she said, looking up into his face. Then her smile turned into a pensive frown. "I should let you go get cleaned up. You're all wet, and you look terrible."

"I have looked much worse." He grinned at her. "I was very surprised to find you waiting, I had not thought to see you so soon. How did you know I would be here early?"

"She didn't." It was Chance's voice, and Jon looked up to see his friend leaning against the window where Hanna had stood before, dressed in his bodyguard uniform. "She's been down here since dinner ended pretending to sketch flutter shuttles in the dark."

"I was not pretending!" Hanna stamped a little foot and turned toward Chance, hands on hips. "I have four pages of shuttle sketches. The artificial lighting with the dark shadows is dramatic." But when Jon hooked an arm around her waist and pulled her back against his chest she added sheepishly, "Although, there is a small possibility the sketches were an excuse to sit here and wait. Just in case." She snuggled against him and laughed self-consciously.

"You received my gift, then?" Jon murmured into the crook of her neck before dropping a kiss there.

Hanna turned in his arms so she faced him again. She seemed thinner, less substantial than he remembered. How was her wound healing? Humans were less resilient than Talessanins. "Yes," she said, beaming up at him. "And I love it. It's a beautiful sketchbook, Jon, I've never owned anything quite like it." Her face went suddenly serious. "I . . . I have something for you, too. But I left it in my rooms."

Jon kissed her forehead. "Perhaps you could go get it. And I will clean up and meet you . . ." he frowned. "No, I must speak with Kamm first. My honor, Hanna, it is important, or I would come to you first and let him wait. I do not know how long I will be. Do not wait for me, I will find you when I am finished, and then I shall be all yours to do with as you wish."

Hanna blushed again. "Promises, promises," she said with an impish grin, and moved away from him.

Jon stared at the mess he had made of her dress. "Hanna," he said, chagrined, "I am so sorry about . . ." he gestured, "the mud."

Hanna looked down at herself and laughed. "It'll wash," she said, "or else it won't, and whoever is picking my clothes for me these days will have learned a valuable lesson about letting me play with nice things. They're all trying to make me into an elegant lady, Jon, but it won't work. I happen to like mud." She grinned at him. "If you still want to find me after you've spoken with Kamm, might I suggest the library as a good place to start looking? I found a book there earlier that I wanted to read, but I got interrupted."

Jon grinned. "The library. I will hurry." He kissed her one more time, savoring her closeness, her scent, her willingness; then he retrieved his bag and headed for his rooms.

Chapter
14

S USAN SHOOK HER HEAD OVER the condition of the red silk
dress but smiled when Hanna told her where the mess had come
from. Hanna showered and put on the clean gown Susan had laid
out and then fidgeted while the maid fussed over her hair again. By the
time she was finished, Hanna was beginning to worry she might not get
to the library before Jon did.

The little platinum mouse gazed wisely out at her when she looked
one last time at the courting knife lying in its case. *Any woman brave
enough to give the Viper a courting knife at all,* it seemed to say, *is audacious enough to give him* this *knife.*

Was she?

She knew what she wanted. Whatever lingering doubts had lurked
around the edges of her soul had been washed away by the plummeting
despair she'd felt when Jon drew back from her at the shuttleport door,
followed by the surge of hope that had flooded through her when he
called her back.

And that kiss!

Yes, she was certain what she wanted. The wanting was gnawing a
hole in her chest. But was she audacious enough to ask for it?

Would she be able to bear it if he refused her? If it turned out this
was just a game for him?

Maybe she should take a few days to think about it, like she'd told Tomin she would. But if she did that, she might lose her nerve. She might get scared and have the knife altered. Or send it back altogether. She might decide it was all too much, too big, too frightening, and she might run away back to her quiet life in Freebridge and try to pretend none of this had ever happened. If she didn't leap now and take the plunge, she might talk herself out of it. She might never know what would've happened if she'd had the courage to just jump.

Yes, it was rash. Yes, it was impulsive. No, she hadn't considered all the ramifications. How could she? Jon's life was so far outside her own experience that she could barely begin to imagine it. But when she was younger, she had taken risks. She had sought out adventures. Back before . . . before the shed. Before Dalathek. That man had taken so much from her. Was she going to let him take this, too?

But what if Jon refused her?

She didn't have time to argue with herself about it anymore, he could be waiting. She closed the case and tucked it into the shoulder bag Susan had acquired for carrying her sketchbook.

The darkness in the library was held at bay only by a few strategically placed reading lights that gave the room a cozy ambiance. One of these hung in the corner with the game board, and one of the two easy chairs was occupied. Kieran looked up and smiled. "Hanna!" she exclaimed. "What a lovely surprise! I was just wishing for some company." She held up a book she'd been reading, and added, "How this writer managed to create a story that is simultaneously incredibly improbable and unbearably trite, I do not know."

Hanna laughed, glad she still wore her translation module. "Kieran, it's good to see you again. I looked for you at dinner last night, and tonight as well, but couldn't find you. It was a big crowd, though."

Kieran sighed. "Yes, well, I dined in my own rooms with a small group of friends who are also not officially here. I am not officially scheduled to arrive until the day after tomorrow, you see, and it would not do for me to make a surprise appearance at dinner." She gestured at the game board. "Is it possible that you have time to let me win another match or two?"

Hanna smiled, looking around at the otherwise empty room. "I'm supposed to be meeting someone here, but I can play until he comes. I'm not sure how long that will be, though." She slid into the chair opposite Kieran, setting her shoulder bag on the floor by her feet.

"Meeting someone in the library at night." Kieran's eyes lit up, and she leaned forward in her seat. "Could it be, by any chance, a romantic assignation?"

Hanna felt her face warm. "Something like that, yes."

"How delightful! You must tell me about him. Is he handsome?" Kieran started setting up her game pieces.

"Very handsome." Hanna smiled at Kieran's enthusiasm. "And kind, and gentle, and generous." Hanna began to place her own little round stones in the starting positions. "And very patient with me."

"Ah," Kieran declared as if pronouncing sentence. "You are still in the early stages of this romance and have not yet discovered your admirer's flaws." She gestured at the game board. "You may begin this time."

Hanna laughed and moved one of her pieces. "Oh, I may have encountered one or two of his flaws. But it doesn't seem right to lay them all out before a third party, especially when he isn't here to defend himself. If he can put up with my flaws, I can put up with his."

Kieran's face softened. "Then he is indeed wise in choosing to court you. Is this an official courtship, or is he still merely a private supplicant?" She moved one of her pieces and frowned. "But you are human. I suppose it is done differently among humans."

Hanna contemplated her pieces. "Well, each human culture has its own traditions. In my culture it's certainly done less formally, but otherwise it's not so very different, I think." She moved a game piece. "However, my current suitor is Talessanin." She watched Kieran. How would her new friend react to this news?

Kieran's eyebrows rose, and she leaned back in her chair. "Is he indeed?" She pursed her lips thoughtfully, then leaned forward and moved a piece on the game board. "I imagine that complicates things somewhat. If I may ask, Hanna, what do you imagine will be the end result of this courtship?"

"That's the big question with courtships, isn't it?" Hanna asked. "Yes, it is a bit complicated, but we are figuring it all out together. I imagine that, in the end, things will either work out, or they won't." She moved another game piece. "And there's really only one way to find out."

"I suppose that is true." Kieran frowned at the game board. "Well, you are certainly figuring this game out, at any rate." She began to move one of her pieces, then put it back and moved a different one. "Perhaps you will introduce your Talessanin suitor to me when he arrives. You have made me quite curious about the man." She leaned back in the chair again, giving Hanna an analytical look. Then her eyes shifted to a spot behind Hanna, near the library door, and her face relaxed into a smile once more. "And perhaps you will allow me to introduce you to my son," she said, "if he will stop lurking in the shadows." Kieran rose to her feet, and Hanna followed suit, turning to see who had come in. "Jon," Kieran said, pride and welcome in her voice, "do come meet my new human friend."

Hanna's stomach lurched.

Jon strode out of the shadows near the doorway, clasped both of Kieran's outstretched hands in his, and placed an affectionate kiss on her cheek. "Hello, Mother." He spoke in Talessanin. "I'm pleased to see that you arrived safely. I wasn't lurking, I only just came in."

Hanna couldn't breathe. Kieran was Jon's mother. That meant . . . it meant . . .

Jon continued, "As it happens, I know Hanna well, though perhaps not as well as I would like to." He turned to Hanna and smiled encouragingly as he held out a hand to her. In English he said, "Thank you for waiting for me, Hanna."

Mechanically, Hanna placed her hand in Jon's. Her heart pounded as she looked from Jon's smiling face to Kieran's stunned expression, and back again. "Jon." Hanna's voice came out a hoarse whisper, and she cleared her throat. "I'm afraid I've been making a terrible fool of myself. I didn't realize . . ." She trailed to a stop, looking back again at Kieran. Jon's mother. The Empress Among the Stars. Hanna's vision began to swim as a wave of dizziness washed over her. She pressed a hand to her forehead, trying to make it stop, but it only got worse, and she felt Jon's arm wrap around her waist as she swayed, and her knees buckled.

"Hanna!" Jon's alarmed voice seemed to come from a distance. "What is happening?"

"Dizzy," she mumbled. "Startled again."

Jon eased her back into her chair, pushing the game table out of the way, scattering the pieces. He knelt on the floor before her as he'd done in the menagerie, tipping her head down to rest on his shoulder, and stroking the back of her neck with his warm webbed fingers. "Slow, deep breaths," he whispered in her ear. "I am sorry, Hanna."

Hanna heard a rustle as the Empress seated herself again in the other chair. The older woman's voice, when she spoke, was carefully flat. "It seems our human friend is somewhat excitable."

"Our human friend," Jon said, his voice tense, "is recovering from a serious injury that required a substantial infusion of synthetic blood. One side effect she is experiencing is dizziness when she is startled. And it would seem that her new Talessanin acquaintance neglected to mention the rather startling fact that she is the Empress."

"Don't be cross, Jon," Hanna said into his shirt. "I'll be fine in a minute. And as you may remember, you neglected to mention a few similarly important facts when I first met you."

Jon chuckled wryly. "You are right." He brought Hanna's hand to his lips and placed a kiss in her palm, folding her fingers around it. "It is a family failing, perhaps."

Hanna laughed softly. "Maybe, but if so, it missed Narista. She's always been unusually forthright with me."

This time Jon's laugh sounded entirely sincere. "So she has."

For several heartbeats no one spoke. Then the Empress said, "Jon, am I to understand that you are the Talessanin suitor who arranged to meet with Hanna tonight?"

Jon's voice was also quiet. "Yes, Mother. I am courting Hanna."

The Empress let out a long, controlled breath. "Kamm told me you had been seeing a young woman during your time here. I am afraid I assumed he meant . . . someone else."

Jon said nothing, but his fingers moved up from Hanna's neck to stroke her hair, and he turned his head to place a kiss just behind her ear.

The Empress spoke again. "Is Hanna aware that it is not legal for you to actually marry her?"

Hanna's head was clearing, and she felt Jon's slight flinch.

"That will change," he said. "If the current amended resolution passes in the upcoming vote, Hanna will be legally as Talessanin as you and I, and able to marry whomever she chooses." He paused, and when he spoke again the tightness was back in his voice. "It would help, perhaps, if the Throne would support the resolution."

The Empress sighed. "I know what it takes for you to ask such a thing of me, Jon. But the Throne is still divided on the human issue."

"And as long as the throne stands divided, so will the Assembly," Jon said, and the tightness in his voice had turned to bitterness.

The Empress was silent for a long moment, then softly said, "And so will you and your lady."

Jon tensed. "I do not require your approval, Mother."

"No," the Empress said quietly. "You never did, did you? But you have it in this, nonetheless."

Her gown rustled again as she stood, and she added, "Hanna, I hope you feel better very soon. And I hope you will still call me Kieran and think of me as your friend." Her footsteps receded in the direction of the library door, and Hanna sat up just in time to see two dark figures detach themselves from the shadows and follow her out.

"Better?" Jon's voice sounded a little rough, and his eyes were sad.

"I'm fine, Jon." Hanna placed a hand against his cheek. "Are you all right?"

Jon smiled sheepishly. "I was not expecting to meet my mother here tonight."

Hanna coughed out a wry laugh. "No, I imagine you weren't. And I didn't expect my new friend to turn out to be your mother." She cleared her throat and shot a glance at the now empty doorway. "But I . . . I'm pretty sure your mother just said she approved of you courting me."

Jon blinked. "I think you are right. I did not expect that either." He grinned, but then his smile turned sad. "Her approval would mean more if she would publicly declare in favor of the resolution on behalf of the Throne. But she will not take an official position on the issue while her husband opposes her. She does not wish to compel him to act against his conscience, so she often allows the Throne to remain officially neutral on issues where they disagree and lets the Assembly decide." He sighed heavily. "This is one of many issues on which the Emperor and I do not agree. But change will come. And we have time, you and I." Silence pressed between them, taut and heavy. Then Jon shifted. "It has been a long day. Perhaps we could speak of more pleasant things for a while." He directed his crooked boyish grin at Hanna. "I believe you said you had something for me. If I kiss you, will you give it to me?"

Hanna laughed. "That sounds like a fair exchange," she said, "but you'll have to get up. It's in my bag, and I can't reach it with you there."

Jon scowled. "I do not want to get up. I like the view from here." He leaned forward to kiss her lightly on the lips. "I can think of very few presents that would be worth getting up for." He kissed her again, more deeply this time.

"Okay," Hanna said, "Stay there, then. I'm not sure you'd even want my present anyway."

Jon shook his head sadly. "But now you have made me curious. What sort of gift does a Mouse give to a Viper?" He braced his hands against the padded arms of the easy chair and heaved himself upright, a grimace of pain flickering across his face as he did so.

"Are you all right?" Hanna's alarm showed in her voice.

"I am well, Hanna, just old, and stiff, and tired from traveling." He straightened tentatively. "There is something about the forming and releasing of a flutter fold that makes the old wound in my hip ache tremendously, and I have been jumping all day."

Hanna frowned. "The same hip with all those bruises? Maybe you should sit down."

Jon eased himself into the chair his mother had vacated and heaved a tired sigh. "There is more than one reason I retired, Hanna; fighting is a young man's game."

Hanna laughed. "You're not that old." She scrutinized him. She hadn't really considered his age before. "You couldn't be older than . . . what . . . thirty five?"

He chuckled. "I am too tired to figure it in Earth years," he murmured, "but yes, about that. Not so old for a farmer, or a diplomat, or a priest, but for a warrior I am ancient." He raised an eyebrow. "And for you . . . ?"

"For me, that's just right." She laughed at his boyish grin and bent to retrieve her shoulder bag. Her hands trembled as she fished out the sleek black knife case, and she took a deep breath to steady herself before moving to stand in front of Jon, holding out the box.

Instead of taking the box, however, Jon put his hands on Hanna's hips and tugged her gently over to sit sideways on his good knee, then curved one of his arms possessively around her middle. "Open it for me?" he asked, a small, mischievous smile on his lips.

A nervous giggle slipped out before Hanna could stop it, and her cheeks warmed. Jon's smile grew bigger. He was gazing intently at her face, and not even looking at the box in her hands.

"All right," Hanna said, looking down at the box so she wouldn't have to meet Jon's eyes. "But if you don't want it, or don't like it, you have to say so. Don't be nice and pretend you do if you don't. I could get a different one, or . . . or something else instead." Jon didn't say anything, so Hanna looked up. He still studied her face, but his eyes were more serious now.

"Do not be so afraid, Little Mouse," he whispered. "If it is from you, I will want it. Whatever it is." He reached a hand up and trailed his fingers across her cheek and down her neck. "Show me?"

Hanna's heart pounded. She took a deep breath and slowly tipped the lid open, turning the box toward Jon. Nothing happened. Was he even looking? She didn't dare glance up to see.

Then Jon shifted under her and drew in a slightly ragged breath. The arm around her waist tightened, and his other hand drifted down from her shoulder, where he'd begun to trace her collarbone. With one careful finger, he brushed the top of the mouse's head, then traced the line of the *taless* leaf knuckle guard. "Hanna . . ." Jon's hoarse whisper trailed off, and Hanna couldn't tell what emotion it carried.

"It's a courting knife," she said, her quiet voice sounding harsh in the sudden, complete stillness. "I know you said it wasn't important, but I thought—"

"I know what it is, Hanna," Jon interrupted. His voice was louder now, but Hanna still couldn't read the intense emotion in it. His hand rose to cup her cheek, and he turned her head until she was looking at him. For a heartbeat, Hanna thought he'd say something else, but he only drew her face slowly to his and kissed her, his lips gentle but eager against hers, his arm around her waist pulling her closer against his body. He drew a shuddering breath, and his kisses became more insistent.

Hanna shifted the knife case to one hand and brought the other up to Jon's face, sliding her fingers down his cheek, as she returned his kisses, and then nudging them around behind his neck under his loose dark hair. One finger brushed against the first *enan* at the top of his dorsal fin; Jon shivered and pulled a little away from her, breathing hard. For a moment he just gazed at her. Then his crooked smile spread across his face, and he looked down at the knife again.

Hanna cleared her throat. "So, I guess you like it, then?"

Jon laughed, a slow, rumbling chuckle Hanna could feel vibrating through his chest. "Hanna, how could you ever think I might not want a courting knife from you?" He tucked a quick kiss into the crook of her neck and lifted the knife from the box, turning it so the mouse's green eyes sparkled in the light from the reading lamp. Hanna reached over and slid the sheath off the knife, revealing the deep green star stone blade. Jon stopped breathing. He shifted his grip so he could study the star at the heart of the courting knife. Then he slid the blade back into the sheath and returned it to its box. "Will you hang it on my belt for me?" he asked softly.

"If you like," Hanna said just as quietly. She kissed him one more time and stood. Jon hoisted himself out of the chair, wincing again as his sore leg took his weight. Hanna frowned. "You should soak that."

"I will," Jon said. "Just now I have more important things to do." He set the box on the chair and offered her the sheathed knife. There was a loop on the back of the sheath to thread the end of a belt through; it wasn't built to clip on and off quickly and easily.

A blush warmed Hanna's cheeks as she reached out to touch his belt. It didn't have the sort of buckle she was accustomed to; instead, the belt looped through a wide ring and wound around in a thick knot with the end hanging down the thigh of his loose trousers. Hanna studied the knot uncertainly, then looked up at Jon's amused expression. He smiled encouragingly, and she turned her attention back to the knot, reaching out tentatively to push the end of the belt back through the knot, while tugging at a loop with her other hand. It took her a couple of tries to get it undone, but she managed, then slipped the sheath of the courting knife over the end of the belt and slid the knife around to Jon's hip. She looped the end of the belt back through the ring but was at a complete loss as to how to reconstruct the knot.

As she hesitated, Jon trailed his fingers along the back of her hand. "Under here." He showed her. "And down through there. And then just give it a tug. You see?" Hanna stepped back, examining her handiwork. It hung crooked. Jon grinned at her. "Leave it," he said. "I like it that way."

He reached out and drew her in for another kiss. "Thank you, Hanna. You could not have given me a more precious gift tonight."

Hanna leaned her forehead against his chest so he wouldn't see the tears she blinked hurriedly from her eyes. "I'm glad you like it." He shifted to take some of the weight off his sore leg. Stepping back, she eyed him critically. "You look exhausted. And when was the last time you ate?"

He looked sheepish. "I am not sure."

Hanna reached a hand up to push his hair back from his face. "You said tonight you'd be all mine to do with as I choose," she said.

Jon looked away, a slight frown tugging his lips down. Was he blushing again? "Hanna . . . I only meant—"

She interrupted him. "What I want tonight is for you to go get something to eat, and have a good soak, and get a full night's rest. We can do something together tomorrow."

Jon's eyes shifted back to Hanna's face, worried, searching for something. A soft smile spread across his face, and he relaxed. "As you wish. May I escort you back to your rooms first?"

"I would like that." Hanna retrieved her bag and, tucking her hand into Jon's, moved toward the door.

Neither of them spoke all the way back to Hanna's rooms in the guest quarters, though several times Hanna caught Jon watching her instead of where he was going, and once he tugged her into a small alcove as they were passing and kissed her until she was breathless and blushing.

He kissed her again outside her door, pulling her close and running his fingers down her back in a way that made her shiver against him. "It is so good to be back," he whispered into her ear, his breath tickling down the side of her neck. "I have longed for this. For you."

Hanna wrapped her arms around him—and tensed as she felt the ridge of his dorsal fin pushing against the back of his shirt. She leaned back enough to get a good look at his face. Thick, dark lines swept away from his eyes, six on each side, out toward his temples, and down over his cheekbones. As she watched, the tracery of smaller lines she'd seen before appeared, breaking across his skin like an intricate blush.

Jon closed his eyes and drew a slow, deep breath, tensing. Then he opened his eyes and leaned forward to brush his lips lightly across hers again. He looked into her eyes for another moment, hesitating, then kissed her again, harder this time, more urgent.

Hanna stepped back. "Jon, I think you should go." Her voice was a shaky whisper.

Jon moved closer. "I do not wish to go." He bent to kiss her neck.

Hanna stepped back again. "But . . . your face." She reached up to brush her fingers down his cheek, tracing one of the dark lines. "Before, you said you wanted—"

"I know," he murmured. "It does not matter. Tonight . . . I think I want this more." He moved closer again.

Hanna retreated another step, and her back met the wall. Her mouth went dry and her heart began to pound. "It will matter to you a great deal tomorrow."

"*You* matter a great deal to me, Hanna." Jon put one hand on the wall beside her head and leaned toward her, pressed against her, his hand moving to the small of her back, pulling her against him, and she felt the trembling tightness of his muscles. "Let me stay a little longer. Please?" As he leaned forward to kiss her again, his other hand reached up to brush a strand of hair away from her cheek.

A wave of white-hot terror engulfed Hanna, filling her nose with the smells of old wood and gasoline before choking off her breath. The splintery roughness of the wood slats in the shed's wall pressed into her back. The taste of blood filled her mouth, as a red haze closed over her vision and the ringing in her ears drowned out all other sounds. A small, strangled whimper escaped her throat. Dalathek's breath was hot against her neck.

It was going to happen again.

Again.

Her hand twitched.

She could move!

No time to think. She smashed her fist into the elbow of the arm he'd braced against the wall, throwing him off balance. Slammed her forehead into his face. Flung herself sideways.

He cried out, staggering back to the other wall of the shed.

Hanna stumbled away from him, ready to run—but she only made it three steps before her legs tangled in her long skirts and she collapsed, sobbing, onto the carpeted floor of the embassy hallway.

The embassy.

Not the shed.

Not Dalathek.

Jon!

She pushed herself up to her hands and knees, choking down the sobs and focusing hard on the nubbiness of the stiff carpeting under her hands to keep herself grounded in the present.

What had she done? Where was Jon?

Adrenaline-fed dizziness washed over her like a tidal wave, and her stomach heaved, spilling its contents all over the carpet in front of her and sending a jolt of pain through her insides. She retched twice more, as the hallway slid relentlessly sideways, and the walls shifted between gray wood slats and flat beige paint.

Where was Jon?

"Hanna?"

It wasn't Jon's voice.

"Hanna! What happened?" Chance. The ever-present bodyguard. *How much had he seen?* A tentative hand patted her shoulder, and she flinched, gagging on the surging scent of gasoline.

"Don't touch me!" she gasped, and Chance backed away.

"What did you do to her, Jon?" Chance's voice sounded confused and alarmed, but the voice in Hanna's ear that translated it into English was flat and emotionless. "I thought I'd give you a little privacy to say good night, I didn't think you'd—"

"I frightened her." Jon's soft, muffled voice came from somewhere close in the shifting, wallowing hallway. "I am a monster, Chance."

"Look at me, Jon. Skip the theatrics and just tell me what—" Chance paused. "Oh. I see." Another pause. When he spoke again there was a hint of laughter in his voice. "Your Little Mouse has teeth."

"Get her maid." Jon's voice was definitely not amused. "Hanna needs help."

The dizziness was beginning to recede when Susan knelt beside Hanna only moments later. "I've sent for Arastan, my lady. What happened?" Susan sounded frightened.

Hanna forced her breathing to slow. She pushed herself away from the mess she'd made on the carpet, leaning her back against the smooth, painted wall and drawing her knees up under the long skirts. "I don't need Arastan," she said, leaning her forehead on her knees. "I just need everyone to leave me alone for a few minutes." She began the calming muscle relaxation exercises and kept her breathing slow, but she couldn't stop herself from shaking. When she opened her eyes a few minutes later, Arastan was bustling around the corner of the hallway. Susan and Chance stood staring awkwardly at each other, and Jon sat with his back against the wall on the other side of the hallway watching Hanna with grim eyes. Blood trickled from his nose and from one corner of his mouth.

What had she done?

Arastan knelt and held her scanner against Hanna's neck.

"I'm fine," Hanna said. "It was just a flashback. I told you about them." She scrubbed the back of one hand across her mouth. "Don't worry, Susan, I'll clean it up."

Susan looked appalled. "You will do no such thing, my lady!"

Arastan said, "Your readings look good as far as I can tell. Sometimes it's hard to say with humans. I'll get rid of that bruise on your forehead and give you a sedative to help you sleep tonight."

"No!" Hanna grabbed the medical advisor's hand. "No sedatives. When the nightmares come, I need to be able to wake up. Go help Jon, he's bleeding."

Arastan gave her another long, analytical once-over and nodded. "Very well. No sedatives. But I will fix the bruise before it sets. You don't need anyone wondering how you got it."

As Arastan stung Hanna's forehead with another shiny medical instrument, Chance glanced nervously up and down the hallway. "Maybe we should go into the sitting room before someone comes along and starts asking uncomfortable questions."

Hanna couldn't help laughing at that. "You mean like the three of you?"

Chance grinned as he scooped her off the floor but said nothing.

When they got into the sitting room, Chance deposited Hanna on one of the sofas and bullied Jon into sitting in one of the chairs so Arastan could look at his injuries. Susan insisted on taking Hanna into the bathroom to clean up, but Hanna sent the maid back into the sitting room to make sure Jon didn't leave before she could talk to him.

When Hanna emerged, clean again, from the bathroom, she ignored the gown Susan had laid out for her on the bed and instead traded her bathrobe for a pair of her own old sweatpants and a tie-dyed t-shirt from home. Then she gave Mr. Bickles a squeeze for luck and went looking for Jon.

He'd pulled one of the easy chairs over in front of the sitting room fireplace and sat leaning forward, elbows on knees, staring into the flames of a newly lit fire. Her courting knife glinted as he turned it over and over in his hands. A tray of untouched food sat on a small table at his elbow. Everyone else was gone, except for Chance, who stood unobtrusively in the shadows on the far side of the room looking out into the courtyard through the French doors.

Hanna's bare feet made almost no sound on the carpet as she crossed the sitting room, but Jon still heard her coming. Before she was halfway there, he shifted in his seat and said, "Hanna. I cannot tell you how sorry I am." He spoke English, but his voice was as empty and emotionless as that of the translation module, and he didn't look at her as he spoke, just stared into the fire.

He kept staring at the fire when she stopped beside his chair.

"Thank you for staying," she said. "I know you're tired, but there are some things I need to say to you that can't wait."

Jon turned the courting knife in his hands. *Why wasn't it still on his belt?*

"I understand," he said softly.

She drew a steadying breath and plunged ahead. "I'm sorry I hurt you. I didn't mean to. It was a flashback. They're a lot like the panic attacks you've seen before, but more intense. I feel as if I am there again, in the middle of it. I can see it, and smell it, and taste it, and reality just goes away for a little while. You were . . . *him*. For a moment. But it wasn't your fault."

"I made it happen." Jon's voice was rough at the edges. "I thought to . . . to court you as humans do, and I . . . I made it happen."

"Dalathek made it happen," Hanna said quietly. "You were just there when it happened this time." She stopped and swallowed hard. "I told you back in the beginning that I wasn't sure I could give you the kind of relationship you want. This is why. It's not that I don't want . . . that kind of relationship. I do. With you. I just honestly don't know if I can.

I don't know how to get around the walls and make it work. The flashbacks are shorter now than they used to be, and I recover more quickly, but they're likely to continue happening sometimes. It isn't cute, and it isn't funny, and it isn't at all attractive. And I completely understand if this is not a mess you want to be involved with. I don't even want to be involved with me half the time myself. But I . . . I hope you still do."

Jon didn't say anything, but the knife stilled in his hands.

He looked up at her. Whatever damage she'd done to his face had been entirely erased by Arastan's ministrations. His expression was carefully blank, but there was something deep in his eyes that looked naked. Vulnerable.

"I thought . . ." His voice came out rough this time. Raw. He cleared his throat. "You are not asking me to return your knife?"

Hanna blinked. "Why would I do that?"

His stony composure cracked, and his face went tight with an emotion that might have been either hope or despair.

"Because I am a monster, Hanna. I am an alien assassin twice your size who is feared across several galaxies, and you have seen me kill people with your own eyes. Because I am entangled in a complicated mess of intergalactic politics that takes me away for long periods of time just when you need me most. Because half my family insists you are not even really a person. Because I almost got you killed." He turned his face away again, staring down at the knife in his hands. "Because I did not stop when you told me to stop. Because I stayed when you asked me to go. Because I make you think of the man who . . . who hurt you. Because—" His voice cut off abruptly, and Hanna saw the muscles in his jaw clench and unclench several times before he went on. "Because you are human, and I am not, and you find my fins and my *tehilethkalan* repulsive. Because . . . because . . ." He made a helpless gesture with his hands. "How many good reasons do you require?"

Hanna stared at him. "Is that what you think?"

He drew a shuddering breath and turned the knife over again, stroking the mouse pommel with one thumb. Hanna knelt in front of him and cupped his big hands between her own. "I am not afraid of you, Jon. I have never in my life felt as safe as I do when I'm with you. If I had just said 'no' instead of hurting you, you would've kissed me one more time and gone. You know you would."

Her hand trembled slightly when she reached up to nudge his hair back from his face, and then let her fingers trail around behind his neck to brush against the first few *enan* and the folded membranes in between. "I find your fins fascinating," she whispered when he shivered at her touch. "And your *tehilethkalan*," her tongue tangled up the word, and she tried again. "Your *tehilethkalan* is possibly the sexiest thing I've ever seen." She leaned forward to kiss his cheek and temple, where faint lines still streaked his skin.

"And," she whispered, "I want to find out what happens after." Jon's eyes rose to meet hers. Bottomless. She cleared her throat. "Just not tonight. I'm not ready. And you want to wait. You know you do. You're just too tired tonight to make good decisions." She shrugged. "If you don't want to do this anymore, I understand. If you want to give my knife back, I'll respect your decision. But I'm not going to ask for it back, Jon. I'm not."

Jon looked down at her, his eyes searching her face. Slowly, he slid off the chair to his knees and wrapped both arms around her. He buried his face in her neck. "Oh Hanna," he whispered. "I thought I had ruined everything."

Chapter 15

HANNA WAS FINISHING HER BREAKFAST the next morning when Chance knocked at her door. "Come now," he said. "There's something you should see." His eyes shone, and he danced from foot to foot like a little boy with a pocket full of frogs.

Hanna swallowed her disappointment that Jon had not come instead and followed Chance into a part of the embassy she hadn't visited previously. It was part of the original embassy ship, and the angles and proportions of the architecture were slightly different from the human-friendly additions that had been constructed after landing. Chance hurried her eagerly along, moving too fast for questions or conversation. Finally, he tugged her through a wide doorway into what seemed to be an arena. The room was shaped like a long oval. Tiers of benches rose up the sides, separated by a waist-high railing from an open space in the center. The ceiling was a high, transparent bubble through which the morning sun shone, illuminating a loose circle of dark figures in the center of the floor and a scattering of watchers in the stands. The handful of men in the arena wore black tooled leather armor that seemed to shimmer slightly, and each wore a black half-mask *enkalan*. The sight made Hanna shiver.

Chance leaned toward her conspiratorially. "It's the Nine Winds. They arrived last night to help with security for the Emperor and Empress. I thought you'd like to see their morning sparring session."

The Nine Winds. The Emperor's personal strike force. These were the men Jon had worked with. Had fought beside. Chance led her down to the row of benches nearest the floor, and the two of them sat to watch.

In the center of the floor, three men in black body armor stood facing each other, taut and wary. The rest of the Winds stood back, watching. After several tense heartbeats, one of the men in the center twitched, and all three exploded into sudden action, twisting and whirling around each other, shifting seamlessly from one motion to the next so fast they seemed almost to be slipping in and out of corporeal reality. Once, Hanna imagined she saw the arm of one man pass right through the abdomen of another without even slowing down.

Abruptly, one of the men flew backward out of the fray and skidded across the floor, blue-white lightning crackling over the surface of his armor. The other two continued their spinning, dizzying dance for only a moment longer before a second man lay on the ground. The victor raised his daggers in the air, acknowledging a silent salute from the watchers. Then he helped his fallen opponents to their feet, and the three of them returned to the center, moving slowly this time while all three combatants and several watchers offered commentary and corrections.

Chance leaned toward Hanna again and said, "The sparring daggers aren't sharp. They incorporate specialized electronic components that interact with the armor's tech and knock combatants down if a blow is struck that would kill or cripple if the weapons were real. It wouldn't do to have the Throne's elite killing each other off just for practice. They can still bruise each other pretty thoroughly, though."

Hanna's brows drew down. "Why daggers?"

He looked at her as if unsure what she was asking.

She shrugged. "What's with all the knives and daggers? I mean, it's not as if you people don't have pulse pistols, and laser cannons, and bullets that see in the dark. Don't you think daggers are a bit primitive for super awesome extraterrestrial ninja warrior people?"

Chance laughed. "Some of it's just cultural. Part of our heritage. But there's a practical reason, too. The more advanced weapons generally work well when you're fighting large-scale battles, but they're likely to get you killed in close combat. For one thing, if you shoot off a pulse weapon too close to a particle field, you're going to get a wave of feedback that will make your weapon explode and cook you where you stand, and when things are moving fast you don't always notice all the particle fields in time. Ballistic weapons don't do that, of course, but the bullets don't penetrate most armor, and they just bounce off particle fields and ricochet around making holes in inconvenient things like life support systems, and bulkheads, and gravity field generators. A pointed weapon like a dagger will penetrate a particle field if it hits point on at the right speed, and it'll go through armor too if you can hit one of the weak points, like the groin, or armpits, or the neck. We use what works."

Hanna leaned back, frowning thoughtfully. "I guess that makes sense. But why not swords, then? I'd think bigger would be better when it comes to that sort of thing."

"Most close combat happens indoors these days. Not enough room to swing a sword effectively."

"But . . ." Hanna frowned. "Okay, you have me there. Daggers it is."

"And throwing knives," Chance said. "And sometimes darts. We can be primitive in all sorts of ways."

Hanna laughed and turned her attention back to the arena, where the men had rearranged themselves for the next match, three against two this time.

After a moment, though, she asked quietly, "Why didn't you just tell me she was the Empress?"

Chance grinned at her and shrugged. "She liked you. I didn't want to make you too nervous to be yourself."

Hanna thought about that as the figures in the arena began shifting cautiously, maneuvering for superior positions. "Well, I suppose nearly fainting in front of the Empress was slightly less humiliating than . . . what happened later with Jon."

Chance was quiet for so long that Hanna looked over at him. His expression was serious and sympathetic as his eyes studied her face. "It wasn't the worst flashback I've seen," he said, "My brother used to have them sometimes. It wasn't your fault. Jon understands."

"You have a brother? You never talk about him."

Now Chance looked away. "Yes, well . . . he died. He led the tech support team for the Winds before me."

"Wait." Hanna twisted in her seat to face him. "You led the tech support team for the Nine Winds? You never talk about that either, you only said you fix things." Chance shrugged and looked self-conscious but didn't say anything. Hanna settled back into her seat. "I never had a brother," she said, "but I always kind of wished I did."

Chance grinned. "I never had a sister," he said, "but if I ever did, I'd want one who wasn't afraid to bloody the Viper's nose for him if he asserted himself too vigorously."

Hanna gaped at him. "That's not what happened at all!"

Chance's grin grew bigger. "Maybe not, but that's the story going around the security office this morning just the same. There are cameras in the corridors, you know."

"Please tell me you're joking."

"I'm afraid not. It's just in the corridors, though, there are no cameras in private rooms unless requested by the occupant. And visual observation only, no audio."

He patted her hand. "Don't worry, the story won't go beyond the security personnel, they only talk amongst themselves; it's a point of honor. And since you had the good sense to land in a blind spot after you tripped, the sentry on duty couldn't see what happened after that until I carried you into your rooms. He thinks you twisted your ankle or something." He leaned back in his seat and nudged her playfully with his elbow. "And now, little sister, they're booking wagers as to whether the Viper's courtship survived his lady's wrath, because they weren't able to get a good view of his face when he left your rooms."

"Oh, you have got to be kidding me." Hanna folded her arms across her chest and rolled her eyes in disgust. "And what was your wager, brother dear?"

Chance mimed righteous indignation. "I would never bet against the Viper," he said solemnly. Then he winked. "Unless I was betting on his lady." Hanna snorted in a very unladylike manner and opened her mouth to speak, but Chance suddenly sat up straight and raised a hand, cutting her off. "Here's what we really came to see," he said, all the teasing gone from his voice. "They invited him to spar with them."

Hanna followed his gaze out to the far side of the arena where a tenth armor-clad figure strode purposefully toward the group in the middle—Jon. He wore his working armor, and even at a distance Hanna could tell he meant business.

One of the Winds barked a command, and the other eight instantly formed up in two lines of four and dropped to their knees facing Jon, heads bowed, right fists held over their hearts. Except . . . one remained standing in his place in the back line, arms folded defiantly across his chest. The leader, presumably the new commander, shook his head at the standing man and went to greet Jon. It was the dance-like greeting between friends and turned into a brotherly embrace before the two parted and spoke for a few minutes.

The defiant man in the back row shifted impatiently a few times and finally seemed to get tired of waiting for the reaction he evidently expected. He left his place in the line and went to stand next to Jon and the commander, gesticulating energetically as he spoke. The commander snapped something at him, but the man held his ground, and after a moment Jon turned to look at the man too, tilting his head to one side as if examining some unusual specimen of insect. Then he shrugged and nodded once.

"What's happening?" Hanna found herself whispering, even though it was unlikely anyone in the arena was close enough to hear her if she spoke aloud.

"He's the new one," Chance murmured. "Jon's replacement. He's very good at fighting, and unfortunately, he knows it. He beat three of the Winds in the trials, and I've heard that only the commander can defeat him one on one now. But he's the only one of the lot who has never been thoroughly thrashed by the Viper, and I guess he thought it would be a good idea to challenge him this morning."

"Challenge! But Chance, Jon's leg! Last night he was limping. What is he thinking?" Hanna heard the alarm in her own voice.

Chance chuckled. "Oh, his leg hurts, but there's no structural damage. Have a little faith in your suitor, Hanna."

The Winds formed their loose ring again, this time with Jon and his challenger in the center. Jon just stood there, arms folded, head tilted, bored amusement in every line of his body. The other man drew his two daggers with a dramatic flourish and struck a dangerous-looking fighter's pose. The commander clapped his hands once, apparently to indicate the beginning of the match, but only the watchers shifted position nervously. The two men in the center of the ring just continued to stare at each other, one the embodiment of violent death, coiled and ready to spring, and the other seeming hardly to notice. Finally, Jon moved a hand up to scratch his nose, and the other man whirled into action, both daggers flashing. Jon took what seemed a casual step to one side and his other hand flashed out once; the challenger collapsed to the floor, electricity sizzling over the surface of his armor. Hanna hadn't even seen Jon draw the sparring dagger he now held in his hand. She gasped at the speed of it all.

"There's a reason they call him the Viper," Chance laughed. "You see? Nothing to worry about. Jon is the best there ever was." He looked at Hanna sideways. "Of course, half his reputation is because of his ridiculous theatrics."

Jon nudged the other man onto his back with his foot and regarded him once again with his head tilted to one side, as if attempting to determine just what sort of idiot the man was. Then he held out a hand to help his opponent up. The challenger just lay there on his back staring up at Jon. Then he rolled over and, without taking Jon's hand, pushed himself up to his knees, bowed his head, and placed his right fist over his heart. Jon patted the man on the shoulder and went to chat with the commander again.

After a moment, the commander barked another order, and the Winds shifted into a wider circle, with only Jon standing in the middle. This time, however, Jon was alert, poised for action, and had both sparring daggers drawn. Only there was no opponent.

Chance sat forward on his seat, a scowl drawing his face tight. "Well now, this is a bit rash," he said.

Puzzled, Hanna leaned forward to see if she could tell what he was scowling at. "I don't understand," she said, "what's he doing?"

"He's taking on all nine of them at once," Chance said. "They used to do that sometimes for fun, but he only won about half the time. And there were only eight of them then. And he's a little out of practice because he's really only had Tomin and me to spar with."

Hanna's mouth fell open, and she stared out into the arena. "All of them?"

"Well, realistically there's only so much space for opponents to close with him, especially without getting in each other's way, so he'll really be fighting only about four or five at any given time. And remember, the daggers aren't sharp, it's only his reputation that's at stake, not his life." Chance stood and stepped up to the railing, and Hanna moved to stand beside him.

This time there was no signal, and Hanna didn't see who started moving first. One moment they all seemed to be standing still, tense, and in the next heartbeat the center of the arena had become a maelstrom of twisting, whirling bodies and flashing steel. A breath later, three men lay sprawled on the floor with flickers of light playing across their armor, and Jon seemed to have disappeared. But then Hanna saw him, half crouched and twisting to kick the feet out from under a fighter on the outside edge of the circle of attackers. The remaining Winds regrouped almost instantly, flowing like water, like air, into a new attack formation, some of them flickering out and reappearing on the other side of Jon. Teleporting. That was how Jon had gotten out of the center so fast. Now five men lay on the ground, leaving only four still circling. They converged on him all at once, daggers glinting in the sunlight, and Jon teleported away again before the two he'd taken down this time even hit the floor.

"That's two ports in less than a minute," Chance muttered. "He can maybe do it one more time, but more than that and the Void-freeze will start causing problems."

The only two men who still faced Jon were the commander and the new man Jon had just defeated. They drifted carefully across the floor, trying to maneuver into flanking positions, and Jon drifted with them, keeping both in his line of sight, angling away from the fallen men and toward the side of the arena where Hanna and Chance watched, breathless.

Another sudden flurry of motion, faster than Hanna's eyes could follow, and the new guy crumpled, leaving just Jon and the commander. The commander grinned and briefly touched the tip of his dagger to his forehead. Jon grinned back and returned the salute. And then the two friends began to dance in earnest, hands and feet flashing, bodies bending and striking, steel meeting steel, with a blurring speed that was beyond the eye's ability to follow. It was terrifying. And beautiful. And it went on and on. Hanna's fingers grew stiff from clutching the railing, and she found herself increasingly breathless as the battle surged back and forth across the floor, drifting ever closer to where she stood watching.

And then, abruptly, it was over. The commander of the Nine Winds skidded across the floor on his back leaving a trail of blue-white sparks, and Jon stood panting, his face a mask of fierce ecstasy, before raising his hands in the air, daggers crossed: the triumphant god of war embodied. Jon was in his element. Without question, this was what he was born to do.

Beside Hanna, Chance shook his head. "Best there ever was," he murmured again. "Gift from the Sower." Hanna let out the breath she hadn't realized she'd been holding. Chance looked over at her and grinned. "And you bloodied his nose, little sister." Hanna stared back at him.

The two of them watched as the figures in the arena picked themselves up and gathered in the center of the floor for follow-up analysis and instruction. When the Winds began to drift off in twos and threes to practice, Jon strode across the floor to where Hanna and Chance stood and stopped in front of Hanna on the other side of the handrail. For a moment, Hanna's breath caught in her throat. Wearing his armor, with his hair pulled back into the complex braids, and still radiating the exhilaration of victory, Jon was rather overwhelming. And the red eye of his *enkalan* sent a shiver down her spine.

"All nine?" Chance chided.

Jon shrugged. "The new one is skilled, but arrogant. The Lord Commander asked me to help demonstrate how his vanity undermines the unit as a whole." Jon placed his hands on the rail on either side of Hanna's and leaned down. "Good morning, Little Mouse. I am glad you are here. When I stopped by your rooms earlier, Susan said you were still sleeping."

Hanna smiled. "You came to see me?"

"I wanted to speak with you." Jon looked sideways at Chance, who rolled his eyes and wandered off to sprawl on one of the tiered benches just out of earshot.

"You sound very serious," Hanna said. "What's wrong?"

Jon looked down and slid one of his hands along the rail until his fingers almost, but not quite, touched hers. "Nothing is wrong," he said, his voice subdued. "It is only . . ." He paused before he looked up, as if gathering his thoughts. His thumb, still cold from the teleports, caressed the edge of Hanna's little finger. "You were right last night. I would have regretted . . . staying. I would like to believe I would have stopped myself before . . . before matters went too far, but if I had not, I would have had regrets. I do not wish ever to regret you, Hanna. Thank you for keeping your head when I lost mine."

Hanna laughed wryly. "Keeping my head? Is that what you call what I did?"

Jon grinned at her, an expression oddly incongruous with the fierce gaze of his *enkalan*. "Flashbacks do not count," he said firmly. Then he shifted and looked uncomfortable. "There is something else." He looked down at their hands. "Tomin is concerned that I may have made some unwarranted assumptions relating to the courting knife you gave me. He explained to me that the reason he procured a personal courting knife for you was that he did not think you had a family crest to put on it. He fears he may not have adequately explained the difference between a generic courting knife and the more personal style."

"He told me," Hanna said slowly, "that there are two uses for knives of the personal sort."

Jon looked up at her and nodded. "They are usually given when a woman wishes to keep the courtship private. I did not think this was your reason last night, but as we have already established, I was feeling rather impulsive last night, and perhaps I should not have assumed that you were as . . . enthusiastic . . . as I was. This morning, I have realized that a number of media correspondents, both human and Talessanin, have arrived at the embassy while I was away, and it occurs to me that perhaps you intended to hint to your high-profile suitor that you would prefer not to be publicly identified as the lady to whom the Viper is paying court."

Hanna smiled shyly and gave a small shrug. "Tomin also told me that they're sometimes given when a lady wants to show a strong preference for a particular suitor, to encourage his courtship." Jon was watching her face closely, and Hanna looked down at their hands so she didn't have to look at his unblinking red eye. "And he explained that the color of the blade on the knife I gave you is a symbol of House Kanestelan, and the *taless* leaves are too, in addition to being fertility symbols. He suggested that I should have the knife altered or replaced rather than give it to you, unless I felt prepared to make a public statement that I never want to have another suitor, and that I . . ." she paused, blushing, her voice trailing off into a shy whisper, " . . . that I am open to the idea of having a family with you." She cleared her throat and tried to speak more firmly. "That's what I meant when I gave you the knife."

Jon was silent for a moment, and Hanna didn't dare to look up at him. Then he whispered, "Not a private courtship?" and his voice thrummed with restrained excitement.

Hanna risked a glance at his face and found his gaze intense above his crooked grin. She smiled back shakily and shrugged. "I don't care who knows you're courting me, Jon, I just wanted you to know how much you mean to me, and that I would like to have a real future with you."

Jon leaned closer, his grin growing even broader. "You are certain, Little Mouse?" He hesitated, studying her face intently, and Hanna wondered what his *enkalan*-enhanced vision might show him about her. When he spoke again, his voice was so low it was almost a whisper, but so resonant it seemed to vibrate in her bones. "Be certain, Hanna, because I am about to kiss you, and there are two people with cameras over there watching us," he glanced sideways. "Once an image like that exists there is no undoing it."

"Is that what this is about?" Hanna laughed softly. "They're going to find out sooner or later, it might as well be now. Whatever happens, we'll deal with it. I'm not going to change my mind." She grinned at him and slid her hands up the warm leather that covered Jon's shoulders until her arms wrapped around his neck. Reckless? Maybe. But if she was going to jump off this cliff, she was jumping *all* the way off.

Jon grinned back at her and moved one hand off the railing to curve around her waist and press her against the hard metal bar as he leaned against it from his side. Then he bent and kissed her until her toes tingled.

As he pulled away from her again, eyes shining triumphantly, he whispered, "That is what I hoped you meant, Hanna."

Someone shouted from the arena, and Hanna looked over Jon's shoulder to see the Commander of the Winds looking expectantly in their direction. "I think they're waiting for you," she whispered.

"I know," Jon whispered back. "They were getting annoying, so I turned off my communicator."

"Maybe you should go."

"I would rather stay."

Hanna laughed. "I think we already had this discussion last night. Besides, I like watching you fight, you're unbelievable."

Jon grinned at her and turned to go. After he'd taken a few steps, though, he strode back, leaned over the railing, and laid his hand against her cheek, drawing her closer. "One more for good fortune," he said and kissed her again.

And that was the picture that dominated the cover of the embassy media office's daily summary report when Tomin slapped it on Hanna's sitting room tea table after dinner that night—Jon bending eagerly down, an impish grin visible beneath the black fangs that curved across his cheek from the edge of his *enkalan*, his hand laid tenderly against Hanna's laughing face as she leaned up to meet him.

Chapter 16

"THAT," TOMIN SAID, HIS VOICE tight and clipped, "went out this morning with the packet flutter." He shoved the media report across the tea table at Hanna and slumped into the chair across from her. "By now it has hit all the near relay hubs and spread across half the Empire."

Hanna picked up the thick, folded stack of pages. "I thought you couldn't send a communication signal through a flutter fold."

Tomin rolled his eyes in exasperation. "You can't. But you can send a low-mass unmanned drone. And you can set up fixed point stations where drones can drop off and pick up message data, which can then be passed from drone to drone, popping back and forth at predetermined intervals. There's a limit to how much data storage you can pack on a small drone without compromising fuel efficiency, especially when you add in the flutter tech, maneuvering drives, shielding, transmitters, and so forth, so private messages have to wait for a transport mail bag. But official communications and important news can be propagated across most of the Empire in a couple of days."

"And Jon kissing me counts as important news?"

"Hanna. He's the *Viper*."

Hanna laid the report back on the table and slid it toward Tomin. "I don't see the problem."

"It would seem," Tomin's voice slid into a sarcastic parody of a newscaster's voice, "that a lady has, at long last, captured the romantic attention of the Kanestelan *Ehr*—the most sought-after bachelor in the Empire. Who could she be? The unknown niece or granddaughter of some minor House, perhaps? As you can see, her face is partially obscured in this photograph by the Viper's hand, so she's quite the tantalizing little mystery."

"So?"

Tomin flipped a few pages on the report and pushed it back to her. "These went out with the evening packet."

There were three photographs on this page. One showed Jon and Hanna from a distance, strolling through the gardens in the embassy courtyard, holding hands. In the second, a gentle-eyed Jon tucked a flower into the elaborately plaited hair of his blushing lady, whose face was now fully revealed. And the third was a close-up of Hanna's courting knife hanging from a chain around Jon's neck, its naked star stone blade gleaming Kanestelan green against his shirt.

"And," Tomin reached across the table to turn another page. "Some enterprising correspondent tracked down the knife's maker out on the Earth orbitals and got all these lovely, detailed images of the thing, along with the news that the piece was commissioned through an unnamed third party, and even the maker doesn't know the identity of the Viper's lady. So, the mystery deepens. Nobody knows who she is, but they now know he's actually *courting* her. Formally. Openly."

Hanna shoved the report back at him. "Well, it's not exactly a secret, Tomin."

"No, not a secret. A mystery. People love a mystery. You'll have everyone's attention after they see that, just because Jon has never allowed his relationships to become public, and nobody knows who you are. Yet."

He reached into an inside pocket of his diplomat's robe and brought out another folded sheet of paper. "This will go out with the morning packets. By the end of tomorrow, half the Empire will have seen it. It'll reach the other half the next day." He laid the page on the table.

Hanna slowly picked up the paper and unfolded it. One photograph showed Jon holding Hanna close, bending to whisper to her as they danced after dinner. Her courting knife hung on his hip, and her hand rested over his heart. The other picture was a close-up of her hand, fingers splayed against the black of Jon's shirt front.

"Mystery turns to scandal," Tomin said grimly, stabbing a finger at the photo of Hanna's hand. "This woman has no finger webbing. Not an obscure aristocratic lady after all, is she? No. This woman—the woman the Viper is courting—is *human*." He slumped back in his chair.

Hanna rolled her eyes. "Tomin, we all knew this was going to happen. It's not like this is a surprise."

He scrubbed both hands over his face. Slowly, he said, "You're right. We knew it would happen. It's just . . . the timing. The circumstances. Public acceptance of this thing would have been hard enough if we'd disclosed it gradually. We could have shown the two of you attending the same events. Sharing interests. Becoming friends. We could have given the public time to get used to the idea and begin to speculate about the possibility of a budding romance. And then when it turned out they were right, they'd feel vindicated. Invested in the success of the relationship. It might have worked. It would have been even better if we waited until *after* humans were granted citizenship. But this?" He waved vaguely at the photos on the table. "You made them think you were a Talessanin noblewoman, and then you dropped a bomb on their heads."

Hanna's mouth dropped open. "I never pretended to be anything I'm not."

"Nobody is going to care whether it was done on purpose. They're just going to be angry that they were deceived. And there are going to be a lot more headlines like that one."

Hanna looked back at the page in her hand. The headline printed down the side of the page was in Talessanin. So was all the type that surrounded the photos. "What does it say?" she asked.

Tomin stared at her a moment, then shook his head wryly. "Never mind. It's not important. I forgot you can't read."

Hanna tossed the page on the table. "I can read just fine, Tomin, when it's printed in English. I'm not stupid."

"No, you're not stupid. I'm sorry. I'm just worried about you. Both of you. I mean, yes, we knew this was bound to happen at some point, I just thought I'd have more time to get some strategies in place. As things are now, with speculation still rampant over Jon's resignation from the Winds, and the Assembly about to vote on that resolution, and media correspondents flocking to Earth anyway for Kamm's ball, I don't know if we can control this, Hanna. And if we can't . . ." Tomin scrubbed a hand over his face. "Well, if we can't, I guess we turn the bow into the storm and see where we wash up. That's about all we *can* do."

"Have you talked to Jon about all this?"

Tomin snorted. "I tried. He doesn't care. He says he's living on Earth, and he'll marry you according to Earth customs if he has to, even if the Empire never recognizes it as legally binding."

Hanna's heart skipped a beat. "He said that?"

"I told you this wasn't frivolous for him." Tomin heaved a tired sigh. "I thought you were going to wait. Think it over. Make sure you knew what you wanted. Maybe have that knife altered. I didn't know you were going to just hand it to him the minute he got back."

"I didn't know that either at the time. But I do know what I want," Hanna said quietly. "Every time he looks at me, I want it more. And the knife is perfect the way it is. I know I'm not very good at the whole publicity game. I haven't exactly had much practice. But I can't just walk away from this, Tomin, I have to see it through. No matter where it washes up." She leaned forward. "So, did you have any actual suggestions, or did you just come here to complain?"

Tomin scrubbed at his face again. "Well, Kamm has assigned me to be your personal public relations representative so you'll have someone looking after your interests. Help me get out in front of this thing, Hanna. Everyone has dark corners. When the media correspondents figure out who you are and go scum chumming, what secrets will come nibbling at the bait?"

Hanna thought it over. "Only a couple of things," she said. "I dropped out of high school without finishing. Took a few classes at a community college after I got my GED and participated in an arts mentoring program for a while, but I never finished college either."

Tomin nodded gravely. "We can handle that. What else?"

"Well . . . when I dropped out, I was in a residential treatment facility for mentally ill people. I . . . I swallowed a lot of pills because I couldn't handle the emotional aftermath of being kidnapped and raped by a crazy alien and then having nobody believe it really happened."

Tomin stared at her. "That happened to you?"

Apparently, Jon and Kamm hadn't shared what she'd told them with Tomin. It was nice to know they could keep a confidence.

She rubbed tiredly at her forehead. "Dalathek. Before the embassy ships came, when the Winds were assigned to the researchers. Before that girl Jon found him with. He . . . he used a memory patch on my parents, and they thought I just made it up. The therapists believed them, and—"

"Hanna." Tomin laid his hand over hers on the table, stopping her. "I'm sorry. I didn't mean that like it sounded. I believe you. I was just surprised. Does . . . does Jon know?"

"Most of it. I didn't tell him about the pills." She pulled away from him. Looked down at her hands as she folded them in her lap. "The records are supposed to be confidential, but I don't know how much that means to Talessanin media correspondents. I'm guessing they have ways of finding things out." She shrugged disconsolately. "I can't make it not have happened."

"We can have your records sanitized. People who know about it might say something, but there will be no way to verify it, and the correspondents know better than to publish unsubstantiated rumors about someone connected with the imperial family." He paused thoughtfully. "Anything else?"

She shrugged. "As far as I know, my father's still out there somewhere. I don't know what he'd say if they tracked him down. I haven't heard from him in years."

Tomin frowned. "Would you like to?"

"No." Hanna looked steadily back at him. "And that's all I can think of."

Tomin nodded. "Thank you, Hanna. I'll be sure to keep you informed."

And he did. The next evening he showed her several photographs and a video documenting that afternoon's official arrival of the Emperor and Empress at Earth's North American embassy and explained that the incident would be particularly tantalizing to purveyors of gossip, because the Empress greeted the Viper's human lady as a close friend, deigning to kiss her fondly on the cheek, while the Emperor did not condescend even to acknowledge the woman's existence.

And the day after that, the reactions started flooding in. According to Tomin, the embassy's summary report carried only the highlights—representative examples of the kinds of narratives that were making the rounds in the media circuit. And according to the report, which Tomin had translated so Hanna could read it herself, the Viper's open courtship of a human woman had taken the media circuit by storm.

The previously obscure Assembly resolution had become the top political story. What was the legal status of the Viper's lady and her people? What *should* it be? Salenia's assertion that humans were merely sub-person, non-sapient, proto-Talessanins seemed to be, as Tomin had said, very much a minority position. But where had humans come from? Why were they so similar to Talessanins? Were they a species in their own right, or just some kind of primitive, mutant Talessanins? How should they be categorized and governed?

An appeal to science unearthed a heated debate over the origin of humans. One side insisted that two separate worlds had produced genetically similar organisms via convergent evolution due to the similar chemistry and climate of the respective homeworlds. The other side favored the notion of a common ancestral race having migrated from one world to the other through a rare, naturally occurring flutter fold, arguing that the differing environmental conditions had then resulted in divergent evolutionary tracks.

Social activists couldn't agree on whether to become involved. Was "the human question" an internal Talessanin dispute to be worked out between the Talessanins with fins (the technologically advanced majority) and those without fins (a more primitive minority sub-culture) without heavy-handed interference from meddling outsiders? Or were humans a separate minority species in need of support from the rest of the Empire's minority species in the face of blatant Talessanin oppression?

And *everyone* seemed to be arguing about whether Hanna and Jon were unlucky lovers kept apart by a legal technicality or an obscene perversion of the natural order.

One particularly pragmatic analyst pointed out that, realistically, the Viper could marry whomever he chose, because after all, who was going to stop him? Hanna laughed when Tomin showed her that one, but she found it all rather overwhelming. She'd known there would probably be paparazzi, at least for a while, until people got over the shock of it, but she hadn't foreseen the magnitude of the political angle.

It only got worse over the next few days. Kamm put a cap on the number of correspondents who could be on planet and in the embassy at the same time, but even so, Hanna couldn't sketch in the courtyard or even walk down a corridor without being trailed by at least three of them. Jon kept being called away for impromptu consultations with the Heads of House and Assembly delegates who had already arrived for the ball. Twice, he was summoned to meet with the Emperor and came back silent and angry until Hanna teased him into laughing again. Perhaps the biggest shock was when the Empress invited herself to Hanna's rooms for tea, along with a wide-eyed gaggle of other Talessanin noblewomen, who watched Hanna like they expected her head to pop off at any moment, but who were suitably impressed with the personal invitation to the ball displayed on Hanna's mantelpiece. She managed to acquit herself with reasonable grace during the visit but had to curl up on the window seat with Mr. Bickles and a cup of herbal tea for an hour afterward to recover.

Fortunately, Jon showed up that evening with a rolling TV cart borrowed from the human wing of the embassy along with a small selection of classic movies that had been donated to the embassy library. They watched *Casablanca* curled up together on her sitting room sofa while Chance and Susan chaperoned a jigsaw puzzle on the other side of the room. That night, she tucked her t-shirt—which still smelled of snuggling with Jon—under her pillow to stave off the nightmares, and she slept better than she had since coming to the embassy.

The next two days were a little better. The intensity of the media's first reaction started to ease off a little, and Hanna managed not to do anything shocking enough to kick it back into high gear. The Assembly was now on the brink of calling a vote on the human question, so Jon was still called away for unexpected meetings, but he carved out as much time for Hanna as he could without offending any voting delegates, and he definitely made those moments count.

Tomin had been right. She *hadn't* seen all the moving parts. But she could certainly feel them spinning around her now, even if she still couldn't see all of them. And she was definitely in over her head; Tomin been right about that, too. But she was determined to learn to swim, because she could not allow herself to sink, and she refused to head back for the shore. Being with Jon was worth it.

Early the third afternoon, Hanna was having a rather tiresome dress fitting with the designer who had been selected from a number of suddenly eager applicants to create her gown for the ball, when a messenger delivered an envelope from Jon. Hanna was invited to attend the opening night of a limited performance of *Romeo and Juliet* that was being presented on one of the Earth orbitals by the British Royal Shakespeare Company in honor of the visiting imperial family as part of a cultural outreach program.

Susan immediately threw everyone out so she could start preparing Hanna for her date. She had Hanna try on gown after gown, even sending off a request for additional options when she realized Hanna had already worn everything in the wardrobe in public at least once. Hanna couldn't help wondering where they were all coming from. Was some poor Talessanin soul popping all over the world in a flutter shuttle collecting every formal designer gown in her size?

In the end, Susan settled on a gown that skimmed Hanna's figure with silver-embroidered black velvet and then dissolved into a layered froth of dark, subtly blue and green chiffon skirts sparkling with what Hanna sincerely hoped were only rhinestones. The sleeves were velvet down to her elbows, where generous gauzy flounces fell shimmering down to blend with the skirt. Hanna found herself feeling terribly self-conscious about the way the gown accentuated her finless forearms. She was terrified that the large, clear stones in the drop earrings were actual diamonds, and was inordinately relieved when Susan fastened only a simple black velvet ribbon around her neck.

By the time Susan finished with her, Hanna was feeling a little faint.

What was she thinking? What was she doing here? This wasn't her. The woman in the mirror looked like some kind of movie star from one of Tiffany's gossip magazines—definitely not like a small-town artist who lived in paint-stained blue jeans and baggy t-shirts and occasionally forgot to buy toilet paper.

She was in so far over her head she didn't even know which way was up anymore.

Chapter
17

HANNA WAS NOT IN HER sitting room when Susan ushered Jon in, but he could see her through the open bedroom door. She stood with her back to him looking into a tall stand mirror. She was utterly breathtaking in the black and silver gown, with the sparkling diamonds clinging to her as if the stars themselves found her irresistible, and Jon paused, hand half raised to knock on the door frame, just to look at her a moment longer.

Perhaps if he had not, if he had just rushed ahead, he would not have noticed the sadly wistful expression on the reflection of Hanna's face in the mirror, or the small, vaguely helpless gesture her hands made just before her eyes refocused and she saw him standing there. The smile that spread across her face then seemed genuine enough, but it held a kind of reserve Jon had not noticed before. He stepped through the doorway and moved to stand behind Hanna, stooping to kiss the back of her neck just above the charming velvet ribbon and savoring the little shiver the action produced in her. She smelled faintly of flowers.

At home, she always smelled of cookies and turpentine.

"Do you like what you see?" he asked softly.

Hanna tilted her head analytically as she checked her gown and hair one more time and studied the dark scrollwork Susan had painted around her eyes. "I never really imagined I could look so . . . refined," she said. "Sometimes I almost don't recognize myself anymore." She smiled as she said it, and Jon might not have heard the soft hollowness in her voice if he had not seen the sadness in her eyes a moment before. Almost didn't recognize herself? Was that the problem? Hanna turned and gave him a teasing smile, twisting enticingly back and forth, and spreading her arms. "Do *you* like what you see?"

Jon grinned and took a step back, making a show of admiring her. "You are mesmerizing, my Hanna," he said. "Truly, a more enchanting lady has never graced the Talessanin court."

Hanna blushed prettily and turned for one last critical look at herself in the mirror. Jon stepped up close behind her, reaching around her waist with one hand, drawing her back to lean against his chest, careful not to muss her hair, while his other hand found her elbow beneath the flounces of her sleeve and trailed down her smooth forearm to find her fingers. He raised her hand to his lips and placed a kiss in her palm, but instead of closing her fingers around it this time, he just held her hand, stroking the delicate lines of her bones under her soft skin. "But Hanna," he kept his voice casual, watching her face in the mirror while pretending to focus on her fingers, "would you think me a complete muck-hearted rogue if I told you I sometimes miss the rainbow trout oven mitts?"

Hanna's eyebrows quirked up, and she blinked. Surprise? Some of the tension melted away from Hanna's back and shoulders, and Jon decided he was guessing in the right direction. "It will not always be like this, Hanna," he said softly. He lowered their still-joined hands and turned her gently to face him. "If Kamm's people do not catch Dalathek soon, I will go hunt him down myself. They captured his flutter craft last night on the border of Kazakhstan. Without help he can't have gone far. And when he has been dealt with, we will go home, you and I. You will show me how to make popcorn, and we will watch movies with our feet on the coffee table."

Hanna gazed at him, an unreadable expression on her face. He thought for a moment that she would say something, but she did not, so he continued, "Perhaps, if I ask nicely, you will allow me to borrow some of your tools to finish the treehouse. I can buy lunch at Mac's for you and your friends to celebrate the sale of your next painting." He let a smile play on his lips as he leaned down to say, "Perhaps you will finally try out my hot tub with more than just your toes."

Hanna pulled away from him, tipping her head down with what sounded like a small exasperated gasp, and for a moment Jon feared he had guessed incorrectly. But Hanna's voice was gentle and affectionate when she said, "You're going to make me smudge my make-up." She fished a small handkerchief out of one of her sleeves and carefully dabbed at her eyes, checking the mirror to make sure she didn't do too much damage to the delicate painted scrollwork. "How did you know I felt homesick tonight?"

Jon shrugged and looked down. "I did not know, Hanna. If I had, perhaps I would have chosen a different gift for you."

How could he not have realized? So much at the embassy was different from what Hanna was accustomed to. And she had not asked to be brought here. How could he never have even thought about what that would feel like for her? She had been taken away from her home, her work, all her familiar things. She couldn't even call her friends. But Jon had thought only of how happy she made him, and never of the price she might be paying for his happiness. Selfish. Thoughtless.

He needed to do better.

But Hanna's eyes lit up, and a smile spread across her face. "You brought me a present?"

"I did," Jon said slowly. "But it is a gift for a lady at court, and I should have brought something to remind you of home. Perhaps I should save it for another time when you will be more in a mood to like it."

Hanna laughed, and her voice was gently teasing when she said, "Don't be silly, Jon. If it is from you, I will like it." It was what he had said when she gave him her courting knife. Then her expression turned saucy. "Besides, you can't tell me you brought me a present, and then not give it to me. It isn't nice." She put her hands on the appealing, velvet-covered curves of her hips and tilted her chin up in playful defiance—a posture which caused delightfully distracting things to happen in the neighborhood of the dress's neckline.

Apparently, Hanna mistook Jon's distraction for hesitation. She grinned mischievously and eyed him up and down. "If you won't give it to me, I bet I can find it and take it anyway." She stepped closer to him and slid her hands up his chest. "Where do Talessanin men keep their pockets?" Her hands moved around to his sides and slid down to his waist and then to his hips, checking for pockets.

In moments, she had turned up a dagger and two of his small throwing knives in addition to her courting knife, and Jon had decided he rather liked being searched by Hanna. In fact, he decided he enjoyed it a little too much to allow it to continue, especially while they were alone and in her bedroom. She had stopped him the last time he'd gotten carried away, but it was not her job to keep his reactions in check. He laughed and caught her hands in his. "Very well," he said, smiling down at her, glad to see the happy gleam back in her eyes. "You win. I will give it to you. Hold out your hand."

Hanna stepped back, a teasing smile tugging at her lips and making her eyes sparkle. She held out an expectant hand, palm up. Jon took it in one of his and turned it over, at the same time shifting the fin spines on his other arm so the silver serpent dropped out of a fold of his fin membrane and into his hand. Carefully, he slid the curling spiral of the serpent's tongue up the mid-finger on Hanna's hand, intrigued by the way her lack of finger webbing allowed the ring to settle all the way down against the base of her finger. The head of the serpent lay across the back of her hand as he coiled the slender, flexible body of the glimmering snake up and around her forearm nearly to her elbow. The coiled links would not have lain so smoothly against her skin if she had fins. He trailed his fingers back again from her elbow to her wrist, marveling at the sleek lines of her human body, before shifting his gaze to Hanna's face.

All the teasing was gone from her expression. Her eyes were wide, and her soft lips parted slightly as Jon released her fingers. She looked back at him for a moment without saying anything, then brought her hand up so she could more closely examine the gleaming, Kanestelan green star stone eyes that stared out from the snake's intricately etched head, and the blood-red ruby that glinted on the back of her finger in the fork at the tip of the snake's curving tongue. She touched a wondering fingertip to the delicately interwoven scale-shaped chain links that formed the body of the snake. Then she looked back at Jon. "It's beautiful," she whispered solemnly. "Thank you, Jon."

"Do you really like it?" Jon asked. "Tomin said you might not, because he learned in the embassy's cultural affairs office that human women generally find snakes repulsive."

Hanna laughed. "Well, this human woman happens to be very fond of snakes. Vipers especially." She wrapped her arms around his middle, tipping her face up for a kiss, which Jon happily provided. Then she tucked her hand into the crook of his elbow and asked, "Shall we go?"

He watched her as they strolled through the embassy toward the shuttleport—to meet *his* friends, *his* family. How long had it been since Hanna spoke to Tiffany and Rachel?

Hanna was welcomed warmly by Jon's mother, by Kamm, and by Tomin and Chance, whom Jon had insisted on bringing as guests. Narista was civil for a change, even introducing Hanna to the nervous lordling she had brought along as an escort. Salenia offered no gesture of greeting at all and made several subtly barbed comments that Hanna pretended not to understand, even though Jon saw by the set of her shoulders and a tensing at the corner of her jaw that she understood perfectly. Salenia's parents, Lord and Lady Trakanaleth, offered Hanna their hands palm down, and Hanna smilingly accepted their disdain even though, having been greeted as a good friend by the Empress herself, she could have insisted on the superior position. Jon's stepfather behaved as if a bad smell had wafted into the room.

They boarded the sleek Imperial flutter shuttle, and Jon watched as Hanna fought to appear calm. She was not widely traveled, he remembered. She had never been off Earth before. In fact, she had told him once during the past few days that she had never even seen an ocean in person. Now that he thought about it, she had been unconscious when she came to the embassy by flutter shuttle, so this might very well be her first real experience of the odd, lurching, ear-popping feeling of passing through a flutter fold.

Her face went pale as the view out the broad windows blurred to the deep, star-studded black of open space. She turned toward the window, pretending to look out, but he could see in her faint reflection in the silica pane that her eyes were closed, and her lips were pressed tightly together. He could feel the tension in her fingers where they were tucked into his elbow. He folded his hand around hers in what he hoped was a comforting manner, but at an angle that rested one of his fingers against the place in her wrist where he could feel her pulse. Her heart raced. Her breathing was slow and even—perhaps calculatedly so. Was she quietly having a panic attack? What had he been thinking bringing her here like this?

Chance was watching him. Jon flashed him the hand signal he would have used in combat to indicate that he would bring up the rear. Chance raised his eyebrows, followed Jon's glance to Hanna, and nodded. As the shuttle nudged up against the orbital's docking portal, Chance leaned over to whisper to Kamm, who nodded once and murmured a quick reply. When the door slid open a moment later, Kamm explained that the rope-lined red carpet pathway that ran the short distance from the docking portal to the theater's entrance was an Earth custom when welcoming the most honored of visitors, and that it was appropriate for them to proceed in order of precedence.

The Emperor and Empress led the way out, smiling at the murmuring masses of people who crowded against the rope barriers, held at bay more by the ominous presence of six of the Winds, in addition to the regular station security, than by the flimsy velvet ropes. When they reached the entryway, where another of the Winds waited in the shadows, Kamm followed, offering an arm to Salenia. This not only kept her from bringing up the rear with Tomin and Chance, but also gave her parents sufficient social stature to walk out next. Chance motioned for Narista and her date to follow them, and Narista glanced hesitantly at Jon, knowing he should have been next even if he had chosen not to take his place behind Kamm. But when Jon nodded, Narista nudged her lordling through the door.

Jon stroked the back of Hanna's hand with his fingers. "Are you ready, Little Mouse?"

She turned her face toward him with a soft smile and a nod. She was still pale, but it seemed the few extra minutes he had bought had helped steady her. A muttering ripple passed through the mass of onlookers as the two of them appeared at the top of the three small steps leading down to the red carpeted pathway, and Hanna froze.

Jon stopped with her, raising a hand in acknowledgment of the crowd. The Viper's appearance often caused a stir, and he was accustomed to the reaction, but what must it be like for Hanna? Hanna lived at the end of a dead-end street and used dates with her stuffed bear as excuses to avoid large gatherings of people. Even at the embassy, where only a few select correspondents were permitted, she had been mostly sheltered from the intergalactic press. Why had he not thought how unsettling this would be for her? He was an inconsiderate fool!

He leaned down and whispered, "My honor, Hanna, it will be quieter inside. We'll be in the Imperial box, away from the crowd." She looked up at him, her eyes wide and frightened, and forced a small smile. Jon whispered again, "Do not look at them. Just focus straight ahead. I will be with you."

Hanna drew a deep breath and gave a slight nod, then moved forward down the steps. Jon stepped with her, and Tomin and Chance followed close behind, drifting out a little to either side as they reached the bottom of the steps and moved onto the red carpet. Around them, imagers flashed and clicked as press correspondents took pictures—still, and moving, flat, and three-dimensional—and voices called out unintelligible questions and comments in a multitude of the Empire's myriad languages.

Hanna slid her hand down from Jon's elbow to take his hand, moving slightly away from him as she did so. She glanced up at him with another tentative smile. The imagers flashed and clicked. She gave a shy wave with her other hand—the one with his snake coiled around her forearm, and the crowd abruptly surged toward them, knocking over some of the rope barriers and pouring out onto the red carpet in front of Hanna and Jon until the Winds managed to intimidate them back into a semblance of order. Jon discovered that he had stepped in front of Hanna, pulling her protectively against his sheltering body with one arm—and that one of his throwing knives was balanced in the fingers of his other hand, poised to fly.

Hanna gave a small, unsteady laugh and said quietly, "This is the first time I've worn short sleeves since they started taking pictures of us. They have proof now that I have no fins. That's all." She patted his shoulder. "Don't kill anyone, okay?"

Jon let go of her and shrugged sheepishly as he tucked his throwing knife away. "My apologies," he said softly. "It is a reflex, the knives. But I rarely kill anyone without orders to do so." He gave her a rakish smile. "Shall we try again?" This time, two of the Winds walked with them down the length of the carpet, and although the imagers clicked, and buzzed, and flashed, everyone stayed behind the ropes.

Jon tucked Hanna into a seat at the edge of the Imperial box, partly sheltered from the staring crowd, and took the seat next to her, blocking the hostile looks directed at her by his stepfather and the Trakanaleths. He was glad when Tomin and Chance dropped into the seats behind him and Hanna, and she relaxed a little in the safe space they helped create for her. He was even more pleased that, long before the end of the first act of the play, Hanna was leaning forward in her seat, bright-eyed and a little breathless, watching the players strut and pose on the stage below; perhaps there would be some enjoyment in the evening for her after all.

The play itself was admirably well-produced. The sword work was a bit rough, of course, but not bad for human performers without proper training. Still, it was a relief when the final curtain fell. The performers returned to the stage for their final bows, and then they and the audience stood in silent respect when the Empress and Emperor stepped up to the railing of the Imperial box to offer a few words of congratulation and gratitude for the excellent performance.

The others in the Imperial party also began to rise and prepare to go. Jon stood and offered a steadying hand to Hanna as she, too, rose from her seat. A rustling murmur rippled out through the watchers when they caught sight of her, and her cheeks flushed a pretty pink. As she stepped toward the back of the box, one of the layered skirts of her dress snagged in a crevice of her seat, causing her to stumble. Jon caught her with both hands around her waist as she fell against him, bracing her hands against his chest. She looked up at him for one startled moment, and then the pink drained from her face as dizziness swept in.

Synthetic blood.

"Do you need to sit down?" Jon whispered.

Hanna leaned her forehead against his chest. "No. It's not as bad as it used to be. Just let me stand still a minute, and it'll pass."

Jon used one hand to motion for Chance to untangle Hanna's dress, and then stroked the back of her neck while she took several slow, deep breaths. Among the spectators below, the murmur grew to a hissing rumble like ocean waves building on a beach, forcing the Emperor to give up trying to make his speech. Jon looked out across the crowd, trying to judge their mood; they seemed excited, but not hostile. Then, from somewhere in the sea of people, someone called out, "Kiss her!" It was impossible to tell who said it, or where it began, but others took up the cry, and in half a moment it had turned into a chant. One of the spotlights from the stage swung smoothly over to illuminate the Imperial box.

Hanna stirred against his chest, and Jon looked down to see her smiling shakily up at him. "Chance is right," she said, just loud enough for him to hear her above the roar from below. "Half your reputation *is* because of the theatrics."

Jon scowled over at Chance, who was in the process of standing up again, having freed Hanna's skirt. What had Chance told Hanna? Chance grinned back at Jon and chanted with the audience, "Kiss her!"

Looking down again at Hanna, Jon saw the color beginning to return to her cheeks. "Better?" he asked.

He did not hear her response, but he saw her lips form the word, "Better."

Tilting his head to one side, Jon smiled at her, feeling suddenly a little shy. "May I?" he asked.

He felt, but could not hear, Hanna's soft laugh. Her voice, when she answered, was barely audible above the sound of the crowd. "You don't need to ask, Jon."

Jon tipped his head down until his forehead rested against Hanna's, and the chanting faded off into a breathless silence. Then he slid his hands around to her back and pulled her against him, as his lips found hers in a long, lingering kiss. The audience erupted in a cacophony of cheers, accompanied by a thunder of knuckles rapping on chairs and feet stomping loudly against the floor.

After a moment, Hanna pulled laughingly away from him and offered a sweet, self-conscious wave to the crowd; the silver snake glittered in the bright beam from the spotlight. Then she took Jon's hand and glided into the shadows at the back of the box, pulling him along in her wake.

As they moved out into the theater's corridor, Jon stepped into the lead, checking to make sure the Winds were in place before guiding the Imperial party swiftly through the media gauntlet and into their waiting flutter shuttle.

The seating in the shuttle had been rearranged into a large conversation grouping, and small tables had been brought out and laid with refreshments. When everyone was aboard, a member of the crew explained that the new arrangement was because their return to the embassy would be slightly delayed as the embassy shuttle port sorted out a small irregularity in security. It was almost certainly nothing more serious than an error in some paperwork, but it was necessary to resolve the matter before the Imperial family returned, just to be safe.

No one spoke as they settled into their seats and picked over the selection of delicacies for something appetizing. It wasn't until the shuttle nudged away from the docking port and drifted out into the star-filled blackness that Salenia broke the quiet. Her voice was syrupy sweet and laced with a subtle venom. "Well," she said brightly, "it would seem we have our very own Romeo and Juliet."

Jon looked up from offering Hanna a tidbit of spiced poultry which she had inexplicably referred to as a buffalo wing. He had seen a buffalo once; they did not have wings. Salenia's parents both looked as if they'd eaten something very sour and unpleasant. The Emperor's face was as dark and tense as an impending storm. Narista only frowned pensively, but her escort looked pale and apprehensive.

Jon's mother broke the tension with a laugh. "Let us hope not," she said, her voice warm, and her gaze fixed on Hanna with what looked like amused affection. "Since they both ended up dead."

The Emperor snorted derisively. "As was fitting, after they betrayed their Houses in such a shameful manner."

"But Father," Narista said gently, "we were told at the very beginning of the play that the stars had marked their love for death in order to heal the breach between the two warring Houses. Is it shameful to be pruned and burned by the Gentle Gardeners in order to restore health to the Sower's garden? If they were marked by fate to love and to die, how were they to escape that outcome? Besides, there is something beautiful about a love so deep that one would wish to die for lack of it."

"It does *sound* beautiful, perhaps," the Empress mused, "but is it not a fragile sort of unenduring beauty if it is built on a selfish disregard for the roots and branches of the lovers? What would have happened to our little Tala if Kamm had taken his life because his dear wife was gone? What would have happened to the Empire? Would it have been beautiful for him to deprive two Houses of a son when they were already grieving the loss of a daughter? If I had died with Jon's father when he went, you never would have been born, my sweet Narista. And if Romeo had been willing to live on, even for just a little while, he would have been rewarded by the return of his lover and a new beginning for their romance. It is better, I think, to build a strong love that can sustain one of the lovers when the universe shakes and the other is gone, than to settle for a love that is merely beautiful and ephemeral."

"Romeo's love was certainly ephemeral." Salenia's eyes were directed pointedly at Jon as she spoke. "At the beginning of the play, he pined and groaned and made himself ill with sorrow, wishing to die for lack of Rosaline's love. Then, one little kiss at a dinner party from a girl he knows nothing about, and suddenly he wants to marry Juliet, and nothing else will do."

Jon's heart began to beat faster. What was Salenia doing? A kiss at a dinner party. That was certainly what had happened in the play, but . . . was Salenia talking about him kissing Hanna at his dinner party? Could she even know about that?

"But Juliet loves him back," Kamm interjected softly, "and Rosaline has only tormented him by keeping him dangling on her line. It makes a difference, Salenia."

"Perhaps Rosaline loves him back as well," Salenia retorted. "Perhaps she meant to tell him so at the very dinner party where he first kissed Juliet. After all, Rosaline has not married anyone else, and as we are told she is one of the most beautiful women in the city, we must suppose there have been other offers. It may be that she has only been concerned about Romeo's tendency to engage in violent exchanges on the streets of Verona and has been waiting for him to grow up and settle down before accepting him. What do you think, Jon?"

Jon remembered, suddenly, the way Salenia had attempted to greet him at that dinner party. She was almost certainly not talking about the play. His pulse quickened. He let his fingers stray to the mouse pommel of Hanna's courting knife. Salenia's eyes followed the motion and narrowed. "Romeo," he began slowly," is a young man at the beginning of the play, but he has loved Rosaline long enough and hard enough to have been chided often by his confessor for his hopeless attachment, and his friends have repeatedly urged him to let go and move on. So it seems to me that Romeo must have been very young indeed when he fell in love with Rosaline. The very young frequently mistake infatuation for love.

Perhaps Romeo has indeed grown up, and learned the difference, and discovered that his infatuation with Rosaline was a tawdry thing compared with his love for Juliet." Salenia's cheeks flushed. Would that be enough to stop her?

No. Salenia went on, her eyes hard and glittering. "Or perhaps what Romeo feels for Juliet is merely lust for that which is forbidden him. After all, the Houses of Romeo and Juliet have held themselves separate from time immemorial, and Romeo knows that a union between him and Juliet must bring instability to his family and could spark rioting in the streets and bring ruin on the whole city. How many people are dead at the end of the play because Romeo must pursue the thing he is told he may not have?" Jon forced himself not to tense. Had Hanna understood what Salenia was suggesting? What would she be thinking of all this?

"It didn't have to bring ruin." Kamm's voice was stern. "It might have brought unity and enduring peace between the Houses if others in their families had not stirred up trouble." He looked pointedly at Salenia.

"There is truth in that," the Empress said quietly, looking at her husband. "Senseless feuds and grudges do harm to the entire society in which they exist, and wise rulers would do well, like the prince in this play, to put an end to the conflict and separation for the good of all. If the prince had taken earlier, more decisive action to end the feud, he might have prevented all the tragedy that followed."

The Emperor's scowl deepened, but he said nothing in reply.

"I think I would've liked the play better if Romeo and Juliet had waited and taken things more slowly and openly," Narista said hurriedly into the silence. She looked puzzled and nervous, as if she felt the undercurrent but could not tell which way it ran. "So much death and grief came from making hasty decisions and keeping secrets. It seems like a high price to pay for just one night of passion when they might've waited, spent a lifetime loving each other, and lived to see their children and grandchildren grow up in peace."

"But why should lovers have to choose one or the other?" Salenia asked. "Some would see a night of passion as a gift between two people, and not as a betrayal of their Houses—especially if an expectation existed, as it did between the lovers in the play, that they'd build a life together afterward." Jon went cold. What was Salenia doing? He dared not look at any of the others.

"Narista makes a good point," he said quietly, choosing his words with care. "The lovers in question thought only of gratifying themselves in the moment and did not consider how their actions might affect the larger course of their lives, or what heartache they might bring to other people. They should have waited."

"Perhaps it is better that they died when they did, then," said Salenia. A tinge of bitterness now colored her voice, as her eyes continued to bore into Jon. "After all, Romeo is fickle and reckless. If they had lived, his unsuspecting lover might've discovered that one night of passion was all Romeo ever really wanted from her, and she might've found herself discarded in favor of another pretty face. Or perhaps Juliet would've found that Romeo's love for Rosaline was not as transient as it might've seemed when he thought he couldn't have her. Perhaps Romeo would've left Juliet for Rosaline if she declared her love for him. What do you think, Jon?"

Jon looked back at Salenia for a long moment, trying to think how to respond. "I think," he said carefully, "that Romeo is a man like other men and has failings enough. It is probably fair to call him reckless, but I do not think he is fickle. His love is not transient when his heart knows where its true home lies. I think love grows best when nurtured with patience between lovers well suited to growing in the same soil, whereas a passion allowed to burn too hot, too soon, may consume the seeds of real love before they are able to take root."

Salenia's eyes snapped fire, but her voice was silky and dark when she said, "And you, Miss Bradley, what do you think of Romeo and his ephemeral passions?"

All eyes shifted to Hanna, waiting for her response. When Jon turned to look at her, Hanna's face bore a small frown, and a tiny line had formed between her brows. Jon wondered how much she had understood of what had passed between him and Salenia. Hanna was no fool; she certainly realized they were not speaking of the play.

After a moment, Hanna leaned back in her seat and offered Salenia a gracious smile. "I think," she said, her voice quiet and deliberate, "that one of the fascinating things about William Shakespeare's work is that the general themes are so easily comprehended by so many people, even when the audience is separated from the author by time and by differences in language and culture. I find that this evening's performance has given me a lot to think about."

A dark pit opened in the bottom of Jon's stomach. Too much. She had understood far too much.

Chapter
18

JON'S HEART POUNDED IN HIS throat, keeping rhythm with the thump of his booted feet on the thin carpet of the corridor as he escorted Hanna back to her rooms from the embassy shuttle port. Chance padded softly behind, keeping a discreet distance until they rounded the final corner, where he stopped and let the two of them go on alone—not quite proper protocol for a Talessanin bodyguard, but close enough, and human customs were different.

Hanna's soft slippers made almost no sound, and even her filmy skirts barely rustled as she walked. She had said nothing since the pilot interrupted Salenia's little drama with an announcement that embassy security had cleared their landing. Her silence was deafening.

She slowed as they approached her door, and Jon slowed with her, wracking his mind for something to say that would not just make everything even worse.

Her fingers paused on the latch, allowing it to confirm her identity. The soft clunk of the bolts releasing and the faint crackle of the particle field dropping embedded themselves into the silence like punctuation marks ending an unspoken sentence. It seemed a heart-pounding eternity before she looked up at him, eyes guarded, smile stiff and uncertain.

"Thank you." Her voice was barely more than a hoarse whisper, but it grated against the silence. She cleared her throat self-consciously and pushed ahead. "The play was amazing. I've never been to a live performance of Shakespeare before, and *Romeo and Juliet* has always been one of my favorites. I—"

She stopped.

Reconsidered.

Her eyes dropped to his chest.

"Thank you." It was that whisper again. She turned back to the door.

That was all? That could not be all.

The latch clicked.

"Hanna . . ." Her name slipped out before Jon had worked out what he might say afterward. She froze with the latch half turned, listening, tense, and Jon scrabbled in his mind for something to say. Something that would fix things between them, something in English that she would understand. *Something.* All he came up with was, "Wait. Please."

Hanna slowly released the latch, and it twisted back into place. But she didn't look at him. And she didn't say anything.

Jon reached out hesitantly, laying his fingers against the back of her elbow. "Perhaps," he began, but still didn't know where to go after that. Her skin was warm and soft, and the flounces of her sleeve brushed against his hand like gentle reproaches. "Perhaps you have questions."

Hanna half turned toward him, but she kept her eyes fixed on the wall beside the door. She opened her mouth, then shook her head and closed it again. But she didn't move to go, so Jon waited. At last she took a deep breath and said, "I have . . . confusions. Nothing as coherent as a question. I don't know how . . ." Her voice trailed off, and something inside her seemed to crumple. She leaned her forehead against the door, and her shoulders drooped. "I'm sorry, Jon," she whispered. "I wish . . ." her voice trailed off again, and Jon felt awkward and unutterably incompetent.

"Could I come in?" He asked softly, barely daring to hope. "Just for a few minutes? Just to talk?"

Hanna drew a deep breath and shot a glance down the hall at Chance before nodding.

Her sitting room was dark and quiet, lit only by the soft moonlight drifting in through the glass doors, until Hanna brushed her hand against the base of a reading lamp on a side table and the bulb flared to life. The light glittered from the silver embroidery on her dress and sparked out from the diamonds. The way that it caught in her chocolate eyes made Jon's heart ache in his chest.

"I told Susan to take the night off," she said, still not quite looking at him. "But I could make some tea, or . . ."

She stopped.

Rubbed at her forehead with fingertips that might have been trembling—he couldn't be sure.

Straightened her shoulders.

More forcefully, she said, "Look, do you mind waiting a minute while I change? I can't think properly in these clothes."

"Of course," he said softly. "I will be right here."

Hanna went into the bedroom, and Jon stared at the back of the closed door for a moment. Then he shook his head and looked around the room for something to do.

He had laid a small fire in the fireplace and was just coaxing a flame into life when the bedroom door slowly opened again. He took a deep breath and turned to face her, still not sure what to say. Or what *she* might say.

Her hair hung loose around her shoulders as she stood in the bedroom doorway, but she still wore the black and silver gown. Her face was tight and miserable, and the dark, painted scrollwork around her eyes had smudged down her cheeks.

She'd been crying.

"Jon . . ." There were still tears in her voice, and her eyes held a desolate desperation. "I'm sorry to ask, but can. . . can you help? I can't twist enough to reach the fasteners without . . . and Susan isn't—" Her voice choked off, and she swallowed hard and drew a shuddering breath.

Jon was beside her almost before he knew he had moved.

"Oh, Hanna, please don't cry." His voice came out a whisper. He raised a hand to brush the tears from her cheek, but she pulled away, turning her back to him. This time he was sure her hand was shaking as she moved her hair to one side, away from the fasteners that ran down the middle of her back, away from the back of her neck, which called to him.

Jon hesitated. If the dress had been made by a human tailor, he thought, it would just have had a zipper running down the back. But zippers were a human invention, and this dress was fashioned in the

Talessanin style, closing with a series of tiny hooks hidden in the seam. His fingers brushed against Hanna's skin as he unfastened the top hook, and his heart beat faster when she shivered at his touch. But then her shoulders shook slightly, and she made a soft, gasping, whimpering sound. She did not welcome his touch tonight. Jon took a deep breath and unhooked the next fastener, and the one after that, trying not to think about what lay underneath—something black and silky. And Hanna.

More hooks. He reached her waist, and her hand caught his. "Thank you," she whispered. "That's enough. I can reach now." She turned to face him, one hand holding the front of her dress in place, eyes wide, cheeks tear-streaked. She cleared her throat. "I'll be right back." And she closed the bedroom door in his face.

Jon blinked and drew a sharp breath. She was intoxicating.

And he was dangerously close to the edge, he realized. This was not a good time to have his judgment impaired by hormonal responses. He spun away from the door and paced across the sitting room to the glass doors. The cool night air on the patio helped clear his head, and he turned his face up to look at Earth's moon, which hung bright and white against the black of the sky. He breathed deeply and let the stillness seep into his mind, into his body, bringing with it the calm clarity that folded around him when he fought, settling it around him like armor.

When he went back inside, Hanna sat on the floor in front of the fireplace, gazing into the flickering flames. She wore a pair of baggy gray trousers and an oversized t-shirt with a large paint stain on one shoulder. Her hair had been twined into a single loose braid that hung down her back, and she had washed all traces of cosmetics from her face. She was so beautiful it hurt to look at her. Jon stepped slowly up and knelt beside her, facing the fire, and for a time the two of them just sat together.

At last, she spoke, her voice soft and faintly dreamy. "You told me she had no romantic claim on you," she said.

"She does not." Jon matched his tone to hers—quiet, gentle. "I have never lied to you." Out of the corner of his eye, Jon saw her turn her head to look at him. He feared he might frighten her if he met her eyes, so he kept his gaze on the fire.

"Maybe not a formal one," she said carefully, and in his peripheral vision he saw her studying his profile. "But there's *something* between you. I see it every time you're with her. And it isn't just her."

Jon shifted, stretching his booted feet out in front of himself, toward the fire, trying to find a comfortable position. "It has been over for a long time."

Hanna studied him. "Will you tell me about her? So I know? I feel like I'm trying to navigate a jungle full of wild animals with a bag over my head."

Jon turned his head to look at her. Would telling her make things better or worse?

What to say?

The truth. She wanted to know. She deserved to know.

"If you like," he said. He shifted again. Then shrugged his shoulders and began. "I have known Salenia my whole life. Our mothers were friends, and her family lived near mine, so we saw each other regularly. She would come to watch me train. She was my partner during dance instruction. She was clever, and I was slow at my studies, so we were often tutored together even though she is a few years younger than I. We were friends before we were . . . anything else. Our parents assumed . . . well, everyone assumed. *We* assumed. She spoke of things we would do someday when I was the emperor, and she was my empress, and at the time, I do not think it occurred to anyone that this might not become so." Jon stopped and glanced at Hanna. She sat gazing into the fire, a thoughtful frown tugging at her lips. But she didn't say anything, so he continued.

"Salenia gave me a courting knife when she was . . ." He stopped to think. "Oh . . . in Earth years I suppose she was sixteen, and I was nineteen. Or thereabouts. I had begun, by then, to speak sometimes of abdicating. Kamm was already so much better suited to governing than I will ever be. And I did not like the way people talked about the conquests I would make as emperor. My father's grandfather was a renowned general in the last great war. My father was Commander of the Nine. And fighting is all I was ever really good at. It was what everyone expected. But war was not what I wanted for the Empire." He glanced sideways at Hanna. She had not moved.

He went on. "Salenia . . . she did not believe I would do it. When I spoke to her of abdicating, she would laugh and tell me not to be ridiculous. I was the rightful emperor; the Sower had planted me in that position for a reason, and the Maker had made me what I am for a reason. I was destined to expand the Empire."

He shook his head sadly. "I do not think she ever really believed in the Sower. But it was the tradition our families followed, so she would speak in that way sometimes. And then she would kiss me, and I liked being kissed, so I would let it go to make her happy.

"I had worn her courting knife for a little over a year when I abdicated. She was furious with me. She said if I would not make her empress she would not marry me. I was hurt by her reaction and stopped wearing her courting knife. But I did not return it, and she did not ask for it back. I kept it through my basic military service, but I only wore it during visits home, when she asked me to." He stopped, looking into the fire, remembering.

Hanna said softly, "Tomin said he'd never seen you wear a courting knife."

Jon sighed. "No, he would not have." He reached for the poker and used it to shift a piece of wood in the fire, sending a shower of sparks up the chimney. "I think Salenia believed I was going through a phase," he continued. "She thought I would retract my abdication, and all would go back to the way it had been—the way she thought it *should* be. No one would have objected. But it would not have been good for the Empire."

He poked at the fire again. "She did not ask me to return her knife until I was inducted into the Winds. I think that was when she finally accepted that my abdication was real, and permanent, and was not going to change. She swore she would never be a widow of the Winds—not many men live to retire from the Winds, you see. And she did not speak to me for a long time after that."

Jon stopped talking. For several long heartbeats there was no sound in the room but the crackling of the fire. Then Hanna shifted, and Jon looked over to find she had drawn her knees up and propped her crossed arms on top of them. Her forehead rested on her arms, but she turned as he watched, and laid her cheek there instead so she could look at him. "There's more," she said. It was a statement, not a question, and Jon nodded.

"There is more. But I have never spoken of it with anyone. It is difficult." He looked away from her. At the fire. At the floor. At the glass doors. Back at the fire again. He drew a deep breath. "The next time I saw her was after I had displaced Dalathek as Commander of the Nine. Kamm told you before how that came about." He stabbed at the fire with the poker. "You must understand, Hanna, that Dalathek was like a father to me. In fact, my stepfather never cared much for me, and Dalathek was the closest thing to a father that I can remember. He taught me to fight. He praised me when I did well. He rebuked me when my behavior was dishonorable. My first real dagger was a gift from him. In many ways, he made me what I am. He was part of me. And until then, I was proud of that. When I discovered what he had done . . ."

He stopped, stabbing again at the fire. He tried to steady his voice, but it came out bitter and hoarse anyway. "When I found that girl—the one he had tortured and . . . and raped"—he glanced at Hanna, but she wasn't looking at him—"it was as if my whole universe came off its hinges. I felt sick. I felt betrayed. I felt . . . polluted. Contagious, even. And I was so very, very angry. When my stepfather refused to believe me, and the Council ruled that it either did not happen, or it did not matter, I felt betrayed again. It was as if everything had turned to quicksand under my feet.

"I challenged Dalathek, thinking either he would die or I would, and I am still not certain which I would have preferred at the time. I lost myself in it. I taunted him. I humiliated him. I wanted to kill him slowly so he would—" He stopped himself. That was not a good path to go down just now. "But my stepfather intervened and, to me, in that frame of mind, it was just another betrayal, another way in which the universe was inside out. But I won the challenge, and Dalathek was banished, and I found myself suddenly the Commander of the Nine. It was not an easy thing. I was new, and I was young, and I was beyond bitter. I had lost myself. It was a dark time."

Jon looked over again at Hanna. Her eyes were soft. Sympathetic. A tiny line had appeared between her brows. Perhaps she knew what it was like to lose herself.

He looked away. Pushed on. "Not long afterward I was at court, where my duties took me more and more often. And one night, Salenia came to me. She did not say anything, she just . . . she kissed me, and . . ." He made a vague gesture with his hand. He laid the poker on the hearth and pulled his knees up, realizing only after he'd done it that he was mimicking Hanna's posture.

He propped an elbow on one knee and leaned his face into the palm of his hand. "She was so . . . familiar. And I needed something to hold on to. I needed to think someone cared. I did not tell her to stop. And she did not tell me to stop. And . . ."

Jon stopped. The fire crackled into the taut silence, and he drew a long, shuddering breath. But he did not continue.

After a moment, Hanna murmured, "And that's what she meant when she spoke of one night of passion."

Several more heartbeats passed before Jon said, "Yes. For a little while everything else went away. Nothing else mattered. It was not better, it was just . . . gone." He shifted. Rubbed at the back of his neck. "Until it was over. It had not fixed anything. And I had used her, and betrayed myself, and dishonored my family, and turned my back on the Sower, and I did not even recognize myself anymore. I had not thought anything could make things worse. But that night did. She has never understood this. It meant something different to her."

He scrubbed both hands back through his hair. "I told you before, Hanna, that I have always wished I might tell my wife, whoever she turns out to be, that I have been faithful to her, even when I did not know who she was. Wishing cannot make it so. I know that. But I *have* been faithful, except for that night. Salenia knew I wanted this. She knew how strongly I felt about it. And she knew I was vulnerable that night. She did it on purpose, Hanna. She knew me better than anyone, and she knew how it would hurt me, and she did it anyway. It was meant to trap me. To force me to take back the throne and make her empress. She whispered to me afterward that if I reclaimed my throne, she would marry me, and if I married her, I would never have betrayed my wife. She said—" He stopped again, staring into the fire.

After a moment, Hanna said, "She had a point."

Jon turned to look at her. "No," he said firmly. "I was with a woman who was not my wife. Marrying her afterward would not have changed that fact." He turned back to stare into the fire. "I am not blameless in this. I could have asked her to leave. *I* could have left. I made my own choices, and I accept my part in it. But that does not change what she did."

He picked up the poker again and gently tapped a blackened piece of wood with the end of it. The stick crumbled into coals at the bottom of the fire. "She offered me her courting knife with the conditions that I give up my place as Commander of the Nine and retract my abdication. I declined her offer. Our families did not know what passed between us, though after what she said tonight they may at least suspect something of the sort. Over the years, they have encouraged us to resume our previous relationship, but since that night I have never asked permission to court her, and she has never offered me her knife. And we have never spoken of it."

"Maybe you should," Hanna said quietly.

Jon poked at the fire again, causing another stick to crumble. "To what purpose?"

Hanna shrugged. "I don't know. To get some clarity. To settle things between you."

Jon looked at her. "Things have been settled between us for a very long time, Hanna. I have clarity. And Salenia does not want me, she wants only to be empress."

"Are you sure?" Hanna shifted position, stretching out her small, bare feet toward the dying fire. She stared into the flames that flickered over the pile of black and red coals. "Whatever she feels for you, Jon, she feels very strongly. What she did on the flutter shuttle tonight—that was a big risk for a woman to take. Especially in front of her parents, and your parents, and . . . and the woman you're openly courting." She paused. Looked at him again, and away. "Surely she knows by now that you won't make her empress. Kamm is the one who could make her empress, but she doesn't pursue Kamm, she pursues you." Hanna looked over at Jon, meeting his eyes. "Relentlessly. I don't know what she was like before I met her, but she's been throwing herself at you ever since your dinner party." She looked away again.

Jon turned so his body was facing Hanna and waited until she looked back at him again. "We have both entertained relationships with other people over the years," he said softly. "She has given courting knives to at least six men that I know of, just in the past year or so. She has not been sitting and waiting for me."

Hanna tilted her head. "Generic family knives, I would guess."

Jon shrugged and looked away. "They are the most common."

"Jon," Hanna said, "Salenia is beautiful. She's intelligent and capable. I gather that her family is very wealthy and well-placed, and that as the *Ahnat* she'll become the Head of her House when she inherits and will wield a great deal of power. She could probably have any man she took a fancy to. Why isn't she married?"

Jon shrugged. "Perhaps she does not wish to be."

"Then why is she pursuing you?"

"Hanna," Jon began.

Hanna cut him off. "Tonight, she said Rosaline loved Romeo and was only waiting for him to stop fighting and settle down. You've left the Winds and built a home to settle in. She as much as said she had planned to speak with you about it at the dinner party. Except I was there that night, and you kissed me instead." Hanna looked away again, her brows furrowing, her mouth drawing down into a frown. "That must've been heartbreaking for her."

"Hanna," Jon tried again.

Again, Hanna cut him off. "And *you* said . . ." Hanna pushed up off the floor and went to stand on the hearth, warming her bare toes by the coals, leaning her forehead against the mantel. "Tonight on the flutter shuttle, you said love works best when it's built over time between people who have a lot in common. And you said you think a passion that moves too quickly will just burn itself out and come to nothing. You and I, Jon . . . even setting aside the fact that I am human and you're Tales-sanin, we only met a couple of months ago. It's not even three weeks since you started actually courting me, and you were gone for part of that. You've worn my knife for what . . . ten days? And it's been . . . intense. Maybe too intense."

She shifted, her small, bare feet silent on the stone of the hearth as she turned more fully away from him. "You and Salenia have shared a lifetime. You share a history. You share a culture. You share family, and friends, and traditions, and inside jokes. You share . . . a lot, I think. Salenia is part of you. When you're with her, there's something between you—something tight, and . . . compelling. Something that ties you to her and leaves me out. Like . . . like . . . secrets."

Hanna turned to face him, her eyes sad and empty. "In all these years, Jon, you haven't accepted a courting knife from anyone else. And you haven't told me you don't want to be with her, you've only said you don't think she wants you."

Jon stood slowly and went to Hanna. He wanted to wrap his arms around her, to hold her close, to tell her she had nothing to fear from Salenia. But she turned away from him, and he had to settle for standing beside her, one hand resting on the small of her back.

"Hanna," he said softly—and this time she didn't interrupt. "I do not want to be with Salenia. If I did, I would be with her now. She did seem to be offering that to me tonight, you are right. But I am here with you, where my heart is." She didn't look at him. She didn't speak. So he went on. "It is true that I have never accepted a courting knife from anyone else. Until you."

He drew a deep breath and let it slowly out before continuing. "At first, after Salenia, I was too lost, too broken inside to think of romance. I needed to learn to lead the Winds. I needed to make peace with myself and to find my place again in the Sower's garden." He shrugged. "And then . . . well, I have made requests that were refused, and I have turned down offers made to me. I have never lacked companionship when I desired it. But my work, and my family, and my reputation have made courtship problematic, and I have not seriously courted anyone since Salenia. But I do not want to court Salenia. I want to court you." He let his fingers trail up her back to the base of her neck. She flinched slightly when his fingers brushed her skin, so he let his hand drop away.

"I said love grows best when nurtured with patience," he went on. "Salenia has always pushed. You have seen her do it. You call it throwing herself at me, but she is that way with everything. When she wants a thing, she grabs at it, and she does not pay attention to the damage she might do with her grabbing. She is spoiled, and demanding, and impulsive, and she does not know how to wait. She thinks waiting—waiting for *anything*—is foolish.

"But she *did* wait, Jon," Hanna murmured. "For you, she waited."

"No. She might have intended to take advantage of my change in circumstances, but she did not wait. It is not in her nature. And she does not want me.

"You are different. You think about consequences. You understand the value of working hard for something. You build things that take time and patience, little by little until something beautiful emerges. You watch. You wait. You nurture the people around you, you do not feed off them. You even care whether Salenia's heart was wounded at the dinner party. That is what I meant, Hanna. I have seen more patience and nurturing from you in the short time I have known you than I have seen Salenia exhibit over her entire life. Time is only time, Hanna. It is not what I meant."

Hanna said nothing. He still couldn't see her face. Did she understand what he was telling her?

"I also said," he continued, "that it is best when lovers are suited to growing in the same soil. Salenia and I did grow up together, and you are right in saying that we have a lot of memories in common. But that is not what I meant either. Salenia . . . she thrives at court. She enjoys the intrigues and manipulations, the elegant parties and formal occasions. That is her element. But it suffocates me. I do not enjoy large gatherings of people, and the intrigues generally seem petty and unnecessary to me.

"I prefer a small home in the country with plenty of trees and a small lake to swim in and no obligation to spend time with anyone I do not care about. She was bored there by the end of the dinner party. But you love it there, Hanna. And you have made it feel even more like a home to me.

"When we were young and talked of having a family together, Salenia always spoke of nursemaids, and nannies, and governesses, and tutors, and all the best of everything for our children. But you, I think, would make them cookies, and read them stories, and tuck them into bed at night with your own hands. That is the kind of soil I wish for my children to grow in, if I ever have any. It is the kind of soil I wish to grow in myself. And I think you and I are well suited, even though we are still getting to know each other."

He reached out tentatively to stroke Hanna's arm with the backs of his fingers, but still she didn't turn toward him. He couldn't read her reaction.

"When I said that a passion too quickly indulged can kill the seeds of love, I did not mean you, Hanna," he continued. "I meant . . . I meant that night with Salenia. I do not really know what was between us before that—assumptions and expectations, certainly, and a long habit of each other. When she cut me off, I missed her deeply. When I opened my door that night and saw her standing there, I was so relieved, so happy to see her. And when she kissed me—well, there was passion then, at least. And if we had only kissed, and talked, and planned, and dreamed a bit, perhaps it would have grown into something more. But that is not what we did. When I see her now, I do not feel relieved and happy. I feel . . . wary. And tired. And I have never felt that passion for her again. I have felt it on a few occasions with other women, though it never came to anything—but never again with Salenia. That is what I meant, Hanna."

Hanna stirred, turning her head just enough to peer sideways at him from under her thick lashes. "Have . . ." she hesitated. "Have you ever . . . felt that way with me?"

Jon opened his mouth, then closed it. He reached over to brush her cheek with his fingers. "Only once," he said.

She turned away. "That night. After I gave you the courting knife."

"I wanted you that night," he admitted softly. "So much I could hardly breathe. But I think perhaps that was a test. I did not think of it that way at the time, but perhaps a part of me wished to see what you would do if you found me weary, and vulnerable, and . . . and wanting you. To see if you would do what she did. To see if I would . . . if I would keep my promises to myself. To the Sower." He sighed. "I am sometimes too impulsive. And not as wise as I would wish to be."

She looked slowly up at him again, studying his face.

He met her eyes as steadily as he could. "But that night is not what I meant, Little Mouse."

Her lips pinched into a puzzled frown.

He wanted to kiss it away, but instead he said, "With you, it began, just a little, when I opened my front door and found you on my porch with a chocolate cake, and it has never gone away since then. Sometimes it sleeps quietly in the center of my soul, and sometimes it flares so bright it is almost unbearable, but it has never gone away. So . . . only once."

Hanna looked down, and Jon thought her cheeks flushed, though it might have been just a shift in the rosy glow the coals were casting on everything. She didn't say anything for a moment. Then she sighed and looked back up at him. Her eyes were sad, and her smile was wry and slightly bitter. "You do have a silver tongue, Jonantathinel *Ehr*," she murmured.

What did that mean?

She turned away from him and took a few steps toward the glass doors, as if looking for a way to escape him. "But there's still something between you and Salenia. Maybe it's been there so long you don't see it anymore. But it's there, and I can't compete with it."

Cold emptiness washed through Jon. What was she saying?

She turned back to face him, keeping her distance, wrapping her arms protectively around herself. She looked so small and unhappy. "I thought," she said, "that giving you a courting knife would help. I thought it would make things clear to . . . to everyone. I thought she would back off, and we'd have the space we need to figure all this out." One of her hands gestured toward her chest, toward him, back again. "But I think it's only made things worse." There was a catch in her voice, and she stopped talking and turned her face toward the ceiling, closing her eyes.

"Hanna . . ." Jon took a step toward her and found that his knees had gone shaky.

What was she saying?

"I don't think I can do this." Her voice trembled.

Were there tears on her cheeks?

Her hands made a helpless, empty gesture. "I can't live through the nightmares every night and fight over you with Salenia every day. It's too much. There are too many battles to fight inside my own head as it is, and every time I turn around, Salenia is there, laughing at me and hinting that she knows you better, that she's had more of you, that you're hers and can never be mine, and . . . and I don't think I can do this."

She folded in on herself, dropping to her knees on the floor. She pressed one of her hands to her face, while the other one clutched at her belly, and her shoulders began to shake silently.

Jon stayed where he was for a moment, trying to remember how to breathe. Then he stepped over to where she knelt and sank to his knees in front of her.

"Hanna . . ." He kept his voice as soft and gentle as he could manage. She had told him this might happen. Back at the beginning of it all in the treehouse she had warned him that she might not be able to do this, that he might get hurt. She had told him again after she gave him the knife. He had no one to blame but himself for the wrenching, twisting, ache that climbed from his belly up into his throat. "Hanna . . . are you saying . . ." He stopped and swallowed hard. "Are you asking me to return your courting knife?"

Hanna's hand dropped away from her face, and she stared at Jon for several interminable heartbeats, her eyes wide and vulnerable. "N-no." Her answer was a stuttered whisper, but it sang through Jon like sunshine through a clear lake, and he started breathing again.

Hanna drew a deep, shuddering breath, and said, "Jon . . . I will never send you away. I promise." Her hand reached out toward him, hovering small and pale in the darkened space between them before coming up to brush against Jon's cheek. "I'm asking you to speak with Salenia." She swallowed hard. "And I'm asking you to finish whatever is between you and her that's unfinished. When you've done that, if you need to be with her, I'll respect your decision, and I won't make a fuss when you return my knife. And if you come back to me, I'll be waiting for you." Her hand flattened against Jon's cheek, and her thumb caressed his lower lip, and for half a breath Jon thought she might kiss him. But she didn't. She said, "Only please don't put me in the middle anymore. It isn't a battle I can fight."

Chapter 19

AFTER JON LEFT, HANNA CHECKED all the locks and had just gone into the kitchen to make some herbal tea when the chimes sounded, announcing a visitor at her door.

Who could possibly be coming to see her now? Had Jon left something behind? Hanna didn't want to see anyone. Not even Jon. She just wanted to go hide in her big bed with Mr. Bickles. Stepping to the corner of the kitchen, she checked the image on the security screen and then, puzzled, set her mug on the counter and went out to answer the door.

Why would Narista come calling?

Narista stared in surprise when Hanna opened the door. Then she looked down, blushing a little. "I'm sorry. I wasn't expecting you, I thought your maid . . ." Her voice trailed off, and she shifted her feet uncomfortably.

Hanna said, "Susan is having a night off." She knew she ought to invite Narista in, but she didn't feel like playing hostess tonight.

Narista took a deep breath and looked Hanna in the eyes. "Is Jon here?"

Hanna rubbed at her forehead with her fingers. "He already left. I'm sorry, I didn't think about a chaperon, but I swear we only talked."

Narista looked confused. Then she smiled sheepishly. "I guess I deserved that." She hesitated, then said, "Look, I'm going about this badly.

I did actually come to see you, Hanna. I was just startled when you answered your own door, and then I wanted to make sure he was gone, and we could speak privately. Could I come in?"

Hanna frowned. "Actually, I was just about to—"

"Please," Narista interrupted. You said once that if I ever had anything to say to you again, I should just knock on your door, and we could talk about it."

Hanna smiled wryly. "Well, I wouldn't want to wake up to another dead mouse. I guess you'd better come in and have your say." She stepped back from the doorway and motioned Narista into the sitting room.

As the door closed behind her, Narista turned to face Hanna, with a nervous smile. "I don't want to take up too much of your time," she said. "I just . . ." She looked at her feet. "I wanted to apologize."

She knelt on the sitting room floor in front of Hanna, drawing a small knife from her pocket and unsheathing it. She placed the knife on the floor between them, clasped her hands behind her back, bowed her head, and said solemnly, "Hanna Bradley, I have brought you pain. I come to know if I can take it away again with me."

She waited.

Hanna stood for a moment, looking down at the kneeling woman. Then she sighed. "Narista, no one has ever taught me this. I guess I should've asked after the last time, but—well, everything has been happening so fast. I don't suppose you'd be willing to tell me what I am expected to do?"

Narista looked up, a cautious smile on her face. "It depends on what you think of me and my apology," she said. "If you don't want to hear it, the civilized thing to do would be to just pick up my knife and hand it back to me without saying anything. But traditionally, you could use my knife to exact whatever justice you thought fitting—cut off my hand, stab me in the eye—although these days that sort of refusal is usually limited to a bit of a nick on the cheek or arm, and even that is considered pretty extreme. But maybe you feel that way about me; I have been truly horrible to you."

She shrugged. "If you're willing to hear what I want to say, you stand or kneel on the floor on the other side of my knife and say, 'Tell me,' and then I say what I did wrong, and try to make things better between us, and ask for your forgiveness. After that, you forgive me. I hope. Or you tell me what else I can do to fix things. Or you can cut me or hand my knife back and throw me out. It's up to you. But I really would appreciate being at least given a chance to apologize." She held Hanna's gaze with her own for a moment longer, then bowed her head again and waited.

Slowly, Hanna walked the few steps that separated them and lowered herself to her knees. "Tell me," she said.

Narista tipped her head up to look at Hanna and brought her hands around from behind her back to rest on her knees. Softly, she said, "Thank you." She drew a deep breath and looked down at her hands. "Hanna, I've been awful to you, and I'm sorry. I allowed myself to be influenced by . . . by other people who also apparently don't know as much about humans as they think they do. But I should've known better, and I accept responsibility for what I did. I've met a few humans from Kamm's embassies, and I've watched entertainment programs with humans in them, but I've never really spent time with one before, and you're not what I expected you to be. I made judgments about you—about your intellect, and your character, and your morals—without even getting to know you. And I was very wrong."

She was quiet for a moment, and Hanna began to say, "Narista, it's—"

"There's more." Narista looked up at her. "I did more than just leave you that dreadful note with the dead mouse. When I saw how Jon acted toward you at his dinner party, I tried to get Kamm to use his authority as Ehrat to intervene. When he wouldn't, I wrote to my father about Jon and you. I think that's why my parents decided to come. I heard you were going to be at that art show, and instead of telling Jon, I arranged for Jon and Salenia to attend together so you'd see them.

"When you came here after . . . after you were hurt, I made you feel unwelcome. When Jon said you'd given him permission to court you, I mocked you. I should've welcomed you, and shown you around, and introduced you to people, and visited you while you were recovering. I should've tried to be your friend. Instead, I undermined you every way I could think of. I even sent a not-so-subtle suggestion to the Council that Jon would be a good resource for information about humans, so they'd call him away. And I shoved Salenia in your face every chance I got. But she and Jon have been dancing circles around each other for years with both families trying to push them together. If Jon wanted Salenia he could've had her already."

Hanna shifted and opened her mouth to respond, but Narista held up her hand. "Please let me finish." She took a deep breath and plunged on. "I think I imagined you were some kind of slutty, opportunistic leech who was slyly worming her way into my brother's affections, and that he was somehow vulnerable to your charms because he'd just left his place with the Winds in order to settle down, and you were the closest female at hand. I did both of you a grave injustice in that. Jon has a great deal more sense than to take up with a woman merely because she's convenient. And you weren't pursuing him, he was pursuing you.

"You make my brother happy, Hanna. I've never seen him smile and laugh as much as he does with you. For as long as I can remember, he's always been very serious, and quiet, and intense. Whatever it is that weighs him down, you make it better. And you're . . . you're nice. I didn't want to like you, but I do. You've never been anything but kind and patient, even when someone tries to provoke you on purpose. That takes a lot of strength of will. I stuck a dead mouse to your door and told you off, and you gave me a muffin. In the menagerie, Salenia said to your face that you were nothing more than Jon's pet plaything, and you just politely excused yourself. Tonight, in the flutter shuttle . . . I would've slapped her if she'd done to me what she did to you. I've been on the wrong side of this thing from the beginning. And I'm sorry. I'd like . . . I'd like for us to be friends. Do you think you can forgive me?"

"You did all those things?" Hanna asked wonderingly.

Narista looked down, and her cheeks flushed as she nodded. "I was a complete sow. I really am so very sorry, Hanna."

Hanna was quiet for a few minutes. Part of her wanted to be angry. Part of her wanted to cry. But most of her was just too wrung out to care what drama Narista had been up to; she just wanted to go to bed. "Well," she said slowly, "I guess I'm glad Jon has a sister who cares enough about him to protect him from slutty opportunistic leeches. And it definitely sounds like it would be safer to be your friend than your enemy."

Narista's eyes flashed to Hanna's face, and she frowned. "Are you saying you forgive me?"

"Sure. Why not. I forgive you."

"That's *it*? You're not even going to shout at me or anything?"

Hanna shrugged. "What would that accomplish?"

Narista grinned sheepishly. "Well, it might make me feel better if you did. And a good, solid slap would probably do wonders for my character development." She picked up her knife and stood. "No wonder Jon likes you so much. You'll forgive anything. I thought for sure you'd be finished with him when he laughed at you in your bathing suit. My brother has a good heart, but sometimes the man just doesn't think."

Hanna, too, rose to her feet. "He made a very thorough apology." She felt her cheeks warm.

Narista's grin widened. "Better than mine?"

Hanna grinned back and shrugged. "Well, he can be very convincing. And he does have a few additional resources at his disposal, being a man."

Narista laughed and smiled fondly. "He can definitely be convincing. And stubborn."

An awkward silence settled between them. Hanna wondered if she should offer Narista a cup of tea or just thank her for her apology and send her on her way. While she was still trying to decide, Narista shifted self-consciously on her feet and said, "If . . . if we're going to be friends, maybe . . . would you maybe let me see your sketches? I really liked that painting Jon bought. And my mother told me you have some very nice drawings of Tala."

Hanna blinked. "You want to see my sketches?"

Narista blushed and looked down, scuffing the toe of one of her slippers against the floor. "I like art. I've seen you around the embassy with your sketchbook, and I wanted to go watch you work, but . . . well, we weren't friends. So now that we are, at least a little, I wondered if . . ." She looked up and saw Hanna's frown. "Never mind. It's probably too much to ask right after telling you I've been trying to get rid of you all this time. I'll just go."

"No, it's not that," Hanna put out a hand to stop Narista as she moved toward the door. If Jon's sister really wanted to be friends, Hanna didn't want to do anything that would change her mind. "It's just that Jon has my sketchbook. The book was a gift from him, you see, and he wanted to see what I've done with it so far. But there hasn't been time to sit down together so I could show him, so when he was here yesterday, I let him take it with him. Otherwise . . ."

"Oh," Narista said with a bright smile. "Well, why don't we go ask him for it?" She leaned toward Hanna conspiratorially. "Maybe we'll catch him doing his drills." When she saw the blank look on Hanna's face, Narista shook her head. "Oh Hanna. I am really going to have to do something about your education. If you had any female Talessanin friends at all they'd have told you that watching fighters work their drills is practically a sport in and of itself. And trying to catch your suitor working his dagger drills is one of the age-old customs of a good Talessanin courtship. It's like a dance in slow motion. In just their *lanat*." She paused, giving Hanna a meaningful gaze.

Hanna gave her a blank look in return. "Their what?"

"Their *lanat*." Narista looked around, as if searching for the right English word. "Loincloth," she said finally.

"Like when they go swimming?" Hanna asked, unsure what Narista was getting at.

Narista shook her head. "Yes. Only so very much not the same thing at all. I guess you have to see it to know what I mean. Come on." She started for the door. Then stopped and glanced at the French doors. "Is it shorter to go across the courtyard?"

Hanna shrugged. "I haven't been to Jon's rooms, I don't really know."

Narista looked dumbfounded. "Never?"

"Well, I've only been here a little while, and Jon was gone most of that first week, and . . ."

"And there I was, imagining you sneaking in his window at night." Narista laughed. "Come on, we'll try the courtyard."

Chapter 20

JON STRODE DOWN THE CORRIDOR and flung open the door to his rooms. He shoved the door shut, pulled off the formal longcoat he had worn to the theater, and hurled it in the direction of one of the bent wood privacy screens that sectioned the great room. Hanna was right about one thing—formal attire was not conducive to clear thinking. Part of him wanted to go straight to Salenia's quarters and tell her exactly what he thought of her little performance. She really had gone too far this time.

He began unbuttoning his shirt as he crossed the room toward the small haven in the corner next to the curving glass wall that overlooked the private garden. He ought to create a permanent haven at home, now that he had a home. A pocket brazier was just not the same.

Hanna was right about something else, too—Salenia had been crossing the line with him for so long that he hardly even noticed anymore. But it was going to stop.

The buttons were irritating. He yanked, and a few popped off, skittering across the tiles. Then he dragged the shirt off over his head and dropped it on the floor. It was good, he decided, that he had told Hanna he would see Salenia in the morning. Tonight, his emotions were still running too hot. Waiting would give him time to calm himself and think what would be best to say.

He stopped at the edge of the prayer rug and rubbed at his bare shoulders with his hands, then bent down to undo the row of clips down the side of one of his boots. He shucked that boot off and pitched it to one side. A moment, and the other followed. He stood still, then, studying the pattern of gold and silver vines that wove across the deep green of the prayer rug. What was his path tonight? Leaves? Fruit? Flowers? Stems? Branching places, he decided. Turning points. Slowly, he crossed the rug, carefully positioning each footstep at a junction in the design where a new branch grew out from the main stem, pausing with each step to ponder the turning points of his life and the choices he had made at each that had led him to this place, this time.

When he reached the small altar stone with its softly glowing brazier, he knelt and contemplated the assortment of *taless* seeds in the bowl. He selected two this time, placed one in front of the other on the brazier, and waited until the white smoke began to curl up from each before spreading his arms, hands open, palms up in supplication, and tipping his face toward the ceiling and the night sky beyond. Both seeds had crumbled to ash in the bottom of the brazier by the time he opened his eyes again, feeling considerably more level-headed. He drew a deep breath and stood, tugging his belt knot loose and slipping Hanna's courting knife free. He raised the platinum mouse to his forehead, touched it to his lips, and held it for a long breath against his chest, before laying it in its black case next to the altar stone.

He began to work the hook fasteners of his trousers as he turned, intending to strip down to his *lanat* for his evening drill work, but froze as the first hook came loose, and straightened, his face going hard and cold.

Across the room, Salenia unfolded herself from one of the cupped and cushioned fishnet seats that hung from the ceiling like a cluster of tilted bird nests and stood. She must've been sitting there the whole time.

"Don't stop on my account," she said, smiling sweetly. "You don't have anything I haven't seen before."

Jon folded his arms across his chest and glowered at her. "How did you get in here?" One of the servants, probably, thinking he was doing Jon a favor. He'd have to talk to Kamm about his staff.

Salenia ignored his question. "We need to talk."

The two stood looking at each other for a long, silent moment. Then Jon rubbed a hand back through his hair. "So, talk."

"Don't you think this farce has gone on long enough, Jon?" Salenia waved an exasperated hand. "You've made your point. That absurd resolution is being taken seriously. What more are you trying to accomplish with this?"

Jon blinked. He tilted his head sideways. "What are you talking about? What am I trying to accomplish with what?"

Salenia gave a sharp, disbelieving bark of a laugh. "This nonsensical propaganda performance you've been engaging in. People are starting to think you actually want to marry that thing."

Jon unfolded his arms and put his hands on his hips, taking a step closer to Salenia so he towered over her. Very slowly and carefully he said, "Salenia, are you speaking of Hanna?"

Salenia's eyes narrowed and her chin came up in haughty defiance. "Why, do you have some other little piece of human gingerbread hiding under your covers that I don't know about? How long do you think I will put up with this? I am not my mother."

"And I am not your father."

"At least my father has the decency to play with his little toy in private. Not you, though. You have to dress yours up, and take it out in public, and flaunt it in my face. You kissed it tonight, Jon. Kissed it! In front of everyone, with me standing right there watching. That disgusting little demonstration of yours at the art exhibit was bad enough. But this—this was beyond vulgar, it was obscene."

Jon's jaw clenched, and he took another step toward Salenia. His voice was low, and flat as ice. "I am *courting* Hanna. I will kiss her wherever and whenever I choose. And if I wish to, and she agrees, I *will* marry her."

Salenia's mouth dropped open, and she stared at him. Then she relaxed and started laughing. "Oh, that's very good. For a moment you almost had even me convinced. But really, I'm tired of your little game, and it's time to let this go."

"This has nothing to do with you, Salenia, and it is certainly not a game. I am courting Hanna Bradley. Every moment I'm with her, I'm more convinced that I do want to marry her, and that if the Sower smiles upon me at all, she will one day be my wife."

"Nothing to do with me?" Salenia's eyes flew wide and her lips compressed. "How *dare* you! *I* am to be your wife. *Me*. I was born to be your wife. I was raised and educated and groomed to be your wife. You and I and both of our families have been planning our marriage for our entire lives. My family's resources have been invested all these years with the assumption that my property and yours would be merged when we married. And now you stand there and tell me you intend to get the laws changed so you can marry some filthy sow human instead, and you say it has nothing to do with me?" Her hand flashed toward Jon's face, and he twisted sideways and back to avoid the slap. Salenia glared and swung at him again. Jon dodged that blow too.

He took a deep breath, fighting to maintain control of his temper. "You and I have never been betrothed, Salenia. Never. And we certainly are no such thing at present. There was a lot of talk when we were children. I courted you for a few years when we were older. But you asked me to return your courting knife when I joined the Winds, and there has been no understanding of any kind between us since then. You know that as well as I do. If you had been suffering under a misconception that a betrothal existed between us, you certainly would not have accepted so many other suitors over the years."

Salenia stepped back, a smug smile toying with her lips. "You've kept track of my suitors?"

Jon rolled his eyes. "Narista felt it necessary to keep me informed. I have never inquired. And I've never felt it necessary to publicize my own relationships."

"What relationships?" Salenia scoffed. "I've never heard of you having any relationships."

"Private relationships. Relationships that are no one else's concern and have nothing to do with you. The fact that our mothers are friends does not obligate me to inform you when I kiss another woman."

She stepped toward him again, pointing an accusing finger at him. "All those years, Jon. All that talk of what we would do when you were the emperor and I was your empress, of when you were my husband and I was your wife, of our home, and our children, and our future together—all of that means *nothing* to you?"

"I made you no promises. And even if I had, I would've been released from them by your request for the return of your courting knife.

I owe you nothing. And you owe me nothing. Marry one of your other suitors." Jon made a dismissive motion with one hand.

Salenia stared at him. "I can't marry someone else." She sank down into the cushions of one of the netted seats. "My father has made it clear to me that if my marriage doesn't result in our House acquiring at least the holdings you inherited from your father, I will lose my place as *Ahnat*. My cousin will become E*hrat* and will inherit all that was to be mine. I will have no home. No House. No name. And no way of supporting myself."

So that was the problem. Jon's anger eased. He turned another cushioned seat to face her and settled into it. "Your father does have a right to choose his successor. But if your chosen husband is unable to support you, you can appeal your inheritance claim with the Throne. My mother may not be able to restore you as *ahnat*, but I would guess she could insist on an *ahn's* portion for you, which from Trakanaleth should be more than sufficient for your needs. And if not, I'm sure she would find another place for you."

Salenia leaned forward in her chair, elbows on her knees, hands clenched into fists.

"You want me to go crawling to the Throne to beg for assistance in obtaining an *ahn's* portion?" she snarled. "I was never even meant to be the Trakanaleth *ahnat*. I was meant to be the Kanestelan empress. I am meant to *occupy* the Throne, not grovel before it. Just as you are destined to be emperor. Can you not see it? Even though you abdicated, the Throne is pulling you in. There is talk—"

Jon cut her off. "It's only talk, Salenia. And it's one of the reasons I left the Winds. I won't let them make me emperor. I wouldn't be the emperor the Empire needs. We've been through all this before."

"Yes, we have. And still you will not listen." She shook her head in frustration. "You are meant to be emperor. Destiny will make you emperor whether you will it or no. It's just the way the currents flow. You've *earned* the Throne now, and you need not accept it as a mere blood inheritance. In all but name you've fulfilled the first condition I required for resuming our courtship. And by leaving your place with the Winds you've fulfilled my second condition. You are mine, Jon. And I'm yours. We were meant to be together. And you know it too. That's why, in all these long years while you were fulfilling my conditions, you've never accepted a courting knife from anyone else."

"But I have," Jon said, his voice soft, but carrying a riptide of ferocity as he leaned forward in his seat. "I've accepted a courting knife from Hanna."

Salenia's face went white except for two bright spots of color high on her cheeks, and she leapt to her feet. "Hanna is a *human*, Jon. It's not even a person. You cannot court your *pet*."

Jon's blood surged again, this time hot and dangerous, and he had to deliberately unclench his teeth to speak. "Hanna is a *person*, no matter what barbarians like your father say. She is an intelligent, creative, compassionate woman, and she makes me feel whole again. I do not require your permission to court her. I do not require your permission to marry her. And you will not come to my rooms like this and speak of Hanna in this manner."

Salenia leered at him. "You didn't object the last time I came to your rooms like this." She closed the few steps between them, standing so close to his knees that he couldn't rise without pushing against her. He leaned back, away from her. Salenia's eyes drilled into his, as her hands went to the silver clasps at the front of her gown. She flicked the first clasp open. Then the next.

Jon frowned at her. "What do you think you're doing, Salenia?"

She flicked open two more clasps. "If you think that vile, squalid little pestilence of a rodent of yours bears any resemblance to a woman, maybe you need to be reminded what a real woman is actually like." She flicked open another clasp with one hand, and with the other, she drew her skirts up out of the way so she could place one knee on Jon's seat next to his hip.

"Stop this." Jon snapped.

"No." She leaned toward him, dress falling open to the waist, exposing bare skin and tantalizing curves, and flicked another clasp. He kept his eyes focused on her face and caught her around the waist, holding her away.

She tucked her other knee up and settled herself astride his lap. "I will not stop. You are mine. And you want me. You just need to be reminded."

She leaned forward and kissed him.

Chapter 21

THE REFRESHING COOLNESS OF THE night breeze began to lift the stifling despondency that had settled over Hanna in the flutter shuttle and clung to her like greasy smoke. As she followed Narista through the embassy courtyard, clusters of bioluminescent plants and fungi added soft pools of blue, and green, and the red of dying coals to the tide of pale moonlight and the occasional supplemental splash of artificial lighting that illuminated the pathways.

She had difficulty keeping track of the turnings but could tell by the positions of some of the more prominent rock features that Narista was guiding her away from the pool and the menagerie and into a part of the great courtyard Hanna had not yet explored. Narista slowed as they turned onto a path that hugged the base of a high stone wall, which was pierced at irregular intervals by decorative iron gates.

Narista paused outside one of the gates. "Jon always stays in the Talessanin guest quarters," she explained. "He doesn't visit often enough to keep rooms in the residential wing—although, maybe that will change now that he's built a home on planet." She fiddled with something Hanna couldn't see in the shadow of the wall, and the gate swung open.

Narista stage whispered, "Here, your education in Talessanin courtship traditions officially begins." She held a conspiratorial finger to her lips and winked at Hanna before leading the way through the gate and closing it behind them. They stood in a private garden planted to resemble a dense forest. Trees grew close together, their branches arching over the narrow flagstone pathway, and thick shrubs and ferns choked the spaces between their trunks. A vine grew up the back of the stone wall, heavy with dark, leathery leaves and drooping flowers that gleamed white in the moonlight.

The path wove and twisted back on itself, transforming the relatively short distance to the building beyond into a long, meandering stroll that probably would've been pleasant in daylight. Normally, Hanna enjoyed forests, but this one was unfamiliar—full of plants she didn't recognize and smells she couldn't place—and sometimes the rippling of the slight breeze among the leaves made a sound like an animal stalking them through the darkness. She shivered and hurried after Narista.

Jon's sister stopped before they rounded the final curve of the forested pathway and motioned Hanna close to whisper, "Just past there the path opens into a cobblestone patio." She pointed, and Hanna could see the edges of a soft, warm light that spilled across an open space. "There's a big window, like a wall of glass with a door opening onto the patio," Narista went on. "Jon usually does his drills in front of the window, where he can see the trees, but sometimes he does them outside. We have to stay in the shadows and be quiet, though, until we want him to notice us, because my brother has ears like a . . ." She paused and frowned. "What is that flying Earth rodent thing that navigates by echolocation?"

"A bat?"

Narista grinned. "Yes. Ears like a bat. So, softly now."

The two of them crept forward. A slab of stone, taller than either of them, stood sentinel at the place where the path opened into the cobbled yard, and Narista crept to the edge, giggling noiselessly and touching a silencing finger again to her lips. Slowly, she leaned to peer around the stone. Then she went rigid and let out a small gasp. Hurriedly, she ducked back behind the slab, clutching at Hanna's arm. "We have to go back," she hissed. "This was a very bad idea."

But Hanna had already leaned past the edge of the stone and stood frozen on the pathway.

The light spilling across the mossy cobblestones did indeed come from a large, curving glass wall, and as Narista had predicted, Hanna could see Jon framed inside the window. He was not doing dagger drills, however. He sat, shirtless, in a sort of net swing piled with cushions, leaning forward and speaking to Salenia. As Hanna watched, Salenia moved to stand directly in front of Jon and began to tug at the front of her gown, releasing the fasteners that held her bodice closed. Jon leaned back in the chair. Salenia pulled her skirts up and slid onto his lap. Jon reached for Salenia as she leaned down to kiss him.

And then everything took a sickly plunge sideways, as a wave of dizziness swept over Hanna. She staggered and slumped to her knees, gasping and struggling to keep from collapsing completely.

Narista reached out to touch her shoulder, but Hanna shook her off.

"This is why you brought me here?" Hanna gasped. "So I'd see this? You and Salenia—I should've known."

"No, Hanna, I—"

"You didn't have to show me, Narista. I'm sure he would've told me tomorrow. I didn't need to see it." She pressed a hand to her forehead and lurched unsteadily to her feet, unwilling to stay where she was even until the dizziness passed.

Narista peered back around the edge of the stone block and inhaled sharply. "Oh Hanna!"

Hanna stumbled back up the path, moving as quickly as she could without tripping.

"Hanna, I didn't know!" Narista's sharp whisper followed her up the path.

Hanna pushed herself faster, swaying and staggering as she ran and silently cursed the winding course she had to take. For a moment, she considered just plunging straight through the undergrowth toward the gate. But that would take even longer than going around all the corners. The dizziness began to lift, and Hanna pushed herself into a jog, not wanting Narista to catch up with her. Tears blurred her vision and trickled down her cheeks.

Chapter 22

JON FROZE, STARTLED. SALENIA'S LIPS were soft and insistent, and the scent of her expensive perfume tugged at something primal inside of him.

What was he supposed to do? No amount of combat training, it seemed, prepared a man for a situation like this; he couldn't very well break her neck or stick a dagger in her belly. How could he stop her without hurting her? He had to do *something*. He couldn't just give in.

Jon clenched his teeth and turned his face away from her. "Salenia," his voice came out low and menacing between his teeth, "if you don't stop, I will have to stop you."

Salenia chuckled softly, and her mouth moved seductively along the line of his jaw. Her teeth nipped gently at his ear, and then she nuzzled into his neck as her hands worked their way across his chest and down his belly.

"Salenia, stop!" Jon felt the rage building inside him. He moved one hand from her waist to push her face away. She twisted in his grasp and pressed her naked breasts against the bare skin of his chest. One of her hands began groping at the fasteners of his trousers.

"Enough!" Jon bellowed. He snatched her groping fingers away with one hand and twined his other hand in her long, red hair, wrenching her backward and off balance.

She slid off his lap and hit the floor, landing on her backside in a pool of skirts.

With an impudent grin, she wrapped both arms around his neck and threw all her weight backward, pulling him over on top of her.

Jon ducked out of her hold and straddled her, pinning her wrists to the floor with his hands. "You *will* stop, Salenia!"

Salenia gazed up at him for a moment, seeming to weigh her options, then relaxed beneath him.

"All right, you win, Jon," she said, a smile playing across her full lips. "You may do whatever you want with me." She wriggled her hips under him suggestively.

"In the name of all the Gentle . . ." Jon wanted to slap her. Instead, he pushed himself to his feet and stormed across the room. He smacked his open palm hard against the wall between the haven and the curving glass of the garden window. He smacked it again. Then he leaned his arm against the wall and rested his forehead on it, breathing deeply and slowly, trying to clear his head.

Chapter
23

HANNA WAS ROUNDING THE LAST corner before the gate when her foot caught on the edge of a flagstone and she fell, ripping a hole in her worn sweatpants and scraping the skin off one knee. As she pushed herself back to her feet, the heels of her hands began to sting where she'd caught herself. They were scratched and bleeding too.

It figured.

She limped to the gate and started groping in the dimness, searching for the latch Narista had used to open it.

Behind her, the undergrowth rustled. A low, clicking chuckle sent a prickle of fear down her spine.

Slowly, she turned her head.

Ferns shifted in the shadows under one of the trees. The clicking chuckle came again. Then a low hissing sound as the *kalakanek* slipped out of the shadows.

The beast crouched on the moonlit path, eyeing her speculatively. It looked bigger somehow, when it wasn't in its cage. It probably outweighed Hanna by a good fifty pounds. The spiky mane on its shoulders quivered and rose, the feathers, or fur, or antennae of it swaying gently as if testing the air. The *kalakanek* snuffled and hissed again, dropping its gaze from her to inspect the place where she'd fallen.

Hanna looked wildly around for something to use as a weapon. A loose stone? A stick? A shovel left by a gardener?

Anything!

She couldn't see a rock smaller than the flagstones, and those were all firmly embedded in the packed dirt of the pathway.

No stray gardening tools.

A stick protruded from beneath a nearby shrub.

Better than nothing.

When she edged toward it, the *kalakanek* raised its head and snuffed at her.

She froze.

It licked its lips and went back to sniffing the flagstones.

Hanna tugged at the stick with her foot. It slid free of the undergrowth without snagging, and relief washed through her.

It wasn't much of a weapon—only about two feet long and a little bigger around than her thumb. But it was broken into a sharp spike on one end. If that thing was going to eat her, she could at least go down fighting. Slowly, she bent to pick it up.

The *kalakanek* cocked its head. A three-pronged tongue flickered out from between its rows of needle-like teeth to lap up a spot of Hanna's blood. A shiver rippled through the spikes of its mane.

Its intense gaze found Hanna again, and it made a soft, high, clucking sound like a deranged chicken. Its ugly head swayed from side to side as it edged closer. The pronged tongue flicked out from between its teeth, as the creature's lips drew back into a manic grin around its tusks.

It lunged forward—only a step or two, testing, but Hanna flinched reflexively, raising the broken end of the stick, clutching it with both hands.

The predator stopped, evaluating its prey. It moved into the open area in front of the gate and circled to one side, drifting closer, cluck-chuckling softly. It was only a few feet from Hanna now, and she knew one good lunge was all it would take for it to be on top of her. But it was wary of her stick.

A stifled shriek startled them both.

The *kalakanek* flicked its gaze toward the sound, but Hanna didn't dare take her eyes off the creature.

Narista's trembling voice came from the last bend in the path. "Hanna? Are you all right?"

The *kalakanek* snuffed again and turned its attention back to Hanna, its tongue flicking out of its mouth toward her.

"Get help," Hanna gasped. "I don't think it will follow you. It wants me. I skinned my knee, and it smells the blood."

Narista whimpered. And went.

Chapter
24

S ALENIA STEPPED UP BEHIND JON and laid a gentle hand against the back of his shoulder. "Let's not fight," she said softly, sounding more subdued. "We can talk about this."

Jon stood still, clenching and unclenching his teeth, trying to think of something to say to her.

Salenia's fingers slid soothingly down his back. It was a familiar sensation—one he had not felt in a very long time, yet one that brought back memory upon memory of other times he and Salenia had disagreed and then made peace. She had not done that since . . . he thought back . . . since before his abdication, surely.

The taut muscles in his back relaxed as her fingertips skimmed over his skin. Something inside him softened too, as the past tugged at him. Maybe Hanna was right; maybe a lingering something did exist between him and Salenia. And maybe it wasn't only on Salenia's side.

Hanna. Memories of her crowded into his mind too—Hanna's fingers tracing the scars across his back in his hot tub while her little mouse feet dangled temptingly in the water beside him. Hanna's fingers tangling with his in the basin at his dinner party. Hanna's fingers tracing the fading lines of his *tehilethkalan* in the embassy's soaking pools. Hanna sitting shyly on his knee and blushing as her fingers tipped back the lid of the black knife case.

"Salenia," he said, keeping his voice slow, deliberate, "I am courting Hanna. I want only Hanna. There is nothing for you here."

As he said the words, the rightness of them settled down through him like pebbles tossed into a clear pool. With Salenia, everything was a contest. Him against her. Attack and response. Maneuvering for position. Strategy and manipulation. It had always been that way with her, as long as he could remember. Sometimes it was a stimulating challenge—she made him think, kept him alert. Other times it seemed an exhausting exercise in futility in which even victory left him discontent. But always there was the underlying tension between rivals. Adversaries. With Hanna, it was different. Hanna was healing. Hanna was like coming home.

Salenia's fingers paused. Her hand flattened against Jon's back and slid around his side to lie against his belly as she shifted closer to him. "You don't really mean that," she crooned.

Strategy and manipulation.

She wrapped her other arm around him too, pressing the length of her body against him, her skin against his skin, her skirts swirling around his ankles.

Had she ever really loved him at all, or had he only ever been a territory to be conquered, a prize to be acquired, a competitor to be bested?

He picked her hand off his belly like a tick, twisting it downward as he turned and caught her elbow with his other hand.

He heard her gasp of pain at the same moment he felt the joint of her wrist reach the limit of its natural motion. He knew how little pressure it would take in this position to do serious damage to the joint. He had crippled men like this before.

"I assure you, Salenia, I mean exactly what I say." Jon spoke with the soft, susurrant intensity of the Viper. "Please listen carefully. I am in love with Hanna. I am courting Hanna. If I am very, very fortunate, I will marry Hanna. There is no place for you in my life. Do you understand?"

"Jon!" Salenia gasped. "You're hurting me."

"Pay attention." Jon leaned closer, pressing ever so slightly harder against Salenia's hand—not enough to do damage, just enough to cause real pain.

She gasped again and sank to her knees on the prayer rug. All the color had drained from her face, and her eyes were wide and fearful. "Jon, please!" she whimpered.

He released some of the pressure but kept his grip firm and his voice calm. "You will never touch me like that again," he said. "Do you understand me?"

Salenia nodded, her breath coming quick and sharp.

Jon continued. "Your behavior toward Hanna will be respectful, and you will never say another disparaging word about her. Do you understand?" Salenia nodded again, but Jon leaned a little closer and pressed her hand down ever so slightly, "Do you?"

"Yes!" Salenia whimpered. "Yes, Jon, I understand!"

He let up slightly on the pressure again. "Excellent," he hissed. "Because if you ever displease me in this manner again, Salenia, I will make sure you wish most desperately that being disowned for marrying the wrong man was the worst thing that ever happened to you." He held Salenia's gaze a moment longer and then released his grip. "Pull yourself together and get out."

Salenia was still fiddling with her clasps when Narista burst in through the door to the garden, eyes wide and frantic.

"Jon!" she panted. "Come now. The *kalakanek* is loose, and it has Hanna!"

Chapter 25

THE KALAKANEK EDGED CLOSER, SHIFTING from side to side. A glob of drool slithered down its tusk and dripped onto the flagstones, and a heavy, sour, animal stench filled the night air.

Hanna backed away until the metal bars of the gate pressed into her back. Could she find the latch, get outside, and close the gate before the thing attacked? She shifted her grip on the stick to one hand and groped behind her with the other, feeling for the gate latch.

The *kalakanek* lunged.

Hanna leapt to one side, whipping her free hand back to the stick, aiming for the animal's gaping mouth. She missed, and something smacked against her thigh, but she focused on the sharp point of the stick as it skittered up the beast's mashed-looking face, caught in folds of skin, and then plunged into one of its wicked eyes.

The creature reared back on its hind legs, nearly pulling the stick from Hanna's grasp, and came down on all fours just out of reach, glaring death at her. Blood dribbled from its eye. Drool dripped from its mouth. Its lips drew back in a tusky, toothy, snarling leer, and it shrieked out the maniacal cackle that had frightened Hanna so much that first time in the menagerie. Then, it crouched to spring again.

Hanna's hands clenched around the stick, suddenly slick with sweat.

Time slowed, focusing to a pinpoint.

The monster launched itself at her, seeming almost to float through the stillness between them, moonlight glinting red off its bloody face, white off its needle teeth.

Hanna's stick drifted up to meet it.

A sizzling bolt of white lightning crackled through the gate behind her, knocking the *kalakanek* backward in mid-spring. Time sped up again as it hit the flagstones and began to writhe. A red-hot glow seemed to light the creature from inside, and it began to melt, oozing blood and offal across the stones.

Hanna's heart pounded even faster, and her breath came in great, heaving sobs as she turned to look behind her.

Chance lowered his pistol and scrabbled for the gate latch. Hanna felt the gate nudge at her from behind but didn't think to move until Chance said, "Hanna, are you all right? I need you to move away from the gate."

Hanna's hands went numb, and the stick clattered onto the stones as she stumbled back.

"Chance!" His name came out as a sobbing gasp. "Oh! Thank you, Chance."

He slipped through the gate. "Are you all right? Did it hurt you?" His eyes scanned her body. "Your leg!" He stepped forward and wrapped an arm around her waist, holding her up.

"I just skinned my knee when I tripped, that's all," Hanna said, looking down at her ripped sweatpants. Then, "Oh. Wow. You'd think that would hurt."

A longer rip had been torn through the thigh of her pants, and the skin underneath was shredded. Blood trickled down her leg in a steady stream and was beginning to pool around her feet.

"That doesn't hurt?" Chance looked even more alarmed. "Hanna, you need to sit down. Right now."

He started speaking rapidly and urgently in Talessainin, and Hanna realized she'd taken her translation module out of her ear earlier when she was taking her makeup off.

"Wh-what?" Hanna stammered.

"Sit down." Chance eased her to the ground and propped her back against the stone wall. Then he produced a knife and began cutting away the torn leg of her pants.

Tiny flickers of silver light twinkled in the undergrowth in front of Hanna and began to flit and flutter around the clearing—some kind of fireflies. Hanna watched them, distracted, while Chance worked. People began to arrive. The first two just materialized out of thin air in front of her. One of them was dressed in black leather and stared at her with a glowing red eye. He had his arm around Arastan, who wore her red medical tunic and trousers, and carried a red bag in one hand and something silvery in the other. As soon as they appeared, Arastan hurried to Hanna and laid a chill hand against her cheek as she began to snap out sharp questions in Talessanin.

Hanna blinked at her. "I don't . . ." she couldn't think of the next word she wanted to say, and the fireflies were so pretty and distracting. She focused on one of the silver sparkles and tried to follow it as it drifted through the air.

Two more people flashed into existence, one black, one red. The red one hurried to kneel by Hanna, and the black one helped his friend move the oozing body of the *kalakanek* out of the way. Hanna lost track of her firefly and began to notice stray details about the people around her. The man in red who was bending over her with a long needle had a large freckle next to his right eyebrow. The blond man in black had a red string tied around the end of one of his braids. Chance's teeth were very white. Jon still wasn't wearing a shirt, and the top two hooks of his pants were undone.

Where had Jon come from?

Narista was crying, and as Hanna looked at her, the fireflies began to swarm around her face.

"Narista," she mumbled, "the fireflies . . ."

"You see fireflies?" Chance asked sharply.

"Silver and blue," Hanna mumbled.

"That's not good," Chance said grimly. He started shouting in Talessanin.

The shouting faded to a strange buzz, and then everything went silent.

And dark.

And very, very cold.

Chapter 26

THE BRIGHT, CHEERFUL LIGHT SHINING through the bedroom window told Hanna it was late morning; maybe early afternoon. Memories of the previous evening twisted in her gut, and she squeezed her eyes shut tighter against the light. It was utterly inexcusable to have sunshine like that on a day like this. Darkness would've been more appropriate. A nice, heavy overcast. And rain. There should at the very least have been lightning. Maybe a good tornado. She was going to have to take that up with the management when she got up. If she ever got up. Maybe she could just stay in bed. Under the covers everything was warm, and soft, and safe. Mr. Bickles made a companionable lump next to her shoulder. If she got up, she'd have to deal with reality. With whatever the *kalakanek* had done to her body. And with what Jon had done to her heart. She wished she'd never met him. It would've been better. Or at least, it would've been easier.

She rolled over and buried her face in the pillow, pulling Mr. Bickles into the crook of her elbow. Her thigh ached a bit as she moved, but otherwise she felt only the kind of stiffness that having been asleep could account for. There should've been pain. Lots of it. Pain would've helped distract her from . . . other things. One would think getting mauled by a monster would at least provide some good, distracting, physical agony.

Life wasn't supposed to just go on as if nothing had happened. Not after a night like last night. If it *was* only last night.

Soft footsteps.

Not Jon! Please don't let Jon be here waiting for me to wake up again!

She didn't want to see Jon. Not now. Maybe not ever.

A gentle hand touched her shoulder. "Hanna?" Arastan's soft voice. Not Jon's. That was a small mercy, anyway. Still, it seemed reality was determined to suck her back in. Why couldn't it just go away and leave her alone?

Hanna rolled to her side and looked up at the medical adviser. "How many days have I been asleep this time?" she asked wearily. She supposed twenty years was too much to hope for.

Arastan gave her a sympathetic smile. "Only since last night. It is now nearly noon."

The medic quickly checked Hanna's vital signs with her scanner and then began an extensive examination in which she jabbed and tickled Hanna's extremities, checked her reflexes, had her watch a moving light, and instructed her to perform specific movements with various parts of her body. Finally, the medical adviser had Hanna sit in one of the cushioned chairs near the bedroom fireplace and pushed up the hem of Hanna's white nightdress to check the injury on her thigh. Hanna was surprised to find that the wounds from the *kalakanek's* teeth were completely healed; only a series of pale streaks and a slight dimpling in the skin showed where the bite had been.

"Does it hurt?" Arastan asked.

"A little," Hanna admitted. "Mostly when I flex the muscles there."

Arastan nodded. "The actual lacerations were only in the skin," she explained. "They didn't extend into the muscle layer, so they were easy to heal. But the venom did some damage to the muscle underneath as it was absorbed into your body. We think regeneration fluid injections will help the muscle continue to heal over time, but we really aren't sure."

Hanna rolled her eyes. "Because I'm a human."

"Well . . . yes," said Arastan. "And because we have very little information about the long-term healing of *kalakanak* bites." She cleared her throat and looked at Hanna for a moment, then moved to sit in the other chair.

"Hanna," she said after she was seated, "I have good news and bad news, as I believe you humans sometimes say."

Hanna shrugged. "Okay, let's have the good news first."

Arastan turned her hands palm up and held them out as if offering Hanna a gift. "It would seem," she said, "that humans have a previously undiscovered resistance to *kalakanek* venom."

Hanna's brow furrowed. "What do you mean?"

Arastan drew a deep breath and lowered her hands to her lap again. "I mean that you are most remarkably well recovered. Most people who have been bitten by a *kalakanek,* even as superficially as you were, do not survive. The venom contains several toxins, some of which affect the victim's nervous system. If treatment isn't given within the first few minutes, it's usually too late; the heart and lungs become paralyzed, and the patient dies. The only good thing about it is that another of the toxins acts as an anesthetic, so death is usually painless."

Hanna stared at her.

Arastan continued. "In those few who have survived, it was necessary to amputate the injured limb, and unfortunately there was always extensive damage to the nervous system, including diminished mental function, total or partial paralysis, and alterations in sensory function such as full or partial blindness, deafness, loss of tactile sensation, and so forth." She leaned back in her seat, spreading her palms again. "However, as far as we can tell, both from nerve scans while you were unconscious, and from the more practical examination I've just performed, your nervous system seems to have survived intact. I've never heard of a complete recovery before. But I've never heard of a human getting bitten before either. It would seem there is some component in your physiology that protected your nervous system from the worst effects of the venom—though clearly you were affected to some degree, since you said the injury didn't hurt, and you were having some visual hallucinations."

Hanna frowned. "The fireflies?"

"There were no fireflies," Arastan said. "They were an indication that the venom had reached your brain, which usually means death is imminent. We thought we had lost you. But here you are." She smiled and shrugged. "Our researchers are most interested in your case. There is, perhaps, a difference in the molecular structure of one of the neurotransmitters that . . ." she trailed off in a musing mutter of medical jargon.

Hanna took a deep breath and rubbed at her forehead with her fingers. "Okay," she said, "so the good news is that I'm alive and more or less intact. What's the bad news?"

Arastan's widening grin seemed entirely inappropriate for the giving of bad news. "Oh," she said, "the bad news is that if hearing the good news makes you want to go get good and drunk—which is what I might very well do if I had been attacked by a *kalakanek* and lived to tell the tale—it probably won't do you any good to try. You were given a large intravenous dose of a broad-spectrum anti-toxin in an attempt to neutralize the venom before the damage became too extensive. We're not sure now whether it did any good or not, but it's going to be in your system for several days before it wears off, and alcohol is one of its favorite things to filter out. The medical staff regrets any inconvenience this may cause you."

Laughing hurt less than Hanna would have expected. Arastan patted her on the shoulder. "Your maid has gone down to the main kitchens for a moment. I don't know if you'd prefer to summon her to help you dress first, but I'm sure your *Ehr* would be very grateful to see how well you've recovered as soon as is convenient for you. He waited to see you the whole time you were in the medical facilities last night and has been out in the sitting room since you were brought back here." Arastan smiled and slipped out through the sitting room door. Through the crack of the door, Hanna caught a glimpse of Jon sprawled in a chair in front of the sitting room fireplace.

Her *Ehr*, Arastan had called him. Hanna felt a gaping wound open somewhere deep inside her. He wasn't her *Ehr*. He belonged to Salenia. Probably he always had. She'd known it since the first time she'd seen them together, that night at the dinner party—midnight and fire, danger and desire. Would Jon just tell her right away, or would he think it kinder to wait until she felt better. Surely he wouldn't make her ask him about it. Hopefully, he'd just get it over with.

And there was no point in her delaying the inevitable either. A new robe made of shimmering deep blue silk hung on the back of the wardrobe door, and she slipped it on over her nightgown, grateful that her abdomen had healed to the point where she could dress at least that much without assistance. She stood for several long, pounding heart-beats with her forehead pressed against the cool wood of the sitting room door and her hand resting on the latch. Then she took a deep breath, twisted the handle, and pushed the door open.

Jon's chair was turned sideways to Hanna. He slouched there, long legs stretched out in front of him, head turned to gaze into the cold ashes of the fire he'd laid last night. He had acquired a clean shirt from somewhere but still wore the same trousers he'd worn to the play last night—a hundred years ago. One elbow was propped on the arm of the chair, and his chin rested on his clenched fist. His other hand rested on one knee, atop Hanna's sketchbook and a familiar narrow black box. He wasn't wearing her knife.

Hanna's heart collapsed in on itself.

"Hanna!" Narista's startled voice came from a seat near the tea table, where she'd apparently been nursing a cup of something hot and—had she been *crying*?

She lurched to her feet. "Hanna, I . . . I am so very sorry. About . . . about everything. I should never have . . ." Her voice trailed off as if she was uncertain how to finish that sentence.

Hanna followed her worried gaze back to Jon. He was looking at her now, his face flat and expressionless, his eyes dark, unreadable.

"Thanks be to the Sower." Chance stood by the French doors. He strode over and dropped to his knees at Hanna's feet, drawing a long, dangerous-looking dagger from one sleeve and offering it to her, laid sideways across his palms. "My lady, I failed you," he said solemnly, looking down at her bare feet. "I offer my life as recompense."

Hanna stared at him, confused. "What? Chance, you saved my life. Put that away."

Chance shook his head. The dagger remained across his palms. "I was your bodyguard. I should've been there. I thought you were settled in your rooms for the night, and I went to see what I could learn about the security irregularity. I didn't know you'd gone out again until one of the guards said he saw you crossing the courtyard with Narista. I came as quickly as I could, but . . ."

Hanna gingerly removed the dagger from his hands. "I never asked you to be my bodyguard," she pointed out. "And you certainly can't be expected to guard me if I sneak out the back way without telling anyone.

I can't even tell you how happy I was to see you. I really thought that thing was going to eat me."

Chance kept his gaze on the floor. "I really thought it *had*," he said softly.

"Well, it didn't. I'm fine. Really. Thanks to you. I couldn't ask for a better brother looking out for me." She sighed. "But it seems we've discovered yet another Talessanin knife ritual I don't know anything about. If I give this dagger back to you, can I trust you not to do anything rash with it?"

Chance studied her face solemnly, making sure she was serious. Then, slowly, his familiar, teasing grin spread across his face. "I would never dare defy a woman who would take on a *kalakanek* with nothing but a bit of a pointy stick, little sister," he said.

Hanna laughed despite herself and gave Chance a playful shove, knocking him off balance as he rose. Then she kissed his cheek. "Thank you, Chance," she said again as she returned his dagger. "Um . . . would you please tell Tomin I'd like to see him as soon as he has a few minutes? I have a favor to ask him."

Chance bowed and went.

Jon had risen from his seat during the exchange and was watching her. *She could drown in those eyes.* She needed to get this over with before she fell in any deeper.

He shifted the black box to one hand and held out her sketchbook with the other. "Narista said you were looking for this." His voice was low. Careful. Laden with some emotion Hanna couldn't put a name to.

"Did she?" Hanna cleared her throat. "What else did she tell you?" She spoke to Jon, but she looked at Narista as she said the words.

"Nothing," Narista murmured. "It was not my place to . . . to . . ." Her voice trailed off as she looked from Hanna to Jon and back. "I should go."

Hanna raised an eyebrow. "Stay. We need a chaperon." She didn't mean to sound bitter.

Narista blushed furiously and shot a longing look at the door. But she stayed.

Jon said softly, "Your sketches are lovely, Hanna. Thank you for allowing me to see." He raised the book a little more, offering it to her.

Hanna's feet wouldn't move. The thought of getting close enough to take the book from him made her feel light-headed. She wanted him to hold her, and kiss her, and call her Little Mouse. She wanted what he'd done with Salenia to not be real. But it *was* real. She'd been there. She'd seen it.

And he was never going to hold her like that again.

She rubbed at her forehead with her fingers. "You can just leave it on the side table."

For a breathless heartbeat he didn't move. Then he nodded and slowly laid the book on the table. His eyes followed his fingers as they trailed along the branches of the tree on the book's cover. "There is something I must tell you," he said.

Hanna couldn't speak. She could barely breathe.

He looked up. Stepped toward her.

She stumbled an involuntary half step back.

Jon froze. Looked down. Miserable. "I am sorry, Hanna. I did not mean to frighten you."

"I'm not afraid of you." Her voice was steadier than she expected. She folded her arms across her chest and let her gaze drop to the knife box in his hand. "Say what you have to say to me."

"Hanna . . ." Her name was a pleading caress. His empty hand rose slightly, reaching toward Hanna, then fell back to his side.

He cleared his throat and took one step closer. This time, Hanna stood her ground.

"You have granted me such an honor in allowing me to court you," he said. "You have made me laugh. You have given me a reason to wake in the morning, and a reason to dream at night. You have made me feel—"

He stopped, looking down again, and swallowed hard. When he looked up, the darkness in his eyes was unbearable. Hanna looked away, looked beyond him into the fireplace at the small, sad heap of ashes there.

"You have been good for me," Jon went on. "But Hanna, it has not been so good for you. I have courted you for only two weeks. A little longer. In that time, you have been taken from your home and your work. You have been abandoned, and insulted, and treated like an animal. And . . . and you have been nearly killed. Twice." He shifted a step closer to her, and again Hanna found herself backing away again. She couldn't look at him.

"Because of me," Jon said. "Dalathek took you to get to me. And now, security tells me someone intentionally removed the *kalakanek* from its cage and freed it in my garden. It was meant for me, Hanna. If Chance had not been there—" His voice cracked, and he swallowed hard. "It would have been too late by the time I arrived. It is not safe for you to be courted by me, Hanna. I make you a target. I put you in danger. How can I say I care for you if I allow these things to happen to you? If I cannot keep you safe?" Hanna glanced up at him. His face was raw, pleading. This time it was Jon who looked away. He held the black box out toward her. "I thank you for the honor of being allowed to court you, Miss Bradley," he said, his voice quiet and formal now, "but I feel it best at this time to return your knife and discontinue our relationship."

Hanna stared at him. An odd, disconnected feeling washed over her. "Your saying," she said slowly, "that you're returning my knife—that you're breaking up with me—for my own good?" Her disbelief showed in her voice. She heard it. He must hear it too. This wasn't what she'd expected him to say. Not at all.

Why had he said nothing about Salenia? Was he trying to protect their privacy? Trying not to hurt Hanna's feelings more than necessary? *Why?*

It didn't matter. One reason was as good as the other. The effect was the same either way. They were finished.

As if last night hadn't been enough to tell her that.

It was all too much. The play. Kissing Jon in the spotlight. Salenia's not-so-subtle insinuations in the shuttle on the way back. Jon's careful fingers sliding down Hanna's back, undoing her dress. "*Only once. . .*" The twin nightmares in the garden—which had been worse, seeing them together through the window or being hunted by the *kalakanek*?

And now *this*? He wasn't even going to be honest with her about his reasons for dumping her?

Maybe this was all her own fault for sending him to Salenia in the first place. Maybe she should have tried to fight for him instead. Or maybe this had been inevitable, and it was good they'd gotten it over with now, before she'd fallen in any deeper.

Whatever the case, it was too much, too fast, too intense. And she couldn't do this.

Jon took another step toward her, holding out the knife case. "Hanna—"

She didn't want to hear whatever he might say next. It was over; that was enough. She turned away from him, back toward the bedroom door. "You can just leave the knife on the table too."

"Hanna!"

The voice that stopped her wasn't Jon's, it was Narista's. Eyes wide, face pale, mouth hanging slightly open, she asked incredulously, "That's all? You're not even going to—"

Hanna cut her off. "No. I'm not. And neither are you."

"But, Hanna . . ." Narista sounded appalled.

"Last night," Hanna said softly, "I promised Jon that if he needed to return my knife, I wouldn't make a fuss about it. He has decided to return my knife. I'm going to keep my promise. And if you really want to be my friend, you'll respect my decision and stay out of this."

Narista gaped at her and began to say something else, but Hanna turned away. "Please go," she said. "Both of you. I'd like to be alone." She walked into her bedroom and shut the door without waiting for a reply.

PART TWO

Chapter
27

THE WORST OF THE WEEPING was over, Hanna thought, and a vague numbness had settled in by the time Tomin came looking for her. Hanna had showered and changed into a long gray t-shirt and pink sweatpants. She'd nibbled at some fruit and toast Susan had brought her. And she'd dragged her battered old suitcase out from the cupboard under the window seat where Susan had stowed it and set it, open, on the end of her bed. Mr. Bickles was tucked into the case next to the sketchbook in its carved wooden box, and Hanna was folding t-shirts when Susan knocked at the bedroom door to announce Tomin's arrival.

"Send him in," Hanna said. Her voice sounded overly abrupt, even to herself. She drew a deep, steadying breath and pulled another t-shirt out of the wardrobe.

Tomin pushed briskly past Susan and wrapped Hanna in an enthusiastic embrace. Then he pulled back and held her at arm's length looking her up and down, and grinning. "You really are okay," he said. "They told us you would be, but I found it hard to believe until Chance came and said you were up and about, and he'd spoken with you." He hugged her again. "I'm so sorry I couldn't come sooner. You and Jon made quite a splash at the Shakespeare performance, and they dragged me back into service over at the media relations office last night to help field all the questions. But don't worry, we didn't tell them very much. You're entitled to a little privacy." He shook his head. "And then with all the excitement over the *kalakanek*—"

"My lady!" Susan interrupted, sounding alarmed. "What are you doing?"

"I'm packing my things," Hanna said, keeping her voice flat and calm. She turned back to the t-shirt she'd begun folding. "Tomin," she said without looking at him, "would you be kind enough to arrange for a flutter shuttle to take me home as soon as possible. It won't take me long to pack." She made the last folds, tucked the shirt on top of the two others already in the suitcase, and looked over her shoulder to see Tomin and Susan both staring at her, open-mouthed.

Tomin recovered first. "What?" he said. "That's the favor you wanted to ask? No. Absolutely not. You can't go home now."

Hanna turned to face him. "Why not?" she asked. "You said I wasn't a prisoner. You said you'd take me home yourself any time I wanted to go. I want to go now."

"Of course you're not a prisoner." Tomin looked confused. "But why? What about Dalathek? It's not safe. Did Jon say—"

"It doesn't matter what Jon says," Hanna interrupted, her voice cold and brusque. "It isn't any of Jon's business what I do anymore."

"But Hanna—" Tomin began. He stopped, as Hanna picked up the black knife box that had been resting on the bed and dumped her courting knife unceremoniously out on the green velvet coverlet.

"I'm going home," she said.

Tomin's face clouded over, and his eyes flashed. "You asked for it back?" His voice was tight and held an undercurrent of fury. "Hanna, we talked about this. I asked you not to hurt him; not to give that thing to him if you weren't serious. You don't understand the things that man has lived through." He put his hands on his hips. "It's been what—a week? And you've already asked him to return it? What kind of—"

"It was Jon's decision," Hanna snapped. "Not mine.

"Jon's decision?" Tomin stared at her. "But that doesn't make any sense."

"You're welcome to take that up with Jon if you'd like. But I'm going home. Are you going to help me, or should I ask someone else to make the arrangements?"

The door chimes sounded. Susan went to see who had come. Tomin stood staring at Hanna, seemingly at a loss for what to say. Hanna went to the wardrobe for another shirt while he decided.

When she turned around again, Kamm was striding through the door waving a sheet of paper, a big smile on his face. "Hanna!" He sounded giddy. "You must see this!" He scooped her up in his arms and whirled her around, then set her back on her feet and planted a big kiss on her cheek. "You are looking remarkably well." He scanned her up and down one more time, then presented the paper to her with a flourish.

Hanna was caught completely off guard. She looked down at the page and had to blink a few times before it came properly into focus. It contained a densely packed collection of scrawling Talessanin print. There was no English. There weren't even any pictures to give her a hint. "Kamm," she said slowly. "You do know I can't read Talessanin, right?"

Kamm stared at her. Then he laughed self-consciously. "I'm sorry, Hanna. How foolish of me." He took the page back from her. "It's from the Chancellor of the Assembly. The resolution passed. Humans are officially designated as a sub-species of Talessanin and as such, are considered persons under the law and full citizens of the Empire Among the Stars." Hanna just stared at him. Kamm went on. "This is because of you, Hanna. You know that, don't you? I've been trying to make this happen for years. But you and Jon have put a face to the human question, and now it has finally happened. They even accepted the amendments Jon proposed when he spoke with the Council, which means humans who have been held as pets are now legally free citizens and are entitled to monetary compensation from their former owners."

"That's great, Kamm." Hanna's voice came out flat and unenthusiastic. She tried to perk it up a little and added, "Really, fantastic news. Thanks for telling me." She went back to folding her t-shirt.

Kamm looked a little deflated. "There are some less advantageous changes as well, of course, and there are lots of small details left to work out. Still, this is good news, Hanna. Very good news. I wanted you to be the first to know."

Hanna turned to face him. "I'm sorry. I really do think that's amazing news. I know it's a big deal, and I'm really glad all your hard work is finally paying off. I know humans will all be safer because of this, and I'm sure it will open up all kinds of opportunities for us, and I'm really incredibly flattered you wanted to tell me first. It's just . . . I'm having a really bad day, Kamm." She looked down at her hands. The t-shirt she'd been folding was a twisted mess. She shook it out and started over.

"But Hanna, don't you see?" Kamm said softly, "There's no reason now that you and Jon can't be together."

Hanna's heart seemed to stop beating for a moment, crushing in on itself. She stared at Kamm. His smile dimmed and turned into a look of puzzled concern. Her heartbeat resumed, a hard, almost brutal throb in her chest. "No reason," she said in a hoarse whisper, "except he doesn't want me anymore." She snatched the courting knife off the coverlet and flung it on the floor at Kamm's feet. Then she went back to packing.

Kamm's stiff, embroidered longcoat rustled as he bent down to pick up the knife. "Hanna," he said slowly. "I don't understand."

Hanna couldn't speak past the choking pulse in her throat. She just shook her head and kept packing.

After a moment, Tomin spoke. "She says it was Jon's decision," he said. "And she wants me to take her home."

"No." Kamm's voice was firm, and his hand caught at Hanna's arm, stopping her. "You can't go home now, Hanna. Dalathek is still out there."

Hanna looked up at him. This time her voice boiled up from inside her and came out sharp and bitter. "You know what happened to me, Kamm." Gently, but firmly, she peeled his fingers off her arm. "For me," she said slowly, deliberately, "Dalathek has been out there every single day of my life since I was seventeen. This isn't so very different." She turned back to her packing. "Send some guards to watch my house if you want. Maybe Dalathek will show up again if I'm there, and you can catch him. But I can't . . . I can't stay here, Kamm."

She looked down at the t-shirt she was holding and realized she'd folded it and refolded it three times already, and it still wasn't right. Susan gently removed it from Hanna's hands. "Please, my lady, let me do that for you."

Hanna snatched the shirt back, clenching her jaw against the tears that threatened to come again. "No, Susan." Her voice was rougher than she intended. "I'm not a lady. I keep telling you. And you are not my maid. I don't want a maid. And I couldn't afford to pay one even if I did." Hanna wasn't really prepared for the look of hurt in Susan's eyes as the maid turned away. She took a deep breath and spoke more gently. "But you are my friend, Susan. I hope. And I'd love for you to come visit me when you have time. I have a little guest room where you could stay. If you want."

Susan turned back, searching Hanna's face. A small, shy smile crept across her lips. "As your friend then, my lady," she said softly, "let me do this for you."

Hanna hesitated a moment longer, but then relented, and nodded her consent. "Only the things that are really mine, though, Susan. None of those gowns you like to dress me up in. I haven't paid for them, I don't have room to store them, and in my real life, there's nowhere for me to wear the things."

Susan frowned at her but nodded.

"Hanna," Kamm said quietly, taking her arm again. "I'm not going to use you as bait. You must stay here until we capture Dalathek."

Hanna shook her arm free of his grip and put her hands on her hips. "I *must*? You've just finished telling me I'm a free citizen of the Empire, Kamm," she said. "Did you mean that, or not?"

"I meant it," Kamm said firmly. "And I won't stop you by force if you insist on going. We can extend Jon's security system to include your property and provide security staff. But Dalathek is crafty. And the security here is better. I'm asking you, as my friend, as my *family's* friend, to stay, just a little longer. Please don't make me tell my daughter her friend with the chocolate cakes was killed by a madman when her father could've stopped it from happening. She's lost too much already."

Hanna gaped at him. She could think of nothing to say.

Kamm went on, his tone softening, but still urgent. "And what about the ball? It's in two days. Because of the timing, it's going to be seen as a celebration of citizenship for humanity. You are the face of humanity to so many of my people now. We need you to be at the ball. There are still so many issues to iron out for humans in the Empire and having you there would help keep the momentum we have gained so recently.

"Don't be ridiculous," Hanna snorted. "Nobody will care whether I'm there or not. The only reason anyone found me interesting was because I was dating Jon."

Tomin was the one who responded. "That might've been true at first, but I've been sitting in the media relations office all night and half of today. They want to know about *you* now, not about your relationship with Jon. It seems a minority rights group that's active in certain parts of the Empire has been using the fact that you were so easily mistaken for a Talessanin noblewoman to push the same-species agenda. Their campaign is what persuaded several of the Delegates in the Assembly to change their minds. And the story of your battle with the *kalakanek* has seeped out somehow during the night and is rapidly being turned into a symbol of the human battle against injustice. Someone even got a photo of the dead *kalakanek* before its body was burned. It hasn't had time to disseminate much yet, but it's really catching hold in the areas it has reached, and in a few more days it will be one of the top media stories. People don't survive a *kalakanek* bite. Except you." Tomin grinned. "I'm sorry, Hanna, but you've become a celebrity completely separate from Jon."

"But that's absurd," Hanna said with a nervous laugh. "Chance killed the *kalakanek*, not me. I'm nobody."

"That's not true, my lady!" Susan clapped a hand over her mouth as if to stop the quiet outburst. But since she was too late, she apparently decided to let the whole thing out. "You are much beloved among those who have lived as property," she said in a rush, "because you have the courage to stand among the Talessanin nobles as an equal. It's one thing to be *told* humans aren't inferior to Talessanins, but *seeing* it is different. Even the human ambassadors defer to the Talessanin nobles. You sit in the library and play *jennan* with the Empress. You order the Viper to leave, and he goes." She shot a glance at Kamm and swallowed hard. "You argue with the Imperial *Ehrat*. You are . . ." Her voice cracked and she stopped. She bowed her head meekly and added only, "It has been an honor to serve you, my lady," before she went back to folding Hanna's t-shirts.

"Please stay for the ball," Kamm said. "It really would make a great difference. And it would give us a few more days to find Dalathek."

"But . . ." Hanna said, flustered. She looked back and forth between Tomin and Kamm. Susan's hands had stilled, and Hanna was sure the woman was listening intently, but she didn't look up. Hanna cleared her throat. "My instructor in the finer points of Talessanin culture," she indicated Tomin, "informs me that proper Talessanin ladies do not attend balls without an escort. I no longer have an escort, and I don't have a father, or uncle, or brother to walk in with instead."

"Nonsense," Kamm said. "A family friend will do as an escort. If my brother is too foolish to take you himself, then you must allow me to escort you. Narista is attending with that fellow she brought to the play last night, so I find myself without a partner. And what better way to celebrate the integration of humans into the Talessanin race than for the Kanestelan *Ehrat* to attend the ball with our new human celebrity." He grinned at Hanna. "Please say yes."

A small gasp came from Susan's direction, and Hanna looked over to see Susan staring at her, eyes wide, hand pressed against her mouth.

Tomin tilted his head and eyed Hanna. "As your instructor in Talessanin culture, Hanna," he said slowly, "I would advise you to accept the offer. After ending a courtship, a Talessanin woman is generally perceived as more desirable if her next escort is socially superior to her former suitor, and as less desirable if her next escort is socially inferior. You are now a Talessanin woman, and the Imperial *Ehrat* is the only man in the Empire who wouldn't be talked of as a step down for a woman after ending a relationship with the Viper. Under the present circumstances, attending the ball with Kamm should establish you as the most desirable woman in the Empire —at least for now. You may find yourself with more admirers than you know what to do with."

Hanna scowled. "I don't want admirers, I want to go home and build canvases."

"On the other hand," Tomin continued as if he hadn't heard her, "there will be people who object strongly to you being given this honor, simply because you're human. Changing a law is not the same as changing the reality of people's attitudes and behavior. It would be interesting to see that friction play out—particularly since you're already viewed by many in the Empire as a surrogate for the human race. When pressure meets opportunity, do humans tuck their tails and flee, or do they step up to the challenge and take their rightful place in Talessanin society?"

Hanna didn't say anything for a few moments. Neither did anyone else. Finally, Hanna rubbed tiredly at her forehead and said, "Fine. You win. I'll stay. Thank you for your offer, Kamm, I'd be honored to attend your ball with you." Then she folded her arms, tilted her chin up defiantly and glared at each of her friends in turn. "But after the ball I'm going home, whether Dalathek has been dealt with or not. Even if I have to walk."

Chapter 28

THE TWO DAYS BEFORE THE ball were every bit as unbearable as Hanna had known they would be. It didn't take long for the denizens of the embassy to pick up on the fact that the Viper no longer wore a courting knife and report that fact to the media corps. According to Tomin, who came to check on her early that first afternoon, the news missed the morning packet flutter, but instead of waiting for the evening packet, some enterprising correspondent paid the captain of a supply transport with a mid-morning departure from the orbital station to drop data at the nearest trade hub. From there, the news was picked up by the communications network and had begun to propagate across the Empire by lunchtime.

Speculation followed rapidly in its wake. Who had dumped whom, and why? Had the Throne put a stop to the arrangement? Had the whole courtship been a sham publicity stunt to draw attention to the issues surrounding the human question? Had Hanna really been just another pet human who took advantage of the new law to abandon her owner? Why was she still in residence at the embassy? The official response from the media relations office, that it was a private matter between the Viper and Miss Bradley, did nothing to quell the gossip.

She kept to her rooms as much as possible, unwilling to face the gauntlet of whispers and stares that followed her down every corridor.

She couldn't bring herself to use the sketchbook Jon had given her, and she feared that if she went to the library she might run into his mother.

She didn't want to see anyone, and when Tomin came for her dance lessons, she sent him away, saying that if she didn't know the steps well enough by now, she never would. She couldn't get out of the interminable last-minute dress fittings, though. And she couldn't bring herself to send Tala away when her little friend came for a visit.

The two of them went into the cramped service kitchen, where Hanna showed the little girl how to make cinnamon rolls, which were declared to be even better than chocolate bundt cake. While the dough rose, they cut chains of hand-holding paper dolls and colored them with the new crayons Tala's father had purchased for her on a recent trip outside the enclave. Hanna taped the chains of little people to the wall above her sitting room fireplace and hoped the tape didn't ruin the paint. Tala's visit cheered her more than she'd have thought it could.

Strangely, Narista's visits cheered her too. At first, Hanna was afraid the woman would want to talk about what happened with Jon, but apparently Narista had decided to honor Hanna's request and stay out of it. Instead, she shared funny stories about the happenings at the embassy and elaborate descriptions of the preparations for the ball.

She stopped by again after dinner, which Hanna took alone in her rooms, using the excuse that she was too tired and sore from the *kalakanek* attack to join the others in the main dining hall. This time, Narista brought a *jennan* board along with more good-natured gossip, and Hanna started to think that maybe Jon's sister actually did genuinely want to be her friend. Not that it really mattered at this point.

Nighttime was the worst. In the dark, the nightmares came with a vengeance, leaving Hanna weeping on the bathroom floor, picking vomit out of her hair in the shower, and obsessively checking all the locks.

Again.

Just one more time.

Just to be sure.

Twice, she thought she saw Dalathek lurking in the courtyard outside her bedroom window—though of course it was just her mind playing tricks on her, and when she pushed the curtain back to look more closely, nothing was there.

Still, she was grateful for the particle field inside the walls of her rooms that Chance had assured her would prevent anyone from teleporting in or using the phase-shifting technology that allowed the Winds to pass through walls and other solid objects. She was glad to know the security codes to her rooms had been changed after the incident with the *kalakanek* so that only a few carefully screened members of the embassy staff could enter, even for cleaning and maintenance, without her express permission. And she was glad she'd been able to convince Susan that she didn't need to stay with her at night. Hanna had been handling the nightmares on her own for half her life. There was nothing Susan could do about them. The pain in Hanna's abdomen when she vomited had eased up considerably, and she preferred not to have an audience.

In the gray hours of dawn, she went for a walk in the courtyard gardens, thinking nobody else would be out so early. For the most part, she was right; the paths were deserted, and the fresh, cool air helped clear away the remnants of the night's troubled dreams. But then she rounded one of the large stone outcroppings and came upon a wide, open space paved in great slabs of smooth flagstone—and froze.

Apparently, the Nine Winds did their morning dagger drills in the courtyard before moving into the arena for sparring practice. And apparently on this particular morning, Jon had joined his old friends in their training again. Narista was right; watching warriors do dagger drills was fascinating. The movements were unimaginably slow, impossibly exact. It was like watching clouds drift through the sky, or shadows creep over grass tickled by a stray, gentle breeze—and yet the movements held an aura of power, of wild violence mastered and bridled to each warrior's will.

And if watching the Winds was fascinating, watching Jon was . . . mesmerizing. His muscles flowed under his skin—bare, but for his *lanat*—as he shifted his weight, ever so gradually, from his back foot to the one in front, simultaneously twisting at the waist with a smooth, restrained motion that kept the daggers balanced on the backs of his outstretched fingers from so much as wobbling. Little by little, he rotated his hands until the dagger grips settled onto his palms, shifted his sculpted body through a graceful, slow-motion pivot that brought both feet together, daggers crossed overhead in the gesture used to signal victory in the sparring matches—like the amen to a prayer offered in motion instead of words.

Hanna only realized she'd been holding her breath when it escaped in a small, awestruck gasp.

Jon's gaze flicked in her direction, and he flinched. One of his daggers glinted in the sun and clattered to the ground. Everyone in the courtyard turned to stare.

Blood rushed to Hanna's face, hot and roaring. She stumbled backward a few steps, then turned and fled behind the stone outcropping. Tears clawed their way up from her stomach, emerging as wrenching sobs, and she sat down hard on a bench, bending forward as a tide of dizziness rose and fell. A small, detached part of her mind tried to figure out exactly why she was crying. Was it the humiliation of him seeing her there? Women were supposed to spy on the men who were courting them, not the men who had dumped them to get back together with their exes. That was certainly part of it but not all. She wept for the loss of him. She wept for the pain of seeing him with Salenia. Some of it was a release of lingering terror from the *kalakanek*. And partly it was because she was just so very, very tired—of everything—and she desperately wanted to go home.

A gentle hand settled on Hanna's shoulder, and she flinched away as she looked up, thinking for a moment that Jon had followed her. But it was only Chance who settled onto the bench next to her. "Ah, little sister," he said, his voice a soothing croon, "you really care for him, don't you?"

Hanna slid away from him along the bench. "I'll get over it," she snapped, angrily wiping the tears from her face.

Chance shook his head. "You shouldn't have to. I don't understand this thing between the two of you. I've never seen Jon behave this way before." He looked musingly up at the sky. "For that matter, I've never seen him drop a dagger before."

"There isn't any 'thing' between Jon and me, Chance." Hanna said. "Not anymore. He gave my knife back. It's all just emotional cleanup at this point."

Chance shifted on the bench. "Why don't you fight for him, Hanna? I don't know why he gave the knife back, but maybe you could—"

Hanna cut him off. "I promised not to make a fuss. And fighting for him would only make it worse, Chance. Jon doesn't want me. He made a choice, and he didn't choose me. If I can accept that, why can't you?" She stood and wrapped her arms around herself. "And I mean no offense, Chance. Truly. You know I trust you with my life, right?" She couldn't look at him. "But if you really think it's necessary for me to have a bodyguard, do you think you could arrange for one who isn't my ex-boyfriend's best friend?"

Chance was quiet for a long moment, and Hanna looked up at him. As she'd feared, there was hurt in his eyes. But he blinked and nodded. "I imagine that is a little . . . awkward for you," he said, standing. "I'll make the appropriate arrangements."

When she got back to her rooms, Susan was shaking out some clothes that a servant had dropped off in a cardboard box. Someone had gone to Hanna's house during the night and brought her shoulder bag with her regular sketchbook and good pencils, along with a couple of pairs of jeans and several shirts without paint stains on them. One was the top she'd worn the time she'd gone to Jon's house to return his jacket, and he'd shown her the treehouse he was building. That was the first time she'd had a panic attack in front of him. The first time he'd held her cradled in his arms and called her Little Mouse.

The faint scent of *taless* seed spice she thought she smelled when she held the fabric to her nose was just wishful thinking, of course. She'd washed it twice since that night at the treehouse, and Jon obviously had better things to do last night—probably with Salenia—than poke through Hanna's closet. But she was grateful to whoever had done it, because being able to dress like herself, even if only in the privacy of her own room, helped her feel more grounded, and having her old sketchbook gave her something to draw in without having to use the one Jon gave her. It wasn't the same as going home, but in a way, it was the next best thing.

After lunch, Narista came again, coaxing Hanna out to soak up the warm afternoon sun on the private patio beyond Hanna's French doors. This time she listened, as Hanna haltingly told her about her life back home. About Tiffany and her crush on the UPS driver who delivered packages at her salon. About Rachel, who was a serious investment broker during the day and a bit of a small-town sorority girl on the weekends. About Mr. Purcell, the art buyer at the gallery where she sold her paintings. About Mrs. Bedella and her prissy tortoiseshell cat.

An hour after Narista left, Chance knocked on Hanna's door to introduce a burly, competent-looking security guard named Kinnen who, Chance assured her, knew his business and would take good care of her. She hoped he didn't get too bored waiting for her to leave her rooms.

Her most unsettling visitor was Kamm. His wasn't a long visit, as he'd really only stopped by to admire the hand-holding paper dolls and ask if Hanna might be willing to share her cinnamon roll recipe with the embassy kitchens for Tala. But the thoughtful way in which he studied her while she wrote down the baking instructions made her nervous, and the quiet solemnity with which he thanked her only made her pulse pound faster. Maybe it was just because he looked so much like his brother. Maybe it was because his air of calm dignity communicated power of a subtler, but no less potent, nature than the aura of danger that seemed to emanate from Jon. Whatever the reason, she was relieved when it was time to see him out.

Halfway to the door he stopped abruptly, and Hanna nearly collided with him as he turned back. His hands caught her shoulders, steadying her, and the intensity in his eyes stopped her heart.

He hesitated. Swallowed hard. Released her. "Forgive me, Hanna, I didn't mean to startle you. I only wondered . . ." He shook his head. "You and my brother—" He cut off as she took a quick step back, wrapping her arms protectively around her body.

"Jon made a choice." It came out too sharp. None of this was Kamm's fault; she shouldn't take it out on him. She scrubbed at her forehead with her fingertips. "I'm sorry. It's just . . ." The words tangled, refusing to line up in any way that might make sense.

"I know," Kamm said gently. His webbed fingers brushed the back of her hand, tangled gently with her own fingers as he drew them away from her face so he could look her in the eyes. He kept her hand in his as he stepped closer. *Too close.* Her heart pounded in her ears.

"It was Jon's decision," he said. "I know that." His other hand came up to brush against her cheek. "And he hurt you, I think. Forgive me, Hanna, I didn't mean to tread so clumsily on feelings that are still so tender. I only wondered . . . do you think there's any chance at all that you and Jon might—"

"No."

"Not ever?"

Hanna pulled away again, turning her back to him. Imperial *Ehrat* or not, she couldn't look at him. She didn't want him to look at her.

Behind her, Kamm shifted and drew a deep breath. "I'm sorry, Hanna. I shouldn't have asked. This must be difficult for you. I . . . I'm sorry."

She was still shaking when the door clicked open behind her, and then shut, and he was gone.

Chapter 29

PREPARING FOR THE BALL TOOK even longer than preparing for Kamm's dinner party had. Susan was practically beside herself as she pulled, and pinned, and twisted Hanna's hair into an elaborate arrangement that incorporated several long black feathers with small, deep red "eyes" at the ends like peacock feathers, and a number of red gemstones that winked and sparked among the looping braids.

It seemed to take hours just for Susan to apply the complex cosmetics to Hanna's face—the rich red lipstick; the smoky, shimmering eye powders; the spider web of intricately painted black filigree that spun outward from Hanna's eyes to drape like lace, across her cheekbones and up to her temples, spilling elegantly down one side of her neck to play in delicate whorls along her collar bone.

The thin black cord that circled Hanna's neck and held the large blood-red stone at the base of her throat was perfectly incorporated into the painted design, and matching stones hung suspended from Hanna's ears by scrolling twists of fine black wire.

Her gown was a work of art. Narrow strips of soft silk formed the bodice, interwoven to resemble the scales of a snake. The weave of the threads within the fabric created a subtle shift in color from black to deep red depending on the angle of the light. A blood-red silk underskirt shimmered through carefully draped, cascading layers of filmy, dark overskirt, and peeked out in startling glimmers when Hanna moved. It was a gown crafted to draw the eye when its wearer was dancing. It was a gown created for dancing with the Viper. Hanna hoped Kamm wouldn't mind too much that his date's gown was made to complement his brother's dress armor; there hadn't been time to have another dress made.

She needn't have worried. When she stepped into the sitting room after Susan announced the arrival of the Honored *Ehrat*, a smile spread across Kamm's face. "You are more beautiful every time I see you, Hanna," he said. "Everyone at the ball will envy me my companion." He'd traded his customary dark green diplomat's robe for a dignified black longcoat with *taless* leaves embroidered in silver down the lapels. An enormous, deep green stone in a highly ornate silvery setting hung from a thick chain around his neck, and Hanna wondered if it was some kind of mark of his rank. She didn't ask, though, just tucked her hand into the elbow of the arm he offered and stepped with him into the inevitable cluster of bodyguards waiting outside her door.

"Tomin has asked me to remind you," Kamm said conversationally as they strolled down the corridor, "that as my chosen companion for the evening, you take my status, socially. He sends you strict instructions not to offer a submissive greeting to anyone but my parents and cautions you to use a greeting of equals only with a very few people whom you know and like." He directed a friendly grin at her. "But honestly, Hanna, as the companion of the Imperial *Ehrat* you can greet people any way you want. You can fling your arms around them and kiss them or spit in their faces if you wish."

He chuckled at Hanna's startled expression. "I should probably mention, though, that there will be a number of human guests present, and they aren't likely to use Talessanin forms of greeting. It has become customary over the years for humans and Talessanins to greet one another on formal occasions with bows and curtsies. If someone does that, just nod your head at them and move on. None of them are as important as they think they are." He waved a dismissive hand. "But you won't need to worry about greetings of any sort from most of the people here. Only those who received a personalized invitation from me are likely to approach you in that way."

"Thank you," Hanna said softly, trying to smile, "I'll try to remember that."

"Tomin also asked me to remind you," Kamm went on, "that because I'm the host, my partner and I are expected to initiate the ball by dancing the first dance while the guests watch. He said to tell you he's arranged with the Master of Musicians for the first dance to be an *aylencanat*, because that's the dance you know best."

Hanna laughed nervously. "He told me all of that this morning. And the part before that with the *taless* seed. Don't worry, I remember." She glanced sideways at him, and said more softly, "I'll do my best not to embarrass you."

Kamm stopped walking and turned to face her. The bodyguards spread out down the corridor in both directions, giving the two of them at least an illusion of privacy. "I'm not the least bit worried about you embarrassing me, Hanna." Kamm's face was earnest, his tone serious. "I truly am only passing on messages from Tomin. Please don't think I meant anything else by what I said."

Hanna looked down, her cheeks warming. "I'm sorry," she stammered, flustered, "I didn't mean . . ." She wasn't sure how to finish that sentence, so she just stopped talking.

After a long, silent moment, she looked up again to see Kamm gazing at her, his head tilted a little to one side, a musing smile playing around his mouth. "I'll do my best not to embarrass you, either," he said softly when her eyes met his. "No matter how tempted I might be. I wonder why I never noticed before what a lovely shade of pink your cheeks turn when you blush." His smile turned into a grin as Hanna's blush deepened, but he didn't say anything else, just turned, and settled Hanna's hand more firmly into the crook of his elbow before continuing down the corridor.

Hanna managed to regain her composure before they ascended a flight of stairs and entered the comfortable drawing room where they were to meet with the rest of the Imperial family and their companions so they could all make their entrance together.

Narista and her escort had already arrived, and Narista had pushed the doors on the far side of the room ajar so she could peer out. She looked around as Kamm and Hanna entered, and excitedly motioned Hanna over to peek out with her.

The doors opened onto a wide balcony that sat above the main entrance to the ballroom. Stairs curved down from each side of the balcony to the floor below. When Hanna had played hide and seek there with Tala and Susan, she hadn't noticed that the walls on three sides could be removed, expanding the already huge room even further. Three levels of broad, colonnaded galleries rose up the sides of the expanded room, and the back wall of the ballroom was completely gone, extending the space out into the main courtyard, which was lit for the occasion with the same floating water lily lanterns that had illuminated Jon's back yard for his dinner party. Soft music drifted from one of the galleries, but it was almost drowned out by the muted rumble of many voices, like the grumbling of ocean waves. Except for the balcony outside the door, the entire massive space was seething with people.

Hanna's heart began to pound. In a little while, all those masses of people—there must be hundreds of them, possibly even thousands—would be staring at her.

She backed away from the door, blinking hard and pressing suddenly trembling fingers to her forehead, mindful not to damage Susan's careful scrollwork designs. A wave of dizziness washed through her, and her knees buckled. Kamm's arm wrapped around her waist as she swayed hard against him. He helped her to a nearby chair and knelt in front of her as she sat on the edge of the seat, shaking, her breaths coming in small, rapid gasps while the panic surged up inside her, hot, and blinding white.

"Hanna, are you all right? What can I do?" Kamm took one of her hands in his.

Hanna knew he meant the gesture to be reassuring, but it made her feel trapped, and she had to grit her teeth and force herself not to jerk away from him. "Sorry," she gasped, trying to make her breaths come more slowly. "Panic attack. Will pass. Just . . ." she squeezed her eyes closed. Trying to talk made it worse, so she stopped. Her heart throbbed in her throat, and the dizziness threatened to drown her.

She couldn't breathe!

"How can I help?" Kamm asked, taking her other hand. "Can I . . . can I get you some water? Or—"

"Stop talking, Kamm. And back off." Jon's voice. How long had Jon been there? Hanna clenched her teeth and leaned forward, trying desperately to stifle the scream that was building inside her. "You too, Narista," Jon continued softly. "Give her some space. She needs to concentrate. If you must do something, go find her some juice or one of those sweets she likes. Something with sugar in it. But save it for after. Leave her alone for now."

Kamm hesitated for several interminable heartbeats, then released both of Hanna's hands and stood, backing away. Some of the suffocating pressure went with him, and relief swept through Hanna. Without his interruptions, she was able to start counting in her head, measuring her breaths, forcing them to slow, feeling the pounding of her heart slow with them.

When she was sufficiently recovered, Hanna straightened in her seat and opened her eyes. Jon stood directly in front of her, several steps away. He was wearing his dress armor, as he had that night at his dinner party. The light shimmered over the scale pattern tooled into the leather and danced among the glossy black beads and feathers that had been worked into his warrior's braids. The war god embodied, she'd thought back then—but that night the impression had been spoiled by his crooked, boyish smile. Nothing marred the image tonight, as he stood with his arms folded, his face carefully blank, towering over everyone else in the room. "Better?" He asked softly, his face betraying no emotion at all.

Hanna nodded once. It was all the answer she could give him. Looking him in the face wrenched at something deep inside her. She glanced over at Kamm, who stood nearby looking far less threatening, and then down at her hands. "I'm sorry," she said. "That happens sometimes."

Kamm dropped slowly back to his knees in front of her. Hesitantly, he brushed the back of one of her hands with a fingertip. "I made it worse, didn't I? I'm sorry."

Hanna took his hand between both of her own and gave it a reassuring squeeze. "You were very kind, Kamm. You couldn't have known. And if I can just sit for a few more minutes, I'll be fine. Really. No harm done." The fingers of his free hand trailed along the back of one of her hands. Kamm's hands were smaller than Jon's, and less calloused, but strong and well-formed, and big enough to easily envelop hers. Concern was written in the tension between his drawn brows. His eyes were green; she hadn't noticed before.

"I didn't realize how hard this would be for you," Kamm murmured. "If you don't want to—"

"No, it's fine," Hanna said. "I need to do hard things. If I spend my whole life hiding because something might trigger an attack, then the fear wins." She took a deep breath and smiled at him. "The fear doesn't get to win. Not tonight."

The door to the corridor opened, and several green-clad servants entered carrying trays of refreshments, which they set on some of the side tables scattered around the room. Narista and her nervous escort went to find something to drink, and after a few minutes Hanna heard the soft thud of Jon's footsteps as he, too, withdrew. He wasn't wearing his working boots, she thought, or she wouldn't have heard him leave.

Kamm stayed where he was. "You're looking better," he commented after a moment, though his voice was still uneasy, and his green eyes still scanned her face.

"I'm fine, Kamm." She touched a finger to the small line that had formed at one corner of his mouth. "You can stop frowning at me now." His mouth curved into a self-conscious half-smile, and the line disappeared.

"Are you truly?" He asked seriously. "Your injuries are not—"

"I'm fine. The knife wound hardly hurts at all anymore except a slight twinge now and then, and the *kalakanek* bite only burns a little when I've been standing too long. I was just caught off-guard by the size of the crowd. I hadn't expected so many. Where did they all come from?"

Kamm shrugged. "Many of the guests have been staying at my other embassies or in accommodations out on the orbitals. There isn't room for all of them to stay here." He looked down at their joined hands. "It was the crowd then?" he asked. "I thought perhaps it was me—something I did." He looked back up at her. "You're not frightened of me, are you Hanna?" There was a hint of pleading in his voice, and something in his eyes demanded an honest answer, not a careless dismissal.

Hanna took a moment to consider. "Yes, I am," she said. "Just a little. You're the Imperial *Ehrat*, Kamm. It would probably be foolish for me not to be a little bit frightened of you. And . . ." she looked down. "You're a man. One I don't know very well. And that always frightens me a bit."

She shrugged and looked back into his eyes. "But you're also my friend, and I've never seen you be anything but kind. I trust you."

Kamm studied her face for a moment. Then he smiled—a real smile this time. "Thank you, Hanna," he said softly. "That is enough for now."

The door opened again, and voices drifted in from the corridor, then hushed. Hanna looked up to see who had come in.

The Emperor and Empress stood just inside the drawing room, with Lord and Lady Trakanaleth close behind. As Hanna watched, Salenia glided through the doorway and stopped next to her parents. All of them stood staring at Kamm and Hanna.

Hanna looked at Kamm. "You should probably get up," she whispered. "I don't think the Imperial *Ehrat* is supposed to kneel in front of anybody."

"It is a little unorthodox," Kamm whispered back, "but under the circumstances it seemed the thing to do." He grinned and winked at her, then slowly rose and went to greet his parents.

Something brushed Hanna's shoulder, and she looked up to find Jon offering her a small crystal cup shaped like a tulip. Her fingers brushed against Jon's as she reflexively reached to take it, and she hoped he'd attribute the trembling of her hand to the remnants of her panic attack. "Thank you," she said quietly and went a little bit numb as her eyes met his. Jon nodded, and kept looking at her, but didn't say anything.

The Emperor's voice rose suddenly above the murmur of other voices in the room. Hanna's translator supplied, " . . . and as Jon is unattached, I am certain he would be glad to escort Salenia." A muscle in Jon's jaw twitched as he looked over to where Salenia waited for him, but otherwise he didn't move.

Hanna looked down at her hands, sipping mechanically from the crystal cup. She couldn't identify the beverage, but it was sweet, and tasted of apricots and some kind of spice she couldn't name. She wondered briefly about its alcohol content, knowing she needed to be careful to keep her mind clear tonight—but then she remembered what Arastan had said about the antitoxin remaining in her system for several days and sucked down a long swallow of the concoction. She wouldn't be able to get drunk tonight, even if she wanted to.

"Are we all ready, then?" the Empress asked.

Chapter 30

EVERYONE IN THE DRAWING ROOM drifted toward the balcony exit. Hanna rose to meet Kamm, who looked her up and down, a worried expression on his face. "Are you recovered?" he asked. "We can wait a little longer if you're not ready."

Hanna took a deep breath. "I'm ready." She smiled to prove it. Kamm smiled back and offered her his arm. He waved a signal to a servant, who pushed the balcony doors open, and the music in the ballroom ended with a flourish, as the rumble of voices dwindled into silence.

The Emperor and Empress walked out first, pausing on the balcony for a moment before descending the steps to the floor below; a massive rustle drifted up to the drawing room as everyone in the crowd bowed and curtsied.

Since Kamm, as host, would go last, Jon was next in order of precedence, and he stepped resolutely toward the balcony. He stopped just inside the doorway, turning to look back, and his eyes met Hanna's. An emotion flickered across his carefully guarded face, gone too quickly for Hanna to understand what it might've been, but leaving her feeling raw and unsettled nonetheless. Jon's gaze dropped away from hers, and he held his arm out for Salenia as he turned back to the balcony doorway. When the couple emerged onto the balcony, a susurrant murmur hummed and whispered through the crowd.

The sound subsided again as Narista walked with her escort out onto the balcony and down the steps to the floor below, and the silence persisted while Lord and Lady Trakanaleth made their entrance.

Kamm held his arm out to Hanna with a reassuring smile. "It will be an *aylencanat*," he reminded her.

"I'll be fine; you'll be there with me." Hanna grinned shakily and tucked her hand into his elbow. "And you've already proven you can catch me before I hit the floor."

Kamm laughed and led Hanna out onto the balcony. For a moment, the breathless silence hovered in the air. Then, a wave of voices washed through the crowd again, growing in volume and resonance as everyone strove to make themselves heard over the noise. Hanna expected the sound to die down again as she and Kamm descended the curving stairs, but it continued to build until it seemed a tangible thing, boiling through the massive space, prodding at Hanna as she moved, step by step, down toward the sea of people. Kamm brushed the back of her hand with his reassuring fingers as they reached the bottom of the stairs. A path had been cleared from the stairs to a low dais in the center of the colonnaded gallery on that level, and as Kamm led her down it, Hanna heard snatches of whispers, most filtered through her translation module.

" . . . courting knife?"

" . . . brother's woman!"

" . . . dares reach so high . . ."

" . . . would his wife have thought?"

" . . . pretty enough, but . . ."

" . . . scandalous . . . "

As they approached the dais, Hanna became aware of the others in the Imperial party watching them. The Empress's gaze was intense and thoughtful, as if planning her next move in a close game of *jennan*. Narista wore a welcoming smile. Jon's face was carefully, utterly blank. Salenia and her mother both looked slightly ill, and the Emperor and Lord Trakanaleth wore matching expressions of sour, angry disapproval. Kamm strolled past them all, seeming not to notice, and led Hanna to the front of the platform, where an ornate brazier rested on a tall stand. Kamm gave Hanna's fingers a gentle squeeze and then raised one hand in the air, commanding silence and attention, as his other hand came to rest in the small of Hanna's back. Quiet descended on the room like an expectant fog.

When Kamm spoke, a hidden amplification system picked up his words and carried them out over the breathless crowd. "My friends," Hanna's translator intoned, "I wish to extend to you my humble gratitude for your assistance in making welcome my parents, Kieransalanesten of House Kanestelan, Empress Among the Stars and her Imperial Consort, the Emperor, on their first visit to this magnificent planet."

A staggering roar of sound—voices, and clapping, and the stomping of feet—erupted from the crowd as the Empress and Emperor stepped forward, smiling, and raising their hands in greeting. From the corner of her eye, Hanna caught the movement of a small, remotely operated camera gliding past the edge of the dais. How many people would be watching this event as the camera's recording rode the packet ships to the relay stations and spread from there out among the distant stars? Kamm raised his hand again, and silence settled over the guests once more.

He continued. "It is also my pleasure to officially announce that the Grand Assembly, with the ratification of the Throne, has established the people of Earth as full citizens of the Empire Among the Stars."

Another roar rose from the crowd, only slightly less enthusiastic than the one before.

Kamm signaled one more time for silence, then raised both arms out to his sides, palms up. "On this historic occasion, I have invited a citizen of Earth, my very good friend, Miss Hanna Bradley, to officiate as we offer tribute on behalf of this great company, as a symbol of our gratitude for the visitation of the Throne, and the joining of humanity with the Talessanin people and with the Empire Among the Stars."

This time there was only a faint ripple of shifting and quickly hushed whispers among the gathered guests. Kamm held his pose, arms outstretched, as Hanna stepped up to the ornate brazier. She carefully picked up the small, round seed that lay nestled in the curve of a silver *taless* leaf and, cupping it in both hands, raised it high above her head—an acknowledgement of something higher, Tomin had explained, of something beyond current understanding. She touched it to her forehead—to clear the mind. She touched it to her lips, inhaling its sweet, spicy scent—to discipline the tongue. She held the seed over her heart—to dedicate the life. Solemnly, she set the seed on the grate at the center of the brazier, careful not to burn her fingers, and waited respectfully until the white, spicy smoke began to curl upward, taking the tribute of the gathered guests with it to drift among the stars. Behind her, Kamm clapped his hands loudly three times, and somewhere above them, the musicians began to play again, this time in the slow, lilting rhythms of an *aylencanat*.

Kamm stepped up beside Hanna and, smiling, took her hand. The two of them walked forward, one on each side of the brazier, their joined hands passing through the smoke of the offering, and the guests drew back, flowing up into the galleries and out into the open court-yard as the *Ehrat* and his companion stepped out among them. By the time Kamm and Hanna reached the center of the great ballroom, a wide, empty space of dance floor awaited them. Kamm drew Hanna into the slow, swaying motions of the dance, his free hand sliding to the small of her back instead of taking her other hand as she expected.

She laid her free hand against his shoulder and leaned in close to whisper, "Did I do it right?"

"Perfectly," Kamm said softly. "Thank you, Hanna." He shifted his hand on her back to hold her there, close to him, and Hanna's cheeks warmed. She looked up in time to see Kamm's smile turn into an impish grin that made her blush even harder. She felt, rather than heard, his low chuckle, and then he shifted his hand again, giving her a little more distance. "Forgive me," he said. "I am in an exceptionally good mood tonight, and I fear it is making me reckless. Seeing you offer the tribute was such a fitting culmination to all these years of work."

Hanna smiled. "It was rather gratifying to hear such a loud cheer when you made your announcement, even though some of the guests didn't look very happy about it."

"It was, wasn't it?" Kamm's shoulder moved beneath Hanna's fingers as he gave a little shrug. "Though I confess I did skew the guest list somewhat in a pro-human direction. And I asked some of the more vocal supporters to stand in strategic locations among the guests to en-courage participation."

"You did?"

Kamm looked sheepish. "Many people's opinions are easily swayed in the direction of what they believe is popular. The video feeds of this evening will be distributed all over the Empire, quite rapidly unless I miss my guess, and I wanted them to present a strong image of enthusiasm toward humanity."

Hanna's mouth dropped open. "You mean you rigged it?"

"A little," Kamm admitted with a wry smile. He shrugged again. "I am a politician, Hanna. I fight different kinds of battles than my brother does, but I do try to use all the weapons available to me as effectively as I'm able."

Hanna thought that over. "Is that what I am, Kamm? A weapon to be used?"

Kamm looked down at her, his eyes troubled and a little sad. "I'd prefer to think of you as a friend and ally," he said, "with your permission."

Hanna studied his face, trying not to lose the rhythm of the music in the process. "I think I'd like that," she said softly.

Silence settled between them, and Hanna looked past Kamm's shoulder as they swayed and turned. Kinnen stood in the ring of people edging the dance floor, along with Kamm's bodyguards and Chance. On the dais, the Imperial party was regally ensconced in comfortable sofas and chairs that had appeared along with small tables bearing trays of food and drink. Salenia sat off to one side by herself. Where was Jon? Surely he wouldn't neglect his lover, even if they hadn't yet made their courtship public. Then she spotted him near the front of the platform with a little girl in a very fancy dress perched on one shoulder.

"Kamm, look!" she exclaimed. "Tala has joined us."

Kamm's green eyes twinkled. "Yes. She was too shy to walk in with us in front of so many people, but Tala isn't one to miss a party."

Tala saw them looking at her and tossed them a kiss just as the music of the dance drew to a close with a flourish.

Kamm removed his hand from Hanna's back, and the two of them inclined their heads toward each other, ending the dance. Hanna turned to move back toward the platform, but Kamm stopped her, his fingers tightening around her hand. "Will you dance the next with me too?" he asked a little breathlessly.

Hanna's brows rose. "Isn't it improper to dance two in a row with a woman you aren't courting?"

He shrugged. "A little." Then his impish grin spread across his face again. "Come be a little improper with me, Hanna. Please?"

Hanna just looked at him for a heartbeat longer, then smiled and shrugged. "All right. Since you asked so nicely."

Kamm waved again at the musicians, and they struck up a tune with a lively, frolicking rhythm. Hanna laughed aloud at Kamm's grin as he caught hold of her waist with both hands, whirled her into the air and down again, and began the twisting, spinning dance, careening with her around the edge of the circle of onlookers. Halfway around, he inserted a broad, flourishing gesture to invite his guests to join in the dance, and in a few more moments, laughing couples were whirling and spinning in a great, revolving loop down the length of the ballroom.

Kamm left a whisper of a kiss on Hanna's cheek when he settled her onto one of the sofas on the dais at the end of that dance and went off to dance the next with his mother. Narista's escort, whose name Hanna still couldn't remember, offered Hanna a bow, blushed deeply, and asked her to dance. Hanna thanked him, but declined, explaining that her injury was troubling her, and promised to dance with him after she'd rested a little. He seemed relieved rather than disappointed and went to ask Salenia to be his partner instead. Hanna wondered why Jon wasn't dancing with Salenia but spotted him after a moment on the dance floor with Tala.

She shifted on the sofa, trying to find a position that made her leg throb a little less urgently, and looked around for something to drink. Her gaze caught on Lord Trakanaleth's face, and her breath caught in her throat. The man's expression vanished almost as soon as Hanna saw it, but it had been unmistakable, and it left her feeling cold and more than a little bit afraid. It went beyond disapproval or contempt. It was hatred—pure, naked, unadulterated hatred.

As she watched, Salenia's father leaned toward the Emperor, who was sitting in the high-backed chair next to him and said something. The Emperor turned to look at Hanna. He didn't bother to hide his disdain as his eyes moved down her body, shrewd and penetrating. Hanna felt exposed. She felt as if the man saw every stray hair, every flaw in her complexion, every ounce of cellulite, every extra curve that had ever made her feel self-conscious. She felt like an animal at auction, judged and found unworthy of even the bother of bidding on. The Emperor said something to his friend, and they both laughed and went back to watching the dancers. But every now and then, out of the corner of her eye, Hanna saw Lord Trakanaleth turn his head to look at her. And every time, it made her blood turn to ice.

A great surge of relief washed through her when the dance ended and the musicians burst into the flurry of wild, running music that signaled the beginning of a *berantelcanat*. It was the dance Jon had performed with Tala at the dinner party, in which each man had to capture a dodging dance partner, and that meant she didn't have to sit and wait for someone to ask her to dance or to work up the nerve to ask someone herself. Out on the dance floor, the couples from the previous dance parted into a whirling, twisting mass of laughing men and women, pursuers and pursued. A few people worked their way to the edges of the crowd, and emerged, breathless, to sit on the chairs and sofas that edged the dance floor, separated into groupings by folding privacy screens. Others, like Hanna, rose and moved toward the dance floor, waiting for an opening in the chaos before plunging in.

As Hanna hesitated on the verge, Tala's high-pitched squeal pierced the growing din. "Miss Bradley!" The child waved enthusiastically as she emerged from the press, perched once again on the shoulder of her tall uncle. His eyes met Hanna's, and for half a heartbeat she forgot how to breathe.

Then a hand clamped down on her wrist, and she spun back as a laughing Narista drew her into the pandemonium on the dance floor. She soon found herself giggling along with Narista as the two of them wove in and out between other twisting, dodging bodies. Couples formed and moved out to stomp and whirl through the complicated steps of the *berantelcanat* in a great ring around the swarm in the center. Narista spotted someone she knew and winked over her shoulder at Hanna before she tapped the young man on the arm. He grinned when he saw Narista and made a grab for her hand. Narista dodged sideways but collided with a lady in a blue dress and momentarily lost her balance. The young man caught her flailing hand and laughed triumphantly as he steadied her. Narista directed a sheepish grin at Hanna, as her new dance partner whirled her up into the air and down, and then drew her off to join the ring of dancers.

Hanna felt movement behind her and slipped sideways, glancing over her shoulder as she dodged. A tall man with blond warrior braids grinned back at her. Why did he seem familiar? She grinned back and ducked behind a broad man in an unfortunate orange longcoat, then twisted away again as that man, too, tried unsuccessfully to capture her hand. An arm wound around her waist, and Hanna gasped, startled, as she was jerked back against someone behind her. Tomin had said the men wouldn't grab anything but a woman's hand in this phase of the dance. She twisted in the man's grasp as he snared her hand and turned her to face him, holding her as if they were dancing, but pressing too close, too hard, crushing her against his body. Lord Trakanaleth smirked suggestively and slid his hand down her back much too far for comfort or courtesy.

"Get your hands off me," Hanna hissed. She squirmed and tried to pull away from him, but his grip was iron.

His smirk turned into a grinning leer, and he laughed. "You are a spirited little thing, aren't you?" Then he leaned down to murmur, "Perhaps when the Kanestelan men are finished passing you around, I'll ask for the loan of you."

Hanna pushed at him again, but he only chuckled. She brought her knee up as hard as she could into the man's groin, and his grip loosened at the same time his face went pale.

She wrenched away, flailing as she lost her balance, and crashed into someone behind her. A large hand closed around one of hers, steadying her, and she looked over her shoulder to see whom she'd run into.

The blond warrior grinned down at her, lifting one hand to push back an unruly braid tied with red string. That's where she'd seen him before—he was in the garden the night of the *kalakanek* attack. But he wasn't the one who had caught her hand. She turned to see who had and found herself face to face with Jon.

Her heart jumped into her throat, and heat rushed to her cheeks.

Jon's face was blank. Unreadable. "Are you all right?" His voice was as void of emotion as his face.

She nodded mutely and glanced down at their joined hands. Was she going to have to dance with him?

"Forgive me," he said. He looked over her head, scanning the milling crowd, then released her hand and gave her a small shove that sent her stumbling sideways again. Another hand closed on hers as she caught her balance, and she looked up into Kamm's concerned face.

"Are you unwell?" he asked, drawing her closer to him. "You look rather pale." He looked over her head in the direction she'd come from, and his brow furrowed. "Did Jon . . ."

Hanna shook her head. She really didn't want to talk about what had just happened. "I tripped," she said. "Sorry." She looked down to where Kamm's hand cradled hers. "Did you want to dance with me?" Kamm scrutinized her a moment longer, as if to make sure she was really okay, and then smiled and spun her into the air.

By the time the *berantelcanat* ended in a flourish of music and a whirl of colored skirts, Hanna could laugh again. She was relieved, though, when the blond warrior, whom Kamm introduced as the new Commander of the Nine, came to ask her for the next dance before she had to go sit down on the dais with Lord Trakanaleth and the Emperor. Hanna supposed she should've recognized the man from the sparring as well as the garden, but he'd been farther away then, and she'd had eyes only for Jon. Three more of the Winds danced with her before Kamm came to claim her again. By then her thigh was burning, and she asked if he'd sit with her instead. Kamm obligingly offered her an arm to lean on and led her back to a sofa on the dais, where he sat with her through two dances before his mother sent him off to dance with Lady Trakanaleth, who seemed out of spirits. Did Lady Trakanaleth know her husband groped other women when he danced with them? But maybe he did that only with human women, whom he didn't consider to be actual people.

As soon as Kamm was gone, the Empress directed a penetrating gaze at Hanna. "Miss Bradley," she began, "I wonder if—"

She cut off, arranging her expression into a pleasant smile as her husband joined her on the sofa, and Lord Trakanaleth eased himself into a nearby armchair. The Empress exchanged pleasantries with the men, and then turned her gaze out to the dance floor, seeming to have forgotten whatever she'd been about to say to Hanna. Neither of the men greeted Hanna; they just leaned back in their seats and stared at her, the Emperor with a scowl and a grim, pinched mouth, and Lord Trakanaleth with a look of predatory speculation.

Only a little bit longer, Hanna reminded herself. *And then I can go home.*

Chapter

31

HANNA JUMPED, STARTLED, AS A hand closed on her shoulder from behind.

"Sorry." Narista smiled sheepishly and waited while Hanna's artificial blood settled before continuing. "I wondered if I could speak with you privately for a moment."

"Of course." Hanna looked up at Narista and then around at the churning mass of people. "Is there somewhere we could go?"

Narista smiled. "Follow me." She plucked two crystal lilies filled with pale pink liquid off a tray and led the way down the gallery to the stairs at the end.

The climb to the third story gallery brought back the ache in Hanna's leg, but she was grateful to get away from the men on the dais. The high gallery was nearly deserted, and fresh air blew in through open doorways that led out at intervals to broad balconies overlooking the courtyard. Even with the back wall open to the night, the room below was filled with the kind of oppressive stuffiness that resulted from too many bodies in too small a space, and the cool breeze on this level began to release some of Hanna's tension as Narista led her out onto one of the balconies.

Vines climbed up the wall outside and trailed over the railing. Delicately carved wooden benches sat with their backs against the wall on either side of the doorway, facing out into the night. It was a perfect spot for stargazing. Hanna sank onto one of the benches, and Narista settled next to her, handing Hanna one of the pink cocktails.

"So, what was it you wanted to talk about?" Hanna sipped tentatively at the stuff in the crystal lily. Strawberry. The taste conjured up a memory of strawberry slushies and popcorn, and Jon sitting on the end of her couch helping her change the batteries in her TV remote. A knot formed in her stomach.

"Not a thing," Narista said with a smile. "I just thought you looked like you needed to get away for a little while."

Hanna couldn't help smiling back at her. "You were right. Thank you, Narista. Parties aren't really my thing."

"Unless," Narista brushed at something on her dress, pointedly not looking at Hanna, "you happened to want to tell someone all about your secret courtship with the Imperial *Ehrat*."

Hanna gaped. "My what?"

"It's the latest rumor," Narista's eyes sparkled with amusement. "Someone probably found out about Jon and Salenia, and it got mangled in the telling and retelling, but the story is that Kamm has been secretly courting you too, and he has stolen you away from Jon. After all, you did have dinner with him while Jon was away, and when you danced a second with him tonight, that proved it." She laughed merrily. "Isn't it delicious?"

Hanna stared at her. "Oh yes," she said, her voice dripping sarcasm, "because after getting dumped by the Emperor's assassin stepson, the smart thing for a girl to do is jump straight into a rebound relationship with the Imperial *Ehrat*." She scoffed. "What kind of idiot do people think I am?"

Narista shot her a defensive scowl. "There's nothing wrong with Kamm. You don't have to talk about him like that."

"I didn't mean it that way." Hanna sighed and rubbed at her forehead. "You're right. There is nothing at all wrong with Kamm. He's smart, and gorgeous, and wealthy, and powerful, and he's a loyal son and brother, and a devoted father to Tala—who is absolutely darling, by the way. I've even seen glimpses of a sense of humor that pops out when he forgets he's being serious. I'm sure he could have any woman he wanted."

"But not you?"

"It's just a silly rumor, Narista. There's nothing to it."

"Because you're not over Jon."

"Because . . ." there were so many reasons Hanna didn't even know where to begin. "For one thing, Kamm would obviously never be interested in someone like me." What man worth having would? Jon certainly wasn't. But she didn't want to talk about that, so she forced a grin and nudged Narista with her elbow. "And for another, his wife will have to be empress. Can you see me as empress? I'd have a panic attack every time someone looked at me sideways. And imagine trying to convince the citizens of the Empire that a human empress was a good idea? They only just decided we qualify as *people*."

Narista shrugged. "If he doesn't marry *somebody*, his sister will have to be empress. You'd make a much better empress than I would. You might have panic attacks, but I have a tendency to jump to the worst possible conclusions about people. That's not a good trait in a ruler. And I can be rather a vengeful sow sometimes." She glanced sideways at Hanna. "I once stuck a dead mouse on a perfectly nice woman's door with a knife just because she didn't have fins."

She sipped pensively at her cocktail. "And as far as the other thing goes . . . well . . . it might not be as difficult as you think. A lot of the non-Talessanin species don't see much difference between Talessanins with fins and ones without; they just didn't want to get involved in what they perceive as an internal Talessanin ethnic issue. A lot of the Talessanin population will follow the Empress on this—if she accepts humans as Talessanins, so will they. Some of them more readily than others, I'll grant you, but the tide there has probably turned with Mother's ratification of the Assembly resolution. And there's a growing faction in the Empire that might actually *welcome* an empress who isn't quite exactly Talessanin in the traditional sense, because they'd see her as a voice for the minority peoples inside an overwhelmingly Talessanin power structure. You might be surprised how much support you'd find. This rumor about you and Kamm is certainly being taken seriously."

"That's ridiculous." Hanna's brows drew together. "But it might explain why your father was glaring at me like he wanted to see me dead."

"My father? I don't think he'd have heard that rumor yet—though he did see you dance the second with Kamm. He looked angry?"

"You didn't notice? I thought that was why you came to rescue me." Hanna shivered. "He wasn't as bad as Lord Trakanaleth, though. I know he's a friend of your family, but . . . well, I'm just glad I'm going home tomorrow, that's all."

Narista shifted on the bench. "He can be a bit sour sometimes," she said. "And I'm not surprised if he hasn't been friendly toward you. He hasn't cared much for humans since his brother got banished because of that human girl. I think that's why he's kept a pet human all these years." She shrugged. "Of course, now he'll have to let her go. And pay her. Maybe he blames you for that."

"Wait," Hanna said. "His brother got banished because of a human girl?"

"You didn't know? That's how Jon became Commander of the Winds. Jon caught Dalathek with a human girl or something and challenged him. Dalathek was my father's best friend ever since they were children, so my father kept Jon from killing Dalathek and banished him instead. But apparently, all the bother was because Dalathek was with a human, and Jon caught him. It seems kind of ironic now. I guess I thought someone would've mentioned it to you."

"Dalathek?" Hanna gaped at Narista. "Dalathek is Lord Trakanaleth's brother?"

"Well, yes." Narista shrugged. "That's how my parents met, actually. After Jon's father died, my mother wanted to get out of the palace for a while—my grandmother was empress at the time, of course, so Mother's duties didn't hold her quite as strongly then. She went to stay with her friend, Lady Trakanaleth, who had recently married. And Lord Trakanaleth's brother, Dalathek, was staying there too, along with his friend, who is now my father. You see? Anyway, Lord Trakanaleth is a bit sensitive on the subject of humans because of his brother. But he'll just have to get over it." She frowned. "Hanna, are you all right?"

Hanna felt sick. *Jon had dumped her for her rapist's niece?*

But that wasn't fair. They had history. And Salenia couldn't help who her uncle was. She sucked in a deep breath, trying to steady herself. "Narista," she said, "Dalathek kidnapped that human girl, and kept her drugged, and raped her. Repeatedly."

"What?" It was Narista's turn to gape. "But . . . Are you certain?" Her cheeks paled in the moonlight.

"Very certain. If you don't believe me, ask Jon. Or Kamm."

"But . . . nobody said anything about . . ." Narista stood and walked to the balcony railing. After a few minutes she turned around. "I was quite young at the time. I guess they wouldn't have told me something like that." She looked shaken.

Hanna coughed out a bitter laugh. "Don't look so shocked, Narista. You knew about Lord Trakanaleth's pet human. I don't imagine he keeps her locked up and drugged so she can't move, and I don't know, maybe he's nicer to her, but how much difference is there, really? Do you think she *volunteered* to be his pet?"

Narista slowly walked back to the bench and sat down. "It was just the way things were," she said softly. "I never met her. I guess I never really thought about it like that."

"No. I don't suppose you did."

An uncomfortable silence settled between the two women, and neither said anything for several minutes. Finally, Narista shifted uneasily on the bench and said, "Hanna . . . I'm sorry. I should've . . . should have . . ." Her voice trailed off, and she turned her hands palm up in a gesture of helpless confusion.

Hanna reached over and patted Narista's hand. "I'm sorry too. It isn't your fault. I shouldn't take it out on you." She looked at Narista. "And I'm glad you told me. I hadn't realized there was a connection. It does help make sense of some things."

"Are we still friends?"

"If you still want to be." Hanna sighed. "If you don't mind, though, could I have a few minutes alone? It's been a rather overwhelming evening."

"Of course." Narista started to leave but stopped with her hand on the doorpost. "Hanna? Um. Maybe you should stay at the embassy a while longer. Until they find Dalathek. What if he—"

"No," Hanna said firmly. "I don't belong here. Kamm asked me to stay for the ball as a favor to him, to keep up the media's interest in humans a little longer. But tomorrow I'm going home." She shook her head and looked out into the night. "I need to go home."

"Because of Jon?"

Hanna didn't answer.

"What if . . ." Narista hesitated. "What if you talked to him. Maybe the two of you could . . . I don't know . . . work things out."

"There's nothing to work out. It's over. He's with Salenia now."

"What if he isn't?"

Hanna wrapped her arms around the ache that rose in her middle. "You saw what I saw. They looked pretty together to me."

"Then, yes. But not since then." Narista perched on the end of the bench. "These past two days, it's almost as if they're avoiding each other. He's not wearing her knife. He didn't even escort her to the ball; he only walked out with her because my father told him to."

"So, it's a private courtship."

"Maybe. But what if it isn't?"

"Then, what? He just *used* her? While he wore my courting knife? And then lied to me about it?"

"He didn't lie to you."

"He didn't tell me the truth. How could I trust him?"

Narista frowned. "Jon is an honorable man."

"I know." Hanna rose and went to the railing, bracing her hands against the cold stone as she surveyed the courtyard below. "So, he *must* be with Salenia. And he didn't tell me because their relationship is private, and none of my business. Maybe they have some issues to sort through. Maybe they're waiting until his sordid little fling with that unfortunate human woman gets swept under the rug of the next news cycle. Whatever. It doesn't matter. It's over between us, and I'm going home."

"But—"

"I'm going home, Narista. Tomorrow. And right now, I'd really like to be alone."

Narista hesitated a moment longer, then left without further comment.

Hanna sat back down on the bench and let the quiet soak into her, calming her jangling nerves. The night air was cool on the balcony, and the sounds of the ball were muted. Hanna watched the lanterns glide in slow, swirling patterns around the courtyard below, and stared up at the stars in the night sky.

How long could she stay here, perched on a ledge between the Earth and the stars, before her disappearance caused problems for Kamm?

Her leg was feeling better, and she'd almost decided to return to the dancing when she heard voices in the gallery beyond the balcony's door—a man and a woman, speaking Talessanin. The words were indistinct near-whispers until Hanna's translation module decided it wasn't tuned properly. Then, it made a slight humming noise, the volume of the Talessanin voices increased, and the module began to translate for her.

"It doesn't change anything," the translator's flat male voice said.

"But Jon," the female voice, just as emotionless, protested, "it's—"

"I meant what I said that night, Salenia," the male voice interrupted. "Nothing is going to change the way I feel about you."

Hanna's heart seized. This was not a conversation she wanted to overhear. She snatched the translation module out of her ear with trembling fingers. The voices continued for a few more minutes, and then footsteps receded rapidly down the gallery.

Just when Hanna's heart began to slow again, a boot scuffed in the open doorway, and Jon stepped out onto the balcony. He strode over to lean both hands on the railing and bowed his head, looking down into the courtyard below.

Had he even noticed her?

Hanna's pulse pounded in her throat, and she barely breathed. She must have made some small noise, though, because Jon started and turned, then straightened as his eyes found her in the shadow beside the door.

Several emotions fought for control of his face as he stepped toward her, but she couldn't make sense of any of them.

"Hanna," he breathed. And then he said something in rapid Talessanin.

Hanna held out her hand, displaying the translation module on her palm. She pointedly tucked it back into her ear and motioned for him to continue.

But Jon didn't repeat whatever he'd said. He just looked at her for a long breath and then said, in English, "I am sorry for intruding, Hanna. I did not know you were here."

"Are you hiding from all the party people again?" Hanna asked softly.

Jon's laugh sounded bitter. "I suppose I am." He gave her a slight bow. "And you have exchanged your dates with Mr. Bickles for dates with the Imperial *Ehrat*. Is he as accommodating about being used as a footrest as Mr. Bickles?"

Hanna rose slowly to her feet. "Jon—"

"Do not worry." His voice had taken on a sharp, self-mocking tone. "I will not attempt any funny business."

"That isn't fair," Hanna whispered.

"No. You are right." Jon said. "I am sorry." His fingers slid into a well-concealed pocket and brought out the thin, black half-mask of his *enkalan*, which he pressed to his face.

He'd said its neural link pierced his skin to connect directly with his facial nerves. Did it hurt?

"Jon—"

"I apologize again for intruding, Miss Bradley." Jon inclined his head. Then he looked up at something above and behind Hanna, and when she blinked, he was gone. Teleported.

She turned and looked up. Jon strode along the ridge of the rooftop, shoulders hunched, head bowed.

Hanna suddenly wanted to be back with people again. She retrieved her glass and stepped back into the gallery, nearly colliding with Kinnen.

The bodyguard had a concerned, uncertain look on his face. "My lady." He bowed. "I wasn't sure if I should— "

"It's all right. He's gone." She handed Kinnen her glass. "Do something with that, will you?" The man ought to perform *some* useful function. She stalked toward the stairs.

By the time she reached the dais again, Hanna's nerves had settled considerably, and Kamm was looking for her. He swept her back onto the dance floor, where the two of them glided through the sedate steps of another of the slower dances Tomin had taught her. Narista's escort claimed her for the next dance, but Kamm was back again for the one after that. In fact, Kamm was rarely far away, and danced with her whenever he could, though he said he'd toyed with her reputation enough for one night already and made sure she had enough other partners to satisfy propriety.

Hanna danced several times with two men Kamm introduced as *ehrs* of other major Houses, as well as good friends. Several of the Assembly Delegates she'd met at Kamm's dinner sought her out. And Hanna was introduced to the President of the United States, who turned out not to be a very good dancer. It was Kamm, however, who escorted her back to the dais when the pain in her leg made her botch too many steps in the dance.

His parents stood near the front of the platform, chatting with Lord Trakanaleth. Narista glided up beside Hanna and was about to say something to her when the Emperor beckoned toward the three of them.

"Come, Narista. I have not danced with my beautiful daughter all evening. You must allow me the privilege before some wild young man runs off with you." He turned to Kamm. "And perhaps you will be kind enough to dance with your mother while I'm off frightening all of your young lords away from your sister." He grinned.

Hanna had never seen him grin.

The grin froze as his gaze settled on her. He glanced uneasily at his wife, then back again to Hanna. "And you, Miss Bradley," he said stiffly, "must dance with our friend, Lord Trakanaleth, so you will not feel abandoned."

Lord Trakanaleth's eyes travelled up and down Hanna's body again, and he smiled in a way that made her skin prickle all over. Dalathek's brother. A man who kept a human woman as a pet. The thought of allowing his hands to touch her again made Hanna feel ill. And her leg burned where the *kalakanek* venom had done its work. She collected herself enough to curtsy unsteadily. "I'm deeply honored, Your Magnificence, but I regret I'm quite fatigued at present and must beg to be excused."

A muscle twitched in the Emperor's jaw. "You are not so fatigued that you cannot stand up for one more dance," he insisted brusquely. "You will dance with Lord Trakanaleth."

"I'm very sorry," Hanna worked to keep her revulsion out of her voice, "but in addition to being fatigued, my injury from the *kalakanek* has become quite painful. I'm afraid it will be impossible for me to dance with Lord Trakanaleth."

The Emperor's face reddened, and he opened his mouth to say something, but Narista interrupted. "Father, the dance is starting. I'm sure Lord Trakanaleth will find a suitable partner."

The Emperor scowled at her and opened his mouth again to speak.

This time it was his wife who intervened. "I am somewhat fatigued myself. I believe I'll sit a while and let Hanna keep me company. Kamm, you must see if you can find Salenia, I don't think you've danced with her yet this evening, and Jon seems to have abandoned her. Perhaps her father knows where she is."

She turned and strode imperiously toward the sofas, and Kamm gave Hanna's hand an encouraging squeeze before nudging her gently in the same direction.

Hanna sank into the chair next to the one in which the Empress had instated herself, and a servant stepped up with a tray of delicacies. While the Empress hesitated over her selection, Tala skipped joyfully over to join them. She bobbed a very pretty curtsy to her indulgent grandmother, who gave the little girl a small chocolate confection to eat, and then, without warning, Tala climbed confidently up onto Hanna's lap.

Hanna winced as the child's weight landed on her sore thigh. "Here, sweetling," she said, shifting Tala to a better position, "sit on this side. That side is still a little sore."

"From the *kalakanek*?" Tala carefully arranged the skirt of her party dress. "When Baba told me it bit you, I thought you were dead," she said, her tone matter-of-fact. "I was very sad."

Hanna smiled reassuringly. "For a while, I thought I was dead too," she said. "But it turns out I'm harder to kill than I look."

Tala turned wide, tired eyes up to Hanna. "My *aman* died," she said. Hanna's translator rendered the word as *mama*.

Hanna nodded solemnly. "Yes," she said. "My mother died too. I miss her."

Tala reached a small hand up to pat Hanna gently on the cheek. Then she settled herself more firmly into Hanna's lap and laid her head on Hanna's shoulder.

Hanna looked up to find the servant offering a drink tray and the Empress regarding her with a troubled expression. She picked up the first crystal flower that came to hand, mostly so the servant would go away and there would be fewer eyes staring at her. It was a tulip and held the same apricot beverage Jon had offered her earlier. Hanna's heart sank like a stone. *Why did everything have to make her think of Jon?* She gritted her teeth and smiled.

"You will be a good mother someday, I think," the Empress said. "Our Tala is fortunate to have you as a friend." Her tone was conversational, but something in her eyes made Hanna uneasy.

Hanna inclined her head. "Thank you, Your Grace," she said. "I have felt fortunate to know Tala. I don't often get to spend time with children, and she has been a delight."

The Empress looked at Tala, then back to Hanna, and when she spoke again, she seemed to be choosing her words very carefully. "I have heard a most interesting rumor tonight," she said, "about a secret her father might be keeping."

Hanna drew a deep breath. "I think I've heard the same rumor," she said slowly, "but not from Kamm."

The Empress tilted her head, weighing Hanna's words. "It is not a secret between Kamm and you?"

"Kamm and I have never discussed anything of the kind."

The Empress relaxed back into the chair, studying Hanna. After a moment she said, "We have been friends of a sort, you and I." She sipped at her drink, directing a penetrating gaze at Hanna. "And you have demonstrated a certain skill at devising clever strategies, and at discerning and circumventing opposing strategies."

"Thank you, Your Grace," Hanna said, uncertain what the Empress expected of her.

The Empress gave a gracious nod; then her eyes narrowed. "I admit I cannot quite make out your current strategy," she said. "But since you and I are friends, of a sort, perhaps you will forgive my candor if I tell you I hope it does not involve pitting my sons against each other."

Hanna blinked. "Against each other? Your Grace, I would never want to see your sons at odds with each other. They play dangerous games with high stakes, and I think they need each other to win. Kamm has been a good friend to me, and Jon was more than that before he decided to end our courtship. I hope nothing but happiness for your sons."

The Empress frowned. "*Jon* decided . . . ?" Her eyes scrutinized Hanna's face. "I find that . . . difficult to believe."

Hanna sighed. "That seems to be the general consensus," she said. "But it is what happened."

"That does alter your game board, doesn't it?" The Empress's frown deepened. "And you must shift your strategy accordingly." Her eyes shifted to Tala, and then back to Hanna's face.

Hanna returned her gaze. "Sometimes the best strategy is to walk away from the game," she said. "I'll be going home tomorrow, where

I intend to build a few more canvases and see how fast I can get more paintings to the gallery without compromising the quality of my work. The leaves will be changing color soon, and I love painting outdoors in the autumn; the scenery is beautiful, the sun isn't so hot, and most of the biting insects die or go dormant for the winter when the first frosts come. With any luck I'll still be able to earn enough to pay my property taxes this year and maybe look into getting a few repairs done on my car. Right now, Your Grace, that is the sum total of my strategy. Your sons are both sensible men, and I'm sure that if any differences have arisen between them, they'll be able to work through them without me."

A slow smile spread across the Empress's face. "I think perhaps that is a wise strategy," she said. "Though I also confess myself a little disappointed to see you go. I have enjoyed watching you play."

The dance ended, and the others came back. Tala had fallen asleep on Hanna's lap, and Kamm apologized and offered to have a servant carry his daughter back to her rooms. When Hanna said she'd rather keep her a little while longer if Kamm didn't mind, the Imperial *Ehrat* smiled and pulled up a chair. The Empress went to dance with her husband, and Hanna and Kamm sat together and talked of little things.

As the ball drew to a close, Kamm summoned one of his bodyguards to carry Tala back to their apartments and led Hanna back to the floor for one last dance. He seemed unusually subdued as the two of them glided through the steps of another *aylencanat,* and as the music wound through its final turnings, he slid his hand further around her back, pulling her close and leaning down to whisper in her ear.

"Please stay, Hanna." He hesitated, then pulled her even closer. "Don't go home tomorrow." There was an unfamiliar urgency in his voice. His hand was warm on her back through her gown, and the fingers of his other hand twined with hers in a way that was uncomfortably close to a caress. It was exactly the sort of pose to feed the rumors about the two of them.

What game was he playing?

The heat of his breath against her neck sent a shiver through her body—a shiver of what? Of fear? Of . . . desire? Hanna honestly didn't know. Her heart pounded. "Kamm . . ." She sounded as breathless and shaky as she felt, caught, as she was, in a current she didn't quite understand. Her hand pushed involuntarily at his shoulder, and he relaxed his hold on her, giving her room to breathe, to think, to look up at his face.

He studied her in return, his eyes serious and intense. After a moment he looked away. "Forgive me, Hanna," he murmured. "Dalathek is still out there, and I worry for you. But I understand why you must go." His eyes flicked unconsciously to one side, and as she turned with the motion of the dance her eyes followed his gaze.

When had Jon returned to the ball?

She stumbled, but Kamm steadied her, then stepped back and bowed as the music—and the ball—came to an end.

Chapter 32

"I THOUGHT I'D FIND YOU HERE." Chance's voice was casual and friendly, as if he'd run into Jon at a port tavern instead of tracking him down on the sloping rooftop of the embassy's kitchens.

Jon glanced up at him but didn't say anything.

What was there to say?

Chance lowered himself to the roof next to Jon. "Rough night," he said. A statement, not a question. When Jon still didn't respond, Chance asked, "Which part was the worst?"

Jon considered, sorting through all the unendurable moments of the excruciating evening in his mind. Hanna turning to Kamm for comfort after her panic attack. Hanna and Kamm dancing an unexpected second, and all the whispered speculation that had generated. His own inability to ask her for even a single dance. The look of horror in her eyes when he had caught her hand during the *berantelcanat*. The wistful expression on Tala's face when she had innocently asked Jon if he thought her baba might marry Miss Bradley. His encounter with Hanna on the balcony after his confrontation with Salenia. That awful, breathless moment during the last dance when Kamm had pulled Hanna to him and bent his head—was it only to whisper to her, or had there been a kiss?

"The tribute," he said finally.

Chance shifted his gaze from the courtyard to Jon's face. "I wouldn't have guessed that one."

"I wanted to teach her that," Jon said softly. "I was waiting for the right time." He looked at his hands so he wouldn't have to meet Chance's eyes. "And Tomin never explains it properly."

Chance was quiet for a long moment. Thoughtful. Then he sighed. "A might-have-been." His voice carried a weight of understanding. "Those can be difficult."

"It is my own doing."

"She might allow you another opportunity if you—"

"That would not be safe for her. Look what has happened to her already because of me."

"Is she safer with your brother?"

"I wish I knew." Jon stared across the courtyard. "I admit I did not foresee that. Perhaps I should have." He shook his head. "They were closing in on Dalathek. I thought they would apprehend him, and she would go back to her home. Her friends."

"I thought so too." Chance stretched his legs out like Jon's. "But there's been no progress since he slipped their net four days ago. We might have to go look for him ourselves."

Jon only grunted in response. When he spoke again, his voice was low and ragged. "Kamm is still in her rooms with her." He waved a hand in the direction of the human guest quarters.

Chance followed Jon's gaze out across the courtyard and then looked back, eyeing Jon's *enkalan* with disapproval. "You can see in her windows from here with that thing?"

"Probably. With the right filters. But I do not wish to violate her privacy, so I have not made the attempt. I can tell he is there by the placement of the sentries."

Chance didn't say anything, but Jon could feel his friend watching him as he stared out across the courtyard. He counted the sentries again, using his *enkalan* to flick his vision into low-light mode and zoom in.

Shadows shifted on the floor just inside the French doors that led to Hanna's sitting room, which was all he could see from here without cheating. Much. Someone was moving around in there. Jon resisted the urge to run the analysis system that would process the angles and proportions of the shadows and project a close approximation of the shapes that were making them. It was none of his business what his brother was doing with Hanna. In her rooms. Alone. In the middle of the night.

"Checking the sentries again?" Chance leaned close, nudging Jon's shoulder hard enough to throw off his line of sight. "All present and accounted for?"

"Yes," Jon muttered, shooting a dark glare at his friend. "Both his and hers. And all the extras."

He pulled his legs up to his chest again and rested his arms across them so he would have something to prop his chin on. That made it easier to keep his field of vision steady when working with long distances and high magnification.

He let out a long breath, trying to make himself relax. "I know the reinforcements are necessary until the investigation into the assassination attempt with the *kalakanek* has been satisfactorily resolved, but I don't like having so many security guards running around who don't know each other well. It would be too easy to insert an assassin."

Chance sighed. "You would know."

"I need to stop doing this." Jon stood and paced a few steps down the ridge of the rooftop.

"Maybe it'll be easier tomorrow when she's gone."

Jon spun to look at his friend. "Gone?"

Chance sat very still, looking up at him. "I thought you knew," he said. "She's going home in the morning."

Jon stared at him. "Why would she go home? Dalathek is still out there."

Chance offered an elaborate shrug. "As it turns out," he said slowly, "someone broke the poor woman's heart, and I guess she doesn't want to loiter about the embassy anymore wasting time pining over him. Believe it or not, she has a life at home that includes activities like not being spied on by her mentally imbalanced former suitor." Chance shot Jon a wicked grin. "Unless, of course, you're deranged enough to follow her home so you can climb in her bedroom window and stare at her while she's sleeping."

"Don't be absurd," Jon muttered. He ran a hand back through his hair, rattling the beaded braids. "I guess that's why Kamm asked permission to station some security personnel at my house."

"Probably," Chance agreed.

Jon paced to the end of the roof and back. "Will you be going?"

Chance shrugged. "Probably." He shifted on the roof. "It would certainly be easier for me to get her attention if I'm there. Especially if you and Kamm are both here."

Jon stopped pacing. "What do you mean?" he demanded.

Chance rose slowly to his feet. "I meant what it sounded like. Don't assume that just because you don't want her, nobody else does either."

"*Want* her!" Jon took a step closer to Chance, his spine stiffening, hands clenching at his sides. His voice went soft and susurrant—the hiss of the Viper. "When did you stop calling her little sister, Chance?"

Chance took a deep breath and shrugged nonchalantly. "If she's being courted by my closest friend, she's like a sister to me," he said. His mouth twisted into an impudent smirk. "If she's not . . . well, then it turns out she doesn't seem so very sisterly after all."

Jon lurched forward another step, looming over Chance. A muscle worked in his jaw. Then he drew a long breath and looked up at the sky. "She would be safer with you." His voice was ragged. "Less of a target." He dropped back to the roof, head bent, shoulders hunched, elbows on knees. "You are skilled with your weapons. And I know you would treat her well."

Chance remained standing a little longer before he slowly lowered himself to the roof and smacked Jon in the shoulder. "What is wrong with you? Of course I don't want to be with Hanna. Not like that. I was just trying to wake you up. You love her. She loves you. The two of you are good together. *You* should be the one going with her when she leaves tomorrow."

Jon choked out a bitter laugh. "I might as well stuff her in a sack and hand her over to Dalathek. Or any of the other murderous lunatics who want revenge on the Viper."

"So instead you're just going to destroy her yourself?" Chance asked. "And butcher your own heart in the process?"

"Better to butcher my own heart than get her killed," Jon said grimly. "And she will recover. She was only splashing in the breakers. I am the one who went in over my head."

Chance shifted on the roof. "I was her bodyguard, Jon. I watched her. I think she was in deeper than that."

"She did not protest when I returned her knife."

"She promised not to."

"She could have said goodbye."

Quiet settled around the two friends again as they stared together at the lights across the courtyard. After a while, Jon said softly, "What can Kamm be doing with her all this time?"

"What would *you* be doing if you were alone with her for that long?"

Chapter 33

HANNA TURNED THE PAGE OF her sketchbook, and Kamm leaned in closer to look at the small, furry animal depicted on the page.

"You've captured its expression perfectly!" The delight in his voice sounded genuine. "That is the exact wide-eyed, perked eared look it gets when something tickles its curiosity. And Tala always giggles when it quirks its whiskers like that."

Imagining the animated excitement of the little girl made Hanna smile. "The keeper had just come with something for it to eat."

Kamm chuckled and told her the name of the animal, as well as its world of origin and a little about its diet and habits, watching with rapt attention as Hanna added notes in the open spaces on the page in her small, neat handwriting.

He'd said he would come in for only a moment, but then asked if she might show him some of her drawings. Hanna couldn't remember quite how they wound up sitting close together on one of the sofas while she turned the pages. She'd lost all track of how long Kamm had spent answering her questions about the animals. But he'd been so kind, and hadn't really seemed in a hurry to go, and Hanna knew she might never get another opportunity to find out what the creatures were called.

"I think that's the last of the menagerie sketches," she said. "Thank you so much for your help. I'm sorry for keeping you so late."

She began to close the cover of the book, but Kamm reached across to place his webbed fingers on the back of her hand. "Don't I get to see the rest?"

Hanna laughed. "At this rate, that would take all night."

Kamm's hand didn't move away. Instead, his forefinger slowly traced the line of her knuckles at the base of her fingers. "Please, Hanna." His voice held a disconcerting, coaxing tone. "Tala is asleep. And for once no one is waiting for me to solve their problems. May I see just a few more? I'm told you have some nice sketches of my daughter."

Hanna smiled self-consciously and looked down at the book in her lap. She nudged his hand away—an action which for some reason she couldn't quite explain made her cheeks warm and her heart beat faster. Then she thumbed through the thick pages, looking for the right place.

When she opened the book to the first sketch of Tala and slid it over to rest on Kamm's knees, his mouth spread into a wide grin. He touched a careful finger to the line of his daughter's cheek, glanced smilingly at Hanna, and turned the page. Here, Hanna had made several sketches of Tala's little hands, trying to capture the gestures she made as she held her books, carefully copied words onto a page, and argued with her tutor. The next few pages had more sketches of her face, as well as smaller detail sketches of her expressive eyes, of her mouth smiling, pouting, biting her lip as she pondered her lesson. The page after that had no sketches, only several lines of neat Talessanin writing.

Kamm's eyes skimmed over the words, and he looked up at Hanna. "Why didn't you ever mention that my mother wanted you to paint a portrait of Tala?"

"I guess I'd forgotten."

Kamm shook his head. "Do you know," he said, "that every other artist in the Empire would trade an arm and several fingers for a commission from the Empress in her own hand?"

Hanna smiled wryly and shrugged. "It was a rather overwhelming week, and I didn't know who she was at the time. She said she wanted a portrait of her granddaughter, and I asked her to write down how to contact her when I was ready to take commissions again."

Kamm tilted his head, a smile playing around his mouth. "Perhaps I could bring Tala to sit for you in a few weeks when you're settled in again at home?"

"I'd like that." Hanna found his gaze disturbingly intense, so she looked back down at the sketchbook as she added, "You should probably have someone call first so I can make sure to be home when you come. I spend a lot of time painting in the field when the weather starts to cool down at the end of summer."

Kamm turned back to the book as well, flipping the pages back to a section where Hanna had sketched the people visiting the art gallery. "Why do you paint so many landscapes?" he asked. "Why not more portraits? You're so good at capturing people." He turned a page. "Even when it's just a few simple lines and very little detail I can tell who some of these are."

When Hanna didn't answer right away, Kamm stopped turning pages and shifted slightly sideways on the sofa where he could see her better. Hanna turned her head away, gazing into the empty fireplace. "It's hard to explain." He didn't say anything, just watched her, waiting for her to continue.

She shrugged. "Art is as much about how you see things as it is about how you translate what you see onto a surface," she said quietly. "For me, anyway. To see a thing properly I have to let all my mental walls down. It's a sort of altered consciousness almost. There's no time, there are no words, not even any thoughts, really—there's only the essence of me, and the essence of the thing I'm drawing, and the longer I look, the harder it becomes to tell where one stops and the other begins.

Sometimes it's fun to do quick sketches like those," she motioned toward the sketchbook, "where I'm only studying the gesture, and I don't have to look at the person too closely, or for too long. And it's easy for me to copy a photograph of a person. That's only the essence of the photograph and the surface appearance of the person. But a portrait painted from a photograph comes out as flat as the photograph. It lacks . . . life.

"Portraits painted from life, though. They're different. To look that deeply into an actual, living person puts me too close to the essence of that person. Sometimes it's fine, like with Tala. Tala is all light and openness inside. She has a deep sorrow, and a loneliness for her mother, but it's a gentle, quiet sorrow, not an angry, violent one. There's nowhere in

Tala for me to become trapped. But some people . . ." Hanna shivered and turned away from him, staring into the cold emptiness of the fireplace. "It's too intimate. There's a point at which it becomes dangerous, where I start to lose pieces of myself. And when I'm in that frame of mind I can't always tell where that line is. And then . . . some people have things inside them that . . . that hurt. Sometimes on purpose." She shook her head, still not looking at him. "That probably doesn't make sense to you. But landscapes are safer. When I get lost in them, I can find my way out again."

For a while, neither of them spoke.

"Do you think you might be willing to paint a portrait of me?" Kamm asked softly. The intensity in his voice nudged Hanna's heart to a faster rhythm.

Slowly, she turned. Studied the curve of his cheekbones. The firm line of his mouth. The strong nose. The arresting green eyes. She let her mind drift, just a little, into that other way of seeing, and other details caught at her—the small, sad line at the corner of his mouth, the crease beginning to form between his brows, the darkness that lay behind the deep Kanestelan green of his eyes. But those were just surface details. Underneath . . .

Her heart began to pound, and she stood. "No." Her voice was firm. "I couldn't paint you, Kamm."

Kamm rose slowly to his feet. "What do you see, Hanna? When you look at me, what do you see?" He held out her sketchbook, and she reached for it, grateful to be able to look at his hands instead of his face.

"The weight of an empire," she said slowly. "Scars left behind by the death of your wife. Decisions you regret." She looked up again at him—not *into* him, just *at* him to gage his reaction to her words. "There's a fierce loyalty to your family but also a vast loneliness. I see reflections of Tala—she softens it for you, I think. And there's something you want desperately and can't have, but I don't know what it is. It . . . hurts to get close to that." Hanna turned away from him and walked to the tea table. "You're a lot like your brother." She set the sketchbook on the table.

After a moment, Kamm said, "And my brother hurt you. Is that why you don't feel safe with me?"

Hanna's soft laugh had a faintly bitter edge to it. "Don't take it personally, Kamm," she said, turning to face him again. "I don't feel truly safe with anybody. I guess I haven't for a long time. I thought I did with Jon, for a while, but it turns out . . ."

She smiled wryly. "I'm not sure I even remember what safe feels like anymore. Most of the time I don't think there even is any such thing as safe." She went back to him and took both of his hands in hers. "But I like you. And I'll try not to hold your brother against you."

Kamm studied her face. Cleared his throat. "That's good. Because I've just realized what an utterly amazing fool my brother really is."

One hand released hers, drifting up to lie against her face as his thumb traced the blush rising on her cheekbone.

Hanna shivered, and he blinked. Let his hand drop. Turned away. "It would be best if I go," he said. "I hope I'll see you in the morning before you leave, but I don't know if I'll be able to make that happen. Things here are . . . complicated, at the moment. But I will call you in a few weeks about the portrait."

He walked to the door, and Hanna trailed behind to see him out. He turned back as he twisted the door latch. "Thank you for tonight, Hanna," he said softly. "I'm glad you decided to stay for the ball."

Hanna smiled shyly up at him. "So am I," she said. "You're a good friend, Kamm."

His smile was faintly sad as he leaned down to kiss her cheek.

After the door closed behind Kamm, Susan emerged from the service kitchen, where she'd gone to hide as soon as Kamm had politely declined Hanna's offer of refreshment.

Between the two of them they managed to unfasten all the impossibly tiny hooks on the dress and to rescue all the jeweled hairpins that had managed to get lost among Hanna's braids and curls. Susan massaged the makeup from Hanna's face with a sweet-smelling cream and sent her off to shower. When she emerged from the bathroom wearing the long, white nightdress Susan had laid out for her, Hanna found a cup of herbal tea along with some kind of Talessanin fruit pastry waiting for her on the tea table.

The two of them walked through the rooms together checking the locks on the doors and windows, before Susan wished Hanna a peaceful night and left for her room in the servants' quarters. The last time they'd go through this ritual, Hanna thought.

She turned off all the lights and sat in the moonlit darkness, sipping her tea, letting the quiet seep into her, and reflecting back on all that had happened since the day she woke up here. In a way it all felt like someone else's dream. Tomorrow she'd go home and pick up the pieces of her own life. She needed to call Mr. Purcell at the gallery and see if there was still a waiting list for her work. She needed to sand the gesso on the canvases she'd begun and put another coat on to dry while she built more frames in her garage. She frowned. She'd have to pay the electric bill. How long had she been here? She'd lost track.

When her plate and cup were empty, she carried them into the kitchen. Tomorrow, she'd have to go back to doing her own dishes. She remembered how shocked Susan had been the first time she found her mistress in the service kitchen, and how the two of them had come to an understanding that Hanna would use the kitchen whenever she liked, but Her Ladyship must never, ever wash up after herself. Hanna smiled at the memory of Susan's scandalized face at the thought of the imperial family's special guest wiping out her own teacup.

As she set the delicate china carefully in the sink, the security box on the wall beside the sitting room door startled her by declaring, with electronic authority, "Confirm level three lockdown." She looked over and saw that the screen showed an outline of a hand, evidently wanting her to press her palm against it to confirm her identity. It amused her more than it should that the handprint outline had finger webbing. But she didn't want a level three lockdown. Level two would keep almost everyone out, but would allow Susan to enter in the morning, as well as allowing access by medical and security personnel with appropriate clearance in case of an emergency. Level three, she'd been informed, would keep out everything short of an actual apocalypse.

"Confirm level three lockdown," the box reiterated. Was it malfunctioning? Or had Susan accidentally selected the wrong option on her way out? Hanna went over to peer at the screen. Several option-selection buttons blinked along the bottom of the screen, but they were labeled in Talessanin, and she had no idea what any of them might do. There was a call button on the side of the thing that Susan had told her would connect her to someone in the security office if she ever needed help with the system. Maybe they could send someone, or just talk her through which options to choose on the screen.

Hanna raised her hand, intending to push the call button, but half-way to the box something she couldn't see clamped down hard on her wrist, shoved her arm sideways, and mashed her palm against the screen. "Level three lockdown confirmed," the machine reported. Hanna tried to jerk her hand off the screen, but the thing around her wrist clamped down even harder. A low chuckle filled the small room, and something dark flickered for a moment in front of Hanna, was gone, and then flickered again, resolving into the shape of a man. He was pressed back into the corner by the security box, and one of his hands was wrapped around her wrist, holding her hand against the screen.

She froze.

Hanna would know that face anywhere. The glowing red eye of his *enkalan* seeped bloody red light across the hard planes of his cheeks, catching on the raised edges of the scar that ran the length of his face, contorting the self-satisfied leer that spread across his cruel mouth. His lips moved, and his voice sounded taut and mocking, a bizarre contrast to the flat, emotionless voice of Hanna's translation module as it intoned, "A little advice for you, Mouse: before you lock all the doors and windows, make sure the threat is on the *outside*."

The security box made a blipping noise. "Miss Bradley, is everything all right?" a voice asked, "We're showing that you instituted a level three—" The voice cut off as Hanna screamed.

Dalathek's other hand clamped hard around Hanna's throat, and he swung her around so her back smacked against the wall. "You should not have done that, Mouse," he hissed. "Not that it will do you any good. They can't get in here now."

Hanna clawed desperately at his fingers with both of her hands, realizing suddenly that he'd let go of the one he'd been holding. She realized why a heartbeat later, when something hard and cold pressed against the side of her neck with a soft hissing sound, and a familiar shaky, weak sensation began to flood through her body. Frantically, she tried to gouge at his eyes with her thumbs, to bring her knee up into his groin—anything that might help her get away from him. But all she succeeded in doing was to stumble clumsily as her hands dropped away from his fingers and her body slumped, limp, against the wall, held up only by Dalathek's hand around her throat.

He leered at her and pressed the length of his body against hers, running his free hand down her chest and around behind her waist, groping at her through the thin fabric of her nightdress. Panic surged up, hot and white, bringing with it a breaking tidal wave of dizziness. Suddenly she was seventeen again—paralyzed, terrified, and alone with *him*. It was going to happen again. And there was nothing she could do to stop it.

Chapter
34

SOMETHING MOVED IN THE SHADOWS across the courtyard, and Jon sat up straighter, watching as several of the sentries glided away from their posts, while those remaining rearranged themselves into a different perimeter pattern.

"Finally," he muttered. "Kamm is leaving."

"Not that it's any of your business," said Chance.

Jon didn't bother to respond to that, but of course Chance was right.

Across the courtyard, Hanna's bedroom window lit up, and shadows danced across the curtains. She would be getting ready for bed.

He remembered helping Hanna with the hooks of her black velvet gown after the Shakespeare performance, the warmth of her skin, the smell of her hair, the soft black silk of her underthings against his fingers.

A picture came into his mind of Kamm's fingers working their way down Hanna's back, freeing the fasteners of her ball gown.

No. Susan was there to help her tonight. And Kamm had already left.

"We should go," he said softly.

But he didn't move. Couldn't take his eyes off the dancing shadows. Which ones were cast by Hanna?

"Yes," Chance said. "We should definitely go."

He didn't move either.

They sat there staring out at the lights on the other side of the moonlit courtyard until, one by one, the window curtains fluttered, as Hanna checked the locks. It was her nightly ritual. He'd seen her do it at home sometimes when he was sitting on his own roof late at night, watching the stars.

Not that he'd been spying on her then, either.

One by one, the lights went dark.

Jon rubbed at his face with both hands. It was hard to think he might never see her again. That his curt encounter with her on the balcony at the ball might be the last time he got to hear her voice.

It was harder still to think he might see her again, smiling in his brother's arms.

But none of that was as hard as standing over her still body watching her bleed out on the street in front of her house. None of it was as hard as kneeling by her in the darkness of the garden with the stench of burnt *kalakanek* in his nose, watching helplessly as its venom took her.

Never again.

He sighed. "We should—"

Chance leapt to his feet, holding one hand to his ear and gesturing for silence with the other. After listening for a moment to his security communicator, he drew a sharp breath. "Can you teleport in that get-up?" He gestured at the dress armor Jon still wore.

Jon was instantly on his feet, gripping Chance by one shoulder. "Where?"

"The corridor outside Hanna's door," Chance said. "Her rooms just went on level three lockdown, and someone heard her scream."

Jon's face darkened as his hand tensed, and then the rooftop was empty.

Chapter 35

HANNA NEARLY THREW UP WHEN Dalathek bent and swung her easily over his shoulder. She supposed that if she were the heroine of a book or movie, this would be the time to say, "You'll never get away with this!" and then wait for some hero to come rescue her. But this was real, and Hanna couldn't even move her lips. And nobody was coming to rescue her. Nobody could get in.

"You might like to know," Dalathek said conversationally, as he carried her through the sitting room, "that I am only being paid to kill you. Anything else I choose to do is purely for my own entertainment." He kicked open the door to the bedroom and turned on the light. "And for the edification of my former pupil." His voice slid down several tones and took on an angry bitterness. "I wish I could see that treacherous snake's face when he finds out what fun you and I have had together without him. Right under his conniving nose." He pitched her unceremoniously onto the bed, where she landed like a sack of potatoes, face-down on the velvet coverlet. "Right where he has undoubtedly fantasized about playing with his little toy himself—even though he's not man enough to actually do it." He shoved at her shoulder and hip, flopping her onto her back, and then leered at her. "I won't have to imagine your face though. You'll be right here, watching me. And I will get to watch you watching."

He unfastened the jacket of his black leather armor and began disconnecting strands of something that led from the jacket to the thin, black shirt he wore underneath. When all the connections were broken, he shrugged out of the jacket and draped it carefully over one of the bedroom chairs. He slid a long blade from a scabbard strapped to his forearm, holding his hands where she could see what he was doing, watching her face intently as he tilted the blade back and forth, letting the light dance up the sinuous curves and glint off the wicked barbs of the dagger. "Shall we play, Little Mouse?"

Hanna's dizziness began to fade, and she found herself clinging desperately to it, trying to hold it between herself and the awful clarity of mind that was seeping in behind it. Dalathek laid the point of the knife just where Hanna's collarbones met, and she wished she could move enough to lunge forward and bury it in her throat, but she was frozen inside herself.

Dalathek grinned at her and drew the tip of the knife down her chest between her breasts. As if from a distance, she heard it slitting the fabric of her nightdress as it went, felt the tip, razor sharp, tickling against her skin. Was it drawing blood, or just skimming the surface? Had he already begun to mark her body as he had so many times, so long ago—and so many nights since then, when she closed her eyes?

She couldn't close her eyes now. She couldn't even look away from him. Her heart beat, her lungs pulled and pushed the air rhythmically in and out, her eyes kept blinking; but she couldn't even look away.

Her breaths came faster, and her heart sped up, pulsing in her ears, urging her to flee. But she only lay there on the bed, staring back at Dalathek. At her nightmare come to life. Did he even remember her? Did he recognize her from before? Or had he done this so many times, to so many women, that she wasn't even a memory to him? His grin widened as his knife reached Hanna's navel. He raised the blade so she could see it again, its tip glistening red as he tilted it to catch the light.

Blood.

But not very much; just a little nick to get him started. He was planning for this to take a while. Dalathek lifted the blade to his mouth and his tongue flicked out, savoring the taste of her blood.

Again.

It was happening again.

Chapter 36

WHEN JON AND CHANCE PORTED into the corridor of the human guest wing, they found Kinnen pacing back and forth in front of Hanna's door, shouting into his communicator. Two black-clad sentries stood by, grim-faced and silent.

"Report," Chance demanded.

"The system went on level three lockdown shortly after the maid left," Kinnen said. "Miss Bradley confirmed with a palm scan, but was probably tricked or coerced, because the only response when the monitoring station checked in with her was a scream. We've been unable to reestablish contact. Nobody saw or heard anything unusual. If abductors are involved, they haven't presented any demands. The windows went opaque when the lockdown was initiated, so we can't see what's going on inside."

"There's no override?"

"Not on level three."

"Where's the control box?" Jon asked. "An unmodulated phase pulse might be able to short it through the wall."

"Interior wall, Honored *Ehr*," Kinnen said. "Between the kitchen and sitting room. Too far in."

"Structural evaluation?" Chance asked.

Kinnen shrugged. "Walls and doors are fully functional blast bulk-head under wood paneling. Windows are ballistic-proof, blast-resistant silica panels with beam absorption. But none of that even matters at this point, because it's all inside the particle field."

"Power source?"

"We've already disconnected it from the main power grid, but there's an internal back-up generator that's good for at least ten days."

"Anchor points?"

"Encased in the foundation block. There are actually eight inter-locking lattices, so the seams are reinforced, and the curvature can't be overextended."

"Eight?" Chance frowned. "Where's the pattern stitcher?"

"In the ceiling, but it's inverted, so it's inside the field."

The three of them stood looking at each other for several interminable heartbeats. Then Jon asked, "What are my odds if I try to port through a set-up like that?"

Chance stared at him. "Don't be a complete idiot, Jon. You won't be any good to Hanna if you're dead."

"What are my odds, Chance?" Jon insisted.

Chance glared at him. "I'd give you about an eighty percent chance of bouncing off and becoming a puddle of jelly on the floor outside Hanna's door."

"And twenty percent to get through?" Jon asked, shifting closer to the door.

Chance grabbed his friend's arm. "And twenty percent to become a carpet stain on the inside. It's no good, Jon. Far too many interstices."

"What, then?" Jon demanded. "How do we get in?"

"Let me think." Chance shoved Jon to one side and began pacing back and forth across the corridor muttering to himself, stopping now and then to draw diagrams in the air with his finger before shaking his head and moving on.

"We don't get in, Honored *Ehr*," Kinnen said grimly. "That's the whole point of having high security suites for paranoid heads of state when they come visiting. Nobody gets in."

Chapter
37

THE DIZZINESS WAS GONE WHEN Dalathek began cutting in earnest, and Hanna felt, with absolute clarity, the stinging trail made by the blade as it glided across her belly—not all the way through the skin, but enough to bleed for him.

Dalathek's smile turned musing as he watched the progress of the knife across her body. He met her eyes again as he ran his tongue down the flat of the blade and held her gaze when he leaned, leering, down to lap blood from her skin. When he raised his head again, a trickle of blood oozed from one corner of his mouth. Her blood. Hanna tried to scream, but all that came out was a pathetic little whimper.

Dalathek grinned, baring red-tinged teeth, and leaned closer to her face, head tilting as if in fascination. He brought the knife up and trailed its tip down the crest of Hanna's cheekbone while his eyes bored back into her own unmoving stare. A warm trickle worked its way down her face and around behind her neck, and she could smell the rising tide of sweet copper in the air. She whimpered again, and her breaths began to come even faster.

The expression on Dalathek's face shifted from fascination into delight. One rough shove shifted Hanna farther onto the bed, and the mattress sank as Dalathek settled one knee beside her hip and planted his hands on either side of her shoulders, stretching his body out above hers—so close; *so* close. His breath trembled hot against her skin as he leaned his face down, inches only above hers. The way he looked at her . . . there was something . . . Hanna's breaths had become rapid gasps, and warm tears mixed with the blood that ran down her face.

Dalathek slowly shifted his weight again, sliding his other knee up between Hanna's thighs, dragging the hem of her nightdress with it. Cool air rose up her legs like icy lake water; there was no way to stop it. Dalathek's eyes eagerly wormed their way past all her mental barriers, penetrating all the way to her core, to her essence. And suddenly, Hanna realized what it was about Dalathek's eyes that she found so disturbing. He saw her. He *saw* her.

Dalathek was an artist. When he began cutting he stopped talking, letting time, and words, and reality slip away, sliding into that other way of seeing things, of merging the essence of the artist with the essence of the subject. She hadn't seen that when she was seventeen, but she saw it now. He was an artist, and her body was his canvas. Or her soul. He laid down an underpainting of terrified anticipation, built up layered glazes of pain and degradation. He carefully worked in dark pigments of humiliation and despair, torment, abandonment, vulnerability. It wasn't about sex for him. It wasn't even about violence. It was about domination of a weaker soul; about mingling his own essence with that of a person in agony, and knowing that he was the cause of that agony; about vicariously experiencing the shades and nuances of human suffering, while remaining detached enough to manipulate them, like layers of paint, like notes of music. The rape and torture were only the tools he employed to create his art. And he was very good at his craft. How many times had he done this? How many women had he raped and maimed to perfect his art?

But now Hanna *saw* him too. And a stillness settled in one corner of her being, making a place for her to hide, to collect the scattered bits of herself, to make a final stand against the fear, against the nightmare. He could rape her. He could kill her. And he would; she knew that. But this much, this part of her, this he could not have. He wasn't going to have all of her. He was not going to win.

Dalathek must have seen her new determination in her eyes because his eyes narrowed, and his leering smirk faded into a disapproving frown. He pushed himself up to his knees, shifting so he straddled her hips, shoving her arms off to the sides, out of his way. One hand flopped against something lumpy and soft; Mr. Bickles. As she recognized her fuzzy pink companion, guardian of her dreams, her hand closed convulsively around his leg, and she came to another realization—the antitoxin she'd been given for the *kalakanek* venom was still in her system, and it was working to counteract whatever Dalathek had used to paralyze her. She opened and closed her hand again, watching Dalathek's face to see if he'd noticed. But his attention was all on the bloody, burning, crosshatching lines he was drawing down her other shoulder.

This time, when the ragged moan escaped from her throat it was not the sad remnants of a scream; it was the leading edge of triumphant laughter. He would almost certainly still kill her, but she was not going to die quietly. And she was going to wreak havoc with his masterpiece.

Chapter 38

CHANCE STOPPED PACING AND STRODE over to the door. He reached out a cautious hand, slowly advancing it until his fingertips met the resistance of the particle field. He lightly stroked his fingers along the surface of the field from side to side, watching closely the glimmering streaks of light that trailed behind his fingers. His hand slid beyond the edge of the door, gliding across the field as it continued along the wall.

"What are you looking for?" Jon asked.

Chance ignored him. "Is it safe to assume this isn't linked to the field of the suite next door?" He asked.

Kinnen frowned and relayed the question to the monitoring station, listened, and repeated the answer to Chance. "The fields of adjacent suites can be joined if the occupants request it. However, the suites on both sides of this one are currently unoccupied. The fields activated when this one went to level three, as an extra security measure, but they're not linked."

"Unoccupied?" Chance frowned. "During the ball? The place is crawling with guests."

Kinnen shrugged. "Most of the human guests shuttled in for the evening and didn't stay over. Those who did are housed on the other end of the facility at the request of the Honored *Ehrat*, in order to give Miss Bradley privacy."

Chance continued down the wall. When he reached the next door, he turned back and went the other way, still watching the light trails glistening in streaks behind his fingers. Jon paced up and down the corridor like a caged animal. There must be something they could do. Some way in. Some way to help Hanna.

Other people began to arrive. Tomin, anxious and agitated. Susan, pale and breathless, tears trickling soundlessly down her cheeks. Kamm in his undertunic and trousers, jaw clenched and eyes flashing, trailed by his regular contingent of bodyguards as well as three of the Winds. They all stayed out of Jon's way, whispering, and gesturing, and uselessly wringing their hands.

Chance stopped halfway to the next door on the other side of Hanna's rooms. He poked at the field again, frowning and leaning closer.

Jon pounced on him. "What is it, Chance? What did you find?"

Chance glanced over his shoulder, his brow furrowed. "Maybe nothing." He turned back to the wall, skimming his fingers over the same patch of particle field again. "No . . . there's something wrong with the pattern here. I think it's joined with the one next door."

"That would show up at the monitoring station," Kinnen said, stepping up beside the other two and frowning at the patch of wall.

Chance skimmed his hand up the wall, picking at the field with one finger, as if teasing a loose thread. "If it's Dalathek," he murmured quietly, "he would have access to teleportation tech?"

Jon shrugged. "He still has his *enkalan*. We saw that when he took Hanna before. I wouldn't be surprised if he managed to take some of his other tech with him when he left."

"We need to get into the suite on this side," Chance said, his voice growing more intense as he continued to pick at the field with his fingers. "I think he left himself a way out. Maybe we can use it to get in."

Kinnen strode quickly to the next door down and pushed the door latch. It didn't move. He swore. "I don't have clearance for this one," he said.

Kamm reached past him, gripped the latch, waited while it scanned his palm, and pushed down. The door swung open, and everyone stood back to let Chance enter first.

Chance strode rapidly to the end of the suite's sitting room closest to Hanna's rooms, and put his hand against the wall. Then he swore. "Of course. It's inside the wall," he said. "I can't feel the field from here." He spun, looking at Kinnen. "I don't suppose it would do any good to tear the wall down?"

Kinnen shook his head ruefully. "More blast bulkhead. The field would be on the other side of it from here. Maybe if we had a week . . ." He rubbed at the back of his neck with one hand. "I might be able to shut down this suite's particle field from the control panel if—"

"No!" Chance was adamant. "Don't touch the control panel!" He stalked back out into the corridor, finding the discrepancy in the pattern again and picking at it, tracing it with his hands up and down the wall, muttering to himself. Finally, his eyes narrowed. "What's up from here?" he asked. "Is there any sort of attic access?"

Again, Kinnen relayed the question. Everyone waited for the answer. Kinnen's lips pressed together as he listened. Then he said, "The architectural plans show a crawl space up there. It's above the ceiling's bulkhead sheeting, so you couldn't break through into Miss Bradley's rooms, but you might be able to find the field up there. If you could get to it—there's no door."

Chance turned to Jon. "Can you make a fold?"

Jon looked up at the ceiling, flicking through several filters and analytical programs in his *enkalan*. "Yes. Bend down." He put a hand on Chance's shoulder as they both dropped into a crouch, and then they were in a cramped, stuffy space where the only light came from the glowing eyes of the snake worked into the back of Jon's dress armor, and the faint trails that pooled around every part of their bodies that touched the surface beneath them. They crouched on top of the particle field.

Jon flicked his vision into low light mode, but there was still nothing to see except the smooth underside of the roof sloping above them, too close for them to stand, the faint haze of a glow emitted by the particle field underneath them, and below that, the smooth, metallic surface of blast bulkhead sheeting. Somewhere below that, someone was hurting Hanna, and Jon could not get in.

Chapter 39

HANNA FOUGHT TO STAY LIMP, not to move, not to flinch, as the knife's blade traced another curving line across her abdomen. She had to wait until more of the drug was out of her system. Even if she were completely unimpaired, Dalathek was still much bigger and stronger than she was. She would have one chance to act. One chance to surprise him. Only one. She must use it well.

The expression in Dalathek's eyes had taken on a dreaming, fanatic quality. His gaze drifted to her abdomen as he trailed a finger through her blood, tracing the patterns he'd made there with his knife. Hanna took advantage of his distraction to test her grip on Mr. Bickles's fuzzy pink leg. Better. Her strength was coming back quickly. But not enough yet. And she didn't know whether the rest of her body would obey her when she moved. There was no way to test her other muscles without him noticing.

Dalathek sucked at his finger, as if sampling some delicacy he was cooking to see if he had the seasoning right. Then he closed his eyes and reached his arms above his head, stretching like a cat, shifting a little on the bed.

Hanna gave her wrist a sharp twist and felt the mechanism click up inside Mr. Bickles's body cavity as the heavy, sharp, hunting knife came loose in its scabbard. She had sewn the knife into Mr. Bickles herself. It had lived in Mr. Bickles's predecessor, and in the bear she'd had before that. The therapist had given that bear to her, saying she could tell it all her problems, and it would never judge her.

But Hanna didn't need a confidant, she needed a weapon. So she'd told the eager salesman at the outdoorsman's shop that her boyfriend was a hunter, and she'd made her own modifications to her therapist's absurd teddy bear. It made her feel—not safe, but safer—to know if her attacker ever returned, she wouldn't be completely defenseless. She began to slide the knife, little by little, free of the bear's overstuffed body, wishing her grip through the stuffed plush wrapped around its hilt was a little more sure.

Dalathek finished his elaborate stretch and turned his gaze back to Hanna's face. He rose higher on his knees, his weight coming up off her hips so she could see better when he began unfastening the front of his trousers. He wanted her to know what was coming next for her.

Hanna's heart pounded, and her breath came in ever more rapid gasps. She was not going to let him do that. It was time, whether her body was ready or not. She could bide her time while he cut her, but she was not going to lie there and let him rape her. Not again. She'd make him kill her first.

Dalathek finished with his fasteners and leered at her, making sure she noticed his obvious arousal, before shifting his weight to one side and shoving her legs farther apart, moving one of his knees back between her thighs.

Hanna eased her hunting knife a little farther out of its scabbard and drew a deep breath, poising herself to strike.

Dalathek shifted his weight to the knee between her thighs and raised his other knee clearly intending to place it next to the first between her legs, using his hands to push the hem of Hanna's nightdress farther up. His eyes devoured the hatred and fear he saw in her eyes, and his leering grin widened, once again baring his bloody teeth as he laughed at her helplessness. Then he glanced down at what he was doing.

Hanna twisted, wrenching with her legs to throw him off balance, while her hand tore the knife from Mr. Bickles's body and plunged it into Dalathek's groin as hard as she could, bringing up her other hand to help, twisting and sawing the blade to work it deeper and deeper into his flesh.

Blood gushed over her hands, hot, and fast, and rhythmic with the beat of Dalathek's heart. She sawed again as he regained his balance and lunged for her, his enraged bellow echoing around the big bedroom. She twisted sideways, trying to get away from him, but he'd come down still straddling one of her legs, and she was pinned underneath him.

The furry grip of the hunting knife was becoming saturated with his blood, and she clutched convulsively at it, pulling it from the ragged wound she'd made. Blood spurted across her face and torso, and made a horrid pattering sound on the coverlet next to her. It washed over her belly, mingling with her own blood and drenching the bed beneath her.

Hanna's mouth drew back in a bloody grin. She'd hit the artery she'd aimed for.

Dalathek's face loomed over her, twisted with pain and fury, but his hands were miraculously empty.

He'd dropped his knife!

Then his empty hands reached out and closed around her throat, squeezing her airway shut, pinching off the blood flow to her brain. "You filthy sow!" He bellowed. "You pestilential human vermin!" His spittle spattered her face. "You. Will. Die!"

Hanna buried her hunting knife in the side of Dalathek's neck and twisted.

His shriek of rage cut off with a sickening gurgle as another great gout of blood sprayed across Hanna's face. Dalathek's grip tightened around Hanna's throat, and his crazed eyes bored into her own. A rushing sound filled her ears, and a red haze began to creep in from the edges of her vision.

She let go of her knife and used both hands to pry at Dalathek's grip, but her fingers only slipped in the blood that now seemed to cover everything. She shoved at his shoulders, beat at his elbows as he slowly collapsed on top of her, but he didn't release his grip.

The red haze grew darker, edging into black, and the roaring in her ears began to coalesce into one long tone, and she could not free herself from Dalathek's death grip on her throat.

Chapter 40

JON MOVED OUT OF THE way and tried to stay quiet as Chance groped across the particle field in the dark crawl space, counting to himself and muttering about lattices and interstices and pattern stitching. After what seemed an interminable time, he stopped, fingers playing across the field on the floor in front of him as if plucking strings on a musical instrument.

"Ha," he said. "Found you." He turned toward Jon. "How well have you kept up the shine on your throwing knives?"

Jon grunted and handed him one.

Chance held the short-handled, leaf-bladed knife close to his other hand as his fingers made the plucking motions, watching the reflection of the light patterns in the polished blade. "I think this will work," he said. "But you have to be ready, because it won't work twice."

"Tell me what to do." Jon's muscles tensed at the prospect of finally being able to take action, and he had to force himself to stillness.

"This field is made up of eight lattices."

"I remember. Hurry."

"Patience. You need to understand what we're doing."

"Hanna."

"I know. But we only have one shot at this, and I haven't got any other ideas."

"Go on."

"Eight lattices," Chance continued. "And this is where they converge. The pattern stitcher is inside the ceiling of Hanna's sitting room, right below this spot. I can feel the edges of all eight lattices. But there's an extra strand woven through some of the interstices here. I think it comes from the field next door. It weaves through the joining between these two lattices"—his fingers tapped a spot on the field, sending shivers of light out from the place—"and keeps them from sealing all the way. The gap isn't big enough to port through as it is, because the strand creates its own junctions and interstices that fill in the space. It's very clever, actually.

"But if I disrupt this strand, it will unravel, and for just a moment there will be a gap big enough to drop a fold through. Just for a moment, though. Then the strand will snap back to its own field, and the lattice edges will seal, and there probably won't be any indication it was ever here. I think it's Dalathek's back door. He probably has some kind of tech tuned to the right frequency to unstitch the strand from the lattice interstices." Jon shifted eagerly, and Chance held up a hand. "But if I disrupt the wrong strand, or if you're not fast enough with the fold, we're either stuck out here with no way in, or we're carpet stains. Understand?"

"We?" Jon frowned. "No. You stay—"

"My life before yours, Commander. Always." Chance's tone left no room for argument. "And I've already lost my brother. I won't lose my new sister too. Do you understand what we're doing or not?"

"I understand," Jon said softly. Time was too precious.

"Good," said Chance. "Now, I'm going to need you to ply the fold before I disrupt the strand, and it needs to be the shortest fold you can manage—just to the middle of the sitting room, or even in the air just below the ceiling, if you can manage that. The fold has to completely release before the strand finishes unstitching from the interstices, or it will cause a feedback loop that will fry us in the Void. So don't try to get fancy with the landing."

"I understand," Jon said again.

Chance nodded solemnly. "Do it now. Tell me when you have it ready."

Jon was motionless as he carefully adjusted port settings with his *enkalan*, shortening the fold path, overriding spatial orientation and proximity safety settings, compensating for a passenger. He began the sequencing that would set the fold but stopped it just before it flicked him into the Void and held it there. Holding a plied fold made it hard to breathe properly. He set his hand against Chance's shoulder and gasped, "Ready."

Chance shifted the throwing knife in his fingers and said, "When I disrupt the strand, a light trail will shoot off in that direction." He waved a hand at one of the walls. "As soon as you see it, drop the fold. Got it?"

"Got it," Jon gasped through clenched teeth. "Do it."

Chance carefully angled the knife blade, and lowered it toward the particle field, using the fingers of his other hand to guide him.

"Hurry," Jon gasped.

The tip of the blade made contact with the field, and light sparked toward the wall. Jon dropped the fold, and the familiar cold of the Void swallowed him for a split second before the sitting room floor smacked him hard in the back, and what remained of his breath whooshed out of him. Reflex kicked in, and he rolled to his feet, dagger hilts settling into his hands as he scanned the room for threats. All was quiet and still, and the only light came from the crack under the door to Hanna's bedroom.

Chance staggered to his feet beside Jon, grinning from ear to ear as he raised his own daggers, crossing them in the victory salute.

Jon nodded grim respect and touched the tip of one dagger to his forehead in response. Then he motioned silently at the service kitchen door. They needed to make sure there was no one in there who might sneak up on them when they were dealing with whatever was going on in the bedroom.

When they were both in position, Jon signaled, and Chance pushed the door open quickly and quietly, going in straight and fast, dropping low. Jon was right behind him, stepping to the side and turning to scan the room, daggers poised for danger.

It was empty.

The two friends moved swiftly back through the sitting room to the bedroom door, taking their positions, pausing to listen. All was silent. On Jon's signal, they went in.

Blood.

So much blood.

Spattered up the wall near the bed. Sprayed out across the pale carpeting. Dripping from the hem of the rumpled velvet coverlet hanging over the side of the bed and pooling on the floor. No one could lose that much blood and live. Jon's heart froze in his chest. He was too late.

Oh, Hanna!

Too late.

A man sprawled on the bed, face-down, relaxed and seemingly unaware of their presence. He'd had his fun and was sleeping it off. Jon motioned for Chance to check the bathroom and began to circle slowly, silently, toward the man on the bed. Was it Dalathek? If anyone could sleep soundly in the middle of carnage like this, it would be Dalathek. He probably thought he had a week or more before the suite's defenses were breached, and could take his time, waiting until the security staff let their guards down before slipping out through his back door.

Jon circled closer to the bed, scanning the room for other threats.

A black body armor jacket was slung across one of the chairs.

A wicked-looking knife lay on the floor in a cluster of blood spatters.

Hanna's small, bare leg, finless and motionless, streaked with blood, protruded from beneath the man's body.

Oh, Little Mouse!

What had been done to her? She'd been alive for it, whatever it was—the blood wouldn't have sprayed like that if her heart hadn't been beating. The shock Jon had felt when he entered the room began to burn off like fog under the scorching heat of his rage.

That man. Would die. Slowly. With great attention to detail. And if it really was Dalathek—

A soft cough. A slow, ragged indrawn breath. The man's shoulders shifted.

Jon raised his daggers.

With a whimpering moan, the man rolled slightly to one side, then settled back into his original position.

Chance moved into Jon's peripheral vision, signaling that the bathroom was empty, and drifted silently into a backup position.

Jon raised his hand to call the attack—

And that's when the screaming started. Raw, feral shrieks. High pitched, like a woman's voice.

Jon froze.

The man's body heaved again, and his head flopped to one side like a ragdoll's.

Dalathek's eyes were wide and staring. Blood tinged with pink foam trickled from one corner of his gaping mouth. Something protruded from his neck. His body convulsed again, with another soul-piercing howl. But . . .

Dalathek was not the one screaming.

Dalathek was clearly dead.

That meant—

"Hanna?" The clench of Jon's heart beginning to beat again pushed her name past his lips in a rough whisper. *She was alive!* He dropped both daggers and rushed to the bed.

Hanna's delicate fingers shoved weakly at the heavy, unmoving corpse that pinned her to the bed. She choked, and her breaths started coming in ragged, gasping sobs. Her eyes flew wide, frenzied and hysterical. Their bloodshot gaze focused on Jon, but he saw no recognition there.

"Get him . . . off me . . ." she pleaded softly. Desperately.

Jon grabbed the back of Dalathek's blood-soaked undertunic and heaved.

Hanna screamed. Flailed.

Chance skidded around the bed as Dalathek's body hit the floor. "Hanna!"

"*Get him off!*" she shrieked.

Jon scooped her up in his arms and stumbled away from the blood-drenched bed before falling to his knees. "Little Mouse," he whispered. It came out like a prayer.

She was alive!

Hanna writhed out of his grasp, slick with the blood that covered her from head to foot. One arm curved protectively over her abdomen, and the other scrubbed at the blood and tore at the tattered remains of the blood-soaked nightdress that tangled around her body.

"Get him off," she moaned. "Get him off, get him off, get him off!"

"Hanna?" Jon touched her gently, trying to draw her out of her terrified hysteria. "Little Mouse?" He couldn't tell how much of the blood was hers. "Are you injured, Little Mouse?" His voice was soothing. Coaxing. "Look at me, Hanna."

"Get him *off*," Hanna sobbed, folding up around herself and rocking with the rhythm of her chant, scrubbing futilely at the blood with one bloody hand. "Get him off, get him off, get him off, get him . . . get him off . . ."

Chance dropped to his knees beside them on the floor. "Dalathek is dead," he reported. "She hit two big arteries, and he bled out. Is she all right?"

Jon looked helplessly at Chance. "She is not responding." He heard the anguish in his own voice.

Chance looked quickly around the room, assessing. "Take her into the shower," he said briskly. "Help her get some of that blood off. I'll let the others in and send for a medic." He placed a comforting hand on Jon's shoulder before heading for the door.

Jon stroked Hanna's bloody cheek with his fingers. "Hanna," he crooned, "Little Mouse, come with me. We will get the blood off. Come with me."

She only rocked and chanted.

Jon gathered her against his chest—so small and fragile—and carried her into the bathroom, into the large, glassed-in shower. The water was already warm when he pushed the lever down, and he held her in the center of the space where the water jets converged. She flinched when the water hit her skin, but her obsessive chanting trailed off, and she turned her face into the spray. Her small hand reached out for the water as if it were a lover, and she relaxed in his arms.

He carefully set her on her feet, supporting her weight, helping her turn so the water sluiced over her body, sending deep red rivulets down the drain. Hanna turned her face upward into the spray, holding both hands out to her sides, palms up as if offering her first true prayer, and he stood behind her, hands on her waist, as if he were her guide, her teacher. His heart pounded in his throat. He missed her like he would miss a piece of himself. Would it always be like this?

But look what he had done to her!

A sizzling pop. Pain stabbed into his shoulder. A thin trail of smoke rose from a hole in his armor. Another pop, and the hole grew larger, smoking at the edges. Water had seeped into his armor and was shorting some of the electrical systems.

Hanna shifted in his arms, taking more of her own weight. She smoothed her hands across her face, then down the front of her body, turning slowly and rubbing at the more stubborn patches of blood.

His armor emitted a loud crackle, and pain seared down Jon's back like a burning whip lash.

He winced, and Hanna turned, as if just realizing he was there. Recognition dawned across her face, and she smiled up at him. A trickle of blood seeped from a shallow cut on her cheek. "Jon," she whispered. "You came for me." Her fingers reached wonderingly for his face, tracing the line of his cheekbone like a blessing. She leaned her cheek against his chest and began to sob.

Jon ran a quick systems check through his *enkalan*. All his armor systems were dark. Burnt out. There shouldn't be any more electrical fires to worry about. He gritted his teeth against the pain and wrapped his arms around Hanna, stroking her back through the wet fabric of the tattered nightdress. "You are safe, Little Mouse," he murmured. "You killed him. You are safe."

Her hair hung loose, heavy with blood and water, down to her shoulders, hiding her face from him. Carefully, he pushed it back, skimming his fingers down the smooth skin of her cheek. Down her neck. With the worst of the blood sluiced off, he could see the bruises forming there. Finger marks. Strangulation marks. That would explain the bloodshot eyes. His fingertips reached her shoulder. Criss-crossing lines sliced into her skin. Like that other girl all those years ago. Was the rest of it the same, too?

He untangled himself from her as gently as he could, stepping back to check for more serious wounds. "How bad is it, Hanna? Let me see," he whispered.

Hanna turned away, putting her back to him, pulling the wreckage of her nightdress closed over her chest and belly—but not before he saw the raw red lines there, and the blood that still seeped out, dyeing the water as it washed down the skirts of her nightdress and into the drain.

"Oh, Little Mouse," he breathed.

This was his fault. This had happened because of him. Gently, he brushed his fingertips along a patch of uninjured skin between her hunched shoulder blades.

She flinched away from his touch, clutching her tatters more tightly around herself, shoulders shaking. "Don't touch me," she rasped. "Don't look at me."

"Honored *Ehr*?" said a trembling voice behind him. "May we be of assistance?" Susan stood at the shower door, holding several towels, and Arastan was rapidly unpacking a medical bag over by the sink.

Jon glanced back at Hanna, who had retreated to the far wall of the shower and stood with her forehead pressed against the smooth glass. She didn't want him there. And Jon couldn't blame her. He had made this happen. And then he'd come too late.

Chapter 41

J ON STRIPPED OFF HIS JACKET as he stalked into the bedroom, wincing when it stuck to the burn down his back, and yanked the electrical connections free of his conductive undertunic without bothering to unfasten them properly. He sank into one of the chairs by the bedroom fireplace, burying his face in his hands. It took much longer than it should have for him to realize that Kamm occupied the chair across from him. Chance sat on the window seat, legs drawn up, looking out the window. Tomin leaned over Dalathek's corpse, which still lay on the floor where Jon had heaved it, though someone had pulled down one of the bed curtains to cover it. Other voices drifted in from the sitting room.

Tomin straightened. "Jon, did you know she had that knife hidden inside her teddy bear?"

Jon frowned. "Knife?" he asked. "In Mr. Bickles?"

Tomin shrugged. "That thing stuck in Dalathek's neck was Mr. Bickles's leg. It has a blade as long as my hand sticking out of it. That's what she killed him with. The sheath is sewn into the teddy bear's body."

Jon stared at him. An odd memory drifted through his mind of that first night after he'd met Hanna. He was sitting on the porch looking at the house across the street, wondering what Hanna would do if he showed up at her door, and Tiffany had said, "Watch out for Mr.

Bickles . . . there's more to that bear than meets the eye." Jon smiled sadly at the memory. There was more to Hanna, too.

"No," he said. "I didn't know. But that would explain the lumps."

Tomin pulled the edge of the bed curtain back over Dalathek's head. "I thought she'd be safe here," he said softly.

Kamm sighed. "She told me she doesn't even remember what safe feels like."

They sat in silence for what seemed a very long time after that, each lost in his own thoughts.

When the bathroom door opened, Jon jumped to his feet, spinning to face Hanna.

But it was only Arastan.

"How is she?" Kamm asked, his voice soft as he rose slowly from his seat.

The medic's shoulders rose and fell wearily. "Multiple lacerations, but they were clean, shallow cuts, and healed nicely with the cell aligner and a little regen fluid. They'll be completely gone by morning. Physically, Hanna will be fine. Mentally—" She sighed and shook her head. "The shock is wearing off, and she is stabilized. But what this will mean for her in the long term, I cannot say. She needs rest."

Kamm took a step closer to Arastan. "The cuts," he said hesitantly, "those were the only . . . injuries?"

Jon looked at Kamm, then turned his gaze on Arastan. "Did he rape her?" his voice came out harsh. "That is what our Honored *Ehrat* wishes to know. Did he rape her while we were all standing out in the corridor wringing our hands?"

Arastan looked back and forth between the brothers. "He did not," she said quietly. Her eyes flicked to the crumpled heap under the bed curtain. "He used a paralytic drug to keep her from moving while he did the cutting. The antitoxin in her system counteracted the drug in time for her to stop him from doing anything else."

Jon sighed and dropped back into his seat, wincing as pain shot up the burn on his back.

Kamm frowned down at him. "Perhaps, healer, you will see what assistance my brother requires?" He turned, without waiting for an answer, and began to pace the length of the room.

Arastan stepped up beside Jon's chair and gently tugged back the burned edges of his undertunic. "What happened?"

"It would seem my dress armor is not waterproof."

Arastan snorted. "Who creates armor for a semi-aquatic warrior and doesn't make it waterproof?" She put her bag down and went to work, muttering about how much easier it was to repair cells that had merely been cut than to heal cells that had been melted or burst or simply burned away. Jon didn't really listen. He had been burned before and knew the routine. The medical attendant had done what she could for him, outside a medical response facility, and was just pulling his undertunic back down over the bandages when the bathroom door opened. Again, Jon leapt to his feet.

This time, it was Susan.

All four of the men in the room watched the maid as she went to the wardrobe and poked around for a few minutes, then went back into the bathroom carrying an armful of clothing. Kamm sank back into his seat. Jon moved to stand next to the fireplace, propping a forearm against the cool stone of the mantel.

When Hanna finally did emerge from the bathroom, Jon couldn't make himself turn to look. He knew it was her. He would recognize her little bare mouse footsteps anywhere. His heart pounded in his throat, but he couldn't look at her. Instead, his eyes followed his brother as Kamm slowly rose and held out a tentative hand. Hanna melted into Kamm's arms, burying her face in his chest as he stroked her hair and murmured softly.

Had they become that close already?

That was none of Jon's business. He gritted his teeth and focused on keeping the air moving in and out of his lungs.

After a moment, Hanna pushed away from Kamm and started across the room toward where Tomin still stood beside Dalathek's covered corpse.

Kamm caught at her hand. "You don't have to do that," he said.

"Yes, I do." Her voice rasped—not surprising, since she'd just been strangled, and then screamed like her soul was on fire because she was trapped under the corpse of the man who had haunted her nightmares all those years.

How could he have allowed this to happen to her?

She dragged the bed curtain off Dalathek, and for several long heart-beats she just stood there, staring at the mess. Then a haunting, high pitched keening sound seeped out of her throat, and she kicked at the corpse with her little foot. Hard. She kicked it again. And again. Then she walked around to the other side and kicked it several more times. When she finished, the keening sound had stopped, and she was breathing hard.

"I win, you filthy animal." she gasped. "You will never touch another woman ever again." She spat in Dalathek's face and kicked him again. "I win!"

Kamm put a gentle hand on her arm and said soothingly, "Come away. Please, Hanna."

She turned a fierce glare on him. "I want his *enkalan*," she said.

"What?" Kamm stared at her.

"I want his *enkalan*," Hanna insisted. She shifted the fire of her gaze to Tomin. "And I want a flutter shuttle. Now. I am not staying here one more minute than I have to."

"But— " Tomin protested.

"Now! Or I will start walking."

Tomin looked levelly back at her for another heartbeat, then bowed, murmured, "Yes, my lady," and headed for the door. Chance muttered something about arranging security and followed.

Kamm put a gentle arm around Hanna's shoulders and tried to steer her toward the sitting room. "It'll be a few minutes. Let's sit down while we—"

"No." Hanna shook him off. "Not until I have his *enkalan*. How does it come off?"

"Hanna—"

"I need it, Kamm. Please." That terrible, broken keening sound played at the edges of her rasping voice again, and a tear rolled down one cheek.

Something inside Jon snapped. He was across the room and on his knees beside the corpse almost before he realized he'd moved. The *enkalan's* dermal bond had partially released, so it came away easily enough, revealing the dark inscription of a one-sided *tehilethkalan* underneath. As Jon drew the long filaments of the neural link out of Dalathek's dark-streaked skin, Kamm made an odd noise in the back of his throat.

Diplomats didn't like to think about the more physical ramifications of soldiering, whether it be the corpses soldiers made or the modifications made to the soldiers.

Jon ignored his brother's reaction. He yanked the other ends of the filaments out of the *enkalan* and snapped both of the insertion needles off at the base. Then he wiped most of the blood off with the edge of the bed curtain and handed the *enkalan* to Kamm.

Kamm held it out to Hanna. "I don't understand," he murmured. "Why do you need this?"

She took the black half-mask and turned it over in her hands. One delicate, webless finger traced the double row of needle teeth along its bottom edge. "It's proof," she said. "When I wake up tomorrow this will all seem like just another nightmare. But if I have his *enkalan*, I'll know it was real, and he's really dead." Her voice snagged, and she cleared her throat. "I need to know he's really dead. I need to know he isn't coming back."

Just another nightmare? What must her nights be like, if this was just another nightmare to her?

Oh, Little Mouse!

Still on his knees, Jon slid one of his daggers free of its sheath. "This was my fault," he said. "All of this was my fault. The first attack. The *kalakanek*. This." He gestured helplessly at the bed, the blood-spattered walls, the still corpse of the man who had been almost a father to him. "None of this would have happened if I had not made you a target. I thought returning your knife would be enough to keep you safe. I was wrong." He laid the dagger across his open palms and held it out to Hanna. "I failed you. I offer my life as recompense."

Hanna stared at him. Her trembling fingers brushed against his palm as she took the dagger. For half a heartbeat, Jon thought she might use it on him. For half a heartbeat, he almost hoped she would; knowing he was the cause of the pain behind her chocolate eyes was unbearable. Instead, she flung it across the room, where it clattered off the mantle and skidded under a chair.

"Don't be stupid, Jon," she rasped. "Bad things happen. They happen to everyone. That's just how life is. Sometimes you can see them coming and try to avoid them, and sometimes they just sneak up on you, no matter how careful you are. "You walked me home to make sure I got there safely; you didn't know Dalathek was going to use me as bait. You weren't the one who turned the *kalakanek* loose. And tonight—well, unless you're who Dalathek meant when he said someone had paid him to kill me, you're not responsible for that either."

Jon stared at her. "Someone paid him to kill you?"

He would find them.

"That's what he said. And not everything has to be about you, Jon. It was probably someone who believes that ridiculous rumor about Kamm courting me and thinks the easiest way to prevent him from threatening the Empire with a human empress would be to just kill me off."

Jon shook his head. It was just as likely that someone was using her to provoke him. "Hanna— "

"Bad things happened to me before I ever even met you. And after I leave here, bad things will go on happening sometimes no matter what else I'm doing with my life. The wiring in my house is old, maybe it'll burn down. I might get hit by a drunk driver on my way home from the library. You can't protect me from everything, Jon. No one can."

Jon stared at her. She was right. Giving her knife back couldn't make her safe. It only meant that when the next bad thing happened, he wouldn't be there to try to stop it or to hold her while she cried afterward. Except . . . she was wrong, too. Wiring could be updated. And the risk of being struck by an intoxicated motorist was greatly reduced if one didn't stand in the middle of the road. Or next to the Viper.

Slowly, he rose to his feet. "Hanna—"

"But none of that really even matters, does it?" she snapped, backing away a step, as if she couldn't bear to be so near him. "Because all this nonsense about keeping me safe is just a stupid excuse. We both know that's not really why you gave my knife back."

Jon frowned. "What do you mean?"

"What do I *mean*?" Hanna gaped at him, incredulous. "I *saw* you, Jon. You and Salenia. I saw you together. I know what you did."

Ice crawled down Jon's spine. How much had she seen?

"No," he whispered. "That was not . . . nothing happened."

"I know what I saw," she snarled. "You had no shirt on. And Salenia's dress was undone down to here." Her finger drew a line down the center of her chest all the way to her waist. "She was sitting on your lap with her skirts pulled up, kissing you. And in the garden, after the *kalakanek*, your pants weren't done up all the way."

She took a step back and folded her arms across her chest like a blast-proof bulkhead. "I promised not to make a fuss if you chose her instead of me, so I didn't say anything. But how can you look me in the face and tell me you broke up with me for my own good, when I saw you with her? You could at least have the guts to tell me the truth."

Something twisted in his belly. Slowly, he said, "I have never lied to you."

"That isn't the same thing as telling me the truth." Her eyes dared him to disagree.

"You are right," he said. "I am sorry." He drew a deep breath and scrubbed one hand back over his hair. "You saw what you said you saw. That is the truth."

Her face went white, and she made a small choking sound as she turned away.

His hand flashed out, catching her elbow. "But it was not what it looked like. That is also the truth."

She shook his hand off and turned back to study his face, eyes skeptical, weighing his words. Hoarsely, she whispered, "It was close enough."

How could he argue with that? He should never have let things with Salenia go that far—especially while he possessed Hanna's courting knife. He should have left as soon as he realized Salenia was in the room. He should have ended things with her more cleanly years ago. It might not have been the kind of betrayal it looked like, but it had been a betrayal all the same. He was a fool.

"I . . . I am sorry, Hanna." *What else could he say?*

"Well, I hope you're very happy together." He couldn't tell if she was being sarcastic, or if she was just tired.

"I am not courting Salenia," he said.

"No?"

"No."

Hanna stared at him. Then she shrugged and shook her head. "Okay. So if you didn't dump me because of Salenia, that means you dumped me because . . . because of *me*." The bitterness in her voice was echoed in her eyes.

Dumped. Such an ugly word.

"I wanted you to be safe."

Hanna shook her head in disgust. "Safe is a lie we tell ourselves so we can sleep at night. There's no such thing as safe. You just didn't want me anymore."

"That is not true."

"If it wasn't true, you'd find a way."

"Hanna—"

"No." She held up a hand, stopping him. "I don't want to hear it. I'm done, Jon. I want my life back. I'm going home. And I don't want to see you again. If you ever really cared anything about me at all, the best way to show it now is to just stay away from me."

She turned toward the door to the sitting room.

"Wait." Kamm blocked her path. "Please don't go."

"I can't stay here."

"We'll find you another room. You don't have to stay in this one. But if someone hired Dalathek to kill you, they're not going to just give up."

Hanna choked out a rasping, incredulous laugh. "And what? I'll be safer at the embassy?" She looked meaningfully around the blood-soaked room. "Really?"

No one had a response to that.

"I'm going home," she said grimly. "You can send some guards if you want, but I'm going home."

Chapter
42

HOME DIDN'T QUITE FEEL LIKE home anymore. Someone had tidied up and dusted. A stack of gossip magazines lay fanned out across the coffee table, the cover of the one on top showing a blow-up of Jon kissing Hanna at the Shakespeare performance. That would be Tiffany's doing. Two piles of mail rested on the kitchen table, junk in one pile, bills in the other. That meant Rachel had been here too—Tiffany would've just chucked it all in a heap.

"Where do you want this?" Chance stood in the kitchen doorway holding her suitcase.

"Just leave it there," Hanna said. "I'll take care of it."

Chance hesitated. "Can I call someone for you? Rachel or Tiffany? You shouldn't be alone."

"It's the middle of the night, Chance. And I like being alone. Alone works for me." She heard the bitter edge in her own voice and sighed. "I'll call them tomorrow."

She moved to the kitchen window, where she could see Kamm's men setting up a perimeter around her house. They'd already checked the inside.

Chance studied her face, eyes troubled. "Is there anything else you need? Anything we can do for you?"

Hanna hesitated, then shrugged. "I could use a ride into town and back tomorrow," she said. "I need groceries, and I probably shouldn't drive until the dizzy spells are completely gone."

Chance nodded. "I'll be staying at Jon's house for a while. Just let me know when you want to go." He started to leave but turned back. "Hanna, I'm sure Jon—"

She jabbed a warning finger at him. "Don't do that, Chance."

He took one step back toward her. "But—"

"Don't. I'm done."

Chance studied her face one more time before his eyes drifted down to where her fingers still clutched Dalathek's *enkalen*. For a moment, she thought he might say something else, but he only nodded, offered a small bow, and strode off through the living room and out into the darkness.

Hanna locked the front door behind him and leaned her back against the inside of it. She felt numb. And empty. And exhausted.

She sighed and dragged the suitcase to her bedroom, where she laid the *enkalan* on top of her dresser and changed into a clean t-shirt and soft leggings. She washed up in the bathroom and stared at herself in the mirror for a long time. She didn't look any different. She'd killed a man; she ought to look different. But she only looked tired.

She scrubbed her hands over her face and went to put a mug of water in the microwave to heat while she checked the locks.

The guest room had been tidied too. And whoever had tidied up in the studio had fished the painting of the misty sunrise at the lake out from behind the cupboard and placed it on the easel. She stood for a moment looking at it, remembering that morning and her encounter with Jon. How long would it be before thinking of him didn't make her feel like she couldn't breathe?

Shaking her head, she flicked the window locks open and then closed again, just to make sure, before she went back to the kitchen for her tea. It was ridiculous, she knew. Dalathek was dead, and the whole place was crawling with alien super-commandos and their high-tech surveillance gadgetry. Jon's particle field had been expanded to include her property. Nothing was coming to get her. But she needed the comfort of routine. Routine was what kept the nightmares at bay.

Mostly.

Chapter
43

THAT NIGHT PASSED.
So did the next.
And the one after that.

Every night, the nightmares came, leaving her huddled in the closet with the door locked or kneeling in the shower picking vomit out of her hair. Again. Sometimes they held only the perennial terrors of the shed. Old wood and gasoline. Dust motes drifting through a knife-blade of sunlight. Blood and pain and heaving, gasping bodies. More often, new horrors crept in. Invisible hands pinning her against the wall. The grate of steel on bone. Choking on a sea of blood atop a green velvet coverlet. Dalathek's dead eyes. Some nights he still wore Jon's face. Sometimes it was Kamm's. Sometimes holding his lifeless *enkalan* was enough to convince herself he wasn't coming back. Sometimes she ached for Mr. Bickles.

Her days, too, settled into a routine. Stretching canvasses. Priming them with gesso. Sighting down the edges of poplar one-by-twos at the lumberyard, checking for warps and knots in the wood she needed to make more stretcher frames. When she had enough canvasses, she packed up her car, got out her old notebooks, and headed out to work in the field, chasing the light, racing the autumn frost as the leaves turned to flame and began to fall. The dizzy spells faded, and the ache in her thigh eased off some.

She might almost have convinced herself that everything was going back to normal, if not for Chance and the other four Talessanin bodyguards hovering stoically around the periphery, keeping the paparazzi at bay with their grim, alien presence. As it was, her life almost didn't seem real—as if she were caught in someone else's dream and couldn't wake up. Especially the day she and her unrelenting entourage stumbled into the stand of aspen trees she'd painted before—the one that now hung on Jon's living room wall. In the solemn silence of the aspen grove, silvery trunks and branches reached heavenward, their fingers lifting golden leaves toward the brilliant blue of the autumn sky like an offering. Like a tribute. Would Jon come back for that painting? Or had he abandoned it like he'd abandoned her?

Sometimes she felt the emptiness of the house across the street as an almost physical pain, even though there were more people living there now than there had been before. Sometimes it felt like home would never truly be home again. Not without Jon there. But it wouldn't feel like home if he was there either. Especially if he brought Salenia with him. He'd said he wasn't courting her, and maybe that was true. But that was probably only a matter of time—the two of them were clearly made for each other. They had all that history together. They had whatever they'd been doing that wasn't what it looked like. They'd sort it out.

Still, home had been home before Jon came, and eventually the wound he had left in her would scar over. Eventually, the paparazzi would get tired of her boring life and go find something else to do, and she could go out with Tiffany and Rachel without worrying that she'd make them targets too. Her life would go on. If she had learned one thing, it was that life went on—brutally, inexorably on—and that eventually, she would be glad of that again.

It was several weeks before Kamm called about Tala's portrait. The swell of excitement that bubbled up in Hanna at the prospect of a visit from her little friend felt good—freeing, somehow, as if it washed away some of the shadows inside her. Kamm said he'd have to send his daughter with one of her tutors because he had meetings he couldn't get out of. And really, Hanna thought she preferred it that way. Kamm was . . . confusing.

She was just taking the last batch of peanut butter cookies out of the oven when the knock came at the door and Chance, who always seemed to be underfoot, went to answer it. It felt good to bake again. She'd avoided doing it since she got home because baking gave her too much time to think. She hadn't wanted to think. She'd just wanted to lose herself in the layers of color and light, where time stopped, and the rest of the world faded away.

Little footsteps thump-skipped across the living room, and Tala wrapped herself around Hanna's waist before she could even put the hot cookie sheet down. She shifted the pan to one hand and held the other out to Chance, who grinned as he tugged her rainbow trout oven mitt off and used it to carry the cookies to the cooling rack on the table. Hanna returned her little friend's hug and—

Her breath caught in her throat as a tall figure stepped through the kitchen doorway. For half a heart-stopping moment, Hanna thought it was Jon. Relief and disappointment flooded through her in equal measures when she realized that, of course, it was only his brother.

"Hello, Hanna."

"Kamm. I . . . um . . . I wasn't expecting you."

"No. Forgive me, I—" He cleared his throat. "There was a last-minute change to my schedule. It's good to see you looking well." His eyes searched her face, as if making sure she really was all right. She knew he received regular reports from her security detail, but he hadn't seen her in person since that blood-soaked night at the embassy. She'd been a mess that night in more ways than one. But he'd held her when she needed it. When Jon had turned away.

Kamm stepped slowly into the kitchen, swinging a bag off one shoulder and onto the floor before offering Hanna his hand, tipped up for the greeting between good friends. Hanna tugged off her other oven mitt to put her hand in his, and he dance-stepped forward, leaning over his daughter's dark head to place a kiss on Hanna's cheek. Almost like a man coming home to his family. Hanna's heart beat faster at the unexpected thought.

Tala squeezed out from between them, skipping over to help Chance with the cookies.

Hanna placed a shy kiss on Kamm's cheek in return. As she began to pull away, Kamm caught her with his other hand at her waist, pulling her closer to whisper, "We've missed you." His breath tickled against her neck, and his voice carried an almost frightening intensity.

Blood rushed to her cheeks and she tensed, flustered.

He released her with a soft chuckle and brushed the backs of his webbed fingers over her cheekbone. "You really do have the most charming blush."

He spared her the necessity of a response by turning away, leaning down to retrieve his bag. "I hope you don't mind, but I brought some work with me. I wonder if you'd be kind enough to allow me the use of your kitchen table while you're working in the studio?"

"Oh . . ." Hanna's mind wouldn't focus, and her lungs seemed to have forgotten what they were for. "Kitchen table. Yes, of course." She backed two steps away from him and nudged past a frowning Chance so she could busy herself helping Tala find a glass of milk to go with her cookies. It gave her a moment to collect herself. What was wrong with her?

While Tala ate her cookies at one end of the table, her father unpacked his bag onto the other. First, a rectangular object about the size of a hardcover book. "Power source," he explained when he caught Hanna watching. She just nodded, and Kamm smiled as he pulled out the next object. It reminded Hanna of a domed glass paperweight she'd seen at her grandmother's house when she was a little girl. Kamm's was larger, though, and was filled with an intricate arrangement of wires and colored blobs, unlike the tiny, carefully arranged dried flowers that had been inside the paperweight. The thing gave off a pulse of blue light when he set it on the power source, and then was still. The only other thing in Kamm's bag turned out to be a fancy case full of papers and writing implements.

While Kamm sorted documents into careful stacks, Tala bounced in her seat, chewing furiously. As soon as she swallowed, she jumped up from the chair, grinned from ear to ear, and clapped her little hands. "Oh Baba! Will you show Miss Bradley the sleepy fishes? Please Baba?"

Kamm's smile seemed a little sheepish as he regarded Hanna for a moment from the corner of his eye. "Very well, little one," he said softly. Then he said something in rapid Talessanin and stroked a finger across the top of the paperweight thing. Inside it, lights flared, gleaming out through the glass. The lights sent color rippling over the walls and ceiling of Hanna's kitchen, creating wavering, shifting patterns of blue and green and gold, as if the kitchen were at the bottom of the sea, with sunlight filtering down through the water. Rocks and corals sculpted of light grew out of the floor, and the languid, sinuous shapes of unfamiliar fishes began to make their way through the air, some gliding, some darting, some settling into the sand on the illusory sea floor.

Tala giggled and spun in place, arms outstretched. "You see, Miss Bradley? It is just like chasing your bubbles!" She leapt toward a nearby fish, swatting it with her little hand. The fish changed color and darted off behind a rock. Tala squealed in delight and scampered after another one.

Hanna smiled, watching the little girl flit laughingly around the kitchen chasing the flickering fishes. After a moment she looked over to see Kamm watching her, a small, pensive smile on his lips. "It's beautiful," Hanna said. "Why does Tala call them sleepy fishes, though? They seem pretty lively to me."

Kamm shrugged. "It's an automatic projection that plays if too much time passes without the unit being used while it is connected to the power source. Tala usually sees it when I'm trying to work while I'm too tired, and I nod off in the middle of something."

Hanna smiled back at him. "When *you're* sleepy." She chuckled. "I see."

Kamm shrugged again and turned his attention to his daughter. "Enough, little one," he said. "I must work, and you must go sit very still for Miss Bradley so she can paint a picture of you." He clapped his hands, and the underwater scene disappeared, replaced abruptly by an array of floating documents and diagrams, some of which had lines drawn between them and what looked like handwritten notes floating in the air around them. Of course, all the writing was in Talessanin, so Hanna had no idea what any of it was about, but it looked important. She took Tala's hand and led her into the studio to see if the children's movies she'd rented could hold the child's attention as well as holographic fishes did.

Tala sat very nicely for an hour while Hanna adjusted the lighting and took some reference snapshots, and then started blocking in the portrait on the canvas. When the little girl began to get fidgety, Hanna said they'd take a break for lunch and sent Tala out to play tag in the yard with Chance.

Kamm's head was bent over the papers spread out across the table, and Hanna tried not to disturb him while she made chicken sandwiches for everyone. When the sandwiches were finished, Kamm still hadn't looked up, and Hanna wasn't sure he'd even noticed she was there. His brows were drawn down and his lips pressed tightly together as he read whatever was on the paper he studied so intently, and now and then his fingers drummed an agitated beat on the tabletop. Hanna packed a stack of sandwiches into her picnic basket along with some plates and cups and a two-liter bottle of rootbeer to take outside for Tala and the bodyguards. She put Kamm's sandwich on a plate and carefully slid it and his glass onto a bare patch on the table, where hopefully he'd discover them when he looked up at some point.

As Hanna turned to go, Kamm's hand reached out, catching her fingers, and Hanna started. Still not looking up from his papers, Kamm drew Hanna's hand to his lips and placed a kiss in her palm. "Thank you, Hanna," he murmured, and leaned his cheek for a moment against her wrist before letting go of her hand. Hanna stood, frozen, waiting for her heart to slow again before taking the picnic outside for the others.

Why did Kamm make her feel so unsettled sometimes? Was it just that his Talessanin manners were familiar enough to put her at ease, while still being foreign enough to catch her off guard sometimes? Was it because she was never quite sure whether he was just being friendly, or actually flirting with her, and she wasn't entirely certain which of those options she'd prefer? Was it because he looked so much like Jon, but wasn't Jon?

She missed Jon. It made her feel foolish. How could she miss him, want him back, after what had happened with Salenia? But she did.

She left the dishes in the sink for later and went outside to let the cool autumn sun chase shadows from the corners of her heart.

Tala sat for another hour after lunch, after which, with her father's distracted permission, she dashed back across the street, trailed by two bodyguards, to play in the unfinished treehouse in Jon's back yard. Hanna retrieved Kamm's empty sandwich plate and glass from the table and added them to the stack of dishes in the sink, before turning on the hot water and adding some soap. Kamm carefully packed up his papers and put his paperweight and its power supply back in the bag. His face was grim, and his shoulders slumped as he stretched and looked around. His expression softened and a smile toyed with the corners of his mouth when he saw Hanna watching him over her shoulder from her place by the sink. Something in his eyes made Hanna's heart start pounding again, and she turned hastily back to the dishes. After a moment she heard the scuff of his booted feet as he crossed the floor to stand beside her.

"Thank you, Hanna," Kamm said softly again. "For everything. You're wonderful with Tala. I can't wait to see the painting." He picked up the dish towel from the counter and began absentmindedly twisting it in his hands. "And it was nice to be able to work uninterrupted for a while."

Hanna pushed the faucet over to fill the other side of the sink with rinse water and set a clean, soapy plate under the stream of water, where the bowl and utensils she'd used to mix the chicken salad already waited. "Did you get a lot accomplished?" She asked.

"I'm not sure. I'm certainly better informed about the matter on which my mother has asked me to render a decision, but I don't feel like I'm any closer to being able to resolve the dispute. It's a complicated situation." Kamm shrugged. "But all of the disputes that are brought to the Throne are complicated. Simple matters are resolved in a lower jurisdiction." He rubbed at the back of his neck and sighed. "I'm sure I'll think of something." He lifted the plate out of the rinse water and began drying it.

"You work too hard," Hanna said softly, sliding another plate into the rinse water.

Kamm was quiet for a time, mechanically drying the dishes as Hanna washed. Then he said, "You're right, of course. I do work too much. Especially at times like this." Hanna waited for him to say more, but he just went on solemnly drying plates. The Imperial *Ehrat*, standing at her sink in her kitchen, solemnly drying her plates.

Finally, Hanna cleared her throat and asked softly, "Times like this?"

Kamm carefully added a plate to the stack of dry ones on the counter.

"On the Talessanin calendar," he said, "it was three years yesterday since my wife died." He shrugged and fished out another plate. "The memories are still tender, and working helps keep me from picking at them."

Hanna stopped washing for a moment and looked up at him. "Oh, Kamm, I'm so sorry."

Kamm turned his head and met her eyes. "Thank you, Hanna," he said softly. He didn't look away again, and Hanna found she couldn't look away either. Neither of them spoke, and after a poignant, awkward moment, Hanna felt her cheeks warm, saw him notice her blush, saw something come into his eyes that she couldn't identify, and couldn't face. She looked back down at her hands and cleared her throat.

"She must've been very beautiful," she said, picking up a cup. "I think maybe Tala has her mouth."

"And her eyebrows," Kamm said in a quiet, musing tone, and Hanna glanced over to see him smiling sadly at the plate in his hands. Kamm continued, "Yes, she was very beautiful. And stubborn." He stacked the plate and fished out the last one.

Hanna put the clean cup into the rinse water. She didn't say anything.

"She wanted a son," he went on after a moment. "But she wasn't strong. She lost three babies before Tala was born." He picked up the cup. "After Tala, her physician said another pregnancy might kill her. But she wanted a son. In my wife's Blood House, inheritance has always passed through the male line." Hanna slid another cup into the rinse water, and Kamm began to dry the one in his hands. "I think she felt inadequate in some way when she couldn't produce a son. But I am of Kanestelan, where inheritance passes to the oldest child. The female line has carried the throne for the last three generations, and we already had a daughter. Narista could've inherited if something had happened to Tala. Or Jon might've been persuaded. Or one of my mother's brothers. There were options. But my wife wanted a son."

They washed and dried cups in silence for a few minutes until Hanna glanced over and saw the grim set of Kamm's mouth and the twitch of the muscle in his jaw as he clenched and unclenched his teeth. He needed to talk about this. "So," she prompted, "you tried to give her what she wanted?"

Kamm shook his head. "I told her I wouldn't put her at risk," he said. "I told her I needed my wife, and Tala needed her mother more than she needed a son. It became a point of contention between us for a time." He stopped. "Where do these go?" he asked gesturing at the stack of plates.

"I can put them away for you." Hanna pointed at a cupboard, and Kamm paced over to open the door. "She said she wanted to make peace," he said into the open cupboard. "She said she'd taken steps to prevent another pregnancy." He stalked across the kitchen again and picked up the stack of plates. "She lied."

Hanna watched silently as he put the plates in the cupboard. "When she became pregnant, she went back to the palace at the Capital so I wouldn't find out what she'd done. She knew I'd be angry with her for deceiving me." He closed the cupboard door and stood for a moment with his hands on the countertop, his back to Hanna. "They sent for me when things began to go badly for her, but she was already gone by the time I got there." Hanna put another clean cup in the rinse water, and Kamm must've heard it clink against the one that was already there, because he pushed away from the counter and returned to the sink to continue drying for her.

"That must've been devastating," Hanna murmured.

After a moment, Kamm said, "It was very difficult. Yes." He pulled a cup from the rinse water. "But it was three years ago. Nearly four Earth years, I suppose. And all the suns in the empire go on rising and setting just the same."

"Life does have a way of going on," Hanna said.

"It does," Kamm agreed. He paused thoughtfully while he fished out another cup, and when he spoke again there was a hint of laughter in his voice. "Especially when everyone you know pushes it forward. They gave me a year to mourn before they began hinting that I should marry again."

Hanna glanced sideways at him, lips quirking into a wryly teasing smile. "An Earth year, or a Talessanin year?" she asked. And then wondered if she was making too light of something that must be painful for him.

But Kamm grinned back at her. "Oh, you know," he said, "whichever is shorter." He shrugged, and chuckled, and went back to drying cups. "To be fair, they do have legitimate concerns. There have been a few times in the Empire's history when a brother and sister have shared the Throne, and Narista would be a fine empress, I think, given the chance to grow up a little more. But it does work better when the Throne is shared between a husband and wife. Tala would be better off with a mother. And I . . ." He set the cup on the counter and frowned, looking over at Hanna. "Well, I work too much. But it is still difficult to let go of the past."

Hanna began washing the last cup. "So, do you think you'll ever remarry?" she asked without looking at him.

"I don't know," Kamm said.

Hanna felt him watching her. She reached to set the cup in the rinse water, and his hand met hers, brushing lightly against her fingers in the water, skin against skin, much as Jon's fingers had sought hers in the wash basin at his dinner party all those weeks ago.

"She would have to be someone very special." Kamm's voice was soft. Gentle. Unsettling.

Hanna pulled her hand away, moving a little more quickly than necessary to let the water out of the sink and wipe off the counter. She finished that, and wiped out the sink, then washed her hands and turned to look for the dish towel to dry them. Kamm held it solemnly out to her. Hanna reached for it, a little hesitant, and Kamm stepped closer, placing the towel in her hands. "Thank you for listening, Hanna," he said. He bent to kiss her cheek and added, "I'll let myself out."

Hanna stood in the middle of her kitchen floor, holding the towel and looking after Kamm. It was several minutes before she noticed Chance leaning against the frame of the door that led to the back yard.

When had he come in?

"Are you all right, Hanna?" he asked, when he saw her looking.

Hanna waved a vague hand at him. "I'm fine." Her voice shook a little when she said it, and Chance straightened and took a step toward her.

"I just . . ." she said. "I can't seem to . . ." She turned, folding the dish towel and setting it on the counter by the sink. "I don't know what . . ." She propped her elbow on the counter and leaned her face into her hand.

Chance stepped slowly up beside her and put a comforting hand on her back. "Ah, little sister," he said quietly, "some days are like that." She turned to him, and he held her while she cried.

Chapter 44

NOTHING LIKE THAT HAPPENED IN the days that followed. Kamm came with Tala for each portrait session but only greeted Hanna as a friend and worked quietly at her kitchen table until Tala was finished for the day. He kept his conversation to safe topics, and he didn't touch her again except for the handclasp and chaste cheek kiss of his friendly greetings. Had he realized the complete emotional collapse that one touch had sent her into and backed off? Or had she only imagined the whole thing? Kamm was confusing.

Tala was distraught that she couldn't take the portrait home with her as soon as the last sitting was over. When Hanna explained that the oil paints would take another week or two to dry to the touch, and that it would be best to wait a few months for them to cure completely so she could apply a protective layer of varnish before they took it home, Tala's smile crumpled into an expression of fretful worry.

"But then, how will we take it with us when we go to live at the Capital?"

Hanna blinked. "You're going to live at the Capital?" Her gaze flicked up to Kamm.

His mouth pinched at the corners, and he watched her face carefully as he said, "This isn't how I intended to tell you. But with the human question more or less resolved, and humans officially accepted into

House Kanestelan, Earth now warrants its own military protection. I don't need to maintain my primary residence here in order to justify using my personal security forces to ward off poachers and discourage outside encroachment. So, Mother has decided that my presence is required at the Capitol."

Something twisted in Hanna's chest, leaving room for an odd emptiness to form. "Oh. Um. How long before you go?"

Why did it matter?

"A couple of weeks."

Hanna nodded numbly. "The . . . um . . . the paint will be dry enough to transport by then, if we wrap it carefully. And I'm sure you can find someone at the Capital who could varnish it for you, when it's ready."

Kamm opened his mouth to say something, but Tala tugged on Hanna's hand, capturing her attention. "You will come and visit us," she declared confidently in her piping voice. "I shall have my own rooms at the palace with my own garden with a splashing pool. *Bahta* Jon will make a new treehouse, and we will have a tea party and make rainbow drawings and . . . and cimmalon rolls, and—"

"Tala," Kamm said, "remember what we talked about."

The little girl deflated. "Invite. Don't order."

"That's right."

In a more subdued tone, Tala said, "Miss Bradley, we would be most pleased if you would come to the Capital for a visit." Then she brightened. Catching Kamm's hand with the one that wasn't holding Hanna's, she said, "And you were going to invite her too, Baba, remember? For pepperonis. You promised." She looked expectantly back and forth between the two of them.

Kamm cleared his throat. "Yes, little one, I remember. Why don't you go see if Chance will take you out to the shuttle while I speak with Miss Bradley."

Tala bounced on her toes and giggled. "Maybe he will carry me upside down."

She tucked Hanna's hand into Kamm's and scampered off, leaving Kamm and Hanna alone in the studio with an awkward silence.

"Tala will miss you." Kamm said softly. "You treat her like a child, not an inconvenient half-grown demigoddess." He gave her hand a gentle squeeze and released it, then shrugged and stuffed his hands into the pockets of the jeans he was wearing. They made him look very human. To the floor, he added, "All of us will miss you."

The gravelly undertone in his voice made Hanna's pulse jump. The empty place in her chest made it hard to breathe.

Before she could think how to respond, he straightened again, smiling. Briskly, he said, "But Chance will be staying at Jon's house for as long as you require security, and Tomin will remain at the embassy, so he'll be able to assist you with . . ."—his eyes met hers, and he faltered—". . . with whatever . . . arrangements you may require. And he can get a message to me if you ever . . ."

He petered out. Swallowed hard. "Truly, Hanna, you would be a welcome visitor at the palace any time you choose. I hope you'll come. But having discharged my mother's commission for Tala's portrait, you are under no obligation to my family, and if, as you said, you just want to put this all behind you so you can have your old life back, I will make sure your wishes are respected."

"Kamm . . ." Hanna's mind couldn't seem to catch up.

"Just think about it. Decide when you're ready. In the meantime, Tala and I are taking Narista to New York next week to eat pepperoni pizzas and visit the Met. Tala asked me to invite you along, since you missed our last trip because . . ." He hesitated and his voice went gentle as he finished, "because Jon was reading you stories."

Hanna's stomach twisted, and she looked down at his brown leather boots.

They took a slow half step closer, and Kamm's fingers brushed her elbow. "He won't be there," he said softly. "He's been off world since you left the embassy. And Salenia has gone back to the Capital. It'll just be the three of us. And you, if you come too."

She looked up into his face. He was standing so close. Close enough she could've leaned against his chest without even moving her feet. He would hold her, if she wanted him to. She could see it in his eyes. And undoubtedly it would feel as good as it had when he'd held her the night she killed Dalathek. But what would it mean if she let him? What would she want it to mean?

She didn't want to think about that. She wasn't ready. And he would be gone in a couple of weeks.

So she just pasted on a smile and said, "I've always wanted to see the Met."

Chapter

45

HANNA SMOOTHED A STRIP OF packing tape down the seam of the cardboard shipping box that formed the last layer of protection around the portrait of Tala. It was strange, she reflected, how oddly out of proportion some events in life turned out to be. An ordinary cardboard box could contain the image of a little girl who would one day rule an empire too vast for the human mind to even comprehend. A simple thing like taking a chocolate bundt cake across the street to welcome a new neighbor could escalate to stabbing a man to death in the high security guest suite of an alien embassy. Bidding farewell to the heir to an intergalactic throne could turn out, as it had the week before, to be as simple as a shy kiss on the cheek of a friend as he cradled his sleeping daughter in his arms.

But soon such matters would be back outside the boundaries of Hanna's life, where they belonged. Jon and Salenia were already gone. Tomin would arrive at any moment to collect the portrait for the Empress. In the morning, Kamm, Tala, and Narista would take a shuttle to the orbital port, where they'd board a long-distance transport to the Empire's capital. And Hanna's world would contract back to the comfortable proportions of Freebridge, of painting simple landscapes and portraits of cats and making sure the property taxes got paid. Yes, there would be some ragged remnants of her grand adventure fluttering on the periphery for a while—nightmares, and paparazzi, and Chance and his commandos holding them at bay. But eventually, all would go back to the way it had been. More or less. And her life would go on. Right now, that was all that she wanted. All she could allow herself to want.

A knock sounded at the front door, and Hanna hollered, "Just let yourself in, Tomin! It isn't locked!"

She had left it that way in a fit of daring, even though it was already dark outside, so she could finish packing the portrait without interruption. It was silly to bother with locks anyway, under the circumstances.

The front door squeaked open and thudded closed, and the thump of booted feet crossed the living room.

"There's a tin of cookies in the kitchen for Tala," Hanna called out. "Can you grab them for me?"

Tomin didn't respond, but the boots thumped into the kitchen and back. Hanna smoothed down the last two strips of tape and slid the oversized box off the worktable. Almost finished. And then she could put all this behind her.

But when she emerged from the studio, Tomin wasn't there. Instead, the Imperial *Ehrat* was poking idly through the collection of odds and ends Hanna displayed on the cheap particle board shelves in her living room.

Hanna's stomach twisted. The portrait box slipped in her grip, and she barely managed to keep it upright as it thumped onto the floor. Numbly, she leaned it against the battered coffee table, which also held the tin of cookies.

Kamm carefully set the conch shell he'd been holding back on the shelf before he moved forward to greet her.

"Forgive me, Hanna," he said. "Tomin was detained with some last-minute arrangements, so I decided to come myself."

He wore a deep green velvet longcoat encrusted with gold embroidered *taless* leaves, and the ornate green stone he'd worn at the ball rested against the black silk of his shirt front. His face was freshly shaven, and his sleeked back hair made her realize just how informally tousled he'd been for the portrait sittings and the trip to the Met. She wished she'd put on something besides old sweatpants and a ratty t-shirt. She wasn't even wearing shoes.

He didn't seem to notice. His fingers rested gently on her waist as he kissed her cheek, and his thigh brushed ever so lightly against hers. Was that intentional? Half an invitation to a lovers' greeting?

Was that what she wanted it to be?

Before she could decide, he released her and stepped back. "It's an interesting collection." He nodded toward the shelves.

"Memories and wishes, mostly," she said, grateful for the distraction. "A few things that are just fun to look at."

Kamm picked up one of her glass-framed pressed plants, turning it over in his hands. "What are these flowers called?" he asked. "They're lovely.

Hanna shifted a little closer to see which one he held. "Those are pansies. They're just simple garden flowers, nothing special. But I've always thought they looked cheerful."

"Simplicity," he mused. "And cheerfulness. That kind of beauty is less common than you might think. And more precious." His gaze shifted to her, and she had the uncomfortable feeling that he wasn't talking only about the pansies.

Her pulse quickened.

"What about this one?" He picked up another framed cluster of flowers and held it out so she could see. "The same blue as the sky, with tiny stars in their hearts."

"Um . . ." She swallowed hard. "They're called forget-me-nots."

Kamm's smile froze on his lips, then turned wry and a little sad as he propped the frame back between the ceramic horse and Hanna's frayed paperback copy of Pride and Prejudice.

When he looked up, she couldn't meet his eyes. She side-stepped around him. Reached over to straighten the old patent medicine bottle. Rubbed some dust off the cover of Great Expectations. Adjusted the fist-sized geode so the purple quartz crystals that sparkled in its cavity would better catch the light.

Kamm studied her where she came to rest, her fingers toying with an ornate, half rusted skeleton key. Slowly, deliberately, he moved in close, placing his hand against the small of her back as he reached past her with his other hand to touch the conch shell he'd been looking at when she came in. "And this?"

If a human man had done that, she'd have thought he was trying to start something. What did it mean from a Talessanin? From Kamm?

"Um." She cleared her throat. "Rachel brought that back for me from her company's team-building trip to the Bahamas last spring. I've always wanted to go to the ocean, but I've never been able to afford the trip, and Rachel said she wanted me to at least be able to hear the ocean whenever I like." She made the mistake of looking up at him over her shoulder.

He was so close!

His lips drew into a puzzled frown, and he tilted his head, a questioning gesture that reminded her too much of Jon.

Her heart pounded in her throat.

"You . . . um . . ." She shifted away from him, picking up the shell to demonstrate. "You hold it up to your ear like this. It sounds like the ocean. Sort of. I'm told." She handed it to Kamm so he could try.

After listening a moment, he smiled. "It does," he said. "A little." He studied her solemnly and handed the shell back to her. As she set it on the shelf, he murmured huskily, "I would've taken you to the ocean, Hanna. You had only to ask."

Cheeks warming, she shot another glance at him over her shoulder. Saw him notice her blush. Saw the intensity it brought into his Kanestelan green eyes. Her knees went rubbery.

She clutched at the edge of a shelf to steady herself, and her clumsy fingers bumped against the scabbard of her courting knife, knocking it off the closed lid of its sleek wooden box. His gaze weighed on her as she picked up the knife and paused, trying to decide whether to put it back on top of the box where she could look at it sometimes or to tuck it out of sight inside.

"I know," she whispered.

Silence.

Then Kamm said softly, "You miss him, don't you?"

Hanna drew a long breath and let it out again, tipping the lid of the box back to reveal the green silk lining. "It doesn't matter."

"It does matter," Kamm said softly. "I know what it is to still love someone who hurt you."

Absently, she slid the blade of the courting knife half free of its sheath and tilted it between her shaking fingers, watching the star dance at the heart of the green stone so she didn't have to look at him.

She drew a shaky breath and swallowed hard. "Why are you here, Kamm?" she asked. "There are a hundred people at the embassy you could've sent instead."

He hesitated. Shifted closer. She could smell the clean scent of his soap over the warm, underlying musk of Talessanin male. One web-fingered hand trailed down her arm from shoulder to elbow, sending shivering tingles down her spine.

Her heart pounded. *He was so close!*

"I wanted to say a proper goodbye," he murmured. "Without hiding behind my daughter. I will miss you, Hanna. And I couldn't leave without at least—" His voice cracked, and he cut himself off. Drew a shuddering breath.

He was Jon's brother.

He was the Imperial *Ehrat*.

He hadn't brought a chaperon!

Unless the bodyguards outside counted. Did they?

"Hanna . . ." He shifted even closer.

Panic exploded inside her, white and hot. Pulse pounding, she twisted to face him, bringing her fisted hands up between them to rest against his chest, ready to push him away.

But she didn't. The fear did *not* get to win. Dalathek did not get to win.

Phantom dust motes danced in the corners of her vision, toying with the scents of old wood and gasoline. She swallowed hard and forced herself to balance on that knife's-edge of panic. Forced herself to breathe until her heart slowed again.

Slowly, she looked up into Kamm's eyes.

He looked back. Questioning. Vulnerable.

"I'll miss you too," she whispered. Whatever chaos churned her emotions in that moment, that much was true.

He cleared his throat and shifted half a step back, opening a little space between them.

She didn't realize until his hand folded around hers that she was still clutching the courting knife, pressing it against his chest.

"Take care, Hanna," he murmured. "This is not a weapon to taunt a man with lightly. He might think you're asking him to court you."

Her heart rolled over in her chest, and her throat closed up. *Was that meant as an invitation?*

Kamm's mouth twisted into a wry, almost bitter smile, and he released her hand, edging back another half step.

"Forgive me," he said gently. "I know you think that rumor was ridiculous."

Was it? It didn't seem that way just now.

"Do . . . do you want to?" The words slipped out before her numb lips could catch them, and her hand jerked reflexively up, angling the knife's pommel toward Kamm.

What was she doing? What if she was wrong? This man was the Imperial Ehrat for mercy's sake! His wife would someday be the empress.

He stared at her. "Do I *want* to?"

"I'm s-sorry," she stammered, letting her hands fall limply to her sides. "I shouldn't have asked. It's just . . . sometimes I've had the impression that you . . . um . . ." Her blush went supernova, and she looked down.

His fingertips grazed her burning cheek, sending panicky little tingles racing down her spine, then came to rest under her chin, coaxing it up so he could see her eyes again. His other hand slid caressingly down her arm and closed around the courting knife. Without breaking eye contact, he slipped it from her unresisting grip and tucked it behind his belt. Then that hand moved to Hanna's waist, and he shifted close again, leaning down to whisper in her ear.

"I have wanted to court you ever since I saw you sitting in the moonlight with Tala drinking imaginary tea."

His breath was warm against her skin as he tilted his head ever so slightly, that Talessanin gesture of questioning, and pressed the soft suggestion of a kiss against her neck.

Hanna's heart stopped beating. She couldn't make her lungs work right. Her knees felt like putty.

"Kamm?" It wasn't a whisper. It was barely even a breath.

He leaned back, looking into her eyes. Hopeful. Afraid.

She didn't know what to say. She couldn't move. Every nerve in her body seemed to thrum in time with her heartbeat. She teetered on the brink of panic, balanced precariously on the thin edge of dust motes, old wood, and gasoline.

He bent to place his next kiss hesitantly, tenderly, on her lips.

Lightning flared through her, and she tensed, bracing against the flashback she was sure would come . . .

but . . .

didn't.

Her lips melted against his, and her heart started up again, pounding in her chest, in her throat, in her temples as she returned his kiss.

His mouth grew more insistent, and his hand on her waist slipped around to her back and up her spine, as if seeking *enan* that weren't there, pulling her against him.

Her own hands slid up his chest, tangled in the embroidered lapels of his longcoat, found the softness of the dark curls that skimmed his shirt collar, the warmth of his skin at the turning of his jaw, the hard smoothness of the first *enan* at the top of his dorsal fin.

He stiffened, every muscle going hard against her body, and pulled back, gasping, eyes closed, fingers trembling against the skin of her neck, the small of her back. As she watched, dark streaks broke across his cheekbones, running down from the corners of his eyes like tears and up toward his temples. Finer lines and softly mottled patches filled the spaces in between.

His *tehilethkalan*. The Talessanin mating mask.

He released a shuddering breath and opened his eyes, studying her face once more. Intense. Asking silent questions she couldn't begin to understand, much less answer. The hand that lay against the side of her face traced a slow line over her shoulder, down her side behind her elbow to her waist, drawing her more firmly against him as he considered whatever he saw in her eyes.

His gaze drifted downward to her lips, and he slid his hands up her body to cradle her face between both palms as he leaned forward for another kiss.

Stopped halfway.

Drew one more ragged breath.

And leaned his forehead against hers instead.

"You are a very dangerous woman, Hanna Bradley," he whispered.

He drew another long breath, as if steadying himself, released her, and straightened. "And I deeply regret that I cannot court you."

Hanna blinked. She must've heard him wrong. Her mind was still tangled in that kiss.

"Wh-what?"

"I want to." His gaze bored into her, searching for something, but not finding it. Committing her to memory. "I thought for a moment that I could. But if you kiss me like that again there will be no going back for me. And we both know that given the choice, I'm not the one you'd pick."

"Kamm—"

"If he were anyone else, I would try to change your mind. I don't think I could, but I would try." He laid her courting knife against her palm and pressed her fingers closed around it, dropping one last kiss along the backs of her knuckles. "But he's my brother, Hanna. I want his happiness as much as I want yours."

Something twisted in the pit of Hanna's stomach. "He returned my knife, Kamm. He doesn't want me anymore."

Kamm made a noise somewhere between a laugh and a moan. "He wants you like he wants to breathe, Hanna. It frightens him." He laid a hand against her cheek, tracing the edge of her bottom lip with his thumb. "And you're not truly finished with him yet either."

"Kamm—"

"Good night, Hanna." A hoarse whisper.

He bent to pick up the portrait and the cookie tin and strode out the front door, leaving it open to the night as Hanna stared, frozen, after him. As he disappeared into the darkness, two bodyguards detached themselves from the night to glide in his wake.

Hanna wrapped her arms around herself and drifted out onto the cool concrete of the porch, peering into the darkness that had swallowed Kamm. She was still shaking.

What just happened?

As she turned to go back inside, something else caught her attention—a darker blackness against the night beyond the light spilling out from her bay window. Someone stood there with his back to her, head bowed, shoulders tight, one hand braced against the wall of her house.

Someone very tall.

Chapter 46

"JON?"

He tensed at the sound of Hanna's voice, but didn't turn.

"How long have you been there?" The pounding of her heart in her throat made it come out like an accusation.

"You offered him a knife. He . . . accepted with enthusiasm." Jon's voice was flat. Expressionless.

The curtain on the bay window wasn't drawn. He would've had a perfect view. And . . . had Kamm seen him out here? Was that what made him change his mind?

She swallowed hard. "Jon, I—"

"You will be happier with him than you would have been with me."

Would have been. Over and done. Her stomach twisted.

"Jon, It's not like—"

"He has been married before and knows how to touch a woman without—"

"I get it, okay? You can stop." If he could interrupt, so could she.

He straightened and turned toward her, folding his arms across his chest. "You did not have a flashback when *he* kissed you like that."

Anger flared in Hanna's stomach. "*He* didn't back me up against a wall. And I've had a little more practice being kissed since that night when you—"

"He will make you a good husband."

"That's *enough!*"

This time, he didn't say anything, just stared back at her in the darkness.

What did he want from her?

"Look, I get it," she snapped. "You approve. Your blessing has been given. You don't want me anymore, so your brother can have me. I get it. You don't have to come here and rub my nose in it."

"That is not—" He stopped. Tried again. "I did not come here to rub . . ." His shoulders slumped, and he scrubbed a hand back through his braids. "I do not know what that means."

The stoic indifference was gone from his voice. He sounded worn out now. Defeated.

"It means . . ." She was too tired for this. Too much had happened too fast. And her bare feet were getting cold. She just wanted to have a bath and a cup of tea, and pretend none of it was real.

She sighed. "It doesn't matter. What are you doing here?" She glanced around the dark yard and peered up the empty street. "And how did you even get here? I thought my bodyguards were supposed to keep people from spying on me."

He kneaded the muscles at the base of his skull with one hand. "I am sorry, Hanna. I did not mean to spy. I intended only to leave that for you and go. Chance gave me permission."

She looked where he was pointing. If she had taken two steps sideways, she would've tripped over the big paperboard gift box that sat next to one of the porch posts—metallic gold, tied shut with a red satin ribbon. But she'd been staring after Kamm like a dazed sheep, so she hadn't even noticed it.

"You couldn't just knock on the front door like a normal person?"

"You said you did not wish to see me again."

Well, that was true. She had said that.

Abruptly, he drew a ragged breath and looked up at the sky. "No. You said that if I ever cared for you, I should stay away. Staying out of sight is not the same thing. I have broken that trust too, I suppose. I just needed to . . . I thought . . ." He looked back at her, shaking his head. "I do not know what I thought. But I did not intend to spy on you. I just . . .

when I arrived, you were . . . I could not . . ." He drew a deep breath. "I am sorry, Hanna."

The weariness in his voice took the edge off her anger, but the choked laugh that escaped her throat still held a bitter edge. "I guess you know how it feels now."

He shook his head. "No. It is not the same. I have no claim on you; you are free to kiss whomever you like. When you saw me with Salenia, I bore your courting knife. What you saw should never have happened. Even if it was not—"

"It doesn't matter." Hanna sighed. She didn't want to fight. It was over; that was enough.

"It does." Jon stepped forward into the light spilling out of the window. His voice held a note of bleak desperation, and his words fell out in a rush. "She was waiting for me. I thought we could talk. Settle things between us. But she caught me off guard, and . . . and then she would not stop when I asked her to stop. I was uncertain what to do, and I let her go too far before I stopped her, because the only way I could think of to make her stop was to hurt and threaten her. I was ashamed. I was afraid that if I told you, you would be angry and think less of me." His voice went softer. Wistful. "I did not want you to think less of me. But that is only an excuse. I should have told you. I am sorry."

She sighed. "You tried. After Dalathek. I wouldn't listen. I'm sorry too."

Silence wedged itself between them, charged and awkward, until Hanna straightened and cleared her throat. "Well . . . um . . . I'm glad we finally got a chance to talk. But I'm sure you have things to do. I don't want to keep you."

She had taken only two steps back toward the refuge of her living room when his hand caught her elbow, and the spiced leather scent of him washed around her, stopping her heart.

"Wait." His voice rasped in his throat. "Hanna . . . will you not open my gift?"

She rubbed at her forehead. What would be the point? Was it supposed to be some kind of apology present? A consolation prize? *No Viper for you, but here's a nice teapot to make you feel better.* Whatever it was, she didn't want it.

She drew a deep breath—a mistake, since it smelled like him—and said, "Why? It doesn't change anything, does it?"

"I have made a mess of this." He let go of her arm and sat down on the edge of the porch, elbows on knees, hands clasped, looking down at the crack in her sidewalk. "I swear by all the Gentle Gardeners, Hanna, I never meant to hurt you."

His voice broke, and he scrubbed one hand back through his braids. Part of Hanna wanted to point out that he had dumped her and demand to know how he *thought* that would make her feel. But he already looked so broken. And he was trying to do a nice thing. And she was too worn down to fight.

She sighed and picked up the box. A beam of soft light from the half open door glinted off the gold paperboard as she sat down beside him.

Inside the box, nestled comfortably in a pile of red tissue paper, lay a big plush teddy bear. His fur was dark—brown or maybe black, it was hard to say in the dimness—and impossibly soft against her suddenly trembling fingers. She held him up, trying unsuccessfully to catch the light better. One leg hung at a slightly stiff angle, and when Hanna gave it a tentative twist, she heard the familiar click of her old scabbard lock.

She swallowed hard. Not a consolation teapot after all—he'd gotten her a replacement for Mr. Bickles. Jon, of all people, would understand how much she missed her comfortable old companion. He always seemed to know what she needed, even when she didn't know herself. Something wrenched inside her. Mr. Bickles wasn't the only companion she missed.

She clenched her teeth, brushing furtively at a stray tear that threatened to escape, covering the movement by twisting sideways to lean against the porch post. Drawing her knees up, propping her bare feet on the porch next to Jon's hip, she cuddled the bear into her chest and buried her face in the top of his head as she had done so many times with Mr. Bickles and his predecessors. He smelled of *taless* spice and leather.

Something warm brushed against her toes. "Strawberries?" Jon's voice was a choked whisper, and his breathing had gone ragged. "Sweet Sower, Hanna, are you trying to kill me?"

Hanna tipped her head up to look at him. He was staring at her feet, which had apparently landed in the beam of light that had glinted off the box a moment ago, making the red and green of her toenail polish seem almost to glow in the darkness.

She laughed wryly. "Tiffany painted them. Tomin smuggled her in yesterday. She wanted to try out a new design, and I didn't think anyone would notice. Or care."

He glanced sharply up at her, then looked more closely, leaning forward in the dark. One big hand came up to brush another sneaky tear from her cheek, and then stayed to cradle the side of her face, warm and strong.

Hanna's heart pounded in her throat, making her breath tremble when she whispered, "Thank you, Jon. For the bear."

"A warrior should not be without her weapon." His hand dropped away, and he leaned his elbows on his knees again as he studied the shadowy sidewalk. "The blood would not come out of the old one. And I could not find a pink one the right size. But this one reminded me of your chocolate cake. I hope . . ." He shook his head and didn't say what he hoped.

She cleared her throat. "He's perfect. I think I'll call him Cupcake."

He nodded, but said nothing, just stared out into the night.

She watched him for a moment, then reached out to lay a hand against his forearm. "Come home, Jon," she whispered. "Please. I miss you."

He laid his other hand over hers and let it rest there a moment before bringing her hand up to his lips and placing a kiss in her palm. He closed her fingers around it and pressed another kiss against the backs of her knuckles.

"I wish I could, Little Mouse," he murmured. "But it would be too dangerous. Dalathek was not the only one who wished me ill. You were right to ask me to stay away. Being near me is not safe."

Hanna stared at him. "Safe? Jon, there's no such thing as safe. But if there were, the safest place in the Empire would be standing beside the Viper."

He shook his head. "I would only make you a target. The risk is too great."

Anger flared again in Hanna's gut, and she pulled her hand away. "That's not for you to decide, though, is it? I'm a big girl, I can choose which risks I'm willing to take."

He straightened, shoulders squaring. "But you cannot choose which risks *I* am willing to take. I could not live with myself if something happened to you because of me. Not again."

"Well, I'm *tired* of nothing happening to me." Hanna pushed herself to her feet. "Nothing happened to me for a long time before you came, and it was like being dead. Maybe I wanted that back then, but I don't anymore. I want to live my life. Yes, there are risks. I almost died three times. But that's not *all* that happened to me. The rest of it was—" Her voice broke, and she clenched her teeth to hold back the hot threat of more tears. Turned away so he wouldn't see the one that escaped. Swallowed. Murmured, "I'm going to die someday either way."

Jon rose slowly and laid a comforting hand on her shoulder. "Kamm is a better choice for you. He has fewer enemies and is surrounded by—"

"That's not your decision to make either, Jonantathinel *Ehr*," she snapped. "You don't get to just hand me off to your brother when you're done with me like you handed over your empire. I am *not* your property."

He had the grace to look startled. "Hanna—"

"And anyway, it doesn't matter. Kamm won't court me either."

"But . . ." Jon looked from Hanna to the bay window and back again. "But I saw him accept—"

"He gave it back."

He stared at her. "Kamm is in love with you. Why would he—"

"Because he knows I'm still in love with his stupid brother."

She didn't run, and she didn't look back; she had at least that shred of self-respect left. It wasn't until her bedroom door was safely shut behind her that her knees gave out and the dam broke. She collapsed against the wall, buried her face in the top of Cupcake's head, and let all the tears come flooding out.

Epilogue

KAMM WAS IN HIS PRIVATE sitting room when Jon returned to the embassy. Tala cuddled in her father's lap as he read to her—an Earth fable about a mermaid who transformed into a human. She'd wheedled Jon into reading it to her enough times for him to recognize it from the sentence or two he caught as he paused in the doorway.

Tala flew to her uncle as soon as she saw him, and he picked her up, tossing her into the air and catching her again in a big, squirming hug. Kamm frowned sternly, and Jon set his niece safely back down on the floor.

The little girl captured his hand in both of hers and, swinging it enthusiastically between them, demanded to know if he wanted one of the cookies Miss Bradley had sent for her. Just the smell coming from the open tin on the side table made his heart clench in on itself. Warm spices. Melted chocolate. *Hanna.*

Fortunately, Tala's nursemaid came to take her to bed before Jon had to actually eat one of the things.

Kamm leaned back into the deep cushions of his low-hanging seat and stretched his legs out in front of himself as he studied Jon. He looked tired.

Jon remained standing and returned his brother's impassive gaze with a blank expression of his own. They hadn't spoken since the night of the embassy ball—and all that had followed. It was difficult to know where to begin.

When the silence stretched too long, Kamm asked quietly, "You've been at the Capital?"

Jon nodded. "And . . . elsewhere."

Kamm waved a hand at the seat across from his. "Report." He sounded as tired as he looked.

But this was, at least, a beginning point Jon could manage. He lowered himself into the indicated seat, sitting on the edge of the cushions with his feet planted firmly on the floor and his elbows propped on his knees. "The integration laws are coming together nicely. Your dinner party with Hanna seems to have made a difference with the Assembly." He felt his lips twist into a sardonic smile. "Perhaps you should have introduced them to a pretty woman a long time ago, instead of sending them all those dried up diplomats."

Kamm's return smile was also wry. "You're probably right." He paused. "And . . . the other thing?"

Jon's smile faded. "Nothing conclusive. He definitely had high-level help getting in. The deep-op techs confirm that he overrode your systems using dark codes. Your people couldn't have stopped it. They did well to detect the irregularity at all. His delivery system used a self-scrubber that filled the infiltration gap in the data and erased all traces of itself down to a sub-structural level except for a few crumbs in an auxiliary redundancy backup that deep-ops used to reconstruct it. Chance might have caught it, had he not been distracted by the *kalakanek*. But I'm glad he was." He met Kamm's eyes and saw in them a shared horror of what might have happened otherwise.

Jon shrugged and went on. "Still, the codes have surfaced and have been logged, and they won't work again. Whoever they belonged to won't get new ones until the next cycle unless they report their action to the Throne. Which seems unlikely under the circumstances. She should be safe enough for now."

"Dark codes." Kamm sighed and scrubbed at his face with his palms. "I confess I had hoped it was just some other disgruntled former acquaintance of yours."

Jon shrugged again. "EtChuk said he found one new bounty on my head, but it was already resolved when he arrived."

"And by resolved, you mean . . . ?"

"Dead men don't pay bounties."

"So not that, then." Kamm leaned forward in his seat. "Well, if he had dark codes, his employer had to be a Head of one of the Great Houses. Or someone they trust with their codes."

"Or someone who stole their codes."

"Dark codes? That would have been reported immediately."

"Probably. But I like to consider all the possibilities."

Kamm thought that over. "So we're left with a Head of House who knew how to contact Dalathek and was willing to burn this cycle's dark codes to get him inside." He frowned. "The choice of Dalathek as the assassin suggests that this was personal and that you were the intended target, at least initially."

Jon nodded solemnly. "The most likely candidates are Mother, the Emperor, and one or the other of the Trakanaleths, though there are a couple of other remote possibilities. The Shadows are looking into it, but we may never know for sure. Especially if it came from the Throne."

Kamm shook his head. "I don't think it was Mother. My inside sources say she called in private favors from several Assembly Delegates to push the resolution through."

"Did she?" Jon let his surprise show in his voice.

"Don't let on that you know; I don't have time to cultivate new sources. But Mother was never opposed to integration, she just wanted Father to come to it in his own time." Kamm shook his head. "She doesn't always show it well, but she wants you to be happy. I don't think it was her."

"And the others?"

A hesitation. "I'm less certain." He thought about it a moment longer, then leaned back in his seat again and changed the subject. "What did Cerulean Stone say?"

Jon stood and went to look out the window that constituted one concave wall of the room. This had been an observation deck when the embassy ship traveled the stars, but now it just looked out into the moonlit darkness of Kamm's private garden. "Cerulean Stone says he's even more convinced than ever that under pressure from the Sovereignist faction, your father has no intention of stepping down when the Empress passes sovereignty to her heir, who is more sympathetic to the

Multiformists. He hopes we might still find a way to avoid civil war. He feels it would help solidify your position if you moved your residence back to the Capital. And"—his heart clenched as he said it—"if you were married."

Kamm waited until Jon glanced at him over his shoulder before saying, "He's probably right."

Jon turned back to the window, gripping the handrail that curved along the inside. He swallowed hard, forcing his voice to come out flat and even as he said the rest. "He asked me to convey his commendation of Hanna as a good choice for your consort."

A brief pause. "He's heard that rumor then."

"He might've started it. With him, it's hard to say."

Kamm grunted. "It would be like him to toss a pebble like that in the pond just to watch how the ripples played out."

Jon slowly raised one shoulder. Let it fall. "He's certainly watching the ripples closely, whether he tossed the pebble or not. He's acutely aware that Hanna is unfamiliar with most of the Empire, and that prejudice against humans exists in some quarters. But he asserts that many in the Empire don't care whether a Talessanin has fins or not, and hinted strongly that some parties who *do* care might welcome an empress who knows what it's like to be a minority outsider."

"She has a quick mind," Kamm observed. "And a compassionate heart." His tone probed for a reaction.

Jon didn't give him one, just continued in that flat, even tone. "He was most impressed with the way she took his foreign appearance in stride and used emotion cues without being prompted. He believes she would adapt well and bring a fresh perspective to the new Throne."

In the window, Kamm's reflection shifted forward in its seat, planting its feet on the floor and leaning its elbows onto its knees.

"I sat at Hanna's kitchen table for four days while she worked on Tala's portrait," Kamm said, "trying to come up with a good way to resolve an inheritance dispute. It involved a mineral-rich planet with a lot of valuable resources, and both parties had equally valid legal claims to it. I could find no grounds on which to base a decision that wouldn't look like arbitrary favoritism. Hanna came into the kitchen to get a glass of water for Tala and asked me what was wrong. When I told her, she asked which of the claimants would treat the people on the planet better. Such an obvious question, but I was so caught up in trying to untangle the legal claims that it hadn't even occurred to me. I spent a little time going through the judicial records, and the decision became a simple one. She would make a spectacular empress."

Jon couldn't make himself respond to that.

Silence settled between them. Tense. Heavy.

It was Jon who eventually broke it. "How long have you been in love with her?"

Kamm sighed. "Since the night of your dinner party. In the tree-house."

The memory of that night made Jon's heart stop beating. *The first time she'd kissed him.*

"But you were there before me," Kamm went on, "so I tried to love her as a sister. At least, until you returned her knife. That made it harder." He paused. Then asked, "When did *you* first love her?"

"She brought me a cake." It came out a hoarse whisper. Jon turned away from the window and leaned his hips back against the railing, arms folded. He tried to keep the emotion from his voice. And failed. "Did she give you the same knife she gave me, or did she have a new one made?"

Kamm sighed. He rose from his seat and went to stand beside Jon, gazing out into the night. "I'm not courting Hanna."

"You gave her knife back. That's not quite the same thing."

"You saw that too?"

"She told me."

Kamm leaned forward, bracing his hands on the railing. "You've spoken with her, then."

"Yes." Jon's gut twisted in on itself.

"About Salenia too?"

"Yes."

"Then why aren't *you* wearing her knife?"

"She'd be better off with you."

Kamm turned to stare at him. "Is that what you told her?" He let out a long breath. In a carefully measured tone, he said, "She doesn't want me, Jon. When she looks at me, she sees only pieces of you incorrectly assembled. When I touch her, she flinches. She—" He stopped, scrubbing one hand back through his hair.

"She kissed you back."

"That was the first time. The *only* time. And it only happened because she thinks she can't have you." He slammed one hand down on the railing so hard it hummed. "Sweet Sower, Jon, go to her. She loves you. She deserves to be happy." He turned away from the window, away from Jon, and paced halfway across the room before he added more quietly, "And so do you. You've had too much of pain and death in your life. You deserve a little love and peace."

Jon turned back to stare at the darkness out the window. "I don't think I know how."

"Jon—"

"No one ever taught me that. My father died. My mother made a new family. My mentor was a monster. Death is all I've ever been good at."

"Then let *her* teach you. But hear me now, brother. If she takes you back, you had better take very good care of her, because I think given time, I might be able to persuade her. And if she ever looks at me the way she used to look at you, I won't be able to step away. Not even for you."

Jon closed his eyes and clenched the railing.

Kamm's boots scuffed against the carpet, and the netting of his chair creaked softly when he sat back down. "You'd have to be a fool not to at least try. And you've never been a fool."

"I *am* a fool," Jon said softly. "A monstrous fool. But I cannot keep putting her in danger." He turned to face his brother, wondering if the hollowness in his heart showed in his face. "You know how to love a woman. As heir to the Throne, you will have the full force of the Empire to keep her safe. And I would rather lose her to you than to someone like Dalathek."

Kamm looked steadily back at him. "You're the Viper in the Night."

"Which only means I have a hundred times more enemies than you."

Kamm held his gaze a little longer before slumping back against the cushions, scrubbing at his face with one hand as he changed the subject. "What else did Cerulean Stone say?"

Jon sighed. Kamm could always tell when he was leaving things out. "He has urged me again to rescind my abdication and seize the Throne while I can still command the loyalty of both factions."

"And you refused again?"

Jon said nothing. His brother should know better than to ask him that.

"I would not oppose you," Kamm said quietly.

"And I will not oppose you," Jon insisted. "My abdication stands. The Empire needs a diplomat on the Throne, Kamm, not a warrior. You know that as well as I do. We decided that together. And I am loyal to the Throne."

"Loyal to the Throne." Kamm shifted in his seat. His frown deepened. "My father is one of your four most likely candidates for the attack, Jon. Three, if we eliminate Mother. What if it was him? What if he still wants her dead?" He leaned forward. "You were his personal assassin for years. There's no one better than you. If he commanded you as his loyal subject to keep Hanna from becoming my empress by killing her, since Dalathek failed, would you do it? Where would your loyalty lie then?"

Jon stiffened, studying his brother's face. Kamm gave nothing away. Slowly, deliberately, Jon said, "I did *not* kill your wife, Kamm. That was only a rumor."

Kamm studied Jon's face in return. "Did he order you to?"

He had never asked the question so directly before. Jon held his face completely, utterly still, and said nothing.

After a moment, Kamm shook his head. "No. I know you can't answer questions like that. Perhaps I'll ask you again when I am emperor and can peer behind the curtain of silence." He looked up at the ceiling as if seeking answers there. "And I know you didn't kill my wife. I had a private comprehensive analysis done after she died. The pregnancy killed her. *I* killed her." He sighed and brought his focus back to Jon. "But that isn't what I asked you. Where would your loyalty lie, Jon?"

Jon studied the carpet. He was silent for a long time.

Kamm waited.

At last, Jon drew a deep breath and said, "I am loyal to the Throne, Kamm. My blood is the blood of two imperial families. I was Commander of the Nine. I live and fight and die for the Throne and for the good of the Empire." He paused and raised a fist to his chest, still not looking at his brother. "But my heart beats for Hanna," he said softly. "Marry her, Kamm. Put her on the Throne, so I never have to choose between the two. Because Sower help me, if your father ever gave me that order, I would kill him. I would rescind my abdication and bring to bear the blood of both my Houses, all the political influence that is mine to command, every friendship I can claim, every personal favor owed to me by every cutthroat brigand in the Empire, every secret piece of blackmail I could whisper, and every breath in my body to keep her safe."

An Invitation From the Author

IF YOU ENJOYED READING THE *Viper's Kiss*, please tell a friend and consider leaving a review on Amazon or Goodreads. Reviews help books gain exposure and sales, and are critical to the success of any book, especially those published by independent authors and small publishers. Even just a line or two can make a big difference.

I also love hearing from my readers directly. Please visit my web site to find contact information or sign up for my Guild to receive periodic email updates. There's also a link to the Guildhall on Facebook, where you can chat with other fans. See you there!

amybeatty.com

Special Thanks

THIS BOOK, LIKE ITS PREDECESSOR, *Dancing with the Viper*, formed part of what I consider my apprenticeship in novel writing. It was the second half (minus a small portion I've reserved for book three in the series) of the first book I wrote. The original ideas from that manuscript are still intact in both books, but the manuscript has been split, unsplit, re-split, developed, and refined from that first step I made into the unexplored darkness of novel-writing. Thus, like *Dancing with the Viper, The Viper's Kiss* has been touched by more helpful hands than I had the sense to keep track of, and it is impossible to give credit to all the places it is due. I remain deeply grateful for the incremental education I received from each of those who left their fingerprints on the story.

Special thanks must be given to my editor, Julie Frederick, who helped me untangle and reweave the threads and pointed out the holes that needed filling. This story would not be what it is without you, Julie.

To my old writing group, Jennifer Jenkins, Lois Brown, and Nichole Van, who took a new writer under their wings and helped me spread my own, thank you. Your encouragement and critique were truly invaluable, and I wish all of you the best on your new adventures.

A big shout-out to my intrepid last round test-readers (whose names I did have the foresight to record—I'm learning!): Laura Rawlins, Talei Lawson, Patrice Ashby, Amy Adams, Jennifer Jenkins, Katrina Frederick, and Carol D'Augostino. This book is better because of you. Thank you.

And, of course, to my family. Thank you doesn't seem enough.

About the Author

AMY BEATTY IS THE AUTHOR of The Vanir Dragon Series and the Viper Series. Her work has been compared to Robert Jordan's, and her debut novel, *Dragon Ascending* (2018) was reviewed by Orson Scott Card (Author of Ender's Game), who recommended it highly, calling it "an extraordinarily entertaining and innovative treatment of dragons."

Amy was raised in the wilds of Yellowstone Park as part of an experiment in combining the genes of a respected biologist with those of a grammar aficionado. She now lives in the mountains of Utah with her husband and two delightfully unconventional children under the benevolent dictatorship of a toy fox terrier who is determined to take over the world one delivery truck at a time.

WORKS BY AMY BEATTY

THE VIPER SERIES
Dancing with the Viper
The Viper's Kiss

Viper Prequel Short Stories:
available at amybeatty.com
The Viper's Egg
A Viper in Her Bosom

THE VANIR DRAGON SERIES
Dragon Ascending

SHORT STORIES
Out of the Fire
Available in the anthology
Of Fae & Fate: Lesser-Known Fairy Tales, Retold
Edited by Beth Buck

www.ingramcontent.com/pod-product-compliance
Lightning Source LLC
Chambersburg PA
CBHW071230250626
47163CB00001B/116